ÖRÆFI
THE WASTELAND

THE
WASTELAND

—

Ófeigur Sigurðsson

TRANSLATED FROM THE ICELANDIC
BY LYTTON SMITH

DEEP VELLUM PUBLISHING

DALLAS, TEXAS

Deep Vellum Publishing

3000 Commerce St., Dallas, Texas 75226

deepvellum.org · @deepvellum

Deep Vellum Publishing is a 501c3
nonprofit literary arts organization founded in 2013.

ISBN: 978-1-941920-67-1 (paperback) | 978-1-941920-68-8 (ebook)
Library of Congress Control Number: 2017938738

—

This book has been translated with financial support from:

Cover design by Anna Zylicz · annazylicz.com
Text set in Bembo, a typeface modeled on typefaces cut by Francesco Griffo for Aldo
Manuzio's printing of *De Aetna* in 1495 in Venice.
Distributed by Consortium Book Sales & Distribution.
Printed in the United States of America on acid-free paper.

CONTENTS

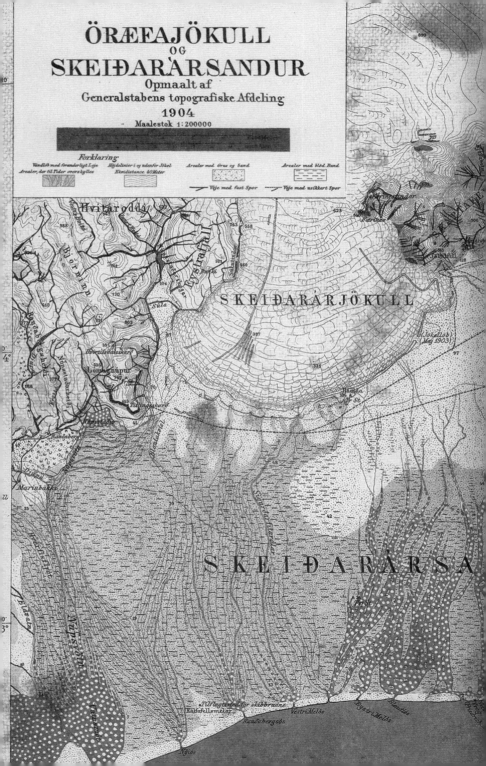

BREIÐAMERKUR
JÖKULL
Hermannaskarð
Máfabygðir
Breiðamerkurmúli
Breiðamerkurfjall
Hrútsfjallstindar
Tjaldskarð
Hvannadalshnúkur
ORÆFAJÖKULL
Skaptafellsjökull
Svínafellsjökull
Hafrafell
Skaptafell
Kristínartindar
Rótarfjallshnúkur
Knappur
Kvíárjökull
Kvísker
BREIÐAMERKUR
Sandfell
Hof
Knappavellir
Knappavallaós
Ingólfshöfði
Skeiðará
Vrag.

PREFACE

The glacier gives back what it takes, they say, eventually brings it to light. Not long ago, pieces of mountaineering gear started appearing from under the glacial ice of Vatnajökull: crampons, a piolet, tent pegs, anchors, a pocket knife, glasses frames, a thermos, a lantern, a corkscrew, a cake slice, sundry other little things—crushed, broken, badly worn down. They were found scattered around a small area, like after a shooting. The objects were brought to the Skaftafell Visitor Center for examination. Some of the items, being monogrammed, were soon identified as the possessions of an Austrian, one Bernharður Fingurbjörg, a man who had gone far out onto Vatnajökull, all alone, undertaking a research expedition, investigating an iceless mountain belt rising from the glacier. It was chiefly the cake slice that identified him as the items' owner: there were still folk alive who remembered the man with the Viennese cream cakes, even though many things had been going on in Öræfi—the Wasteland—around the time Bernharður was traveling. I met him in 2003 during his trip to Iceland; we were fellow passengers on a bus east to Öræfi. He went up to the mountains and onto the glacier while I stayed in the lowlands; we never met again. An extensive search by farmers and a rescue team at the time came up empty-handed. One of the objects the glacier coughed up was a strongbox, more or less intact; the park ranger broke into it and saw it was filled with papers and writings. Glancing quickly inside, she didn't look further than to see the box contained a long letter written by Bernharður Fingurbjörg. The park ranger sent me the box; the letter was addressed to me.

Auth.

I

DREAMS

Ingolf landed at the place which is now called Ingolf's Head
(Ingólfshöfði).

Landnámabók (The Book of Settlements)

I was past exhaustion, the Austrian toponymist Bernharður Fingurbjörg wrote in his letter to me, spring 2003. I crawled, Bernharður went on, into the Skaftafell Visitor Center, where I promptly lost consciousness. When I came to, a crowd of people was staring at me, but no one came over to help; my head was swimming; there was a large, open wound in my thigh, reminiscent of a caldera, and I thought I saw glowing lava well from it, a burning current pouring itself out like a serpent writhing up my spinal cord toward my head, which was becoming a seething magma chamber. I was delirious. For a long time, no one did anything, then, finally, after much staring and gesturing, a doctor was called; she happened to be on a camping trip with her family in Skaftafell at the time and came running full tilt to attend to me. I cannot find my mother, I told the doctor in my delirium, I cannot find my mother, I remember saying. I started to cry.

The doctor asked for clean linens and towels, a dishcloth, some organic soap, ethanol, toothpaste, whey, sugar, Brennivín, and an interpreter. The staff jumped to their feet and bounded in all directions at her requests. I heard it all at the periphery of my senses, from deep within my coma, and I saw it all before me,

I saw the rich flora of the valley opening up for me, dripping butter from every blade of grass, and I said: Butter drips from every blade!... People flocked around me in the Visitor Center, I could hear myself talking a soup of nonsense, the doctor again calling for an interpreter so she could understand what I had to say.

I later learned that this doctor was, in fact, a veterinarian, one of national reputation: Dr. Lassi, the district veterinarian from Suðurland, a superheroine in thick wax coat and cape, wearing high leather boots and with a bottle-green felt hat on her head. Dr. Lassi said that it was beyond real that I'd emerged alive from the mountains without the rest of my party, given how badly my thigh was injured. I will help you find your mother, she said, stroking me, rubbing me like a newborn calf—all this Bernharður wrote in his letter to me that spring.

When the interpreter got there, people noticed a strange expression on her face; she alone understood the fantastical tosh bubbling from me, the things Dr. Lassi later recorded in her report—although I *was* speaking splendid Icelandic (for my father is Icelandic, and had used his mother tongue around me and my brother so we could talk to our relatives), there now erupted a flood of delirious German words, or rather Austrian, or, even more accurately, Viennese, to be precise, all a mumbled babble and humming, a soft lowing mix of various languages. Someone brought woolen fabrics and Dr. Lassi wrapped me tenderly, saying, I'm swaddling you like a little boy going to sleep, I'll watch over you, you're my little bundle.

The Alpine Child, as the doctor's report sometimes calls me, was taken by hay-cart over to the hotel in Freysnes, followed by a whole herd of people, according to the report, people who didn't want to stop looking at me. The hotel in Freysnes is big and expansive and dependable and the cleanest building in the region, even though the roof had recently blown off, and rain would pour into the rooms on the top floor. The big old place had been warped at the foundations by the terrible power of gale force storms, and several people were at work with backhoes and tractors and bulldozers pushing the building back into shape. The patient couldn't very well be treated in the Skaftafell Visitor Center due to the abundance of sweaty tourists and because the air there was clogged with ancient, greasy, frying juices; all the restrooms were piss-stained and shit-marked. Dr. Lassi had no intention of dealing with an open wound in such conditions, and so I woke with the dew, as the saying goes, to find myself on a rattling hay-wagon; I saw that my leg had turned icy blue, splotched with white. Salmon pink pus bubbled from the wound. I thought I saw a snake crawling about in there, a fur hat on his head, a pipe in his mouth.

Dr. Lassi seemed familiar with the antiseptic revolution brought about by the Hungarian obstetrician Dr. Semmelweis, I mused there in the hay-wagon, how he saved countless lives with hand-washing and good hygiene for mother and newborn alike; perhaps Dr. Lassi knows Dr. Semmelweis through the French writer Louis-Ferdinand Céline, as I do: Céline wrote an important essay about Semmelweis when he qualified as an obstetrician, *La vie et l'oeuvre de Philippe Ignace Semmelweis*, really more a literary than a medical text, I thought in the hay-wagon on my way to Freysnes, many good writers have been doctors, these professions are by nature similar ...

It's the custom in Öræfi to make do with whatever lies to hand, and Dr. Lassi was well acquainted with that region, having steeped herself in regional life; during her vacations at the Skaftafell campsite with her family and camper van she considered herself a true Öræfing. They would arrive early each spring before lambing started, a time when there were few tourists around. This year, their vacation had run together with Easter, which fell later than normal. Dr. Lassi didn't hesitate in her task, injecting me with horse tranquilizer via a horse syringe, the sight of which turned me white: I've dosed you with the butter-drug, my friend, said Dr. Lassi, and you'll feel a little numb, beyond cares; you're heading to another world but remaining with us still, watch carefully now, watch everything carefully and then tell me what you see.

The patient's case revolves around a significant injury to his leg, Dr. Lassi wrote shortly after in her report: the foot had frostbite and septicemia, and gangrene had begun to develop in the upper thigh, an ugly fleshrot known as coldburn had entered the bone; a large chunk had been bitten out of the thigh, probably several days ago, in a bad frost, Dr. Lassi's report concludes. I examined the wound and saw at once the bite was from something with straight teeth, not canines, thought it can hardly have been *a man* who bit this kid in the leg, wrote Dr. Lassi, unless it was someone with an oddly large mouth, like Mick Jagger, though it's highly unlikely he's on a trip to East Skaftafell at this very moment, nor would such a decent man turn utterly brutal without warning, though given he's been out west sailing a little cutter recently the possibility can't be entirely ruled out, not that you'd find a cutter amid the black sands here, with all the surf and oceanic erosion—no, some wild animal bit the boy, some *highly-evolved wild animal with transverse-ridged teeth* ... Dr. Lassi jotted the three periods of an ellipsis in her report; the interpreter was standing right there, some timid country girl. What's the guy saying? Dr. Lassi asked the interpreter and the interpreter pricked up her ears: He's telling his mom not to go over to some green Mercedes Benz, he's repeating that phrase again and again, he's looking for her and can't find her.

Dr. Lassi and the interpreter scanned their eyes over me a long time, their garrulous patient, until Dr. Lassi became angry at the continual delay in fetching clean towels and the rest of the things for which she'd asked; lacking what she needed, she started taking off her own clothes. Underneath she was wearing gray woolen underwear and some kind of tank top; she tried to remove my pants but couldn't do it without causing me great pain so she vigorously cut the pants' legs open with a pocket knife. Dr. Lassi slipped off her underclothes and made a tourniquet above the wound using her bra, untying the scarf I'd bound there to cut off my circulation, a scarf now thick with coagulated blood. Dr. Lassi was in good shape, and people were embarrassed at suddenly having a naked lady there inside the hotel room. She cried out for vodka and whiskey and Brennivín and spirits and toothpaste and any books that could be found out here, maps, almanacs ... everything! shouted Dr. Lassi. People leapt to their feet and disappeared about the hotel, searching in the kitchen and the toilets, opening all the cupboards, going into bedrooms; someone picked up the phone and made a call. Amid all this a bottle came flying, as if summoned by the shouting itself, responding of its own accord...Dr. Lassi plucked it out the air and upturned it over her underwear, cleaning the thigh with great care and devotion; she took a decent swig herself then poured the dregs sensually into my mouth, as though I was her lover dying in a mountain cabin...After finishing up, Dr. Lassi got to her feet; she wrapped herself in her wax overcoat to hide her nakedness and looked at everyone with large, predatory eyes.

In Dr. Lassi's report there are arguments about how it wouldn't have served any purpose to call an ambulance: since the community was reunified, it's 350 kilometers to the nearest hospital, a 12-hour drive given how much there is to see on the way, things one simply has to stop and examine, all kinds of natural wonders which no one could remain unmoved by— and the helicopter was busy out west in the fjords doing something with the Viking Task Force, shooting rogue cattle or else out with reporters, capturing images of Mick Jagger some damn place, Dr. Lassi writes, and there's no port anywhere in Suðurland, just immense breakers crashing over the sands and across the wilderness; in order to steer a ship to land here, you'd need to know by heart an essay written by the "fire cleric" Jón Steingrímsson, *Um að ýta og lenda í brimsjó fyrir söndum* ("On Steering and Landing a Ship on Waveswept Sands")—an essay everyone has neglected over the years; the article isn't part of the education curriculum and the consequences for today's travelers are most grave.

Dr. Lassi asked for all the toothpaste in the hotel: once gathered, the toothpaste was to be squeezed out of the tubes into a large bowl; she also needed a trowel or tile float. Several people got to work on this. These tubes are appallingly tiny, said Dr. Lassi. And then Dr. Lassi needed a saw: she stretched out her hand, looked up to the heavens and asked for a saw but no saw appeared in her palm; there wasn't a saw to be found at the hotel in Freysnes, which shocked many people. No saw? I have saws a-plenty at home, said old Muggur, the farmer from Bölti, if we were at my house, you could have your pick of saws, Dr. Lassi, I have all kinds of saws, wood saws, hacksaws, wheel saws, a saber saw, a table saw, a chainsaw... At the hotel, there were blunt, non-serrated kitchen knives of every kind (only soft food was served there) and a number of wickedly sharp pocket knives, whetted on emery, all arrayed on a tray the local farmers offered to Dr. Lassi so she could carry out her mission; Flosi from Svínafell said that perhaps there might be an angle grinder in his jeep, could she possibly make use of such a thing?...That'll do it! Dr. Lassi's exclamation echoed around the hotel, already wobbling on its foundation, the patient is totally out of it...What did you give the fellow? demanded Jakob from Jökullfell quietly, why does it smell of hay? It's butyric acid! cried Dr. Lassi, made from silage, a domestic-designed and produced medicine, often used in date rape; even if the good gentleman is half-awake, he won't remember anything after the operation, won't feel a thing during it, all because of how effective the medicine is. Flosi from Svínafell came back from his vehicle; the angle grinder leapt to life and the hotel splattered with red gore; people felt the mountains dim and the glacier cracking and the sands moaning... Dr. Lassi was dexterous with the angle grinder, taking the leg off at the asshole and scrotum with swift hacks. It saved the tourist's life, Dr. Lassi writes a little further on in her report, and it was necessary—because of the acute abscesses, infections, deep freezing and frost and fleshrot and coldburn—to entirely sever one of his ass cheeks, and also his penis; the tourist was then sewn back together with twine sterilized in Brennivín; his asshole was saved, although it would have been safer to take that, too, Dr. Lassi writes in her report, before proceeding to provide a literary survey of the local region.

Rumor has it that Dr. Lassi sent the pecker into town on a bus, rolled in cellophane and packed in a cooler to preserve it. The package was addressed to an acquaintance of hers at the Icelandic Phallological Museum, describing this gift as a contribution to high culture and urging the Minister, the warrior queen of Icelandic culture, to take this thing ceremoniously from its cooler and hand it off to the superintendent of the Phallological Museum with a little speech. The ceremony was shown prime time on the national news. There's no leg museum and no buttock museum, said the Minister of Education, but we're proud of the Phallological Museum. Back east in Öræfi, there was nothing for it but to discard the leg and ass-cheek in the trash incinerator at Svínafell, an incinerator which heats the swimming pool Flosalaug, wafting a grilling smell over the countryside in the spring breeze, a pungent mix of smoke and soot and trash fumes.

The nasal-voiced regional reporter from the State Broadcasting Service in Suðurland reached Öræfi despite sandstorms at Skeiðarársand that rendered his car entirely plain, stripping all its markings; he interviewed Dr. Lassi after news of this mysterious accident spread, asking about the vet's impressive initiative and the case of the man whose life Dr. Lassi had worked so remarkably to save, the Alpine Child. In an interview broadcast via telephone, Dr. Lassi said she had no choice but to amputate ... dismember, whispered the language consultant at the State Broadcasting Company into the small headphone in the regional news correspondent's ear ... *dismemberment*, repeated the language consultant in the ear of the correspondent ... dismemberment, blurted out the correspondent in front of Dr. Lassi ... the dismemberment of the Alpine Child at the hotel in Freysnes, said Dr. Lassi, I was forced to take off a leg, I had no time to lose if the youth was going to live. Dr. Lassi showed the correspondent the leg and butt check, lifted the piece up and shook it a little bit and let it crackle over the microphone where it rattled the wider population, it'll be discarded in the trash incinerator, Dr. Lassi told the radio listeners, to heat up Flosalaug, which is usually heated with tourist trash but the tourists won't have arrived this early in the spring, they arrive with the migratory birds ... this is energy ... trash is energy ... all matter is energy, she said, somewhat off track ... but the nasal regional correspondent from the State Broadcasting Service asked, energetically: Is it fun being a veterinarian? Yes, it's fun, said Dr. Lassi, when things are going well. Then they went around the hotel and showed the correspondent the sights, the blood-drenched angle grinder and the maids cleaning the wallpaper. Is it true a sheep bit this man? asked the correspondent, but Dr. Lassi replied carefully that the man had encountered a flock of wild sheep some place up in Öræfi, the Wasteland, where they had been all winter or even for several winters, Dr. Lassi said, and that's a violation of the law, I cannot say for how many centuries the laws have been broken here in the country ... but as to whether a wild sheep bit the man, I cannot say: I don't know what bit him, but something did. At the end of the interview the correspondent explained somewhat frankly the journey the penis had made by bus to Reykjavík, its warm reception, and the place of honor it could expect there in the capital's culture.

Dr. Lassi settled down in the Öræfi region while she attended her patient at the hotel in Freysnes, ordering her family to stick around in the tent trailer at Skaftafell and not to trouble themselves, no matter what happened. I must write my report, Dr. Lassi told her family; she had resolved to find out what had happened in the wilderness, where the traveling Alpiner had been, where he came from ... It's not possible to saw off someone's leg and save their life and then just walk away; that would be unethical, writes Dr. Lassi in her report ... How educated are you!? Dr. Lassi shouted at me like I was deaf from the pain in my leg, no longer a leg but a phantom limb, that was the first thing she wanted to know ... how educated is he!? Dr. Lassi shouted at the interpreter, who she felt was being sluggish, reluctant to translate ... He's a graduate student, the interpreter reported to Dr. Lassi, he's studying in the Department of Nordic Studies at the University of Vienna ... And what's he doing there!? asked Dr. Lassi, loud and clear. He's looking for his mother ... no, wait, he's writing a dissertation in Toponymy? *Toponymy?* Toponymy? Well, fine, but is that really a field of study these days? Dr. Lassi asked the interpreter... And does "the kid" have a name? He's called Bernharður, the interpreter said to Dr. Lassi, Bernharður Fingurbjörg, from Vienna.

The interpreter worked on the report with Dr. Lassi, Bernharður wrote in his letter, passing on the words I spoke there on my sick bed at the hotel in Freysnes. The interpreter had a hidden narrative gift, filtering out all the delirious babble and needless descriptions; she weaved together a pithy narrative, an escalating, logical sequence of events. Dr. Lassi found it highly compelling and envisioned publishing the report in the *Journal of Agriculture* or even submitting the report to the great agricultural paper *Freyja* or publishing it in *Friends of the Animals* or just in *Nature Papers*; she imagined, too, getting to know the interpreter rather better, though Dr. Lassi didn't yet know if the shy country girl had any lesbian inclinations.

I wanted to reach Mávabyggðir, said Bernharður, Dr. Lassi's report says, and stay there a while to study the place names, their origins and local forms; my intention was to go from Mávabyggðir over to the pass, Hermannskarð, where Captain J. P. Koch and his companions went on their 1903 expedition to measure the ice shelf at Öræfajökull, those preeminent men after whom the pass is named. I was planning to celebrate the 100th anniversary of their expedition there, and then to go up to Tjaldskarð, the valley up from the glacial shield volcano, between two peaks, where Captain Koch spent two weeks in a tent in a variety of weather conditions, knuckling down to his research during the periods he could not be outside taking measurements. One day, as he was sitting writing in the tent, hoarfrost and a heavy snowstorm outside, he saw that the oilcan had sprung a leak and so he and his companion, Þorsteinn, would need to fetch a new one from down in the settlement, and return the horse they had with them since they were no longer using it and all it was doing was risking death. They dressed and hurried away from their spot, following an ancient, perilous way down the precipitous, fissure-ridden Virkisjökull, the horse with them; Virkisjökull is a tumultuous glacial cascade that descends from high cliffs, a difficult and obstructed glacier, and visibility was low due to fog and rain as they were coming down. They descended to the valley Hvannadalur, where in the old days people picked angelica; it was a long trip, Koch and Þorsteinn went with their horse over the great belt of rocks the glacier had created, tracing a slender path of loose stones at the bottom of a precipitous landslide, with sheer drops down into gaping fissures, I will need to go carefully once I get there, I thought to myself, Captain Koch and Þorsteinn headed to the cave Flosahellur on the way because Koch wanted to examine it; it's great to be here, Captain Koch said in Flosahellur, Bernharður said, Dr. Lassi wrote. From there Captain Koch and Þorsteinn headed down a peat landslip to the lowlands, then down the mountain to get supplies at Svínafell. There was a man there with a newly-acquired wooden leg: not long before he had been out to the shore with three other men hunting seal. They were caught in extreme weather and frost and blown off their path; two of them were lost for good while the third made it home to Svínafell, about 40 kilometers away, with tremendous difficulty: the leg had frostbite and so was sawn off, the stump bound together, and a peg leg made from driftwood, a boot painted on it. Koch and Þorsteinn paused briefly, wolfed down some provisions, gulped down coffee, got a new can and rushed back that very same day, the same route up Öræfajökull;

no-one would do such a thing nowadays. I planned to descend the glacier this way and make a research expedition to Svínafell and confirm J. P. Koch's measurement of Öræfajökull, although all the time I was worried about how I would fare with the horses and my traveling trunk, a large wooden box; I would find a way when it came to it, having never been there before and knowing nothing about the way it was, but I had to go if it were at all possible. Captain Koch had taken a horse down there so I knew it was possible, and I was of the mind that someone ought to traverse the same route in the year 2103 to remember Captain Koch and the 200th anniversary of his expedition, though probably everyone will have forgotten him by then. Place names, though, last forever. On this trip there were many names to encounter: for example, Fingurbjörg, or Finger Rock, the name Captain Koch gave to the large rounded rock on Mávabyggðir, or The Place Gulls Settled; Hermannskarð, The Soldiers' Pass, the gap through the glacier the soldiers took on the way to Öræfajökull; Tjaldskarð, the Tent Pass, where they were situated when measuring Öræfajökull; and Þuríðartindur, a large and beautiful mountain peak named after Þuríði Guðmundsdóttir from Skaftafell, Þorsteinn's sister; under this rock Koch and he enjoyed the pancakes she had baked for them as provisions, and they were so grateful to her for the delicacies that they made her immortal in the peak's name. I found for my part that the way to the glacier from Mávabyggðir through Hermannskarð went on rather too long; I was crushed by gnashing hoarfog on the glacier, by fierce gusts; I did not want to believe that I was lost and walked for many days on my skis going short distances in adverse conditions;

most of the time I hunkered down inside my trunk, which suited me fine, until the storms and blizzards worsened and one by one I lost my horses, a disaster, I was morose at having taken them with me out on the glacier, I became estranged to myself—this was a travail I had dreamed about for such a long time, the idea of the expedition had become the idea of myself, my identity, but as soon as my dream was coming true, I was a stranger. The last horse, the one that drew the trunk, disappeared, the trunk along with him, with it all the data for my thesis. Unless the data reappears in fifty years' time somewhere, at glacial speed. Probably, I took a wrong turn on Hermannskarð and went a long way out onto the glacier, thinking myself safely and correctly almost arrived at a settlement. I reached instead a luxuriant valley surrounded by cliffs that I clambered down; I could not find this valley on a map and there were no external landmarks visible from within it, neither peaks nor elevations—it was as if the land had suddenly slipped apart and up sprang a luxuriant valley full of forest, heather-moss and grasses inside the glacier. A rollicking sense of joy seized me, both at having gotten off the glacier alive and at possibly being in an unknown valley, one which would be named for me, *Bernharðsdalur*, it would be a real boon for my dissertation, would bowl over the professors in the toponymy department at the University of Vienna, I would become a toponymist and explorer ... these days, it's rare to get a place named after you.

In the valley my compass got completely confused, utterly unable to function, the arrow turning circles at lightning speed, then the compass stopped and pointed resolutely right at me, no matter how I twisted myself about and tried to wrestle myself ahead of the arrow. I attempted that for a while. After the compass stilled, I marveled at all the rich vegetation, the valley's fragrance, its weather, here in the middle of powerful Vatnajökull. I sat beside a little spring and washed my feet. From there I saw where sheep, long-legged and almost like steinbocks, grazed on the slope; they seemed to glisten. There were rams so obese and rotund that they resembled wethers more than sheep, heavy and sluggish; when the herd became aware of me it startled; the animals began to stamp their feet and the mountains resounded with the noise; it was like darkness crashing into the valley, amazingly intense in contrast to the twenty-four-hour sun that shines this time of year in this latitude. And then a hundred glowing eyes were approaching in darkness. I became so horrified that I lost my faculties and lay prone beside the spring, my whole body going to sleep. I did not lose consciousness; on the contrary, I was too alert, hyper-aware yet paralyzed physically, I felt able to engage everything in the whole world, to hear everything, to see everything, to feel everything; I saw the black sky and the sun enormously large behind the darkness, all a burning fire, I felt myself flying through space as though sallying on in a dream, suddenly a piercingly bright light appeared and the sun was directly over me, stifling hot, I had the notion to remove my clothes and immerse myself in the spring, but then I saw a single fearsome ram standing over me, bleating loud and cruel and biting my leg, but he vanished just as suddenly as he appeared. I was slow to re-orient myself and struggled to shift. I first tried crawling, then hopped a while on one leg, supporting myself with a staff;

a blizzard struck and the lush valley immediately became sub-merged in snow and slush, such that I had great difficulty keep-ing myself upright in the snow and not being submerged in slush; I sweated buckets causing a thick armor of ice to fasten itself to my clothes, leaving me board-stiff. My leg was numb, lead-heavy, useless; I felt like a weighted-down sled was tied around me, or a horse and carriage, or that my leg was terribly long, unman-ageable, and in this fashion I climbed up the rocks and scree out from the valley, like this I crawled along the ice for a long time, like this I crawled over the hills, like this I crawled across rivers and streams, like this I crawled through forests—and like this I crawled back to civilization.

This happened on Holy Thursday. On Good Friday, 18th April 2003, Bernharður Fingurbjörg crawled into the Skaftafell Visitor Center, Dr. Lassi writes in her report, telling the inter-preter: I have no option but to believe you what you're saying, or else the ground beneath my feet will open up, but I am going to make it my immediate mission once I reach Reykjavík to sign up for German language courses in the Continuing Education Department at the University of Iceland in order to read Goethe in the original and talk to all these tourists.

†

The farmers who owned land and had pastures in the wasteland, Öræfi, took offence when the evening radio news reported wild animals up in the mountains; an emergency farmers' council took place in the dining room of the hotel at Freysnes early Saturday morning. This disgrace needs to be wiped out, Dr. Lassi writes in her report. The meeting was attended by the District Magistrate of East Skaftafell; he stood up first and spoke, not needing to ask for quiet because there was absolute silence in the room before he said: A herd is on the loose in the National Park. And so his speech ended. Well, said Runólfur from Mýr, that's not good. No, it's not, said Flosi from Svínafell. Well...Tempers flared, the report says, they went absolutely crazy by Öræfi standards, although an unfamiliar visitor could have mistaken it for meditation class. The animals are probably on the Skaftafell slopes, didn't the lad come down that way? He came down the glacier at Morsárdalur, said Jakob from Jökulfell, falling asleep in mid-sentence... Didn't this little punk head to Mávabyggðir without letting anyone know about his trip and without a sure sense of his route, said old Muggur from Bölti; he deserved to die. He must have gone directly from Mávabyggðir straight across the glacier to descend at Morsárdalur. But where did he get himself bitten? Or is it something other than a bite, Dr. Lassi? asked the magistrate. Perhaps this wild sheep is from Núpsstaður, having wandered from Eystrafjall over the glacier and into the National Park, said Odd from Gröf. Oh-oh, this is all just speculation, the magistrate said. Some were convinced the sheep belonged to Jakob from Jökulfell, it's your sheep, Jakob, said the farmers from Mýr, or at least it's on your land. This is not my land, Jakob said, this is State land. From one perspective that's not really so, Bjarni from Nes chimed in, this is the land of the Lord our Creator and it's the duty of all of us, Jakob, to herd together...These are State sheep, said someone, and where is the State shepherd? (laughter) Well,

well, said the magistrate ... wouldn't it be best to saunter up there in the morning and see what we can find. Has anyone heard the forecast? Of course everyone had listened to the weather report; they knew the weather by heart going back decades.

It is a *humanitarian duty* of farmers to retrieve sheep from the mountains, I said in a maternal manner at the meeting in the dining room of the hotel in Freysnes, wrote Dr. Lassi in her report, just as the National Society for the Prevention of Cruelty to Animals requires all farmers to do, it's *horfellislögin*, an old and just law meaning farmers must ensure sheep have shelter and winter fodder: what is there for sheep to eat up on the glacier? They cannot simply eat up the whole of Skaftafell forest and Bæjarstaðar forest and Núpsstaðar forest, or why would tourists want to come to see the National Park then? The black desert sands? ... Besides, grazing is prohibited in the area. You must retrieve the livestock and prevent it from suffering; it must not go wild over winter, for it will be cold, it will be hungry, it will suffer because of your negligence and lack of culture; such a thing cannot be tolerated, it is *inhumane*, I said at the meeting, so says the law of the land and so agreed the farmers, more or less, with much mumbling and muttering, resolving to go out on a well-manned mission to the countryside to fetch the sheep from off the slopes, to save it and bring it into human hands ... that is, to the slaughterhouse.

I knew several of the people present at the meeting thanks to my work in the region, the report continues. Flosi from Svínafell is not a tall man, but strong and powerful, big-boned, reasonable, quiet, reminiscent of Japanese ancient emperors; Flosi never feels pain even though he has repeatedly been badly hurt working on the farm, *merely a scratch* is what he called a bloody dent in his shin the time a horse kicked him—someone asked at the dinner table why his pants were wet with blood, why there was a big puddle under the table that the children were sliding about in ... I saw steaming coffee poured over his hand when the cup overflowed, but he did not notice the difference, and once I witnessed the trunk of the old Volvo he used for saddle storage get slammed shut on his fingers; when asked if it hurt, he said: there's no damage ... I thought, this man cannot recognize pain, but I did not know the Öræfi region well then, I had only just started working at the vet's office, he must feel the way other men do but just does not like to show it, not in front of others nor to himself. One time, up in the mountains, a fox bit Flosi on the thumb and would not let go. Flosi strangled the fox with his free hand and walked for a whole day with the dead fox dangling on his thumb. He grew tired of the carcass by nightfall so cut the head off the fox and slept like that through the night; the next day he finally gave up on the head, cutting off his thumb with a pocket knife at the breakfast table. Muggur from Bólti was at the meeting, a hot-tempered fellow, gruff, someone with whom few dared speak, neither at the meeting at the hotel in Freysnes nor outside, old Muggur is broad-shouldered and repulsive, with a glowering face and a paltry scraggle of toothbrush beard, eyes like ball-bearings, loud-mouthed, impulsive, he once got struck by lightning when he was laying telephone lines across Skeiðarársandur, he fell screaming down from the pole, some eighteen feet; he simply got up unharmed, but steam rose up off him, however, and his fellow workers' eyes smarted; they noticed he smelled like a grill, and that gave them hunger pangs. At seventy years old he took a charging bull in a chokehold and flipped it over, a bull which had gored three teenagers and done some serious damage, Muggur held the beast down and stuck a lynch-pin through its nostril and fastened it to the back of the tractor and dragged it home to his house; the bull has been tame ever since, friendly, even.

In Öræfi the weather can be awful, Dr. Lassi's report says, everything gets blown away, things which people in other parts of the country would never imagine could blow away. During a great sandstorm rocks fly about and then a boulder flings through the air and shatters everything in its path. One time, the fresh hay-bales were being protected from the weather, tied onto a truck so they would not blow away; that night, the truck was blown on top of the haystack, which was lying under it like a squashed cranefly when the men came out to the farmyard the next morning. Not long ago, a tractor was blown out of the farmyard in Svínafell and flew over the nearby houses. In Svínafell there was a church once; that got blown away. A new church was built but it flew away, too, so people stopped bothering to have a church in Svínafell. Here in Öræfi, cars blow off the road like empty plastic bags; bus windows explode in a hail of rocks and the lacerated tourists on board freeze to death, perishing in large numbers; afterward, a new highway gets unrolled like a licorice curl, slung across the sand. One time, the farmers clubbed together; they were getting tired of visitors to the region constantly being killed by the slightest gust, so they flew to Germany and bought a tank from the military and transported it back to Öræfi; the tank is a tremendous, heavy vehicle which proves successful when it's necessary to go out onto the sand in bad weather to collect trapped people. At first, the Öræfings simply used the tank as a school bus, but Runki from Destrikt had once been on a course with the Regional Rescue team and decreed that the tank could only be used in storms, whether for transporting children from school, fetching old people from a crumpled bus, or bringing dead tourists to the Visitor Center. Runki from Destrikt is not from these parts and his mentality is very different from the Öræfings: an uneasy man, he took the tank under his command, saying it seemed like the Öræfings wanted to use the tank in mild weather to drive sheep to pasture or kids to school, to cruise around, count birds, survey the sand... at the time Runki invited everyone to a summit at the hotel in Freysnes, wanting to establish a special regional rescue force with the tank at its heart. There was certainly a need, the countryside was full of tourists run amok, ever since the river, Skeiðará, was bridged once the National Park was established at Skaftafell, something he considered entirely outrageous... a National Park! Instead of utilizing the country, Runki from Destrikt said at that meeting, Dr. Lassi wrote in the report, everything these days gets protected, he said, are they going to protect foxes next!? Minks!? Today, farmers can't think about cattle or agriculture, they're always having to deal with tourists, the tourists want to camp in the hayfields, they want to go horse riding, they want to poke around the farm, they want to birth a lamb, they want to drive a tractor, they want to make hay, they want to stay on the farm, they want to eat lamb for dinner, to eat with the family, to experience a real country atmosphere, coffee and toast in the morning, helping with farm chores; they start driving after us, they ideally want to become the farmer himself during their damn vacations! And, of course, they get in the way! *I* never get any peace, said Runki, you can't move without a busload of tourists taking your picture, whether you're mowing a field or pissing against a wall, better to have sheep in Skaftafell rather than these tourists who trample all over everything, that way the national park would be protected because this nation lives on sheep, at one time there were herds on the slopes and now tourists go walking with their worthless currency in all directions! ... (they all had to think a bit to understand this last assertion) ... you cannot survive on beauty alone; if anything defines beauty, it's livestock on a mountain.

The old farmers, Flosi from Svínafell and Muggur from Bölti and Jakob from Jökulfell, had all of a sudden become Tourist Service Farmers and Regional Rescue members and had ill accepted their lot. They tootled about the beach and slopes in the tank and herded sheep, no matter what Runki said. Öræfings are used to heavy vehicles; during World War Two all kinds of powerful off-road vehicles came into being (nothing advances technology better than war); pictures of this apparatus appeared in newspapers and magazines and some of them spread east into Öræfi, which gave rise to the idea that it might be possible to get such a vehicle to Skeiðarársand, the most rugged place in all the Nordic countries. A debate took place and a parliamentary resolution was agreed; a large barge with caterpillar tracks was brought in and transported east over the sands. This astonishing machine was christened Water Dragon, a name soon simplified to the Dragon; it puttered across rivers and was able to ferry large commodities, implements, and building materials. Afloat, the belts functioned like oars, but it was difficult to control, taking considerable practice to master the Dragon. In the wake of this, Jón from Austurbær brought the first car to the region and, taking his lead from the Dragon, he placed empty barrels under the car and floated it across the river. The Dragon reigned over the beach in the years after the war until modernity arrived in the form of bridges, killing off culture entirely. The Dragon got worn down traversing the sand and was costly to run; it did not provide public transportation and was chiefly used to search for the treasure ship that was supposedly somewhere on the sands.

The Tvísker Brothers came to the meeting at Freysnes— Hálfdán, Helgi, Sigurður, and Flosi—even though they didn't own cattle and aren't farmers but self-taught scientists; they were planning to use their trip to collect insects, count birds, observe plants, and measure the glacier. Hálfdán is a naturalist, Helgi an inventor, Sigurður a scholar, and Flosi a glaciologist. Then there was Fippi from Núpsstaður, crossing Skeiðarársand in his old Willis, made in 1953, an SUV that has lasted half a century because it doesn't have a computer in it, Dr. Lassi wrote, computers have destroyed modern cars, every year brings ever greater luxury and ever more junk.

Some claimed the wild herd belonged to Fippi from Núpsstaður, who welcomed the damage to the National Park, that these were the notorious wild sheep from Núpsstaðurskógar's forests. Fippi wasn't inclined to respond, having told people a thousand times already that the whole herd population was annihilated in a blizzard from the north and by blinding weather and by falling from the cliffs above the farm; they were all killed at once in the late nineteenth century. These days, a great flood of travelers can be found about the farmyards of Núpsstaður, with tourists wandering off in all directions and popping up at the windows. People come to see the old houses and the chapel dating back to the sixteenth century and the hundred-year-old hermit Filippus Hannesson, the son of the rural mailman Hannes Jónsson; tourism has transformed him into a museum exhibit. Fippi felt he couldn't refuse to go on the round-up; you never know where you stand with a wild beast, he said, sarcastically, though it's probably not a wild beast after all, but a very everyday animal. The wild Núpsstaðarskógar herds were quite special, a highly evolved stock, the report continued, they would stay out grazing in the mountain woods the whole year round, and were on the glacier, too, for centuries, perhaps as far back as the Settlement— there were rarely humans about and the animals lived their lives undisturbed in the wilderness, growing fat, sizeable animals yet less well-built than other sheep, because their organs never grew larger than standard lambs' organs; they were noticeably long-legged, typically multi-colored, mottled, thick-necked and big-horned, they had abundant wool, so thick it never dangled down or lagged like wool on today's adult sheep. Heavyset, they were uncontrollable because of their cautiousness; it was hard to catch them, they would leap onto the glacier, jump in rivers, and dive off cliffs to certain death rather than fall into human hands. The farmers in Núpsstaður would only allow themselves to seek a single sheep for food, and they did so for centuries, making the hazardous journey, an adventure, in harmony with nature. When I briefly visited Fippi, wanting to inquire about the wild herds so that I could write an article for *Agricultural News*, he said that so much nonsense had been said and written about the wild animals of Núpsstaður that I might as well just write whatever I felt like, giving me poetic license where his animals were concerned. Though the plan was to write a scientific report for *Agricultural News,* the idea popped into my mind that I should write a novel about the wild herd. But how do you write a novel about wild sheep? I thought, as I stood with Fippi in the farmyard. We locked eyes. Fippi is, like his father Hannes the rural mail carrier, oddly short and slim. People were often amazed to see the Willis on the sands: it would seem empty and gave rise to numerous ghost stories. Tourists often turned up at the Skaftafell Visitor Center greatly disturbed after going out to see the sands, not so much because they'd been caught in a sandstorm in a rental car whose paint was stripped off by the weather, but because they'd met the old Willis in the dark, yellow and red and bearing the number Z221 and with no one behind the wheel!

At Núpsstaður, the last town before you go out onto Skeiðarársand, is Lómagnúpur, a sheer rockface rising 700 meters from sea level, wrote Dr. Lassi in the report; rational, intelligent men grow fearful and awestruck in his shadow, for inside Lómagnúpur lives the giant Járngrím; he appears to people who perish on the sand. It's said that men are doomed if they merely see him; below Lómagnúpur raging whirlwinds whip up and no-one is worthy of mercy. One time, the farmer at Núpsstaður was fetching water in pails down in the mudflats under the overhang, but as he came back up with his full pails a whirlwind whipped up and swirled him up in the air, face-to-face with the rock's highest edge, then twirled him about and around and downward, slow and slower still until he was standing in front of his cowshed door, not a drop lost from his buckets.

Fippi's father, Hannes Jónsson, the rural mail carrier in the Skaftafell area, was known across the land as a heroic traveler, a man as modest and humble as Núpsstaður men tend to be, making nothing of the mortal danger he was placed in by his hazardous journeys across sands and glacial rivers and glacial scree; such stories had to be dragged out of him, like leading a ram to slaughter; he was tortured into writing about his journey over the glacier when the Skeiðará flooded in 1934, an enormous flood; at the time, Hannes was in Öræfi and wanted to cross the sand to deliver his mail and get back in time for Easter, but the sand was practically impassable because of the swelling water, so he detoured across the glacier while the flooding was at its peak, gushing so much water and glacial material and so many icebergs that the Skeidará measured forty kilometers wide across the sand, tumbling along carrying icebergs the size of apartment buildings like little ice cubes; telephone poles were washed away and even the highway, everything in the river's way. Hannes went above this roaring glacial scree, right over the ebb, with the flood booming under his feet across the ice which had turned blood red from the ash columns steaming off the glacier as it towered over the mailman, all flecked with lightning and glare and flashes and thunderous booms and raining sand; the whole time large pieces would break off the glacier around him and where he'd just this second stepped peat-gray flumes flecked with cudbear-red spouted up in the mist. New cracks opened everywhere about him; he had to crawl between them amid the raucous noise, hearing all kinds of murmurations, but he safely crossed with his deliveries, traversing the sands and rivers and glaciers and mountains and forests between Skaftafell and Núpsstaðarskógar, a journey which took eighteen hours and meant he could return home by Easter Sunday. More than once he was prevailed upon to write an account of this journey, and you have to read between the lines in his narrative, which is known by different titles: *Minor Incidents during a Pleasant Journey* or *An Unremarkable Hike*.

Freysnes lies between Skaftafell and Svínafell, Dr. Lassi's report explains at the end of the regional description, since the report was intended for both academic and popular audiences. No-one had lived in Freysnes since that fateful year, 1362: the ruins of dwellings lay about Freysnes for all time, or at least until they were leveled to the ground by a bulldozer one fine winter's day, and today no one knows where the ruins are. More than that: the ruins are a source of shame in the region. Ragnar, the farmer at Skaftafell, sold his land to the State in 1966 so that Skaftafell could become a National Park and so the Icelandic population, not just farmers and their friends and family, could enjoy its natural beauty, an unsurpassed beauty, and it was agreed it should belong to the populace—in fact, Skaftafell's beauty should belong to humanity as a whole, said Ragnar. Everything was changing and few people kept up the traditions. Farming was declining even as tourists started streaming toward Öræfi now the Skeiðará had been bridged on Iceland's National Day,

1974, completing a ring road around the entire country; that year marked 1100 years since Settlement and there were magnificent celebrations. Farming wasn't to be allowed within the Park, for it does not suit the tourism industry; the hotel in Freysnes was designated for those who didn't want to, or couldn't, camp in tents within Skaftafell National Park, such as the elderly and the elegant; Freysnes' beauty is comparable to Skaftafell's. And now all kinds of little houses stand in ancient Freysnes, dotted around the big structure, which has wobbled on its foundation: decorated, furnished prefabs and containers tourists can use, Dr. Lassi wrote; Icelandic ingenuity can change trash skips into hotels.

Documents flooded into the hotel room in the form of books and magazines while Bernharður slept. The chronicles record that one morning in 1362 *Knappafells glacier exploded and spewed over the Lómagnúpur sands and carried everything off into the sea,* thirty fathoms deep: deposits of large rocks, water flumes, sand floods, volcanic detritus, falling rocks, and gray mud left behind desolated sands. The Province was destroyed, all its people and creatures annihilated; no sheep or cattle survived, no creatures left alive anywhere in the province around the glacier, both the historical chronicles and contemporary accounts agree, volcanic material fell everywhere, surging in such great abundance out to sea that ships could not navigate; the corpses of people and animals washed up on beaches far and wide, alongside debris and other rubbish; the bodies were cooked and tender and the flesh so loose on the bones it fell apart. This was the most destructive and fatal volcanic eruption in the history of Iceland, one of the greatest tephra eruptions anywhere on Earth in the last millennium;

the eruption surprised everyone with its so-called *gusthlaup*, the latest scholarly theories contend in a back issue of *Nature Studies*, Dr. Lassi wrote, sweaty with excitement at the surge of evidence the interpreter dumped onto the table beside her, seventy farms were destroyed in one moment that morning, a *gusthlaup* rushing with tremendous speed down the steep mountainsides, taking with it seventeen churches copiously furnished with books, vestments, bells, chalices, and other belongings; nothing survived of this thriving civilization. Beauty and fertility instantly turned forbidding and barren in this storm of destruction, the area now a gaping wound; even the place names were scraped off the land, and everything had to be named fresh when the settlements snuck back in fifty years later, humans bedding down on the new land like fragile plants; Hérað, the Province, became Öræfi, the Wasteland; Klofajökull became Vatnajökull; Lómagnúpssandur became Skeiðarársandur; Knappafellsjökull became Öræfajökull; Knappafell became Hnappavellir; Tvísker became Kvísker... N.B: I should put that in a table as a convenience to readers of the report, Dr. Lassi had written, the amputation of place names and their transformation—you'll like this, Bernharður, you place-name-pervert! Dr. Lassi said, loud and clear.

What the hell is a *gusthlaup*? Dr. Lassi asked the interpreter, I keep writing this damn word in the report, taking it from the accounts that stream in here, but I have no idea what a gusthlaup is! The interpreter replied that she didn't know what gusthlaup meant. Get Hálfdán from Tvísker! Dr. Lassi ordered the interpreter, he's down at the meeting, no, Hálfdán is the ornithologist... Sigurður! Fetch me Sigurður, or whichever of the brothers is the geologist? Just get any of them, they must all know the word, they're so learned, these people, and it has to be clear in the narrative.

No area has ever endured such an extensive natural disaster as Hérað did in 1362, Dr. Lassi's report says, drawing on her sources, fire came up from the glacier, bringing a torrent of burning ash that destroyed all the farms and wiped out the countryside. What's called a pyroclastic flow, or *gusthlaup,* sparkling clouds of poison together with masses of staggeringly hot air rushing down the mountain slopes in the first hours of the eruption, burning everything in an instant, damaging anything living. Oxygen was used up; flesh burnt away. Exactly what happened to Pompeii in ancient times happened to Hérað in 1362...a *gusthlaup*...The Province became Öræfi—the Wasteland...violent fires melted the glacier and ice water ran down the mountain across the plains carrying burning sludge...Legend has it that a lone shepherd on Svínafell heard a crack, then another crack and then said he would not wait for the third crack but rushed boldly up to that part of Svínafell known as Flosihellir, the place he kept his swine, a hairy boar, broad-shouldered and with human intelligence; the boar discovered a cave where large truffle mushrooms grew, and the storm spewed over the countryside and water and mud flowed over everything and over half the mountain and up to the cave, gray and discomforting; the shepherd and his boar alone survived the disaster, gobbling up the truffles in Flosihellir for six months straight, making them quite dyspeptic. When people later investigated the region, they saw that everything on the mountain had burned up and a meter-thick layer of toxic ash lay over it; a lizard-green haze hovered still, and in it long worms swam, the Annals say, the steam debilitated the searchers' pupils so they saw everything upside down and contrary to what anyone else saw; this continued for a long time, and what was gray and black seemed friendly and green. Butter drips from every blade of grass, the new settlers said, as a new beauty sprang up.

What is it exactly that happens in a *gusthlaup*, Interpreter? Dr. Lassi asked the interpreter, it is incomprehensible to me, yet Dr. Lassi did not wait for a response, dashing onward in her writing, Interpreter constantly running to fetch books and sources and maps all throughout the hotel ... Here it is! shouted Dr. Lassi and papers and documents swirl up in the air ... The sources say a *gusthlaup* results from an explosion in a crater, some resistance is required causing the debris to storm down the side of the volcano, not straight up in the air ... but what is the *gust*? Interpreter ...! What do we make of the gust!? Ask those Tvísker brothers about the gust ... no, here it is, there's an article in *Skaftfellingur* about it, let us see ... *gust* is basically lahar fire-cloud, what the French scientists call *nuées ardentes*, that's the *gust* in *gusthlaup*, a plume of smoke and mud, heavy with a burning eruption of gravel and fiery gas, and the gust—the flow—descended the mountain on its fatal journey, destroying everything before it, all the buildings in the Province, all the people and all living creatures, laying waste the whole area in an instant. No one had time to flee, no one knew what was coming and no one knew what had happened, everything became petrified, cast in molds in an instant as ash and friable pumice fell over everything, covering the dead in a dusty veil. Everything lay motionless for fifty years—and then a new settlement began! Dr. Lassi said aloud at the same time as she wrote it in her report.

Who originally settled Öræfi!? Dr. Lassi asked the Interpreter, that must be in my report, my Interpreter, I was even thinking that it would be neat to start the report with it, what do you think?... Isn't that neat?...Wasn't it Ingólfur Arnarson!? I'll be damned, that's ideal! Dr. Lassi enthused, how exceedingly elegant that the report begin with the first settler in Iceland. This report of mine will appear in countless magazines and be translated into many languages, Dr. Lassi remarked to the Interpreter; it will garner international attention. *Ingólf landed at the place which is now called Ingólf's Head*... that's how a report like this should start, my dear Interpreter, said Dr. Lassi, how does *Landnámabók* put it? Where is *Landnámabók, The Book of the Settlement,* when one needs it? Back home up on a shelf! What use is it there? Surely there's not a copy in the hotel? It *should* be here at the hotel, every hotel should have *Landnámabók* in the bedroom drawers and not the *Bible,* for *Landnámabók* is the Icelandic Bible ... from now on I will always travel with *Landnámabók* on me! Dr. Lassi said, it is simply common sense! And good mental health, Interpreter...a damn powerful opening for this report! ... But Ingólf the settler did not settle in Öræfi, and it wasn't called Öræfi at the time, it wasn't called anything, as far as is known, Dr. Lassi wrote, unless some Irish hermit called the area something. Ingólf stayed here one or two winters, along with his retinue; he had thrown his chieftain's pillars overboard, as was the custom, and ordered his servants to find where the columns had come ashore. It was beautiful to look out upon what is now Öræfi, for the province was blessed in its weather, woods flourished and tall grasses and people weren't in favor of going to find the columns, they wanted to stay in the region, and the area was soon given its distinguished name, Héraðð, because butter dripped from every blade here where there's now sand and desolation, where once there was a little glacier and enchanting valley a sinister glacier crawls its desolating way. Back then, seals slept calmly on the shore amid the driftwood; out on the promontory there was an abundance of birds and eggs, fish in the sea, trout in the rivers and water. The Province was paradise, and so there was some disappointment when the pillars were discovered at Reykjavík, though the warm hot springs somewhat enticed the sensualists among them. It's an unfortunate thing, said Karli, Ingólf's slave, traversing a bountiful region merely to build on an inhospitable headland; in Reykjavík cold winds blow, it's all bare gravel and naked ridges and insistent drizzle. This stubborn settler's household lamented leaving the area, which was still nameless, regretted adhering to the high pillar tradition, giving their fate to the roll of a dice—what sort of nonsense this religious idiot believes, the slaves muttered among themselves, not understanding their chieftain's actions; the slaves got angry with the gods and the gods got immediately angry back at them, their anger a thousand-fold—and so a curse has lain on the land and its inhabitants ever since, the region scattered widely with supernatural spirits, harbingers of the gods' anger, the scourge of men; horrors often bombarded the country, settlements were destroyed time and again by earthquakes, volcanic eruptions, and floods, especially in the South, close to Ingólf's original settlement. But Ingólf's steadfastness saved his progeny from a cruel fate: he followed the gods' will, abandoned the fertile slopes and fair ground at the foot of the glacier and took the sparse, unprotected land near Reykjavík, Dr. Lassi wrote, cribbing generously from her sources, not giving the slightest thought to quotation marks, because in 1362 Öræfajökull annihilated Hérað. Believe you me, serfs, I chose to leave Norway, said Ingólf. Don't talk to us about *choice*, said the slave Karli, you can shove your pillars you know where. Ingólf settled up at Arnarhvoll from where he looked sadly across the fjord; he did not feel like beating the slave. Go, then, Ingólf said to Karli, take a maid as a servant, go settle some land, build a farm, multiply, go fish for happiness with greed's leaky net—but never return to me unless you are ready to die.

Should we have built a settlement on the cliff in Hérað? Ingólf asked his wife, Hallveig, at Arnarhvol, the area was certainly beautiful to look upon, but the pillars came ashore here in Reykjavík, here where there are hot springs, clean water, fish in the lakes and birds on the cliffs, a perfect harbor, fjords and green islands and spectacular views, the gods wanted this, I could not have imagined that before as we put to sea, we must make ourselves a settlement here, never return to Norway, here we will thrive in peace. So who took the land in Hérað? It will be interesting to see... Now, dear Interpreter, Dr. Lassi said, fetch me someone who knows all about the Skaftafell district, one of those Tvísker brothers, most likely Sigurður, he is such a knowledgeable guy, I can feel my report flourishing, I can sense the material simmering inside me, from settlement to present day, I just need to vent it, to give it form, this could even become a whole book, and a book entirely unlike anything anyone has ever written in Iceland, a medical history of Bernharður with biographical overtones yet mostly about the wound to his thigh and the amputation; a medical history with a biographical element but all wrapped up in national lore, even, my darling, global sensibilities, yes, yes indeed, I see it all flashing clearly before me, this book will not become irrelevant, the way books do because they are so homogeneous these days, only ever about some*one*, any *one* thing you could sum up in one sentence, as writers do when they're asked what their book is about, What's your book about? they're asked, it's about this, the authors answer, sure of their facts, but when I get asked what my book is about I'm going to answer with a single word: *everything*, everything, it is a global report about an individual and the world, about things in the world, all that's subjective in the world... but what the hell should the book be called? Help me now, Interpreter, what to call this child? Our thing, it needs to be something subtle, but also descriptive, like Dismemberment... listen up, that's it! Spare your brain cells, we've got our title, *Dismemberment*, no, stop entirely now, damn, that is a fine title, a keeper, alright by me, as people say nowadays; it just struck me suddenly from the realm of ideas like lightning strikes in the darkness of night in the wasteland! Above me a blinding, gloomy storm cloud grows, brimful of ideas, making lightning flash through the sky! Dr. Lassi said—and there I was, lying there listening to this conversation in order to memorize it, one side effect of butyric acid, Dr. Lassi said, is that everything that comes before the senses gets committed to memory: first butyric acid causes amnesia, then the *super-memory* in the body and brain get embarrassed and want to compensate a thousand-fold...

37

Report

about

DISMEMBERMENT

Biography (of sorts)
Medical history with national
& global information written by
Dr. Lassi

That's what the book will be called, Dr. Lassi told The Interpreter, when the report is published in book form after having appeared in all the world's major magazines. Or might it be better to call the piece *Amputation*? That's more stylish and sophisticated...Am–puta–tion: *am*... I always have the radio set to AM; puta means whore and I love whores; -tion is action and we must act!... no, better to phrase it like this:

Report

about

Amputation & Castration

&

bio

graphic

medical history

with national and

international information

which was written down verified by trusty

sources by the country's infamous regional

doctor Lassi

or is that too much? she asked as she wrote out the title on a sheet of paper and lost herself in it—but The Interpreter was itching, pulling at her skirt because she needed to fetch Sigurður Tvísker from down in the dining room...You must help me with this, Interpreter dear...Dr. Lassi read her mind and body language and told her to forget Sigurður for now, for the thing now is to write, don't hunt down Sigurður immediately, but go away all the same, I'll call you later if the patient babbles anything, right now I'm going to write a bit of the report, I've got my inspiration, although it's strange how profound I am in your presence, it's like you blow power and spiritedness into me—yes, you'll have to be here while I write this report, I can pay you an inconsequential amount, how lucky I am to have you to turn to, I meet so many varied people from day to day in my line of work, I'm always on the go between farms in Suðurland, I have to geld here and dismember there, so I'm exhausted when I come home...my wife, I have to say, is an energy–suck; I get paralyzed in body and soul around her, so she can do whatever she wants with me, I become an object without will in her hands, she controls everything throughout our house and I'm just like a sausage over in the corner, first she drains all the energy from me, all vitality, then she can be in charge of everything in the household—but if I had a person like you around, life would be a thrill, would be fecund, you are an *energista* my dearest Interpreter, that's what I'll call you, you can see how imaginative I am around you, starting to create words, perhaps I'm inclined to pursue the humanities more than the medical sciences since I'm so smart as to be able to create concepts, that would be better for me, but stop prattling on like this, Interpreter, and fetch Sigurður, didn't I ask you to? No, wait, what's that Bernharður is burbling, just when I'm about to write, he's squandering my inspiration, go get him water if he's asking for water! then bring some more Brennivín for me, just order me a bottle at the bar, the bartender knows me if there's any trouble, I'll go see him tonight and pay the bill with my caresses, if he calls them caresses ... No, don't! Interpreter mine, if Bernharður says something remarkable we cannot afford to miss the information for the report, it might suffer perforations because of that, grow thin and full of holes, that's not good science, the report must be tight and consistent ... sorry I am tired, keep an eye on the bleeding while I write, I couldn't write if you went, I'd get so afraid he'd say something and we'd miss it, it could be the core of the report, so we must not miss anything, nudge me if you see his bandage getting wet, if that happens we must add more toothpaste to the wound, now I'm going to write a bit, I always dreamed of writing, I'm always just about to write something more, there's just never any time, there's always things disturbing one, it's like no one wants anyone to write, I always dreamed of becoming a writer, in some ways it's childish to be a veterinarian, it's what I always replied when I was asked as a child what I was going to be when I grew up, I said *vet* but thought *writer*, because people reacted to it better, I didn't have to listen to some long-winded rebuttal; once when I was ten years old I asked my big brother for the loan of a two-króna coin and I bought a notepad and pen, I assumed the pose and felt the beauty of the world surrounding me as I began to stab the pen down, letters beginning to arrange themselves, the words taking shape from each other on the page, meaning accruing, the world opening up! Something so great, so different from what I'd ever experienced: I felt I'd become a magic-woman, a witch, even— but my mother looked over my shoulder and saw the top of the page with, in capital letters, *The Biography of Lassi the Veterinarian, by herself,* and she exploded with laughter and the whole family burst out laughing and the whole world exploded in laughter, tickled by these fantasies of mine, dead already, it became an entertaining story at every family event and all kinds of uncles and aunts with unfamiliar faces asked me about it and laughed this vile laughter that masked envy and greed; that went on for years, ever thus, ever the same, a mask for envy and greed, it's still this way, indisposition, envy, and greed, people haven't thought up anything new under the sun to torment me with. I long since ceased going to those ill-conceived family get-togethers. I've dismembered myself from my family, I turned into a teenager determined to rise from my dream's death so I could have my revenge on my family; I began studying to be a veterinarian, but deep down I was planning to become a writer and record my own life as a veterinarian and how frustrating my family is, how narrow-minded and judgmental, I have always felt that *art* runs in my blood even though there are no artistic neurons anywhere in my family, I'm so very different from them. Now, finally, now my parents are dead, I will allow my dream to come true, for why haven't I done it before? In reality, it isn't possible to do anything in this world until everyone is dead and one finally gets some peace—when all those who have placed obligations on your shoulders are finally dead, you are free and can make your dreams come true, although then you'd be alone in the world, unable to achieve anything. I never wanted children, just to be kind to animals and care for them in this evil human world, prevent them from suffering and cruelty, but it's proved impossible to escape my family, I've been forced to cause many animals to suffer and worse, so much worse, I have been forced to castrate them and kill them, to castrate animals, Interpreter, that is an unspeakable horror … and I cannot get out of this, it has often occurred to me to castrate myself as a deliberate punishment, a payment for all the eunuchs I have made, to remove my uterus, because these are undeniably crimes, crimes against animals, crimes against nature, crimes against life and crimes against God! …You have selected a good job, how noble it is to interpret between people in this post-Babylonian world of ours, Dr. Lassi said, her face clouding as she looked wearily up at the ceiling light, causing shadows to thread shallow wrinkles around her eyes, making her look intensely disordered and cruel, her youth and dreams eaten up the way suburban street systems eat up nature. I have sometimes looked at myself, feeling a pressing need to justify myself, to have self-belief after a hard day at work, and have told myself I'm an interpreter, interpreting between humans and animals, and my wife tells me to cook and clean, she does it indirectly, I come home and nothing has happened at home since the morning, she has been at home all day watching TV, she commands me, dead tired, to cook and clean and I tell her I'm an interpreter between humans and animals, and then I clean and cook food and do it with good graces … but I'm no interpreter, I'm more like a predatory animal, this job isn't the way children imagine it, I

think all veterinarians planned to become veterinarians as
children and fixated on the dream and never found a new dream
amid the idea-destroying weight of their home environment; it is
a dream that arises when children have somewhat lost faith in
humanity or, more accurately, their parents, who are humanity's
representatives among children, and so children stop loving
mankind, their parents, because they see their parents as
executioners; instead, they direct their love to animals, to the
animal kingdom, children find harmony with dumb animals and
their suffering, although they're not dumb, all animals have their
own language and gestures, it's just the *interpreters* are missing, not
yet arrived, if I can't understand German or Viennese, how can I
understand pig? And when I step into my childhood dream of
giving animals my love, I find I must castrate and kill them,
castrate them and kill them, day in and day out, inject them full
of drugs and filth; the childhood dream bursts in the adult
nightmare, for veterinarians and for everybody else ... the adult
world is horribly brutish, my Interpreter, it is too late for me to
become an author, if my dream had been nurtured when I started
my biography at nine years old, I would have become a writer,
everyone is always trying to destroy others' dreams, my parents
destroyed my dream by making fun of it, instead of encouraging
it, you must start early if you want to flourish as an artist, there's
no time for anything else, you need to start your education at an
early age and never stop, I am not talking about school education
but self-study, the peace to pursue one's interests like the Tvísker
brothers have been able to, having never busied themselves with
farming except for sheer pleasure, they would not be the scientists

and artists they are today if they had been required to farm or carry out some other duty; if I'd been invited to write the story of my life when I was a little girl I'd have become an author and lived my dream instead of living in a nightmare as a vet, unceasing, how badly I've spent my time, spent my life badly ... and now I'm hungry, can you fetch sandwiches or something, and get Sigurður on the way, my Interpreter, sandwiches now and Sigurður from Tvísker, now we need to put the big truck in the report, I first need to disperse my thoughts before I can collect myself in intense concentration, I don't feel I can write right now, perhaps I can glean something from Sigurður while we have ourselves some sandwiches, put the time to use, instead of eating while staring into the air, we can find out something useful about the history of the Skaftafell district, perhaps when the phone lines were laid across Skeiðarársand, I don't want salad or anything like that, just ham and pineapple, I think gleaning Sigurður's words would be a glacial marker on the way to bringing the report to fruition, crossing the choppy, moving glacier that is writing, preferably white bread, and I could become a writer and stop having to castrate and kill animals, but my real dream, my dream is to get out of my dream, though then someone will take my place and continue to torment the animals, so it's just as well that I do it, I want the sandwich toasted, animal suffering is a cog in the mechanism of society, you can't stop the wheels, although that sanctimonious bore is always saying so on the radio, over and again, that reedy-voiced little fatso, can't remember his name, also a jug of water and some glasses, Sigurður's full of interesting information, he's a really good and talented man, no ketchup or anything disgusting like that, it's staggering that these Tvísker siblings are such intelligent people, perhaps it's because they don't waste their time farming but attend to their studies, I wish *I* could lose myself in study, you hear farmers and farm-dwellers say, but we need to attend to the livestock, attend to the livestock and attend to the livestock, always on the run from studying, or how else would we all live? Interpreter, off you go now, it's just that everyone wants to be like them, like those gifted fellows without progeny, it's said there's mental illness in the family, now I'm going to stop castrating and killing and I'm going to apply myself to study, apply myself to creative writing, my dearest lady, my man! Applying oneself to writing is the most exalted and most sinful thing, worse than castrating and killing, I'm headed out of the ashes and into the fire, but who settled Öræfi? I'm going to ask Sigurður as we eat a sandwich, I know Ingólf Arnarson lived here a year or two at Ingólfshöfði but scholars don't consider that settlement, so what's settlement? My books are all at home, I want to travel with my books, to install bookshelves in the folding camper or pop-up camper or whatever it's called, but my wife denies me even that, I was going to pack several essential books for the journey to Öræfi, including *The Settlement of Skaftafell & its Governing* by Einar Öl. Sveinsson, that first-class piece by a first-class scholar of those first-class pillars, it would have been better to leave a toothbrush than *The Settlement of Skaftafell & its Governing*, I've read it before, but a long time ago, I know the book well but that's not the point, I've brushed my teeth often enough, I would not have to disturb Sigurður if I had the book, you follow, although everyone benefits from disturbing

Sigurður, one grows more accomplished from proximity to him, a man spends his time well in the presence of smart people it says in *The Brothers Karamazov*, something like that comes to mind, I cannot remember who said it, whether it was Ivan or Alosja rather than Dimitri, it would have been good, time well-spent, looking that up, my wife took all the books out the camper van and put them back in their places in my office, she considers books to be furniture, or junk, she said that the family was headed on a trip together and I was not going alone on an outing with my books—but what family? Just her and her abominable poodle, I admittedly neglect them for my work, my endless work trips that take me the length and breadth of Suðurland, and, yes, by reading when I'm finally back home, it's possible to watch TV together but not to read books together, unless we each read to one another, though I do not want to hear my wife spoiling the text of *The Settlement of Skaftafell & its Governing* by Einar Ól. Sveinsson, destroying a book which is so precious to me, she goes back to the TV and lies about all day and stares at it in the campsite between browsing about the Visitor Center, looking at postcards, lapping down ice creams, shitting in the bathroom ... In modern society, we have to do everything ourselves, so there's no way for anyone to become a real writer or real scholar, let alone a polymath, no one in modern times has the potential to become a generalist, that's the past, it's not so much that infinite specialization has set knowledge and science and philosophy into the shredder, rendering science nothing but a pile of strips nowadays, it's rather there is no time, they are clever, those brothers Tvísker, they divided the studying between them so that together they are one great polymath; you have no time in these modern times, you have to do everything yourself, despite all the machines, appliances, all this stuff which makes you think you don't have to do anything except be a master of all of it, cradling oneself in a rocking chair and sucking a pipe and thinking about the deeper questions of existence or even trifling questions, modern appliances let you think they are doing it all and that you yourself have nothing to do, but a person is constantly in a frenzy in their household, if you aren't constantly in a frenzy the appliances send you an accusing glance so you are always guilty of not being in a frenzy with the appliances, and when you're in a frenzy over these domestic devices, you're guilty of not doing your literature and science, of not using the time to gain knowledge instead of being this damned slave to domestic appliances, for modern man is a slave to technology, to nothing else, everything intended to relieve human activity has made it heavier: as well as needing to know everything, you need to do everything yourself, in the past there were many people in a home and each had their role, now everyone is alone at home and has the task of doing everything; in fact, no one is at home any longer because all of us are out serving the State. Where formerly one cooked dinner, another tidied, one raised the kids, the shepherd herded the sheep, things were clear, now everything is so unclear, now everyone feels insulted, particularly women if reminded of a domestic role, there cannot be any division of labor, everyone has to do everything, know everything, and no one can be at home during the day because that would be State inequality, though no one does anything and no one can be anything but a domestic slave and nothing sensible comes from nothing… it will be nice to meet Sigurður from Tvísker, I want to tell him I've been a subscriber to his magazine *Skaftfellingur* from the beginning, although my wife was against it, because we aren't from Skaftafell district but rather Rangárvalla district, so couldn't I subscribe to *Rangvellingur?* But there is no magazine called *Rangvellingur*, there is the magazine *Árnesingur* from Árnes district but I don't care to read it, then there's the magazine *Goðasteinn* which Þórður published out in Skógar, a regional magazine for Rangvellings which bridges the gap between Rangárvalla district and Skaftafell district, a truly wonderful magazine in every way, especially the old issues, as always, I was a subscriber for a bit, kept it a secret from my wife, who thought it too extravagant to subscribe to both journals, even though she buys tons of magazines, ones that are *for the sake of the household*, she said, useful magazines everyone could enjoy, magazines one could look at but not just ones for me alone, my magazines were magazines for eccentrics and oddbirds, my wife said, and there was little point saying I got neither pleasure nor use out of her *Life, Modern Living, The Week, Betrayal & Treachery, House & Dwellings, Massage & Home Living, Drink & Luxury, Seen and Heard, Scent & Smell, Domesticity, Improvability, The Ball of Yarn & Its Fate* and so on and so forth, this bloody woman's garbage, what's more, she wanted to subscribe to *Channel 2*, that's where I had to draw a line! What about subscribing to *National Geographic?* I asked, isn't it fascinating? but she indicated that it isn't… I want to tell Sigurður from Tvísker that *Skaftfellingur* is an outstanding magazine and I found his articles the most interesting, most informative and best written, I would like to tell him without any posturing, without buttering him up or getting caught up in affectations, I want to tell him this sincerely because I feel this is so profound, always, one is always playing some role, no matter what one does, no matter what one says; I will absolutely be putting on a pose, to my own inconvenience, when I tell Sigurður how much his writing affects me; I need to make sure I'm understood, to get the truth across I need to play a certain role. Strangely, when I'm castrating and killing I need to be in a role, identity is nothing but a role, I'm not the same at work as when I'm home with my family, sometimes you take the embers of your work-self home, which doesn't sit well with those playing their home roles—it's like a character caught between plays, but these are always our roles, oh, how exhausting they are, each role altering with each repetition, becoming a distortion of itself: something existed once but repetition has distorted it. I gear myself up for the role of speaking with the Minister of Agriculture and the Minister of Agriculture gears himself up for the role of talking to me, this preparation takes place backstage. Being yourself is definitely a role. I can only castrate and kill when I'm in my work role, a government service role, a domestic service role, talking to my mother, or making love, I can only castrate and kill if I am in my work role, and believe me, I am quite trained in this, one role takes over from another, you don't like yourself in every role, in my home I'm barely a person, my wife sucks so much energy that I can't wait to leave home for work, the worst thing is that I'm my best self in the role of the veterinarian, castrating and killing, in those moments I'm so strong, straightforward and purposeful, no nonsense, all the world in its right order, things working logically by themselves, the universe stable ... of course the world is not at all in safe order and nothing is logical and nothing stable, I do what I need to, though deep down I despise my veterinarian role above all, perhaps that's how it is with everything, that what you most love you hate in your heart, a subject authors understand, don't they have a love-hate relationship with their fictions? So I've heard, and I thought it strange at first but now I understand it, for that's how I am these days, my friend, a person in a role, empty inside from having devoted her life to castrating and killing, all as part of her own dream ... I'm not a veterinarian, I'm an executioner ...

It was Hrolllaugur from Mæri, the Interpreter interrupted, Hrolllaugur from Mæri settled Skaftafell district.

What's that!? ... Hrolllaugur! Wait there, I'll write it down immediately, said Dr. Lassi, I knew that, surely, it had just been taken from me ... Hrolllaugur ... with three l-s? really? Meaning "shivering-in-a-pool"? Where's the pen and notepad, it's sopping, covered with the tourist's blood ... Hrolllaugur from Mæri ... my friend ... the hot spring must have been cold in Mæri so the little guy got chills ... the dick ... his dick shrank, ha ha ha, that's why he called Hrolllaugur, I'm going to put this theory in the report, but how fares the patient and where are the sandwiches? Seems like he's doing fine, the buttery butyric acid has helped him settle his own new land ... and Sigurður? ... did you hear, he's shivering, fetch a blanket! The right thing would be to fill Flosalaug full of chlorine and alcohol and throw him in the deep end with a barrel and a life preserver, as I speak his leg and buttock are being incinerated so the pool should be warm and cozy, that would take the chilll out of the settlller... might we not say that the penis is addicted to colonization?... well, what's the deal with that... no dicks in my life, fortunately, when they come my way I tend to cut them off and throw them in the trash, interpreter, you queen of language, are there many words in Icelandic, or any other languages, with three l-s in a row? I can think of one: loyalty points, no no no, there's only one l at a time, where did that come from? I don't even know what loyalty points are or how they're relevant, I'm falling into a trance... it is best to have a pen and notepad handy, yes, I know that loyalty points are what people get when they leave the country by plane, which makes them doubly contrary to Hrolllaugur from Mæri, since Hrolllaugur reached land by ship... with his three ellls...

Ballless, said the Interpreter.

What about being ballless? Dr. Lassi asked, is the patient saying something about being ballless? Maybe he wants to know where his balls are?

There are three ells in ballless, said the Interpreter, like in Hrolllaugur from Mæri. Though I think it's spelled with just two ells, Hrollaugur...

Shiver-eyes! cried Dr. Lassi, by which I infer that his eyes experienced tremoring, perhaps from light-sensitivity or suffering from chronic myoclonic twitches?... Anyway, you were saying?

I was just going to say that Hrollaugur was the brother of Hrólf, Duke of Normandy, the one known as Hrólf the Expeditionary, the subject of many stories in the ancient Nordic legendary sagas.

Oh yes, they're so entertaining! You have them here?

This fellow Göngu-Hrólf, or Rolf the Walker, the brother of the Hrollaugur who settled in the Skaftafell district, Dr. Lassi's report explained, is one of France's national heroes, known as Rollon—he was called Hrólf and he spoke Icelandic but the French could not say Hrólf in a normal fashion, and called him Rollon, likely because he always smelled clean and fresh. Hrólf the Expeditionary was a great viking and outlaw; with his army he gained control of part of Russia, as told in *Heimskringla* by Snorri Sturluson and the Sagas, and he toured various lands, accruing gold, marrying princesses, fighting for England, storming into France, waging war in Paris, becoming Earl of what is now called Normandy, owing to the fact that the area was settled by Norwegians. Hrólf the Walker was Rúðu-Earl, the Earl based in Rúðu, which the French call Rouen; he defended France against an invasion of Danish Vikings, and from Hrólf the Expeditionary descend Norman earls and all the English kings—so Hrollaugur's brother is a French national hero, the ancestor of the British royal family...

Hold on, what's that the little punk is muttering, interrupting our scholarship? It's about that horny hussy he met in Skaftafell? Horny-Edda, the park ranger, I think she's hanging about down here still in the dining room, feeling like it's her duty to watch over him—but I will not allow people to press in here, teeming with bacteria and filth, who knows where their fingers have been, visits must be controlled, remember Dr. Semmelweis! But the little hornbud will get to meet her eunuch, we don't stand in the way of love, isn't that so, my Interpreter? ... no matter how trashy she is ... oh, what glory to be a lesbian!

†

I arrived in Skaftafell by bus from Reykjavík on Friday 11th April, Bernharður said, Dr. Lassi wrote in her report, the air was relatively cool and a warm sun shone that day in Öræfi. I wheeled my trunk to one edge of the campsite, which was largely empty; I had plenty of space. I was having a very impressionable day, and when she came by to charge me for the night on the campsite, I was immediately brought outside myself, transported by the uncontrollable beauty confronting me, and I don't know if I've yet fully returned to myself, I feel like I'm still out in the other world into which that beauty cast me, where I want to be, unleaving: there is love, everything there transcends explanation, everything becomes feeling, everything is muteness, deafness, sightless, I hardly knew whether I was in this world or another, I was intoxicated, absolutely beside myself and yet right up close to the core of my being; how remarkable that when a person is outside themselves they also become the very kernel of their own existence. I looked at the ground so it wouldn't be quite so obvious to her how desperate I was, desperate because of something immaterial, an emptiness which came upon me, and she came to me and I felt a stinging, tingling sensation amplify in my stomach, I had no time to recover or gather myself, I ran a comb through my shock of hair, she was asking for my payment and the evening sun was on her face, Hvannadalshnúkur in the background, her cheeks flushed and glowing in the spring scents, nature come to life, she is the beauty within beauty, I thought, and I dived into my trunk, hunting for money to pay her—I invited the park ranger inside my trunk for caraway liquor while she waited, so she wasn't standing there shivering, the weather cold though the sun shone, and she agreed, she said there was no need to hurry, there wasn't that much to do this early in spring, I let the way she spoke go to my head, her voice ever so slightly broken, husky, seductive, I said I had been introduced to this liquor the previous day and was taken with it, I love caraway, said the park ranger, she introduced herself as Edda, I do not know what came over me, maybe it was a fear of science, I don't know, my heart raged violently in my ribs like a caged mink, like a mink driven crazy by cruelty, like a mink which wants to bite the farmer in the throat and kill all birds and destroy the Icelandic ecosystem! ... I introduced myself and there was this abominable burning in my chest and I began to tremble, succumbing to spasms, tugging at anything I could reach, this always happens when I'm infatuated, surely she has a boyfriend called Snorri or something, I thought, you cannot touch her, you must not think about it, I said to myself, unless she touches you first, first, I have to stop trembling, my teeth need to stop clattering so I can talk, I was looking for my money but I had no idea what I was doing, I was going to split asunder with all this emotion, I could not keep myself together, my rift plates were transverse, I myself was the glowing magma and I was running in all directions, the kernel that is missing from the upper atmosphere ... Edda blushed and smiled, she is a Nordic beauty with perfect teeth, I thought, though I did not want to think it, a fine-figured bird, I was on fire with infatuation and death, charm gusted off her, I had invited her into the trunk and she had accepted. My penis is getting hard, I said, and she began to laugh. That night we lay together in the trunk and I fervently longed for the new day to never come, wishing I could stay in her arms until the destruction of the earth.

Kindly fetch the strumpet if he is so infatuated with her, Dr. Lassi told the Interpreter, it'll help with his recovery. The eunuch doesn't lack an erotic sensibility! We also have to allow some damn visits since we have transformed the hotel into a hospital ... then we can change the hotel in Freysnes into a research center, too, because this is the site of an ancient farmstead and I am planning to finish the report while we wait for the amputee and his paramour ... it's just as good to have a visitor now as at a later time ... it makes sense to let Edda be the first to tackle him today, he seems obsessed with her, he is always mentioning her in his delirium, she clearly occupies a place in his heart, remind me to have a section in the report about love, I tend to forget it and go directly to the erotic.

In the trunk, Edda got all steamed up, breathing excitedly. I had not been with a woman for quite some time and was worried I wouldn't measure up, wouldn't be able to perform adequately, to lick her up until she was all done, I couldn't quell my thoughts, relax, said Edda, sensing my tension, telling me to be calm, I lay on my stomach and she massaged me, massaged my tremors away, I tried to plot out my moves, the techniques I should use, but that terrified me, the park ranger told me to relax, enjoy it, enjoy it, said Edda, just to hear her speaking those words in that voluptuous voice, it was like all the liquid had been wrung from my brain and sucked out of my head, down my spine to spit out my penis—all the burdens, the despair and anxiety, the evident embarrassment. Contentment flourished in my heart and joy filled my breast with its perfumed fragrance; in my mind I began to cartwheel up Mávabyggðir where I threw myself into a hidden crevasse to wait out a happy death worshipping the marvelous monstress Horny-Edda and all the world's goddesses!... Sorrow gets stored up in the scrotum, Edda said, lying in the trunk, as does joy. After a brief moment, something took shape in my body, a feeling deep inside me that resembled swamplight; it slowly grew into a veil of mist, will-of-the-wisp enveloping me, then the fire broke out again and momentarily lit up the trunk from within, and then came the pyroclastic flow and so did I, utterly...ash and gravel...Edda spent the night with me in the trunk, but I woke her with my mouth's caresses and she sighed loudly as she came out of her dream, she asked me to come inside her at once, I slipped my penis in and kissed her firm breasts and in response her nipples hardened and reddened, I nibbled at her nipples, Bernharður was saying, I nibbled at her nipples, he kept repeating, I nibbled at her nipples! That's what he's shouting, the Interpreter said...please stop, said Dr. Lassi, go on...Edda's body tremored in response and she wrapped her legs around me, I thrust deep into her and she sighed so loud it rang out in the night's silence across the Skaftafell campsite, she yelled yes, she screamed, she orgasmed and began to cry, we held each other tight, lying in a still embrace; some mysterious barrier, some dam inside me, had weakened, I felt I could no longer be as objective as I once had been, no longer a body; instead, I'd become subjective, a spirit, I felt I'd touched some ancient ecstasy, had left my body, up to now I'd been a bound manuscript but I'd become oral folklore... *Ek em súbjektíf,* I said to Edda, and tremblingly clutched for the caraway liquor, serving us drinks in two cups. She clinked my glass and said: better than prayer. I shook so much Brennivín slopped from the shot glass and Edda had to tip my head back and pour it down my throat. I was trembling all over and shaking, spitting the liquor out my nostrils—but then I swiftly calmed, my emotions bursting out so that I felt like I'd vanished into her wonderful being, disappeared from my own being, become the core of myself, I shook with fear, the slightest movement sent electric currents streaming through my mind, we locked eyes and I found security and beauty and terrific sexiness in her sensual eyes, she was so sturdy and compact, soft and firm, we were in thought and then she was on top of me, I was worried whether she was satisfied, she shook herself and groaned softly, then the sighs increased until finally the violent shaking overtook the trunk once again… we fell asleep wrapped around each other. Mávabyggðir could wait.

After resting, satisfied, I found myself brimming with a great store of ideas and noted them frantically in my notebook through the night while Edda slept. I lacked an introduction to my essay on Mávabyggðir and sat on the bed in the morning sun beneath the glorious mountain. Place names often describe the terrain or soil, I wrote in the notebook, place names can describe local conditions or landmarks themselves; really, one could say the place names *are* the landmark, symbolically; they are often formed by the lay of the land or its landmarks, the shape or relation of one place to another, they often give the hint of mineral strata or some other geological formations, or vegetation, they might describe color, can be metaphorical names, symbols, they are boundary markers, shore markers, the boundaries of pastures, they are taken from livestock, wildlife, from farming, from work methods or procedures, shipping routes and anchor points, trails, plentiful resources, travelogues, sundry incidents and events, battles, weather patterns, temporal markers, legends and oral histories, the names of people, doppelgangers, references to pagan religion, to Christian faith, the Church, political assemblies; place names are set upon landmarks and landmarks show people the way; place names are a testament to the people who settle a land or region, to their life, work, and thoughts; place names are precious cultural histories documenting ancient eras, our attitudes today, and a view to the future; place names are themselves people.

I heated up some coffee and put a big layer-cake on the table to mark the occasion of this glorious day of the Lord. A breakfast for heroes! I shouted to wake up Snorri's-Edda. She stirred and said in a low voice: How many books you have in your trunk … She fumbled about, as though trying to get her bearings with what had happened. What, are they all *national studies*? Yes, I said, I got them at the used-and-rare bookstore, Bragi, my friend helped me choose them, more or less chose them all for me. A lot was going on around the Skaftafell campsite. Are there many people at the campsite? I asked. She answered that there were, relative to the time of year. It's good to sleep in a tent, I said but Edda was staring dejectedly at the tart, her expression somewhat ambiguous, though you need a good tent, emerging from a tent is like being born, which makes sleeping in a tent the closest thing to undoing our amnesia about the time we spent in our mother's womb; it's important that the tent is good, made of decent material, who wants their mother's womb to be made of nylon and to crinkle relentlessly? What about this trunk of yours? asked Edda, isn't it like being born from your father's asshole when you clamber out into the new day? ... the trunk is made of beech, it's a durable wood but lightweight, I said, pouring a cup of coffee for her, cutting a large cake slice for that amazing body, then I asked her, suddenly sniffling: Is it fun, being a park ranger? ...Yes, said Edda, it's decent when things are going well, and it always goes well; you meet all kinds of fun people at the campsite, and get to observe the country's economic development and the deterioration in taste, how the more a person moves away from nature, the more he desires it. At first, everyone came with cotton tents or tents made from sailcloth, natural materials that breathed well and kept the wet away; at one time, the tents didn't even have a floor, and that's how people slept best—they were A-shaped, so no pools of water formed on them, and they broke the wind well—but then they were no longer good enough and people began to bring all kinds of deformed tent shapes, an imitation of the mistakes of the city suburbs during the '80s, domed bays here and outcroppings there, it was a difficult task, tenting such tents, people spent all day at it, not to mention packing them back away; it was a significant commitment, the whole weekend was spent attending to the tent. Next, one began to see pop-up campers, trailers attached to the back of a car out of which one unfolded a tent, in theory with a single gesture, although in reality that one gesture became a thousand; the advantage was that the tent didn't take up space in the car but hung there behind it. A year later, the nation became slightly richer and pop-up campers became shelters, that is, much larger trailers, sometimes larger than the cars themselves; you hauled the shelter directly out from the trailer with a crank instead of flipping it open. The people in these shelter houses were so elegant that they looked down on the people in pop-up campers, who must be poor folk unable to keep up with the times; the shelter people couldn't begin to imagine the era of national shame when families had stayed in ordinary tents on their travels, with all those incomprehensible poles and pillars; now you just gave it one crank *et voilà*—but many people got trapped in these shelter-houses when they lay down together and a lot of well-to-do people lost fingers; for a time, it was absolutely a status symbol to be missing a finger, it meant you probably had a shelter-house. But economic development outpaced status symbols, Snorri's-Edda said, and the shelter-houses were still a kind of tent the men had to fold out from a trailer and the women were always afraid of them, worried about getting pinched by them or crumpled up into the structure or even shut inside and the men stopped bothering to listen to their nagging, and they very well did collapse in and the whole family was stuck in the trailer, a very scary experience, I've had to rescue many people from their trailers. A year later, no one had them, except caravaners, which left people free of the banality of tents and all that fussing, is it the case that now things are made from plastic and take people ever further into modernity? A year later, one could see more and more mobile homes, where the trailer is merged with the car; some people feel that's a step down, that the mobile homes have a boorish quality, that it's just more plastic rubbish designed for tropical weather, but we have seen it blow up everywhere, exploding all through the district, and now the situation is marked by a certain uncertainty: people do not know how to sleep when traveling. Who knows; perhaps everyone in future will have a trunk like yours.

†

Ever since Bernharður Fingurbjörg, as a young boy, saw the discussion in *National Geographic* about Öræfi, Vatnajökull and its expanse, Dr. Lassi wrote in the report, he dreamed of going to Iceland. The magazine featured large images of Jökulfell, Skaftafell, Hafrafell, Svínafell, and Sandfell; interviews with ancient farmers; pictures of sealers and the skin-curing process; of bird-hunters, abseiling and taking eggs (they were poor farmers in remote areas getting hold of what food they could); there were discussions of handicraft and homemade work equipment; of horses on the sands; of the dying art of riding horses through the glacial waters. It was like the end of beauty, Bernharður says, though I didn't think so back then, I discovered it inside me later, it is only now that I've put that feeling into words. And then the ring road was opened up and bridges crisscrossed the sand and Öræfi was run together with the world after 1100 years of solitude: the district was opened up and simultaneously destroyed. I have to go to Öræfi, I kept telling myself and later I managed to create a link to my studies. I have always subscribed to *National Geographic*; its spines were the yellow glow of my childhood. The Iceland issue summarized glacial exploration history, documenting the first trip the doctor Sveinn Pálsson took onto Öræfajökull; he was my boyhood hero simply because of this one short passage about him in the issue, a passage I read a thousand times—I was probably the only kid in the whole of Austria who was bothered about the 18th century Icelandic physician Sveinn Pálsson, the only one who had him as a hero or knew who he was, even. My father had a great affection for him, owned his books, quoted his diaries and his travel narrative, which we had in our home. I decided to start keeping a diary, too, and become a bit scientific in my own life. I began to write small travelogues on the way to school, all the names of the streets I passed, what time I arrived at an intersection, when I left and when I arrived at my destination, I recorded the weather, light, temperature, distance, all the detours home, I wrote down all the names of the streets in Innere Stadt, first it was all extremely imperfect, but gradually I trained myself, I wanted to become a doctor and explorer and naturalist like Sveinn Pálsson, the first to walk on Öræfajökull. The Iceland issue quoted old writings, included old black-and-white photos of research expeditions from the early 20th century, discussed J.P. Koch's surveying of Skeiðarársand and Öræfajökull in 1903 and his collaboration with Dr. Wegener, the situation of the tectonic plates in Iceland, how the country is at the fracture between the North American plate and the Eurasian plate, all those frightful volcanic eruptions which destroyed settlements and human beings through the ages—ever since then I wanted to go to Iceland and walk around the mountains in Öræfi, the Wasteland, get into all of it … I later saw that behind all of this lay, of course, the father of mountain-going, *Benedict de Saussure*, his alpine spirit hovered over the waters of my youth, Benedict de Saussure was a contemporary and model for Sveinn Pálsson, this poor Icelandic farmer's son wanted to be like Benedict de Saussure, the true aristocrat among Geneva citizens who sacrificed his working potential and intelligence for mankind. I also found out that Sveinn Pálsson check-mated his mentor on one crucial point, though never received recognition for it: Sveinn Pálsson was the first to grasp the nature of advancing glaciers, a problem with which people had long wrestled. He presented his theory in his book *Glacier Writings* along with a study of glaciology; if it had been printed right away in 1795, it would have become the foundational article for the academic community; Sveinn Pálsson is the secret father of glacial studies. In *Glacier Writings* it states, according to *National Geographic*, that farmers in Öræfi had for centuries known the glaciers' character; though it was said that Sveinn had been the first to set foot on Öræfajökull, the Öræfings had long gone out onto the glacier, though only if they had an errand, not for fun like nowadays; they knew the languor which seizes you as you head over the top of the crater, what's now called Antarctic stare. Sveinn was first and foremost a doctor, he translated *Core Questions in Health* by Dr. Bernharður Faust, which came out around 1800 and was on my father's bookshelves along with *Travelogue* and *Glacier Writings*. In Faust's book, in a chapter about traveling that I used to prepare for my Iceland journey and glacier hiking, it says: What should you do if you get frostbite? Avoid going into a warm building, or near a hot flame. What instead? The frostbitten limb needs submerging in ice-cold water, or to be packed in ice and snow, until it has completely thawed, and life and feeling return to it. Wouldn't the pain be intense? Yes, deeply painful, but you must do it anyway, because the limb, which otherwise might have been forfeit, will come to life again and heal completely if you follow this method.

From *National Geographic* I got a love of maps: the magazine often came with maps that I hung on my wall while my peers hung posters of singers and band photos from magazines like Bravo and Popcorn. I was teased for my interest in maps, always being asked if I needed to find my way home to my mother, which often upset me. The map of Öræfi held the place of honor: it was drawn by the Danish captain J. P. Koch in 1903. One gloomy day in my room, I saw my name on the map; I was startled, uncontrollably happy, afraid. *Fingurbjörg*, it was within Mávabyggðir, inside Vatnajökull, in Öræfi; J. P. Koch had been there and there I too would go, I want to go to Fingurbjörg in Mávabyggðir, I later said to my professor in the Nordic Studies Department at the University of Vienna. I read up on local knowledge, I groped around in the books in the library of the Nordic Studies Department, in one source or other I stumbled on the fact that, despite the name, no gulls live in Mávabyggðir, and I had trouble believing it, there must formerly have been some avian settlers who gave rise to the place name, in the 18th century *Travelogue of Eggert and Bjarni,* which the library had in Danish, German, French, and English, I found out that there had still been gulls living at Mávabyggðir back then, and I also read about wild sheep, how there were two strains still alive in Iceland, in Núpsstaðarskógar and far out on the glacier at Mávabyggðir. I felt a burning need to study the history and the meanings of the place name *Mávabyggðir*, I would defend my doctoral thesis on this, resolve all the uncertainty, go to Iceland and climb Fingurbjörg and investigate Mávabyggðir deep inside the glacier, taking samples of rocks and soil, looking into the relationship of folklore and place names, and also conduct, if it warranted space in the thesis, a comparative grammatical study of mountain place names in Öræfi and Týrol, using the teachings of the Swiss linguist Ferdinand de Saussure as a guiding light. My professor at the Nordic Studies Department jumped head height with joy when I brought him the topic, Bernharður said on his sickbed in Freysnes, wrote Dr. Lassi.

So far I had been considered eccentric for having Iceland on the brain: a certain shame has afflicted Nordic Studies since the Nazi era; the field has been cursed since that time. Now, though, interest has re-arisen around the world, mainly in medieval Icelandic literature and Nordic mythology, although these topics are not absolutely *the foundation of the State* like they were the last time they were in fashion. I was always fond of *Burnt-Njal's Saga* in my classes in the Nordic Studies Department; my father had the Halldór Laxness edition of the story in Icelandic, featuring large, beautiful pictures that enchanted me; he had given me it in German, *Die Saga vom Weisen Njal* (1978), when he became aware of my interest through *National Geographic*. I became obsessed with Suðurland, I pored over the map, I dreamt dreams about Flosi, the ruler of Svínafell, I dreamt dreams about Flosi's dream when the giant Járngrímur appeared to him and said that poisonous serpents would rise up, how he enumerated all those who were doomed, except in my dream he named the names of the classmates who teased me, I told them that they would all die and I believe that has for the most part come to pass. I felt connected to Flosi from Svínafell, how he was sucked into a scenario that he did not understand and how he responded by putting on traveling pants, a sort of medieval leggings, and headed off on foot from Svínafell across the lava and sand and glacial lakes for several hundreds of miles—my professor in Nordic Studies was astonished at this and danced with joy and fury and went pirouetting down the columned hall, up until now Flosi has been a villain! ha ha ha! said the professor, Flosi who went on the journey to torch the dwelling at Bergþórshvol, burning up Njal and his wife and family and many other people, Flosi's an arsonist and villain! the professor retorted and laughed loudly and rolled around the room, but I maintained Flosi was human, perhaps *all too human*, he goes along with or rather gets *caught up* in the plot and acts against his better judgment, he is forced to bow before customs and habits that actually displease him, he is out of keeping with his time, under the yoke of civilization, I said to my professor who now had stopped dancing and giggling and was stood bent over the pages on the big lectern, the time still hasn't come for a Nietzschean interpretation of ancient Icelandic literature, he said, nor Freudian neither ... Flosi is by nature a chieftain, a bellwether, I said, that makes him an *empath* ...Well, said the professor, have it your way. So I went and wrote a master's thesis about the place names in *Burnt-Njal's Saga*.

I wanted to wend my way onto the glacier, standing down on the plain near the Visitor Center in Skaftafell and looking at the mountains and glaciers towering over the country, this beautiful monster that could destroy everything at any moment, I went out on the sand, watching from there; I pored over the map in my trunk, stored the place names in my memory, went out and matched the map to the territory; the glaciers had retreated drastically in the hundred years since Captain Koch measured Öræfi in 1903. I had read that the way up to Mávabyggðir is to follow the so-called *moraine streaks* in the glacier that originate at Mávabyggðir and reach down to the plains, known as the Mávabyggðarönd, although they are really a belt of rocks which the advancing glacier ferries from the mountains down to the lowlands; you can establish the direction of glacial movement using these streaks. There was no hope left and I knew I had to study my maps well to orient myself better for the trip.

Hafrafell is a hideous mountain, I said to Snorri's-Edda when I re-entered the trunk and pored over the map, Bernharður said, and the author of this report can agree with that, Dr. Lassi wrote, having subsequently gone on a journey to hunt the wild sheep with the farmers in Öræfi, as discussed in greater detail later in this report. Hafrafell separates Skaftafellsjökull and Svínafellsjökull, but until almost the middle of the previous century the glaciers proceeded together in front of Hafrafell and sealed off the mountain, creating a very good highland pasture, which is still the reality, but the glaciers have now retreated to such an extent that Hafrafell protrudes into the country, surrounded by moraine; sky-high, sheer, rough-edged, like a rusty knife thrust out of the glacier. In Hafrafell there is a treasure trove of place names for you to investigate, said Snorri's-Edda, because animals have gone about there since the settlement. I go on the livestock round-up there every autumn and am beginning to know it a bit; it's impossible if no one knows place names, for then shepherding is pointless and hopeless. We opened the trunk up and gazed out at Hafrafell. Evil rocks, for sure, said Snorri's-Edda, impassable, up there on the mountain ridges are pillars known as the Upper Men and the Front Men because they seem like people standing there, visible far and wide, the key characteristic of Hafrafell, some people call them the Upper and Lower Men but that is not right, it's Upper and Front Men, although the front men *are* below the upper men. I tried to note down everything Snorri's-Edda said, looking at the mountain and the map and scribbling, there is also *Illagil*, or Evil Gully, and *Einstigir*, the Narrow Stair, and *Stóraskarð*, the Great Chasm, and *Langagil*, Long Gully, you need to know that when herding in the round-up, if you want to send someone somewhere quick then everyone needs to know what direction to go in, there's *Grjótdal*, the Stony Valley, and in Grjótdal the extremely high cliffs are called *Svarthamrar*, Sheer Black, they face westward, under which is *Ból*, the Shaft: once, two youths of around twenty from Svínafell went hunting animals one winter, one of them plunged from the precipitous cliff, falling hundreds of meters, but he landed in a snowdrift which was piled high; he escaped with a shattered foot, but there was too little daylight left to get help from home at Svínafell and the boy was not equipped to lay out in the frost overnight so the story goes that his companion took him on his back and carried him all the way to Svínafell, what's more the Svínafellers are as strong as giants, said Snorri's-Edda, said Bernharður, wrote

Dr. Lassi, sweaty and barely keeping up. First you think: why would animals live on this mountain where there's nothing but scree and stones, after all, on the way to the mountain there are many grassy slopes, for example, one that's simply called *Torfur*, or The Turf, on the east side of the mountain and not visible from here, then there's *Meingil*, where a man once plunged to his death when his staff broke, he fell all the way down the glacier, then there are also the grassy *Kviar* and *Rák* over there, where the path goes up from Svarthamradal and over to Svarthamra, from where the boy fell, further in, the place name opposite to the west is Fauskagljúfur...What is *fauskur*? I asked, I don't know the word. It's rotten wood, said Snorri's-Edda, sometimes they say about old men that they are *fauskar* if they are somewhat stiff and formal, in Fauskagljúfur they have unearthed the remains of an ancient forest. High up between the Upper and Front Men lies *Fles*, there are awe-inspiring views from there and you are among giant-settlements, Fles is springy turf, it's good pasture so the sheep seek it out. Far away from Skeiðarársandur, Hafrafell seems small, a tuff protruding from Öræfajökull, but when you get nearer Hafrafell appears impossible and untouchable, all cut up by precipitous ravines which are rightly called *Illuklettar*, the Evil Rocks, it is impassable, starvation and a death sentence await you there, no one does go there, you can see from here that transverse from Illuklettar there's a mysterious X, a symbol marked by a guardian land-spirit so that no one may pass; when we herders go up to Svínafellsheið and over the glacier to Hafrafell, although it's possible to go right up the ridge between the Front and Upper Men, I would never chase sheep into Illuklettar, said Snorri's-

Edda, I'm greatly fearful of this mysterious X, what is it a symbol for? On Hafrafell, tourists are in grave danger of being swept down in a landslide from above to a death deep on the glaciers that flow either side of the mountain—once the mountain was encircled by glacier completely, but the glacier's retreated so it's possible to drive up to it—these glaciers have swallowed their share of tourists and experienced mountaineers; their metallic equipment comes to light 50 years later, flattened and crumpled, an indication of the ice's power. No human remains ever come to light. It's as though the ice wants to hold onto bodies but to spew back metal; the metal debris is all on display at the Visitor Center in Skaftafell, and people are drawn to look into the display box, to see death itself, the abyss arranged in a clinical display case: your powerlessness in the face of nature spills over you, and you just want to crawl into your tent and never come out again...the glacier gives back, or so say the Öræfings, said Snorri's-Edda in the trunk.

After hearing this, all that wonderful information about Hafrafell and the mountain's death grip attached itself to me, reeled me in, as we lay there together in an embrace in trunk, I dozed and as I did the mystical X in Illuklettar appeared to me, gleaming, butter was gushing from it, I jumped up and went out while Edda slept, the dusky night wrapped the surroundings in silence and stillness, all was still and quiet, it was just starting when I reached the glacier, I put on my crampons and went up on it, dark cracks swallowed me hook line and sinker and I breathed the cold rising from the depths, this great serpent occasionally hissed and sputtered, how coarse and uneven his scales were, he was going to snatch me, and I was ready, I was happy, I had nothing left to do in the world, I could fall into the crevasse, go into the mountain, settle down in Illuklettar and walk with the dead and with herders' ghosts and alongside angels and monsters... I saw something glittering on the ice and went over, it was some object, an old tent peg, an old dented tent peg on a glacier, I looked up at the rough serpent-scraper as he crawled down the cliff belt on top of the breadth of ice, he's traveled a long way, I thought of the men in the tent the glacier swallowed, those for whom this tent peg had served some role, they disappeared up there somewhere, now nothing was left of their existence save a single tent peg, old and dented; perhaps these men had climbed all the major peaks of the world, used the best equipment, here they were now, eaten out of their skin and hair, the glacier returning only this one transformed tent peg... Creeping glaciers crawl along like living creatures, I thought about the glacier, contemplating the tent peg while Edda slept in the trunk, these creatures breathe, move forward, recede, they moan and groan all of a sudden; when I came back I awoke Edda, I told her that glaciers were serpents.

Where were you? asked Edda.

I went to look at Hafrafell and Illuklettar and the mystical X, I went out looking for my mother.

To look for your mom? Is she lost there? Shall we call the rescue team? she asked sleep-addled, the Dragon, the armored tank? ... huh?

She was attacked, a long time ago, when I was little, she and her sister were here on a trip and her sister was killed, my mother savagely beaten, she never recovered, in truth it destroyed our lives, my father says she was never the same again after the attack... I found this on the glacier, I said, and handed her the tent peg.

That's horrible, she said, and took the tent peg, began to examine it distractedly, then with great awareness and intent, what did you say, your mother was murdered...

Her little sister was murdered, my mother savagely beaten, I said, and shakily cut a cake slice, my teeth chattering; I had fallen in love. You should have the tent peg, I said.

I'm not going to put it in the display case in the Visitor Center though it's my duty to, she said, I don't plan to send it to Þórði in Skógar either, nor the Settlement museum in Höfn, nor to the National Museum, I'm not going to show it to anyone but I'll keep this mysterious treasure here with me instead and think of you, said Snorri's-Edda in the trunk, Bernharður said, and the Interpreter interpreted, Dr. Lassi wrote in the report, or so Bernharður wrote to me in a letter, spring 2003.

II

TREASURES

You're not the first person whose leg has had to be sawn off, Dr. Lassi said by way of comforting me, Bernharður wrote in his letter, though you are the first one I have had to dismember, and in impressive style, even if I say so myself. Sigurður from Tvísker told me that amputations were common in this area in bygone times: men would frequently get frostbite on their winter journeys, in rivers or from a heavy frost, in the mountains or on the sands or at the shore; their limbs would be damaged by the frostbite, blackened and burned by the hoar. These days, we know that was caused by rotting flesh in the limb, dead or decaying flesh, sometimes called coldburn—and people are still always needing amputation, but less can be lopped off, and it's no longer remarkable, there's a whole community of amputees, you're going to do very well as an amputated person, Bernharður, you'll get to have fun choosing a prosthetic limb from Össur, these days they're custom-made—but what dull times we live in as far as language goes, *custom-made*, such an odd way to put it—I think it's actually best to get a wooden leg, my dear fellow, you can ask old Muggur from Bölti to construct it for you, he's a carpenter highly-esteemed throughout Öræfi, I recommend wooden legs made from birch, which is lightweight wood, durable, it is used for pointed staffs, you could even ask Muggur to put a point on your wooden leg, you'd be really agile in a landslide, stable out on the glacier, fashionable on the city sidewalks. Sigurður told me that on the eve of January 20th, 1903, a German ship got stranded on the shore at Svínafell, a ship called *Friedrich Albert*, a bottom trawler, a kind of vessel very unpopular with Icelanders because they scraped the sea bottom, destroying fishing grounds, although Icelanders changed their tune on such bottom trawlers as soon as they succeeded with the very same ships themselves, and most people have scraped the bottom ever since. This icy and black January night in 1903, the ship stranded on Svínafell shore and the twelve-member crew made it onto the land with great difficulty, and they loitered there, stuck on the beach until light began to appear late in the morning and the stranded men were at last able to see around them: when the Germans saw Öræfajökull they were terrified by the threat of this colossus appearing before them on the shore, Öræfi, they could not imagine any settlement existed here, only desolation and death, and they decided to stay in the west on the shore furthest from Öræfajökull and try to build a shelter; that seemed to them the easier and smoother plan, but it was a big mistake, Sigurður said, they did not know the beach lay on a great estuary and the whole of Skeiðarársandur lay before them; if they had kept on in the direction of the glacier they would have reached a settlement within a day, that's what the heroic Kári Sölmundarson did when he broke his ship to pieces on the promontory at Ingólfshöfði and walked to Svínafell in a snowstorm, as *Burnt-Njal's Saga* tells us, reconciling there with Flosi and marrying his first cousin; Kári settled in Öræfi, and from him extends a large, beautiful family tree with many stately men. This was the first registered shipwreck in Skaftafell district since the division of the country into administrative hundreds, but the shipwrecked Germans on the *Friedrich Albert* were not familiar with Öræfi the way Kári was: they continued *west* along the coast, an entirely impassable route along which the quicksand sucked the men's strength so that they grew exhausted after just a short distance, hungry, cold, and despairing, walking on quicksand is miserable, mortally dangerous, and there are many quagmires here—so they returned to the ship, from which they managed to rescue an inconsequential amount of food; they made a fresh attempt the next day to head west; day after day they made attempts to go west across the sand away from their wreck, but each time they had to return to the ship because the route was blocked. The First Mate went crazy, tearing himself away from the group, taking three crew members with him, rushing out into the sands. One day as the shipwrecked men were trying their hand at the estuary they saw two crew members wandering about, confused and perplexed; a third sailor was stuck in the mud, delirious, and he died shortly afterward, the same day as the chief engineer succumbed to cold and weakness; the First Mate was never seen again. After a week at the spot where they'd wrecked, a week of unsuccessful attempts to get past the sand, the shipwrecked men hauled material off the trawler with great difficulty and built a raft; they dragged the raft across the shore and went past the glacial estuary and the sea marshes. On 30th January, after three days straining on the sand with the raft, ten days after the stranding, the men reached a small farm, Orrustustað; by then, they had surmounted over forty kilometers. At Orrustustað lived a solitary farmer with only one leg; he was very happy to welcome them, as they'd hoped, and afforded them all the kindness and food available, because Skaftfellings are hospitable people. The district doctor, who was an excellent surgeon and courteous to all men, came the same day at full speed; some of the shipwrecked men had frostbite and gangrene and the district doctor was kept busy through the day sawing off their limbs to save their lives: he put the men to sleep with chloroform, cut, flayed, sawed and sewed the stubs with patches of flesh, as many feet as fingers lay about the living space, which was becoming more of an abattoir; from the five men who had frostbite he took eight feet plus all the toes from two other feet; thanks to his methods, the shipwrecked men returned to full health and happiness in a short time. They were grateful and fortunate and hospitable themselves, humble and polite like Skaftfellings, because such behavior is highly contagious. At the same time, a corpse was found, driven in from the sea near the coast; people believed it was the First Mate but the skin on his face was so damaged by frostbite that he was unrecognizable. Another body washed up on the shore at Tvísker. When the strandees returned to Germany, the most talented Continental doctors hurried to examine how the amputations had been carried out by the primitive northern people, suspecting they might need to fix things, and the event was written up in the newspapers, becoming exceedingly famous throughout the continent, because the German doctors were amazed to see how neatly everything had been done, and how well the wounds had healed; it was said in the press that the amputations had been performed as if by the most skilled European physicians, and so the district doctor from Skaftafell was honored with the Prussian Medal of the Red Eagle Order.

Yes, 1903 was an eventful year in Öræfi, said Sigurður, Dr. Lassi said, and I had to write it all down, the wreck in January, the Skeiðará flooding in May, the greatest jökulhlaup the oldest residents had ever seen, known since then as the Stórahlaup, the Great Flood, the subject of numerous reports. The Skeiðará had been dry for several months' time so the Öræfings knew a flood was coming, but no one had any idea how big the flood would be: the water gushed out from cracks which had opened in the glacier and jets poured down in high pillars as everything moved in angry tremors, the region quivering, the houses shaking, window panes shattering as icebergs rolled about the sand; heavy thuds were heard all about Suðurland, heard many hundreds of kilometers away, and the flooding caused a tidal wave along the whole coastline so that ships enjoying a smooth sea suddenly found themselves in the greatest danger. Next, fire burst out from the glacier and the flames shot high into the air; a dark, gray-black, thick cloud formed, dominating the sky, an alarming mushroom rapidly growing, and lightning flashed and lit up the night, a cold, metallic light striking the ground and water, while the ash plume clung to the slopes, causing ash to fall onto the settlements. After the flood, giant blocks of ice littered the sand, taking many years to melt, and creating in their wake dangerous kettle deperessions in the sand. The fire burnt in the glacier until the following year and killed much of the livestock due to the dust steaming off the fire—especially horses, far and wide across the country.

Sigurður got the story about the wreck of the *Friedrich Albert* from a report written by a lieutenant in the land surveying division of the military General Staff, one Captain J. P. Koch; he alone noted it down at the time, although something was mentioned in the newspapers in the south. At the time, Captain Koch was in Öræfi surveying and drafting, and he interviewed the shipwrecked men and fit the shipwreck story together into a geodetic report for the Danish General Staff and the Royal Scientific Company. The report was called *About the Activities of the Land Surveying Department of the Military General Staff in Iceland*, by J. P. Koch, Lieutenant, *Surveying & Preparing Maps on Skeiðarársand & Öræfajökull, summer, 1903*. I know Captain Koch well, Bernharður said, Dr. Lassi recorded in her report, I read about him in an old *National Geographic*, so I felt at home in his book *Durch die Weiße Wüste*, that is, *Across the White Wilderness*: the expedition over the high glaciers of North Greenland with Icelandic horses in 1912–1913. It had a tremendous influence on me; the scientists' mission was to investigate a snowless landmass inside the glacier and go where no one had gone before. With them went one Doctor Wegener, a meteorologist, which was then a new scientific field: he had the year before articulated a theory of tectonic plates which did not become widely accepted until much later; he went on to become one of the most famous scientists of the 20th century. Wegener discovered the existence of tectonic plates while he stood at Þingvellir chit-chatting with Koch and looking at the Almannagjá Rift; they were talking about the adoption of

Christianity in the year 1000, or so the story goes, and the division between the pagans and Christians, which caused the idea of tectonic divisions to rise up for Wegener, and the basis of tectonic plate theory surfaced in his mind. All modern earth sciences are based on this idea. The Icelander Vigfús Sigurðsson was also with them, a mail carrier and carpenter; ten years later, when they went out onto Grænlandsjökull, Captain Koch and Dr. Wegener and Vigfús brought along Icelandic horses to use on the Greenland ice instead of sled dogs like everybody else did. Captain Koch was fascinated by the Icelandic horse and had proven its excellence transporting heavy scientific equipment across a glacier on large sleds; he practiced for his Greenland expedition on Vatnajökull, crossing over it and back with horses, no small achievement. When Captain Koch and Dr. Wegener and Vigfús the carpenter and mail carrier arrived in North Greenland in mid-summer the horses had a funny feeling about all this and ran off; Captain Koch sent Vigfús after them and Vigfús only retrieved five of the sixteen horses. Those five were greatly exhausted because the trio had tremendous baggage with them: materials for building and food for 16 horses. Koch had always taken a lot of luggage but this time he took 20,000 kilograms of luggage to accompany him for the 1,200 kilometers across Greenland, a journey that took an entire year; nobody can top that, no other traveler. It took the expeditionaries nearly three months to ferry luggage from the port up to the glacier's snout, where they built a cabin on the advancing glacier, naming it The City and placing two chimneys on it—The City had a paraffin stove that heated almost too well, it was often 20-degree weather in the hut when it was 50 degrees below zero outside. They settled in and stayed there for the winter. They all got to know one another well, becoming close to their comrades: the Icelandic sheepdog Glói, who was along with them, a joyful and grateful dog but something of a prankster; the remaining horses Gráni, Brúnka, Fucksrauður, Kavalíer, and Pólaris. Little Glói held up their morale although he was often scolded. One time, he shit in Wegener's hat. They had playing cards, but never played them, instead using the time to read scientific books and novels and educate themselves and nurture their souls; Koch and Wegener played chess on Sunday evenings, Koch tells us in his travel book *Across the White Wilderness*, said Bernharður, Dr. Lassi wrote. In autumn, when it got light briefly around midday, they took advantage of the time for measurements outdoors and Wegener took photographs, but otherwise they were mostly in the cabin during the winter, while storms raged outside, 50 degrees below zero, frostbite threatening. At Christmas, they gave each other gifts and drank champagne and smoked cigars they had brought along as a festive treat; they ate chocolate, strawberry jam, and apricots. There was one window in the cabin and they had potted plants Koch's wife had sent along with them, artificial, of course, but they gave the cabin a homely feel, which mattered: they hung up pictures that gave them heart through the winter conditions, an image of the king, of a flowering apple tree, of their wives. All this helped to make the long winter on the glacier in this eternal darkness and hoarfrost more bearable. Wegener photographed the Northern Lights, Koch used shadows to measure the Earth's circumference and examined the zodiacal light, or swordlight, as it's known. They would head out and make large holes, seven meters deep, and examine the snow strata, seeing how the snow became ice, an old riddle people had tried to solve ever since Sveinn Pálsson and de Saussure in the eighteenth century. They made observations about mirages and photographs; Wegener had to take off his gloves in 50 degrees below zero when he photographed these phenomena, Koch recounts in his book, phenomena like the reflection of light from the snow, the forms of snow crystals and ice crystals, various twilight phenomena. They suffered frostbite and burns alternately; they were fortunate not to lose fingers or toes, or entire limbs. During the winter Koch fell into a crevasse and landed on a ledge twelve meters down, breaking a leg in the fall; for much of that winter he lay in the cabin like in a lair, unsure about making the trip over the glacier. In the spring of the following year, when it finally got light, Koch was healthy again and they went out on to the glacier. Koch and Wegener did not tire of wondering at and admiring the life forms on the coast of the Arctic region: there were walruses, polar bears, musk ox, foxes, lemmings, and snow hares, in which Glói showed great interest, running after them wherever he saw them, amusing the men. When they reached the upper glacier, life was rather scarce; a lone snow bunting followed them through the storms all the way across the white wilderness, much to their delight. Vigfús shot several foxes at the beginning of journey and Koch got two fleas from one of the foxes, storing them in his luggage so the fleas came with him right across the glacial north of Greenland; any-thing for science, he thought to himself. This white desert, Captain Koch said to Dr. Wegener up on the high glacier,

Bernharður said, reminds me of Skeiðarásandur when I was measuring it ten years ago, spring, 1903. I withstood heavy sandstorms on Skeiðarásandur to take measurements; I made an attempt to travel the glacier by horse when I was surveying Öræfajökull and had to proceed precariously, but man learns little by little. We are going to prove to the world the superior qualities of the Icelandic horse, Wegener. Captain Koch collected all the place names in Öræfi from the most knowledgeable people in the region so they could be set on the maps that were made based on his observations, the so-called *General Staff Maps,* the first accurate maps of the land and certainly the most beautiful ever drawn, still very useful even though the glaciers have retreated and new areas been identified. I have the article about Captain Koch in *National Geographic* to thank for the fact that I wanted to become a toponymist and explorer; in reality, I had my mother to thank for giving me a subscription to National Geographic for my birthday when I was 6 years old, though in reality it was a consolation because she was going on a long journey with her sister, leaving me behind with my father, or rather a nanny, because he was never at home; perhaps I was just alone with *National Geographic,* a yellow spine glowing on the nightstand, and there I began to develop my strongest desires and fantasies. I read the retelling of Captain Koch's journey a hundred times and I always had *Across the White Wilderness* to hand. The Greenland expedition of Captain Koch and Dr. Wegener with their twenty metric tons of luggage for scientific research proved more difficult than they had expected, like any real expedition: they proceeded in a line, Vigfús going first, then the horse Gráni with the compass sled; Gráni was a good riding horse, a gæðing, a unique horse in many respects, versatile and wise; next came Koch with his horse Pólaris and the lightest sled; then Brúnka with his sled; then Wegener with Fucksrauður; Kavalíer brought up the rear. The drive was difficult and the horses became exhausted and fell in turn, each at the others' feet; I cried while reading, I cried at school when I thought about the horses, I cried time out of mind, I was sure that the horses who fled upon landing in Greenland had seen the time to come and that's why they ran off. Pólaris gave up first, after a month-long hike, on May 15th; he was shot; the Kavalíer fell on May 20th and was shot; Brúnka was shot June 4th; finally Fucksrauður on June 11th. Gráni had to make it all the way west across the glacier because he was the best horse, the apple of Vigfús' eye, a magnificent horse, the best water horse, the best glacier horse, the most cherished, Captain Koch writes in *Across the White Wilderness*, he grew seriously ill and struck the men as almost deranged from hunger and exertion; Gráni was set on the sled which the men pulled in despair, the whole world turned upside down; they wanted to find him a pasture where he would rebound and the merit of an Icelandic horse for a glacier adventure would be proven, but unfortunately that was not to be: he was shot July 4th, and was soon lying down on the empty ground. They had to leave Gráni back on the glacier ridge when they crossed it, fashioning for him there an unadorned resting place for eternity. Over the next day they suffered great disorientation and many obstacles; they created a cairn and stocked it with all the scientific data and logbooks and tools, leaving them there— they would have to search for it later if they were spared, or others arriving in future would find the data and process it. Out of food now, they sought for some, any settlement in West Greenland, but were faced with an endless, hopeless wide expanse ... There was only one thing to do to survive: they killed their dear friend Glói the dog and ate him. Just as Koch popped the first bite of dog soup into his mouth, a terrible sadness in his heart because he was a great animal lover and was tired of this dirty work of always having to shoot animals and sacrifice them to science, just as Koch stuck into his mouth the first bite of little Glói—Glói who had been so kind and entertaining and who had walked with them over the upper glaciers of Greenland along the 77th latitude at 50 degrees below zero through many storms and endless difficulties, poor little Glói who had shit in Wegener's wool hat, Glói who would gad about restlessly at night, in and out of the tent on the middle of the glacier so we were all kept awake—Captain Koch thinks of all this as he takes his first bite of dog soup, of poor little Glói who got locked outside out in the middle of the night during a storm when he went to piss and couldn't wake Koch so gnawed a big hole in the tent to get back in and everyone got so angry with him but Glói just slept soundly as the men slaved away repairing the tent in the middle of the night, and Koch slipped the first bite into his mouth, surprised and ashamed at how tasty the meat was, how delicious the soup was, and just then he saw a boat on the fjord: the men and the expedition were saved.

Koch and Wegener worked on their data, becoming famous although now they're forgotten; at the time the scientific world was open to the results of such studies, open to endeavor, open to sacrifices, open to Captain Koch and Dr. Wegener; the world was open to dead horses, open to fleas on a fox Vigfús shot, open to a snow bunting following them across the glacier all winter, the world was open to 20,000 kilos of luggage, the world was open to Vigfús who received 100 photographs from the trip on glass plates as a gift from Wegener and who lectured throughout Iceland and was always called Vigfús the Greenland Adventurer.

Across the White Wilderness is a tragedy about animals on a glacier, said Bernharður, how they are sacrificed in the interests of science, how the Icelandic horses dwindled in number one by one; it is the story of the equipment, the story of the clothing, the story of the baggage, the story of those twenty tons, the story of frost; the scientific work itself Captain Koch leaves for a second report, published in scientific journals. *Across the White Wilderness* is a travel narrative, a tragedy of poor little Glói who was taken and eaten in the end when it was unnecessary. No one could go on this expedition nowadays as they did then. They went across unknown lands, but unknown lands no longer exist, except perhaps underwater and subglacial (for now). As they traveled across the zone of accumulation, the upper glacier, they gave the places names, nothing vain like Koch Peak or Wegener Heath and Vigfús Rock or the like, but modest and practical, The Point, Touchstone, Cold Ridge, features along the way that they agreed upon and could reference as they explored the land and ferried stuff to a new camp. Captain Koch likely acquired this way of thinking about place names in Öræfi when he was surveying there, a place where men are reasonable and practical, on Öræfajökull many of the places are named after Koch's expedition, like Hermannaskarð and Tjaldskarð, although the soldiers passed through and the tents were set up there in the middle of Öræfajökull for no longer than 1903, even if several people have stayed there before and after. Captain Koch's expedition was in the service of science, unlike most other expeditions which are in the service of vanity or nothing at all. Science for its own sake, Koch wrote in *Across the White Wilderness*, Bernharður said, science for its own sake does not have utility as its goal, but is instead concerned with ethical values.

†

The Alpiner Bernharður Fingurbjörg was born in Vienna on November 2nd, 1975, Dr. Lassi wrote in the report, on the so-called Day of the Dead, the Mass of All-Souls; what's more, his father was a well-educated diplomat in the Foreign Service in Sweden, Nikulás Fingurbjörg, an Icelandic man of high birth, tall and with light brown hair. His mother was of Swiss parentage, Marie Luce Geist, a stout woman with an agile face who became subdued later in life. She studied in Vienna and got a good job at the Ministry of Foreign Affairs in the city immediately after graduating from the law department at the University the year Bernharður was born. Bernharður said that his father studied in Málmey (Swedish: *Malmö*) and was a successful, bright, and well-respected student. He had a family there, a wife and five children, siblings Bernharður has never met. My mother was an elegant, single twenty-something woman, an important person in the Ministry, Bernharður said; she worked on various in-house tasks and in 1973 my father was there for a cocktail party held by the European Free Trade Association; he met my mother, was immediately attracted to her, as she was to him, even though he was much older, and they slept together that night in his hotel room. That's how my older brother was conceived, Tómas. They didn't meet again until two years later, at an EFTA conference in Brussels in early 1975; they became infatuated with each other that night. "EFTA love," was the way my mother described it to me some time later, it was an EFTA love night when you were conceived, my dear son, said my father, after which he returned to his family in Sweden and probably told his wife the conference had been successful. That fall, I came into the world. My parents continued to meet several times a year at conferences across European cities; enthusiasm, love, and respect burrowed deeper into their hearts, paralleling the way the EFTA agreement was taking hold in Europe, a valid counterweight to the European Union. But Marie Luce had less and less patience for this double life while Nikulás constantly tried to do his bit and end the duplicity; each year my father promised her everything. Finally, in 1979, he decided to divorce his *boring spouse* and leave their *boring children* in Sweden, as he called them sometimes, wrapped in the comforter late in the evening at a conference at the Hotel Plaza, and start living with his mountain goat, as he called Marie Luce. My father was fifty when he started his life over again in a new place; he always said he hated Malmö but loved Vienna, he often did so in Icelandic to Tómas and I, and I tried to imagine the ghost-family he'd left, but I never conjured up a mental image. These people were paternal shadows, Bernharður said, Dr. Lassi wrote. Up to their necks in *amor*, Nikulás Fingurbjörg and Marie Luce Geist decided to settle in Vienna, having married in a small church near Lake Vierwaldstättersee, a ceremony attended only by the Geist family. Marie Luce had a decent position in the Ministry of Foreign Affairs, so they could afford a large and beautiful home at Freyung 7 in Vienna, above the famous *Kräuterhaus*, an herbalist store which has plied its trade there for 200 years; the home had enormous cabinets and numerous drawers, beautiful interiors, a good energy, sweet aromas; it fulfilled my parents' dream of living in Innere Stadt, year after year they'd dreamed of it, lying in each other's embrace in hotel rooms all over Europe after having made love, I want to live in *Innere Stadt*, my father is supposed to have said, in Innere Stadt where all the old, fashionable people in Vienna lived, but now there are only tourists, the gentry has fled; my parents were tourists in the world of aristocracy, my father wanted them to become aristocrats, but my mother said it wasn't possible, it doesn't happen that way, Nikulás my dear, nobility is *inherited*, not learned, you should know that, we'll never be anything but imitation aristocrats in a tourist world in Innere Stadt, my mother said despondently; when they moved to Freyung in 1980 all the aristocrats were moving away or dying, strange things happen when tourism increases, and even more astounding was the lack of interest philosophers showed in the changes happening in moral standards, the way everything was becoming desolate: cities, nature, human beings, stories, Innere Stadt had emptied out, perhaps there aren't any philosophers any longer, the city's heart had hollowed out, the tourists were getting an education, were maturing, but the inhabitants had become uneducated and immature, everything was standardized and empty, people had been tossed aside, visitors paid their hosts no heed, not knowing who they were, and then they weren't there, the guests ate cakes and left their plates lying about ... I grew up in a large apartment above the herbalists on Freyung 7, a large neoclassical building from around 1700, near the historic square in the old town where there are several old palaces and where there has always been a thriving market atmosphere; the area formerly belonging to the monks, street artists and aristocrats of the square, and that's the way it still was in my childhood. I was planning to either become a monk, a street artist, or an aristocrat—or all of them. The tourists came to Freyung to see the monks, street artists, and the aristocracy, but only saw other tourists looking for monks, street artists, and aristocrats. When my parents sacrificed their lives for the apartment they thought that their position would be secure among old aristocratic families, but it takes more than an apartment to climb the social ladder, even if an apartment can guarantee a family a financial safety net. All those living in the building were respectable citizens with PhDs in law or other profitable areas, highly-esteemed in society. Out the window on the other side of the street was Batthyany Palace itself, and there on the ground floor my friend Norbert had his antique store, I was a fixture there, a gray cat in and around the ancient books and maps and old-city photos. Next to the palace is the Constitutional Law Court, a rather dull building that it is elegant in the ancient Greek style, the way courthouses in general are; stretching off from the square is the beautiful Fountain of Austria;

a female statue rises out of it, a symbol for the Austrian State, *Austria*, a figure for Hapsburg rule. Directly on the other side of the square is the passage to the palace market, where we knew all the traders. Today there's an organic market at Freyung Square on weekends and you always sees the same people, the last people left in the neighborhood, older people from all walks of life gathered in the afternoon to drink organic beer or organic pear schnapps or organic white wine or organic wine or organic juice; these are the last aristocrats with their high moral fiber and their inner lamentations about the workers and the high-end winos; there you'll find organic cheeses and organic sausages, vegetables, spices, oils, honey, olives, even organic toys. People from the neighborhood meet in the square to talk about old times, about a world gone by, and to buy rural wares. Occasionally hooves can be heard clicking along the cobbled streets with rich tourists trying to look natural in the faux-imperial chariots the horses pull; the tourists end up looking awkward and helpless. On Saturdays I would sit there and drink pear schnapps and eat Tyrolean *gröstl*, a potato dish my mother often made when I was little, with bacon, sauerkraut, juniper berries, and caraway, and then I would feel at home on Freyung with its aroma of herbs, with its watering posts where dogs and horses can get a drink on a hot day, where the clock chime in the basilica, also known as the Scottish Church or the Scottish Cloister; it was attached to our house, and we attended church every Sunday morning before taking coffee with the Church board afterward: it was of the utmost importance to know the priest, to be in good standing, as it should be: that contributes to one's ability to feel at ease, respected in society, at one with other good citizens, having found a foothold in civilization—but such ease is fleeting, as all ease is. I never missed a church visit because along with the coffee you always got moist cake, which I guess is why I've become a real cake fiend. The Scottish Church beside our house was originally a monastery, founded by Scottish monks of the order of St. Columbcille more than a thousand years ago; my mother said I was baptized after the holy Bernharður who was bishop of Vienna in the Middle Ages. Bishop Bernharður went out into the wide world as a young man and fought in the army of Charlemagne, the father of Europe, said my mother, Charlemagne conquered countries and baptized people. St. Bernharður later lost his appetite for war after his parents died, and so he joined the monastery. He is the patron of those who till the ground, or so my mother said on Sundays, when there was a certain sanctity at home I liked, calm, peace, space, learning. I have always loved Sundays, the way I feel secure with my mother. I was going to become a monk, says Bernharður, a monk, an itinerant, and aristocrat, because I easily tired of this tumbling world.

Bernharður Fingurbjörg is 198 centimeters tall, Dr. Lassi wrote in her report, 64 kilos, he is gangling, ruddy, curly-haired and unkempt, pale and a bit freckly, large-mouthed, gap-toothed, green-eyed, with an intense, dewy gaze, a joyful, determined countenance, protruding ears, a large head, a slender neck, long, distinctive limbs over which he has little control. It will do him good to lie there a few months and rest so that his muscles and bones get re-acquainted while his wounds heal. He uses thick glasses because he is very far-sighted, +5 on the left, +6.5 on the right, his eyes seem massive in the glasses, heavy glasses that slip down to the tip of his nose. He has a long stride but a rather stiff walk. He is wearing high-laced military boots laced on top of his pants; a raincoat and cream yellow shirt. Generally neat, he is somehow inherently chaotic; he wore a bow tie on the glacier. Several of his characteristics would be a model for young people.

Despite growing up in a staid home among distinguished tea drinkers and medicinal-plant aficionados from the herbalists on the ground level, there was always some underlying turbulence, some instability, as in all homes, Dr. Lassi reported. A dark sadness hung below the houses, underneath the city. Tómas, my older brother, hung himself in the living room one cold winter night in 1982 in the middle of the week, said Bernharður, he was nine years old, it was an accident, we brothers were alone at home playing, I went over to him and cut him down with my father's razor and carried him to bed and set him up there, I was numb-mouthed, weak-kneed, I lay in bed with him and held him and cried, there was no one I could notify and nothing occurred to me, although I do not know how well I remember all this, I don't know what is dream and what distorted memory, it would have been good if the world had stood still, it was evening, the monks next door had probably gone to bed, I could just lie there with him and nothing would ever happen again in the world. I must have fallen asleep because our mother was in the doorway, calling my dad, telling him to come and see us there together, the brothers; they had been out to dinner and the theater.

My mother sought salvation from the so-called Benedictine house in the monastery; there, she was offered Christian trauma counseling and psychotherapy. She got more and more involved in church business, and it seemed to do her good; she did a lot of good work there. The summer after Tómas died, my mother went to Iceland with her sister. She did not come back the same. That's what my father always said. I was in constant conflict with my father, most of it good-natured. And yet I was hardly ever around my parents throughout adolescence: they were busy at work and with their social life, while I was utterly distracted, wandering aimlessly around town. I was, however, a good student; I applied to the Nordic Studies Department at the University. When I announced this to my father, he said: Tómas would have become the Austrian Foreign Minister. Then he started asking, day after day: How are you going to support yourself? A subsidy from the state? I thought you wanted to become a diplomat like me, you've always wanted to travel, diplomats travel a lot, I have already put in a good word for you at the State Department, there's a post waiting for you, of course you'd begin with something general first, like I did, sorting documents, answering the phone, something like that and before you know it, you'll be the assistant to the Foreign Minister...Who'll pay for the apartment when we're dead and gone? What does a toponymist do anyway? Teach? Examine maps?...Humanities? Bernharður, how can you do this to me? We haven't managed to set aside as much as we planned to...toponymy, of all things... I plucked up my courage and asked my father: You work on relationships, right? As a diplomat and ambassador? Toponymy is the same, I said. What do you mean? asked my father mildly; he was adept at holding conversations using Socratic methods and getting you into trouble. Place names are relationships, I said, place names are the conversations people have across a country, they spring up between people in a country, for example, property rights, natural structures, stories, business transactions, even military actions, toponymists play an important role in military affairs just like regular diplomats, toponymists are the land's diplomats, I said, making every effort to please my father. I read in *National Geographic*, I said, that it is a tradition between fathers and sons in Iceland to study place names; the fathers tell their children about the place names, teaching them, that's how it's been since the Settlement...Well, fine, said my father, have it your way...I wanted to deviate from my parents' path, I didn't want to go into management science or study law or become a public relations stooge or project manager or diplomat, spending my whole life climbing the rankings within the European Union ambassadorial system, as had been mapped out for me, inheriting the apartment after having sent my parents to a faux-Chinese luxury retirement home in the Alps, a place with the most expensive view in Austria, finally free, free slaves missing their oppressor, mournful dogs living in financial security and stability, neither secure nor stable but dangling there like the sword of Damocles...you should never do what's expected of you; there's always another path through life than the one before you. I wanted to look at maps and work with words but didn't dare say so directly; I always dreamed of being a hobo, as they call it here in the square, I'm going to become a monk and hobo, I told my parents when I was little. That's a difficult prospect and an unhealthy one, my mother said; you must foster your name's reputation, my father said with a mixture of regional pride and urban arrogance ... I don't give a shit about that! I said, startling my parents with my remark.

The funeral took place in the church on Freyvangur; the monks sang Haydn's *Stabat Mater*, always a favorite of my mother, she finally got to mourn her son, and when I think about it today, I find it grotesque that my mother stood weeping beside the coffin and let them sing that song; at the least, it was highly morbid. I remember I sat hardly daring to breathe. I did not cry. I thought about all his stuff I was going to own even as I knew I could not show that I coveted it. Perhaps it was entirely normal, yet I felt an uncontrollable anticipation, I was delighted my brother was dead and the grief that went with that gnawed at me. I watched my mother weeping in her black garments, saw how she avoided looking at me, avoided me, in fact, like I wasn't there, or she was already gone. Dad focused on supporting her, distressed and wrinkled. Our relatives, all black-clad and with umbrellas, were afraid to make eye contact: every one of them, my grandmother and grandfather, too, avoided looking at me or being near me. The church was filled with frightened eyes avoiding me. This was all my fault.

Why was I so different from my parents? They wanted me to be the Austrian Foreign Minister, but I wanted to become a hobo; that was my response to the pressure, to hurry in another direction entirely. In truth, I'm no different from them, but I want to be different. They want everything fine and clean and expensive and high-quality; I have things that are coarse, dirty and cheap, though also high-quality. I don't want anything they want, I refuse to follow their path—but can this be the only train of thought regarding independence, being contrary to one's parents? Doesn't it cut any deeper? When I think I'm renouncing my parents, going my own way and acting of my own will, I'm actually denying myself, going the way they have gone, and unthinkingly. Everyone rebels against their parents, it lasts but a short time, naively short, it doesn't amount to anything but frustration—yet from this naivety and frustration I'm going to make my career... I know and understand misfortune, was brought up by her, that's what I'm trying to avoid, trying to retrieve my mother's happiness, taken away on Freyung and in Öræfi, the Wasteland. I always pity my mother, it's easy to honor her as the commandments demand because she supports everything I do, she understands my impatience because it's hers, too. She was born in the mountains, and people born in the mountains can't sit still all their lives in an office, they squirm under their skin, yearning for adventure. My father often spoke through her, her personality disappearing for periods. My mother, said Bernharður, is a fine person. But too delicate for the world, Dr. Lassi wrote. Tómas's death was unbearable, and she never recovered from what happened in Iceland; my mother turned gray, stayed out a long time inside the large markets, where she would break down weeping and need help getting back out. She would wander around downtown alone, depressingly dressed, she withered and dried up, my father had to help her with things, picking up domestic chores, barely concealing his frustration—he wanted to be king of the household. My mother wanted to follow her son across the great divide, she loved Tómas as much as a delicate person is able to, with bottomless sacrifices and with weakness. My mother got lost in the haze and I could rarely find her after that, I became a teenager and drowned myself in studies, I had to get away, I wanted to go to Iceland where my mother had been, I had to get out onto Vatnajökull, get inside old issues of *National Geographic*, I had to find my mother in Mávabyggðir... after Tómas's death, I avoided my mother the way she avoided the world, her grief was too big. When she returned from Iceland, she'd become a shadow, a delicate ghost, a fragile ghost, a character of dust... I couldn't follow Tómas into emptiness the way my mother did; I was stuck in the ice cave of reality.

†

I do not know whether he'll ever have the chance to return to Vienna, to Freyvangur, Dr. Lassi remarked to the Interpreter, he'll probably die here in Freysnes, ho–hum, there are worse places to die, he'd already have been dead if I hadn't amputated him and castrated him. We doctors have a duty to extend life, and though I've gelded this man, some beautiful girl just must come visit him, it is surely *love* if a dashing woman visits a eunuch, there's the woman from the Skaftafell Visitor Center, the park ranger, a damn horny creature, stout and broad, Edda, a country girl, a shepherdess, no?... I'll almost have tears in my eyes when Edda visits her eunuch, such beautiful, beautiful love—then I think with horror of my nagging old biddy in the camper van, no, shush, I can't say that, maybe if I saw off my breasts using the angle grinder my big buxom girl will love me; self-dismemberment arouses love better than anything, at least for a while. I don't know what it would take for me to love her, perhaps sawing off her head, I'm sure if she got killed I'd love her, for the first time I'd really love her with all my heart, that's how love goes, it compensates, I would fall in love with the memory of my old nag, for then you have a free hand, a free heart to shape another person's character in your memory, it's not difficult, it happens automatically and unconsciously and so I would love her and she would have loved me ... from the other side ... I fear love is only possible after death, at least I struggle to have relationships with the living, Interpreter, oh, I guess I love that hag of mine a little bit, late at night, in twilight ... I've begun to disappear into her hulking bosom in order to maintain my mental health, that's that state I'm in, Interpreter, my work causes me so much stress and strain that I could never get through the day if I did not have them at home, those blessed breasts, weighty hunks, if I didn't have them to come home to after castrating and killing animals I would lose my wits, for sure; I could never cut off and anesthetize animals without my voluptuous vixen ... Edda seems to have more than a little crush on this Bernharður, right? She probably loves him more now that I've cut off his leg, and even more since I sawed off his ass cheek, and still more because I chopped off his pecker, she'll love him most of all when he's dead, for that's when love finally becomes coherent, permanent, and unshakable; she can love him dead her whole life, so it would be really good for Edda if Bernharður kicks the bucket, she'd be able to bathe herself in lovesickness for the rest of her days ... but if Bernharður survives, she'll quickly tire of him.

Let me tell you this, my dear Bernharður, Dr. Lassi said, nudging the Interpreter, your legs got all wet and you got frost-bite and that causes gangrene; when gangrene gets into the limbs, amputation is the only way, the only way, my friend. Let me tell you a story from my region that should cheer you up. Once upon a time, some brothers were making a journey one winter night; it was very frosty, this was back in 1629, my friend, sixteen-hundred-and-twenty-nine, how about that, and the brothers were on horseback, they needed to cross bodies of water that hadn't fro-zen over and so their hands and feet got wet. They started fool-ing around: it was a starlit night, the northern lights crackling in the heavens and the glacier fluorescent through the whole night, gleaming, cracking; they didn't feel like going home immedi-ately but instead lay about in the snow and drank liquor and watched the stars, composing verses about the sky's beauty and love's transience; and then they were weary of all this beauty and hale-heartiness, and they dozed off. This took place on Gagnheið; Jón Espólín writes about it in the sixth chapter of his *Yearbook*, along with many other extreme events he got from old annals and all kinds of esoteric documents, you can quite imag-ine! Now, the brothers wake up with their feet frozen to the ground and are truly startled; after some time, they're able to roll over and tear themselves free, causing ribbons of skin to peel off, stuck to the frozen ground. They crawl painfully to the nearest town, having lost their horses in their drunken tomfoolery, they crawl all the way to Þingvellir and arrive, exhausted, at a farm-yard; a doctor lives there and he leaps up when he sees them, he bundles them into his living space and saws off their legs. They lay there a long time through winter and go around on wooden legs the rest of their lives; one of the brothers lost all his fingers as well, but still manages to write reams by binding a feather pen to his stump; he was prolific with his pen, in all senses: the counts of Rosencrone are his descendants.

Our toponymist flew with an Austrian airline to Copenhagen on Thursday April 10th at 09:40, Dr. Lassi wrote in her report, following the Interpreter's lead; when Bernharður checked in, he asked for an aisle seat as close to the front as possible, so that he could make a speedy exit on landing; on the other hand, if he was going to survive a crash, he thought, he would need to sit at the back of the plane, something he'd seen in the movies: a crash throws everyone forward in a vehicle, crushing what's up front—but it was an unbearable confinement, sitting in back. He asked for a seat with space for his long shanks. It couldn't be done. Bernharður didn't fare well on planes, he needed to walk around the earth and have a panorama, he couldn't deal with being strapped into a tube at a great height. Do you have a suitcase? asked the counter clerk. No, a trunk, said Bernharður. Then he had to go to another counter which handled oversize baggage because the trunk was never going to fit on the conveyor belt. Bernharður headed there; his tomb-like trunk raised suspicions. The customs officers sighed and asked Bernharður to open this colossus. Its contents were recorded: 40 pcs. assorted boxes, 40 pcs. cardboard, 4 large sheets of paper, 20 notebooks, 4 cartons of ink cartridges, 1¾ pounds of sailmaker's twine, 1 pound of combed cotton, 3¾ pounds *aqua fortis*, i.e. nitric acid, bottled, 30 pcs. pig bladders, 10 pcs. jars, 80 cakes, a patterned silver cake slice, a prized treasure inscribed with gothic lettering,

Geist, a travel barometer with a thermometer, a thermometer in a case, fish baskets made of iron, a 600-metre long cable, coiled in a bag, a shaft-less rock hammer, some loose raisins.

Bernharður had to accept seat 17D if he was going to investigate Mávabyggðir; it was a rather small plane and he did not know how he felt about that, it was both good and bad. He sat in his seat, fastened the belt and picked up the book he had long ago decided to read on the plane, *Tonio Kröger* by Thomas Mann, a book he read every time he flew: if he was going to die, he would die with Thomas Mann. He was glad that this small plane had no televisions to annoy him, that pleased him so much the crying baby in the seat across the aisle had no effect on him. He looked over at the parents and gave them a smile to let them know they wouldn't have to worry about him, they weren't disturbing him from reading. He was met by the young mother's downcast expression; she had seemingly given up on her child, she looked hopelessly up into the air, making a show of her weariness, lost in her own self-pity. Bernharður occasionally snuck a stealthy look out the corner of his eye; the young father seemed to be doing everything for their child, perhaps this was an instance of the tender Scandinavian man he had read about in magazines? From Copenhagen, the alpine youth and toponymical scientist took an Icelandair plane arriving in Keflavík, Iceland at 15:45; he would reach Reykjavík around dinner time. The vessel felt pervasively chaotic, everyone utterly helpless to hide the fact that flying a winged cylinder over a large body of water amounts to obvious mortal danger. The flight attendants covered their fear with excess makeup, and pushed the carts selling fake luxuries with great fervor, desperate and nervy; the attendants were smooth and fawning on the surface, but hard and ice-cold underneath, I thought when I looked up from *Tonio Kröger*, said Bernharður, why isn't there a diverting sort of flea market on board planes instead of this consumerist horror show, why don't the flight attendants proceed down the aisle pumping a street organ while a monkey in a yellow vest and red fez jumps between the seats, snatching money and ruffling the passengers' hair? The time would fly and everyone would die laughing... then he managed to concentrate a bit and finished *Tonio Kröger* just before landing. He has always felt this was a book about him, Dr. Lassi added. It was almost a disappointment when the plane landed safely on the ground rather than crashing, burning, into the ocean; he had prepared himself to accept that fate with the help of eight glasses of cumin-flavored Brennivín, an Icelandic schnapps with which he was immediately infatuated. Relieved, he unfastened his seat belt and slunk wriggling out of this sardine tin.

How was he dressed for the trip? Dr. Lassi asked the Interpreter, taking a great but knowing risk by disrupting the flow of truth and deep knowledge from the toponymist through the interpreter to her, to her pen and her report. Bernharður was wearing the same clothes as now, says the Interpreter and Dr. Lassi wrote this down after looking suspiciously at the Interpreter: laced-up Austrian army boots, he is saying he always wears laced-up army boots in the mountains, though it was a tedious business at the airports, having to take off his shoes at security screening, these new procedures, bizarre ones, I would have been better off taking a train to the Netherlands and a cargo ship from Rotterdam to Iceland where I would have been able to sit and write in my cabin and stroll around on deck and smoke a pipe instead of having to keep taking off my laced-up army boots for screening and be proactively terrorized and demoralized, said Bernharður, Dr. Lassi wrote. His green pantaloons made of fine wool, the ones he wears all the time; a coarse woolen jacket with many deep pockets always full of all kinds of stuff, a snuff handkerchief, a harmonica, a pocket knife, a notebook, a pencil stub, some fountain pens, a bird whistle, sunglasses, a comb. He wore a cream shirt and a spotted red bow-tie, a dirty v-shaped diamond-pattern sweater, a large vest with stuffed pockets containing snippets of letters with addresses and phone numbers and ideas; a loose scarf; and, on top of everything else, his raincoat. My mother always taught me to dress elegantly for a journey, Bernharður said; before going through customs I struggled out of my coat and put it on my left hand and pulled the trunk behind me, I did my best to look like a Central European intellectual, which I was and am, I wanted to look like it was Thomas Mann coming to Iceland or Thomas Bernharður or Stefan Zweig or Arthur Schnitzler, but the Icelandic customs officer apparently had no knowledge of the Central European intelligentsia and took me aside. Right away I fished out *Écrits de linguistique générale* by the Swiss linguist Ferdinand de Saussure, although it's not really by him; I handed the officer the book and a conciliatory handshake, this is a gift and a hand of friendship, I said in Icelandic but he considered this act of friendship suspicious and immediately led me into an interrogation room, where he asked about my business in Iceland, I said I was an Austrian toponymist on the way east to Öræfi to record place names in Mávabyggðir and to follow my mother's path, though she had a nasty experience there; he recoiled at that and returned my passport to me. I was a bit sheepish that I hadn't belched this out earlier. He knew the Öræfi region well, this customs official, asking who I staying with, I said I didn't know anyone in Öræfi and was planning to go to the campsite at the Skaftafell Visitor Center; happy days, said the customs official, good times are coming your way, say hello to everyone in Öræfi for me, I'm really jealous, soon I'll get my summer vacation and head, of course, to Skaftafell National Park, the best place to be, perhaps I'll see you there? said the customs officer, and he examined my gift, proud, happy, and bemused: *Écrits de linguistique générale* by the Swiss linguist Ferdinand de Saussure, though in fact it's not really by him.

When Bernharður finally emerged from the terminal, a strong wind blew against him; he had a hard time getting out the revolving door and got stuck there, the door would not budge, it was going to crush him to death, this door means to crush me to death! I yelled, said Bernharður, but then the wind stopped blowing against the door and began to suck instead, causing Bernharður to fly out the revolving door with his trunk, out onto the sidewalk, where an enormous bus stood purring. It surprised him how cold the air was, as if he had had a bitter candy or a Salem cigarette, everything was covered in cold menthol, it occurred to Bernharður that there must be large eucalyptus trees nearby, though that wasn't likely given that the terminal faced lavafields in every direction, with not a single tree as far as the eye could see, except for several small aspens in beds by the parking lot, there for no one's benefit or enjoyment. The bus idling there was headed to Reykjavík and Bernharður crawled into the luggage compartment and holed up there among the bags; there are few nicer things than lying on bags, he thought, on top of a luggage pile, he also enjoyed lying on piles of clothes, and piles in general; when traveling he would empty the contents of his trunk into the middle of a floor and lie down to sleep on the pile or else simply sleep inside the trunk. The pot-bellied bus driver with mirrored sunglasses spotted the gangling Austrian and asked him to kindly get out of the compartment, pay his fare, and move up to the seats. It's horrible how brusque everyone is here, I said to myself, Bernharður said, he was quite contrary about getting on the bus, which he felt was designed for dwarves: why are the seats in airplanes and buses always so small? he asked the bus driver, the bigger the vehicles, the less space between seats, people always get less and less as vehicles get larger and larger, this bloody bus is only for dwarves. Get up there with you if you're coming! barked the bus driver, or I'll call the police.

The bus was a pain. From the city bus station, Bernharður went up Njarðargata and to the guesthouse Norðurljós on Freyjugata, where he got a small room up in the attic, Dr. Lassi wrote. The guesthouse is an excellent stone house from 1946 (it says so on the exterior, according to Bernharður), probably built with war profits and located in the heart of the residential area in the city center, the so-called Neighborhood of the Gods where the streets bear the names of Norse gods and goddesses as enumerated in Snorri's *Prose Edda*. The room cheered Bernharður although it was very small and for the most part all roof, meaning he had to bow and stoop; the attic window faced Freyjugata, and he could see into an interesting sculpture garden he wanted to explore, Einar Jónsson's sculpture garden. The room held a narrow, mustard-colored bed with a beautifully-woven woolen spread; the toponymist's extremities hung off the end when he threw himself down on it. There was a bedside table made of teak, a small desk, a simple wooden chair, a sink and a mirror, perfect, Bernharður said to himself, a communal toilet and shower along the hallway, but Bernharður did not come all the way to Iceland to bathe and sit on the toilet, he was headed on a research trip up to Mávabyggðir to gather place names, or to *experience place names,* as he put it, according to the Interpreter, he set his toiletries by the sink, washed his face with cold water, splashed water through his wild and curly mop of hair using a narrow-toothed comb, he wet the comb well and brushed his hair again, it resembled a stormy sea, he brushed his teeth thoroughly and carefully with salt toothpaste, washed his mouth with Listerine, looked at himself in the mirror, feeling the alcohol and eucalyptus do its work, then he spit it into the sink and took a few deep breaths; he got some shaving cream and rubbed it onto his cheeks with a brush before shaving with a razor, taking his time, making two passes until his skin was completely smooth. He took out a large bottle of 4711 cologne, loosened the cap and poured a puddle in the palm of his hand; he rubbed his hands together well, slapped himself lightly on the cheeks, rubbed it on the back of his neck, massaged his temples and allowed the essential oils and herbs in the cologne to infiltrate his thin skin. This is good for one's sanity, he thought every time he performed this ritual, he rubbed his temples slowly and gently, it increases one's well-being and enhances cognition, according to research, then he covered his nose with his palm and breathed the alcohol and citrus fragrance deeply, clearing his airways so that he felt his brain open wide. This is how he adjusted to travel. Then he opened the cumin-flavor Brennivín bottle he'd purchased in duty-free and filled his glass halfway there at the sink, then downed it in three gulps. After this, Bernharður felt fit as a fiddle, ready to head out.

Bernharður had no option but to stay in Reykjavík for a night before taking the bus east to Öræfi, since the bus did not leave until the next morning. He decided to pass the time walking around town and looking at signs, *the city's place names*, he could see a supermarket outside on the corner and thought to himself it would be nice to have some basic food supplies in the room, perhaps; he checked with the woman who ran the guest house and she pointed out a shared kitchen in the basement where he could store food in the fridge and cook something, just behave like you're at home, the proprietess said. Bernharður was repulsed at the thought of a common kitchen and probably didn't manage to hide that from her, given the way he recoiled; best just to have some snacks up in my room and entirely circumvent this kitchen, he thought. The little supermarket on the corner was called *Matur & Myndir, Food & Films* and Bernharður thought it was a great wonder, combining a grocery store with a movie rental place. At the very moment he walked through the door on the corner, he suddenly had a vision of cells damaged by a virus in the body of Western civilization. Inside Food & Films Bernharður bought some *Finn Crisp* crispbread, on the grounds that he'd come to a Nordic country, and crispbread is a characteristic Nordic food, or so he'd read in *National Geographic* at some point. Having picked up the original flavor Finn Crisp and carefully read the label, contentedly noting that the crispbread contained only rye, water, salt and yeast, he noticed another flavor, *caraway*, which is cumin, and he immediately swapped them out. Then he picked out the packet of butter in the most old-fashioned packaging, butter containing only cream and salt, the way butter ought to, not a pile of garbage as is usually the case, butter isn't butter any more, he thought, but a heap of garbage, and so is cheese, he said aloud to himself in Food & Films, it would be nice to have cheese, but what cheese? After a long study of the small cheese selection it seemed to him like he was going around in circles, he could feel despair beginning to well up within him, and as he was about to return the stick of butter to the refrigerator, he spotted the maribo cheese, cumin-flavored, and that decided it; he paid for the three products at the cash register, happy with his purchase. He took the groceries to his guesthouse, up to his room.

Cumin, Bernharður said, I love cumin, I'm going to eat cumin crispbread with cumin cheese while I drink cumin liquor. I was besotted with Icelandic cumin, feeling lucky to get to taste it. It's called caraway in English, they stick to that, but *cumin* in Icelandic, German and Yiddish calls it cross-cumin, kreuzkümmel. An Icelandic man lived at Guesthouse Northern Lights, and not as a tourist; his was the room opposite mine up in the attic and his door was wide open. He was a bit of a wretch to look at, a vagabond who introduced himself simply as Guest; he popped his head into my room and immediately clocked that all my food contained cumin. He went back over to his place and returned with a jar full of cumin seeds, a gift for me. This is Icelandic cumin, said Guest, I collected it out on Viðey where it grows wild; the story goes that Skúli, the Chief Magistrate, sowed it in the 18th century. You can keep it, I have plenty. You're called Guest, I said, and you're a guest at the guesthouse; my mother's name is Geist. I showed him the cake slice, which I was using for the butter, it's engraved with my mother's family name, it makes me wonder whether being a guest is the same thing as being a spirit or ghost. Guest joined right in and a cheer washed over him. I asked Guest to suggest a good bar in town and to tell me some things I could do in Reykjavík, a place with which I was completely unfamiliar. Come in, said Guest, cumin! I went into his room. Yes, he said, he'd like to show me the city; he was interested in toponymy. We did justice to the schnapps as we had a cumin chat in his room. He'd apparently been living there for some time: you couldn't move for books and stacks of paper; bookshelves reached from floor to ceiling, which was higher than head height; in all the nooks and crannies there were stacks of books, the bed was unmade, a filthy sheet covered only half the mattress; his comforter was blue. Empty beer bottles were thick-packed on the bedside table, together with a full ashtray; under the sloping ceiling was an old and dusty pump organ. Norðurljós is a good guesthouse, said Guest, there's always several writers or would-be poets living here in winter, unemployed, and from time to time psychiatric patients, junkies, students, tourists ... I suffer an eternal displacement thanks to the tourist industry's gold rush, said Guest; I lived next to the guesthouse but my home was swallowed up when it enlarged itself due to that infestation; there was little I could do about it, it happens repeatedly, everywhere I go, I've lived in three places here on Freyjugata, each for a short time, the neighborhood's residents are all moving away but I decided to stubbornly remain and bed down with the virus, myself and my things as a kind of curse... I stood and scanned the book titles, Bernharður said, and noticed a picture on the wall, on it was written *ICELAND 874–1874*; between the dates, a long-haired woman with a sword sat on top of a glacier, and above her was a shining star; below, in the center, was a map of the country, and around the country you could see bull, eagle, dragon, and giant with a big staff; at the bottom I saw the name Ingólf Arnarson. Who made this picture, I asked, what is it? It's a paean to Iceland by Benedikt Gröndal, said Guest, a memorial card to a thousand years of settlement in the country; that's the mountain-lady, Iceland's female spirit. He sat down at the organ on a small stool; in your honor, he said, I'll play and sing *Psalm over Wine*, to the tune of Joseph Haydn. Next he played *Sing Praise to God* and some hymns I didn't know. Then he sat on the carpeted floor, lit a cigarette, leaned back on a tower of books and said: I adore cumin.

As afternoon wore on, the cumin lovers forayed over to a hostelry called *Circus*, Dr. Lassi wrote, giving the report a sprinkle of saga style because she was always reading the sagas, Circus is an ugly junk-hut of a bar on Klapparstígur, dark and shady inside, where they found some pitiful creatures playing pinball and drinking beer; a sad but homely atmosphere prevailed, and there was no discernible difference between bartender and customer, they ran together like so much does nowadays, the ununiformed bartender playing pinball along with the customers, they all greeted Guest like a colleague though he turned out to be a regular there and actually used that as his name, The Regular. He crossed over to the other side of the bar to serve us. I asked whether they might have any cumin beer, which cheered The Regular up no end; he asked at once whether I'd tasted such a beer some place? I said I hadn't, it might perhaps be too much, and I leant against the bar; on the other hand, I was starting to connect cumin, *caraway*, with everything Nordic, getting carried away because German and Hungarian and Finnish and Yiddish and Icelandic are the only languages in the world which call *kúmen* cumin, as I said to The Regular, all other languages follow the Latin model, where the stem is *carvi*, which the Anglo-Saxons heard as *caraway*. Deep down the Icelandic coast is a red fish, said The Regular, called *karfi*; it's almost the color of the packaging on the Finnish crispbread called *Finn Crisp caraway!* ... I had a poetic etymology conversation with The Regular. At Circus, I got what one might call a *poetic sensation* as I noted a spiritual connection between toponymy and etymology; they are both the story of words, of the novels inside words, perhaps—it was that sort of feeling.

The bartender was occupied with his pinball but The Regular substituted now and then, pouring drinks for the few patrons who sat at the bowed bar. I noticed they were putting drinks on their tabs, they were probably all regulars. There was something appealing about my neighbor's face: it was not at all ugly, and some unshakable happiness shone through the sad darkness of the bright blue eyes. The Regular asked my purpose in being in Iceland, and I could easily have led the conversation toward ontology and protected myself from inquisition; however, I answered the question straight, I was headed to Öræfi to research the place names I was writing about for my doctoral thesis in the Nordic Studies Department in the University of Vienna, I wanted to experience them physically, to go into Mávabyggðir and climb Fingurbjörg because my name was Fingurbjörg; you might call it self-searching, I'm going to Mávabyggðir to find myself because I'm lost in the world.

I know Öræfi well, said The Regular mildly, because I went there a lot as a kid. It seemed strange to me, almost suspicious, that The Regular should be familiar with Öræfi, and be living at Guesthouse Northern Lights on Freyjugata, in the room opposite mine—but he for his part seemed still warier and more suspicious and got hung up for a long time on the fact that I lived on Freyung in Vienna and had come to Reykjavík to stay on Freyjugata; he could not stop asking exactly where Freyung in Vienna was located, he regularly came back to this connection between Freyung and Freyjugata, fixated on it.

To head over into Öræfi—but what do you know about Öræfi? The Regular asked. Not much, I replied, and then he was angry and called me a tosser...You can be such a tosser, Bernharður, said The Regular, tosser!...surely you aren't so witless as to plan to gad about around Eastern Skaftafell without having read *The Regional Development of Eastern Skaftafell District Vol. I–III* carefully!?...He tugged at me, saying we had to supply me with some essentials for my trip east to Mávabyggðir. What books did you bring with you on the journey?... None, I answered, embarrassed, but I've read some stuff, I subscribe to *National Geographic*, there are sometimes articles about Iceland in there. You are rushing to your death! said The Regular, let's go to Bragi and stock you up, off you go and get your trunk so we can stack the books in it, he said like an officer, so I dashed to Freyjugata and fetched the trunk and sped back down to Klapparstígur again. The Regular was stood outside waiting and led me across the street to where the rare-and-used bookstore Bragi sits on the corner. All the bookstores except one have been destroyed by tourism, said The Regular, the bookstores don't sell books anymore, just souvenirs and junk, the only actual bookstore left in Reykjavík is the second-hand bookstore Bragi, look here, he said, pointing to the doorbell, a true wonder, the offices of Skaftafell National Park, which is in Öræfi, are here on Klapparstígur in Reykjavík, above the bookstore Bragi, it's a symbol, I should say, an omen, at the very least a mystery, I sometimes give myself up to life's wonders, Freyung and Freyjugata and all that, the bookstore Bragi and the National Park... The Regular was well known in the second-hand bookstore and we got a tremendous reception, everything was very cozy, the radio set to Radio 1, an aroma that was part-book mold, part-dust and part-incense, there were cigarettes burning in ashtrays, we were both invited to take some snuff and enjoy a shot of liquor, dogs waddled between the bookshelves like wolves in a hall of mirrors or were sleeping on the carpet between the book boxes, a large green parrot stood at the cash register and counted while cats padded sleepily about on top of the shelves. We were sucked into the atmosphere. The Regular drew me right away to the section containing national lore, here's a swarm of good books, he said, we need books about Öræfi and not tourist books, either, but books written by local people at the very kernel of culture! Or by a folklore scholar, someone who is stuck inside the subject and cannot get out. The Regular suggested he ought to choose books for me and that he would translate them for me letter by letter; I liked the generosity in that, even if The Regular had not yet managed to absorb the fact that I spoke Icelandic—we had been conversing in Icelandic this whole time. First, he took down a book called *Fjöll og Firnindi,* that is, *Mountains and Wilderness,* and said we were fortunate to have it, it would be best if he guided me through the book before I headed east, inside were stories of Stefán Filippusson recorded by Árni Óli, and few give a better account than Stefán Filippusson, said The Regular; the next book he selected was simply called *Skaftafell: Aspects from the History of Family Dwellings and Work Customs* by Þórður Tómasson from Skógar—he knows everything! The Regular said of Þórður Tómasson from Skógar, even when he doesn't know something, he still knows it; the magazine *Skaftafellingur* is like that, too, it contains many well-written articles, chiefly by the Tvísker brothers, especially Sigurður, we'll buy everything written by them, you'll enjoy reading about wild sheep in Núpstaður in books like *Skaftafell Pass Folklore* by Guðmundur from Hoffell, that's one you should buy whenever you come across it even if is a bit expensive at that moment; gift it when you have extra copies, spread the knowledge, said The Regular, always spread the knowledge. Now let's hustle over to the travel section, I don't want to be seen in this section so let's be quick, The Regular fished from one large stack the *Icelandic Travel Association Yearbook* from 1979; Sigurður from Tvísker wrote this, and there's much excellent information about the Öræfi region, said The Regular; however, even more essential is the 1937 *Yearbook* concerning the Eastern Skaftafell district; you can nourish yourself on the true Öræfi spirit inside that, because back then the rivers weren't bridged—the older the better, you must have *The Travelogue of Sveinn Pálsson*, which is excellently written, Sveinn Pálsson was a very remarkable eighteenth-century physician and writer, said The Regular, I wish he was rather better known, Sveinn Pálsson had great affection for Jón Einarsson from Skaftafell, no less important a man, Bernharður, you simply must know about him if you plan to set foot in Öræfi, Jón Einarsson from Skaftafell made *Sjónabók*, or *Patternbook*, one of the greatest works of art in Iceland, although few know it, I think there probably aren't more than ten to fifteen people in the whole world who know Jón Einarsson from Skaftafell's *Sjónabók*, which is a shame for Icelandic culture, although it is equally wonderful having a valuable and hidden treasure, Jón Einarsson from Skaftafell, remember that... well, and Eggert Ólafsson, Sveinn Pálsson's spiritual mentor, mentor to all Icelandic scholars since 1800; he had a great affection for Einar, the father of Jón from Skaftafell, the infamous Einar from Skaftafell, the very same, he knew everyone, Eggert visited with him over a span of forty years and Sveinn visited his son Jon, if this is getting confusing I can repeat it all night, Eggert visited Einar, Sveinn visited Jón, there's something very special about arriving in Skaftafell because it's one of the most remote places in the world, and father and son were some of the best carpenters and artists in Iceland ever, completely self-taught, which is traditional in Öræfi, though now there's no self-educated folks, everyone's just uneducated, said The Regular, in *The Travelogue of Sveinn Pálsson* you can read how Jón had, using his own diligence and ability, learned Latin, Greek, and Hebrew grammar at an early age from books he borrowed here and there, being too poor to acquire his own books, although he created the most beautiful artist's book in the Nordic countries, little Jón studied Latin and Greek and Hebrew grammar from others' books and was inquisitive whenever the opportunity offered; more than this, little Jón also spoke German and Danish, he studied basic surgical methods, phlebotomy, and wound-binding, he knew botany through and through, so Sveinn Pálsson tells us about Jón Einarsson, The Regular said, but most of all he was a great carpenter, he learned that from his father Einar, an art-smith; father and son built many valuable treasures as well as instruments and tools, sundials and compasses, which are also great treasures, they fashioned guns and gave them to their neighbors to protect against polar bears and to help with subsistence; these guns were considered exceptional, nothing like them had ever been seen, foreign chieftains came to town to press hard for the two, Einar and Jón from Skaftafell, to fashion more guns, but the two of them were busy with arts other than the art of war. It was hard to be a farmer in Skaftafell, the so-called "little ice age" had recently begun, Öræfajökull had erupted in 1727 and had laid waste the countryside for the second time since the Settlement, destroying fields and grazing pastures, the river, the Skeiðará has always been the greatest destroyer of the country, that untameable river smears sand and gravel over the guts of the land, laying waste whatever it runs across. Father-and-son went around the sands on a four-wheel, sail-powered carriage, hunting seal and foraging driftwood on the shore; on their sand-ship the two hustled widely about the district and had a great deal of sport and adventure, but I do not know if I have time to recite and translate the whole *Travelogue of Sveinn Pálsson* into English for you, or into German, because it is long and fairly comprehensive; but hold on, I've been speaking Icelandic all along, The Regular said, finally noticing I knew Icelandic. Let's scram from the travel section and go back to folklore, there are many books you need to have with you in your trunk, *The Settlement History of Eastern Skaftafell District I–III*, for example, *Industry in Eastern Skaftafell District, Commerce in Eastern Skaftafell District, Transportation in Eastern Skaftafell District, Press On*, the history of Eastern Skaftafell District, *Aspects of Öræfi*, and *The War of Water: The History of the Skeiðarárjökull Flood & Grímsvatn Eruption*, also the *Biography of Ragnar from Skaftafell*, the *Biography of Þorleif from Hólum*, and *Skaftafell in Öræfi: Iceland's Thousand Years*, and many other good books.

Jæja, shorty, said Bragi the bookseller to us as he transcribed the prices written in pencil in the books' flyleaves; I had mentally tallied that the amount was getting pretty high, something which caused me anxiety. What studies are you completing? Bragi asked.

We're self-educators, said The Regular, answering for both of us.

Jæja, of course, Bragi responded.

What do we owe for this stack? The Regular asked.

Nothing at all, said Bragi.

No, how can that be?

You've brought us your custom long enough, replied Bragi.

I *never* have to pay for books here, said The Regular, except something nominal, it is *I* who must owe you after getting free books for twenty years, how can you make a living with such a bad business model?

Just pay something next time, said Bragi, sucking up a tremendous heap of Icelandic snuff from the back of his hand.

Maybe there will be no next time! The Regular said angrily.

Jæja, anything else, lads? Bragi said politely, then faded into a pyramid of books.

Since then, I've thought a lot about this singular Icelandic word, *jæja*, and I had it in mind to write a short essay about it as something of a "place name" in the language, a landmark denoting the end of travel, the city limits, as it were. You always know you're close to your base port in conversation when someone says *jæja*; it's the last communicative landmark, the last cairn, before you reach home, the first as you set out from home. Perhaps it's a sign one is lost.

Jæja, said The Regular, this is a good haul, he's so generous, Bragi the bookseller, as you saw, now let's quench our thirst, I always get thirsty for beer when I go to bookshops, especially second-hand bookstores, most likely it's the dust, but I've also heard there's a particular fungus that lives in the bodies of ancient books and humans alike, and it is *that* and not the human himself which wants its thirst satisfied with a beer; this fungus which lives inside people is itself a person, truly, I've started calling him

Gerjólf Yeastwolf, because yeast—*ger*—and hops are important food for this fungus: white sugar and white flour and white paper are his favorite food, and words, too, I've named this word-fungus Gerjólf as a play on Germania, Germany's the site of the greatest ger-mania, total yeast-fervor, in Germania there's a lot of beer and the fungus is strong there, the people sour.

When we walked back into Circus again, the place had radically altered. Huh, they've completely renovated, said The Regular, and it was true, Bernharður said, there were now dizzyingly high ceilings and expansive space from wall to wall; in the heights crystal chandeliers hung, their bling glittering; around the crowns circled canaries and butterflies and dragonflies all singing hymns and patriotic verses in chorus. There was a cross-vaulted-ceiling made from Iceland spar; obsidian pillars descended to a floor cut from gabbro rock; on the vaulted ceilings you could see frescos by Jóhannes Kjarval depicting the settlement of Iceland, the establishment of Parliament at Þingvellir, the conversion to Christianity, Snorri Sturluson at his studies and being beheaded, the civil war during the Age of the Sturlungs replete with rock-throwing, rapes, eye-gouging, castrations and the resulting loss of independence into the hands of the Norwegian king. On the walls, large pictures hung in gold-adorned frames showing ancient heroes and queens of Nordic countries; the walls themselves were carved with story motifs from large wars that had been fought in ancient times, images so polished that they reflected one another in a set of distorted self-images. This calls for champagne! The Regular said, not some damn beer swill. We perched ourselves at the glass-encrusted bar which extended as far as the eye could see, curving at the ends toward a hall of mirrors; one got dizzy looking along it. Such mirror scenes are known in Gauloise as *mise en abyme*, said The Regular, one of the very greatest wonders of the world, a gap in eternity. The servers were dressed in red tuxedos made from Icelandic twill colored with the blood of wild animals, the blood of the wild sheep at Núpsstaðar, a color so pure and mellow that it was almost as though the servers were transparent, smears of red fog, the silver trays seemed to fly themselves around the room like UFOs. The servers' hair was slicked back with brilliantine and they had tremendous sideburns; monkeys clambered up to whisper orders into their ears in Turkish. All around the drinking hall well-to-do people sat and poured champagne and nibbled on sheeps' heads from bellwethers who had enjoyed extremely good lives; all day long the country's leading intellectuals sat there reading the papers alongside solitary winos while misfortunates bumbled in, having procured a drink. Everyone was welcome. The server returned with a bottle of champagne and he slowly and carefully vacuumed the bottle with a hand vacuum before washing it with 8.2 degree Celsius temperature water and telling us in Latin that the bottle had been stored at the bottom of Gvendarbrunna for 1100 years to cool, that it was the champagne bottle the settler Ingólfur Arnarson brought to the land with him then lost when trying to toast the settlement in Reykjavík and never found, as *Landnámabók* records, and everything has gone downhill from that moment, but Ingólf made a head start on getting merry before the feasting. The bottle was found in a spring during the anniversary year, 1974, when citizens were celebrating 1100 years of settlement in Iceland and some went diving in search of the old money that gets thrown into Gvendarbrunna, the Reykjavík wells. Extraordinary amounts of all kinds of debris were found, enough to explode the capacity of the National Museum; this was among the bottles found but the staff at the National Museum did not pay attention to this particular bottle and planned to smash it against the wall, this was before recycling was in the picture; the owner of Circus got to pick it up instead, and it's been down in the cellar here since, 200 meters deep for thirty years, collecting substantial dust though the president of the republic has called every day asking after it and offering ever larger and more terrifying sums for it because all the world's kings and queens and princesses and emperors and their spouses are on the way to visit him at Bessastaðir and he lacks any decent champagne and he wants to be fashionable...We'll take it, said The Regular to the server, gratie, vale, bitte sehr! inflammatus et accensus![1] ...Then the server said with panache: Quando corpus morietur fac ut animae donetur paradisi gloria.[2] Amen, said The Regular.

The champagne was ruthless and we became very merry. I'm not going to read all the books for you, The Regular said at Circus, but will begin by directing you to the chapter "Among Wild Sheep" in the book *Mountains and Wilderness*, there, Árni Óli has written down the story of the mountain hero, the giant of stories, Stefán Filippusson: *Once upon a time in the autumn,* translated The Regular, *I got a message from Jón on Núpsstaður, that*

---

1. Into the bright conflagration!
2. When the body dies, may my soul be granted the glory of paradise.

I should go for him to Eystrafjall and make coals. There were bunches of wood from the spring. This struck me as a beautiful start, exciting me; The Regular read the whole chapter for me, translating wild sheep into English, because he distrusted my Icelandic knowledge, The Regular was unbudging, which I guess is the nature of regulars; even as more and more people came to the drinking house and the babble the people were making inside rose steadily, intensifying the joy of life until the murmuring enveloped the room and reverberated around the walls, he was determined to continue translating, reading me selected sections of the books we had bought in the secondhand bookshop, Bragi, he read me the story of Sigurður from Tvísker out of the book *Hikes and Round-Ups I*, subtitled *Night Under a Glacier*, about the time Sigurður sang a paean to life the time he got stuck deep inside a glacial fissure. In the fall of 1936, when Sigurður was a young boy, he and a companion were out seeking two sheep that had not come down from the cliffs; there was significant snow on the mountain and the paths were dangerous and that morning Sigurður's mother had said he needed two scarves and so he did; Sigurður tied a second scarf on his head on top of his thick, goatskin-lined hat; he was wearing two new socks, sealskin shoes with the fur on the inside, thick woolen underwear, an overshirt made of thick khaki, a wool sweater, overalls made of coarse Nankin cotton, a waterproof storm jacket on top of all this; under everything, against his chest, he'd stuffed hay for the sheep to chew, and thus Sigurður was excellently warmly dressed, so much that his companion laughed when they met at six in the morning, saying he looked like a pregnant cod. There was snow on the ground, it was 6 degrees below zero with a biting north wind, according to Sigurður's account, and though the sheep were on the cliff, thanks to the amount of snow and the impassible path they had great difficulty getting to them without going under the cliffs, where they had to contend with steep scree and loose-graveled rocks as well as narrow channels filled with snow, occasional turfs of heather and patches of grass, all extremely steep and unstable; a belt of steep cliffs ran down the slopes and, on the other side, gliding far below, slept the glittering green creeping glacier, marked and ugly with its countless cracks, leaks, and incomprehensible hollows. There in the channels between the ridges Sigurður said to his companion: anyone who fell down there would probably be done for. Yes, his companion replied, he would certainly tell no more stories. Just then Sigurður heard a crack; looking up he saw the snowdrift above breaking, he heard his companion say Well. And then the avalanche took Sigurður and hurled him down the hillside bundled in snow; he let go of the rope so he would not pull his partner with him in the flood, he lost his staff so he couldn't steer himself, Sigurður rushed down head first and launched with catastrophic speed toward the belt of rocks, everyone has to die sometime, he thought amid the avalanche, seeing the cliffs hurtling past him, and suddenly he was wondering if people were less severely injured in a fall if they were completely powerless, so Sigurður made himself completely powerless, as he reached the belt of rocks he thrust his hips slightly and then he was in the air, head first, he ended up far below the cliffs in the first fissure between the mountains and the glacier, one millimeter either way and it would all have been very different. He startled, breathless and coughing, having hardly breathed on the way down. He had been forced into a narrow space, and he began to try to move, but it was like concrete poured into a mold; he discovered, however, that he was unharmed and knew he was under a glacier. I will certainly not get to tell any more tales, he thought. Then he decided to spend his time in spiritual reflection and began to sing hymns, full-throated and with all his heart, this kept him warm and his mind came back into balance: the days were short and no one would look for him until the next morning, night lay ahead and he was restrained here, face down in this fissure, the ice a cold comforter—but the fact that he was so well dressed came in handy now, he had not even lost his hat because the second scarf secured it to his head. Still, he was not optimistic he would live through the night; many days might elapse before he was found, perhaps he'd never be found, would slowly and quietly die a natural death and be crushed under the glacier, that would doubtless be a painless death, thought Sigurður, he would fall asleep and never wake up again, he felt for the people at home, his mother, he would prefer never to be found if he wasn't going to survive this, that there be no signs he had survived the fall, it was devastating to think his friends and families might realize he had survived a long time down there. It was so black at night that it didn't make a difference whether he had his eyes open or closed, and then the ice around him began to melt a little and he was able to get partly free; he managed to slip both hands together and sang *Now I Lay My Eyes Again*, then fell asleep, waking up, intensely cold, to the sight of a bright beam on the glacier as he looked down, his chest facing the surface; he thought the light a sign of death and uttered the psalmist Hallgrím Pétursson's words: *Come to me, as you list*. It is even possible, he thought, I will die here, let it be swift. But this was not death coming, at least not for Sigurður, it was the northern lights in the deep darkness of night, illuminating the glacier, and he let the light course through him, he sang hymns with all his might and quickly warmed up, then it was midnight and he started to get wet, he passed the night this way, falling asleep several times but singing in between them; in the morning he was able to rip off his backpack and free himself a little more; the day began to brighten, the snow melted above him and he could look around a bit; his right foot, however, was as in a vise, he felt a cold wind all around him and saw that he had come to rest in a narrow crevasse, his ice cave. Sometime in the morning, as he was singing *Praise Be to God*, he heard his name called, he heard his brother calling and he immediately called back, some time later he saw his brother lowered into the crevasse, are you all right, he asked, yes, I think so, said Sigurður, immediately work started to free him from his prison and it took a while, the frozen ground was hard and difficult to break apart, then his brother reached into the cave and extended his hand and pulled him nearer; he tied a band under his shoulders, then the others dragged the two up, rescued Sigurður from the fissure where he had been confined upside down a whole day and night, twenty-eight meters down. His mother had dreamed that night that he lay in a channel, able to breathe but suffering badly. Sigurður was driven home on a sleigh, helpless but chattering away, and the farm was joyful that evening; he was able to write again by the fourth day and walk unassisted after a week; within the month, he was practically as good as before.

Next, The Regular enthusiastically read in my ear the 1979 *Travel Association Yearbook,* by the same Sigurður from Tvísker who sang hymns to save his life, and as we were finishing the chapter "Historical Outline" and just about to get to the section "Looking around Öræfi," The Regular finally gave up and looked disapprovingly at our surroundings.

Then an idea occurred to him; he rang a little copper bell to summon the bartender, who didn't hear over the hubbub in the hall, so The Regular took a champagne bottle and struck it against the big ship's bell that was hanging above the bar; the bottle shattered yet the ball rang loudly, causing everyone in the place to briefly fall silent and the server to come running at a hard sprint.

The Regular suggested he forgo the DJ and let him have some time at the microphone, he wanted to read the patrons the 1979 *Travel Association Yearbook,* by Sigurður from Tvísker, in Icelandic, our dying language, The Regular told the server in Latin, so that this multinational crew, this assortment of tourists, people from the music and fashion industries, so-called art students and international students, visiting writers and guest professors and all the world's guests might get to relax and to use the reading as a motivation for learning the country's language, from now until the clock strikes twelve: the party right now doesn't offer much in the way of education.

I don't know we're expecting a DJ, the server answered in Latin, but we're expecting our chamber orchestra, and they start at midnight; until then you're most welcome to edify the guests; I'm all for learning.

What's on the program tonight? The Regular asked.

Stabat Mater by the maestro Joseph Haydn, answered the server, these are our Haydn days.

Haydn days? The Regular asked.

Quite right, mon signor, answered the server. What did you say you're going to read?

"Looking Around Öræfi" by Sigurður from Tvísker.

I'm not sure this is the right audience for regional stories and provincial descriptions, said the server.

Then all the more need for it! The Regular said.

The Regular was given a microphone and he read a story by Sigurður from Tvísker, based on an account in Fitja Chronicle but peppered with his own embellishments. He improvised as he read: it was an account of the time the Dutch gold ship *Het Wapen van Amsterdam* was driven across the Atlantic Ocean by storms until it stranded at the mouth of the Skeiðará in Öræfi, September, 1667; it was the most modern and most luxurious ship in the Dutch commercial fleet and was returning from the East Indies, namely Batavia, in Java, awash with colonial goods; the ship was massive, with forty cannons to fend off pirates, 300 crew members, *Het Wapen* was not a warship but a cargo ship, The Regular announced, a so-called *flute*; back then, the British and Dutch were fighting a war, so ships couldn't sail via the English Channel but had to go north, past Scotland; there, they often got caught in strong headwinds, and so the *Het Wapen* was driven several days northwest and the sea flooded over it, breaking both mast and rudder; it got separated from the rest of the commercial fleet and ended up stranded at low tide in Öræfi at night during a sharp southeast wind and rainstorms; 240 people were killed either at the water's edge or on the freezing sands; sixty survived. Work started immediately trying to save the cargo of jewels, treasures from the east, uncut diamonds, gold, pearls, silver and copper, scarlet, decorative and luxurious garments, chintz, I don't know what that is, carbuncle, I don't know what that is either, silk and linen and all kinds of assorted curtains and blankets, worth forty-eight barrels of gold in total, or so everyone says, according to the Fitja Chronicle, never since the land was settled had a ship with such precious cargo reached Iceland; the ship was freighted with 40 tonnes of copper meant for church bells in Europe, and Sigurður calculated that on board the *Het Wapen van Amsterdam* was 550 tons of black and white pepper, The Regular said into the microphone, and a grumbling started up in the room at the sound of these figures, pepper was expensive in Europe but all the aristocrats competed to have the most pepper at their table; also on the ship were 35 tons of cloves, 17 tons of cinnamon, 10 tons of peanuts, 10 tons of sugar, 65 tons of Indian redwood, clubs or staffs (5 tons), indigo dye (5 tons), hardwood (5 tons), tin from Malakka (5 tons), 4 tons of cotton yarn, 3 tons of Japanese camphor and Persian silk (3 tons), the Fitja Chronicle says, Sigurður says in the *Travel Association Yearbook* (1979), The Regular said at Circus to what was now a great tumult all around the room; also, part of the cargo was saltpeter and all kinds of spices and pigments, and on board there was a large number of civets from which people take the secretions from a special gland to use for perfume, a joy to Parisian halls. It's said there was a black on board who swam like a fish, rescuing sixty of the 300-man crew; the rest died of cold and exhaustion, wearing only silk garments; the black man trod water a long time, transporting people to the beach one by one, and men actually stood there in shirts or nightgowns alone in the icy rain storm at night on the sand; many of them froze to death, they were all confused and helpless, some went to try to find a settlement, the black man swam ashore with the captain who was fat and cumbersome and had pockets full of gold and diamonds and pearls; this black fellow was so exhausted that he came ashore with the captain and fell down at once and died; he was buried in a gravel hillock and the place was afterward known as *Skollamelur*. The captain never returned to the Netherlands; nothing is known of his fate. Bodies lay scattered on the sand by the time the farmers reached the place; there was one prone form, dressed in black, a man who'd gone weeping around gathering gold and precious stones, only to succumb to a natural death. The Öræfings saved all those who were still alive and dispersed the seafarers across the country. One Dutch survivor came to like Öræfi so much he stayed for the rest of his life; he was called Pétur Jakobsson, and he is the progenitor of a large family descended from various women. He was a good carpenter and he settled in Skaftafell. He learned construction from the Skaftafell farmers and they from him, for Pétur had sturdy tools and instruments he'd taken from the ship; together they built a sail-powered wagon, and the Öræfings went flying across the countryside in this four-wheeler; such land ships were a popular sport in the Netherlands in the seventeenth century, but the development of this vehicle ended after a fatal accident involving the wagon, the brother of Jón Einarsson from Skaftafell died in this accident and the Skaftafellings, having lost such a respected youth, lost their appetite for the invention; they hadn't been particularly given over to the thrill of speed in the first place. Impoverished people went riding about in silks, clad in fine clothes; they were considered quite striking, although they were clothed like this out of lack rather than for ornamentation or extravagance: no other material was available, so housewives had silk sheets and the Öræfings slept in them for a long time. Ever since, this great wreck occasionally emits a strong spice smell across Öræfi; the smell stems from a gold ship that no one knows how to find in the sand. Even today people go snouting about on the sand hunting for treasure and digging holes and channels far and wide and wandering around with metal detectors like idiots...

Kiddi! The Regular screamed into the microphone, startling everyone; a young man could be seen walking across the marble floor, wearing a waist-length leather jacket with oversize cuffs, a turned-up collar and a hat at a jaunty slant on his head; he smiled, flashing his broken incisors. Kiddi is a born-and-bred Öræfing, The Regular announced over the microphone to Circus, and everyone seemed impressed and clapped; Kiddi got a little shy at this, laughing softly, with an ironic expression; he took off his hat and put it on the bar... So, so, so, so said Kiddi, er, truly... er, just finished renovating everything...The Regular flung the microphone away with a crash and a ringing and hugged Kiddi close; they sat at the bar and the server went up into a castle up in the air in order to turn down the audio track. And so we stayed silent for many hours, drinking champagne and gazing out at a mesmerizing splendor of bottles behind the bar; we were all in a row, talking telepathically, which is an art among the Öræfings:

when Kiddi rings me, The Regular said telepathically, he doesn't say anything into the phone, when he calls his grandfather in Svínafell, they are silent together a long time, even asleep, and they're getting honest, quality time, sincere conversation.

✝

When I think about the prospectors on Skeiðarársandur, said The Regular, floating his thoughts over, a gusty wind blows through my mind, I get filled with a furious desire to look for gold on the sands, I'm ready to sacrifice everything, no matter if there's no hope of finding anything in that barren place; it's not the gold itself: there's sand and adventure, the search for the ship, the search itself, man himself, whenever I'm sad I think of the gold ship *Het Wapen van Amsterdam*, when I'm sad, I think of the black fellow ignominiously buried in Skollamelur, how he rescued the crew, how he sacrificed himself, I think of the people looking for the gold ship, and I'm reminded how delightfully absurd life is: the unbearable initial excitement when gold prospectors first head out, full of dreams and passions, onto the sands; they labor there, enjoying themselves, the public watching their excitement, constantly following what they're up to out on the sand, hailing them, curious local folk and traveling reporters alike, the prospectors are always having to answer the same questions, are always equally intense, equally full of life. Gradually, they gain a fuller and richer knowledge than any of them could have imagined they would. The search becomes their life goal, year after year they're out on the sand, shoveling, their hopes never hobbled by the impressive competitors around them; after three decades of searching they strike something hard down there, they rear up desperately, convinced the ship has been found, the whole nation gets excited, I was six, I think, said The Regular, when the papers reported the gold ship had been found, I was really excited and wanted to go out onto Skeiðarársand, ever since I was six I've had Skeiðarársand on the brain—these prospectors, thirty meters deep after thirty years of searching with shovels, excavators, magnets, metal detectors, and all the gadgets available—but it turned out to be a rusty German trawler from 1903 ... how hope and greed go together, do they not! The Regular said, how far down it is to the depths of happiness from surface joy; surmounting life's passions and goals is a deep need to dig. That's the way it is to fall in love, it's energizing, you escape out onto the sand with a metal detector and shovel, ready to sacrifice everything and hunker down on the sand like a dragon on treasure; love overwhelms you, lets nothing else in, makes you want to get to know every hillock and every rise, every grain of sand, digging and digging, your dreams leading you astray, people are soon demolishing the landscape, destroying nature, and then from the sand emerges a rusty German trawler from 1903 named *Friedrich Albert,* from Geestemünde, the worst wreck in Skaftafell in recent times, although many hundreds of ships have been stranded here ... that's love! said The Regular: a man exhaling before this rusty German trawler, almost completely mad with embarrassment and frustration and anger, shattered to his very core—but then when everyone is done making fun of him, the man goes to examine the wreck, which proves quite remarkable, with significant characters caught up in it, the wreck is connected with a big tragedy, you might empathize, feel this surge of emotion, providing you're open to that ... it's easy to fall in love with the beauty of Skaftafell in Öræfi, said The Regular, most of those who head there want to return again and again, Öræfi haunts you, as you get to know the region better you love it more and more, you feel you have a share in her beauty because she has aroused such interest in you, humans don't own beauty but beauty owns humanity, Öræfi becomes part of you, of your self-esteem, you're the most fortunate man in the world, getting to hunt around on the sand, in the mountains or on the glacier; when I was on this trail, I told myself I could subsist on beauty alone, and perhaps you'll say something similar yourself in Öræfi—but beauty can turn against you, she's cruel, suddenly you want to throw yourself off a cliff or hurl yourself into a waterfall or toss yourself into a glacial crevasse because you understand nothing about beauty, because she awakens an intolerable grief inside you; you're happy now so it doesn't matter what happens to you, perhaps the best place for a happy man is in a glacial crevasse, perhaps happiness lives there, in the heart of horror. Times change, or everything changes but time stands still, something happens that's altogether different from what was expected, the same family lived in Skaftafell from the settlement until the National Park was established and the ring road opened in 1974, for 1100 years the same family lived in Skaftafell, until the sequence was broken by incursions into the beauty, probably everything since then amounts to the destruction of Öræfi due to relentless tourism and the decline of agricultural society, due to natural disasters, but what do I know? said

The Regular, one simply has to accept what happens, whether shipwrecks or technological advances, you cannot always resist everything, otherwise I'd be perpetually toiling against everything. I'm against innovation, I want everything as it was, for example, particular men were against the telephone coming to Öræfi at the beginning of the twentieth century, being against such so-called progress is often held up as an example of amusement and stupidity, not wanting to be subject to a pretextless system, remaining unbowed before authority, corporations, the masses, the executioners, I'm afraid I would have been against the telephone at the time, would've considered the phone no less a disaster than the eruption in 1362 which made a desert out of settlements for fifty years. I actually believe the telephone marked the beginning of the region's utter destruction for all time: the telephone transformed Öræfi into something else, perverted it, and the cellphone does the same thing to humanity in our time, a man with a cellphone is no longer a man but a perversion of man, everything that has been achieved through progress, The Regular said telepathically at Circus, has proved a deterioration, always the talk of progress is the talk of deterioration. I'm considered abnormal because I don't walk about with a cellphone, I'm suspicious because I don't walk about with a cellphone, I'm antisocial because I don't walk about with a cellphone, I'm guilty because I don't walk about with a cellphone, arrogant, boring, putting on airs, old-fashioned because I choose not to walk about with a cellphone, but that's jealousy and envy. I miss everything and have no friends but I do not complain because my nervous system doesn't suffer me to walk about with a cellphone, I don't travel that way for the sake of my health, for quality of life reasons, I cannot imagine having a cellphone with me, I wouldn't be able to write, I can't think and write when something is constantly looming, the thought that someone is going to poke me in the back, there's no peace, the phone companies are tyrants, they choke and kill and bury all the studies that demonstrate the harmfulness of the mobile phone, both mentally and physically, going around with a cellphone is like walking in shackles, I prefer to roam free and wild and be hated rather than to be constrained and subservient and loved, I'm despised because it isn't possible to reach me in an instant, at times that suit others rather than me, having a cell phone is being operated by remote control, remotely controlled by network operators, remotely controlled by the whole of society, I don't want to walk in shackles, a remote-controlled slave to the cell companies, they've destroyed me plenty on many occasions, wasted enough of my time and thought, cleaned me out of enough money, those comedians Halli and Laddi aren't at all right when they say phones save time, no, phones *waste* time, phones destroy your time, your spirit, and your body even when they don't ring, it's enough it might and you know it, being aware of your phone eats away at your time, spirit, and body; progress is nothing less than the annihilation of humanity and the earth, a person's conscious mind celebrates progress but their subconscious knows it constitutes destruction and doesn't dare bring that knowledge to the surface, represses it, the awareness of progress as annihilation gets suppressed so you can survive suffering via deception: better to live an illusion than die in truth, that's the definition of a cellphone, the network operators confuse people over the meaning of concepts, the way all tyrants maintain their power over the populace, tyrants change language in order to abuse power, Victor Klemperer studied linguistic abuses by the Third Reich, *Lingua Tertii Imperii*; LTI can be applied to the phone companies, to all big business, but no one dares investigate, people walk around shackled by the telecommunication companies, believing themselves free, money gets vacuumed up from people under the pretext that they're free, but no one is free because everyone around them has a cell, everywhere. It's not like hearing people talk, having conversations, hearing someone talking on the phone is intolerable, hearing someone speaking on the phone out in the street, on the bus, in a bank, a café, or worst, in one's home, your consciousness suffers severe pain, loud complaints from the realm of the dead, what a fate, always having to talk on the phone, even in movies everyone is always blabbering on phones, there's never anyone there, we're all at 30m deep in the sand, an iron heap of disappointment, the phone has eliminated focus, cellphones kill the spirit no one had to begin with, destroy the body no one had, destroy the life no one had, humanity was nothing anyway, the phone lays waste to reality and that's absolutely fine so let's get more champagne and toast our cells ... Servus!

God is perversion, The Regular said, after having gulped down the glass of champagne in one go, *and the clouds are the dust from his feet*, as the Old Testament Book of Nahum states, form and time are the conclusion, the perversion, the eternity, the road to the source, what everyone most fears; the maternal womb, Bernharður, my dear cumin friend, that's the gateway into the perversion, it's your origin, death, immorality, and god... Now, the Chamber Orchestra is setting up, they're going to play *Stabat Mater* by Haydn, not *Stabat Mater* by Vivaldi or Pergolesi, Haydn but not Palestrina and not Scarlatti, Haydn instead, these are the designated Haydn days... on the other hand, it'd be refreshing to have some death metal on the turntable about now, but that's probably not possible in a public space, have you noticed how boring reality is, Bernharður? An intricate weft of domination and aggression, leaving you unable to do what you want; in real life a man is never alone, never a wilderness, a man is in a settlement of boredom, it would be too stressful to put death metal on the turntable if not everyone's into it, but then again no one listens to death metal except perhaps one or two teenagers who are neither old nor mature enough to be here inside this stately place, death metal is one of the most challenging genres of music that ever existed, in death metal there are swift chapter divisions and the feelings and emotions lie deep, the way burning magma does, down in the dark glow of the human soul, apathetic and venting simultaneously. Death metal is reminiscent of Bach, Beethoven, and Vivaldi, I want to say Haydn, too, but I cannot say Haydn this and Haydn the other, though it's fun to say his name, Haydn, Haydn, Haydn, it's like swallowing grapes whole, it's better to say Bach, Beethoven, and Vivaldi, although Haydn is the emperor of classical music. Most people insist on a wide separation between death metal and Bach, Beethoven, and Vivaldi, they consider death metal childish and classical music mature, but it's a short leap, in one sense childishness is a kind of advanced state, the sound differs, that's all, though admittedly there's no composer in death metal equivalent to Bach, Beethoven, and Vivaldi, much less Haydn, but there's still a connection between so-called classical music and death metal as art forms; actually, I've never been able to call classical music classical music, The Regular opined, music genres come and go, the sound wakes and reverberates, what is *genre*, really?...genre is a tree...Now the orchestra is beginning *Stabat Mater* by Haydn...what a welter of pure grief, I feel like I never get closer to the nature of dreams than when I'm listening to good music, dreams are superior to waking because they are nearer to chaos, to the source, to perversion, god, eternal life, one fishes deep down in the abyss of the upper atmosphere, in emotions, futile memories, in absurdities pregnant with meaning...waking now seems rather eccentric compared to sleeping's sensual oblivion...There's no music anymore, just repetition and perversion, death metal ended music, was both its nadir and peak, the last remnants of the form: western music reached its pinnacle with *Sturm und Drang*, deteriorated from there all the way to death metal and flowed out onto the sand, in 1989 the album *Altar of Madness* by the band Morbid Angel came out; never before had such crazy energy surged out of speakers anywhere on the planet, it scraped deep inside you, direct contact with the depths, with rusted demersal trawlers sunk into the sand, and then this new *genre*, death metal, evolved with considerable power: two years later the masterpiece emerges, *Blessed Are the Sick*, a work of art, a masterwork, The Regular said, using telepathy in order that everyone could enjoy the orchestra and choir on stage performing *Stabat Mater* by Joseph Haydn, it was the beginning and the end, all masterpieces are serpents, they bite their own tails, and exist in isolation, they give nothing away except pleasure and death, vital pleasures but lacking in creative interest, the serpent eats itself and becomes a world unto itself, negative, unable to reproduce or approach any significance, only able to enjoy the inverse of time, caught between pleasure and forgetting its trials out there in the world, set apart from the sensations of life; the album art for *Blessed Are the Sick* is graced with a painting by the Belgian artist and symbolist Jean Delville, *Les trésors de Satan,* which hangs in Brussels in the *Museé royaux des Beaux-Arts de Belgique*, Belgium, or, as I call it, Bulgeum, museums and arts the heaving bodies full of fries and mayonnaise and waffles and cream ... I've twice been to Bulgeum, and have made a beeline for the *Museum of Beautiful Art* with the sole purpose of seeing this picture, but both times they were working on the roof of the museum in the room where the picture normally hangs so it had been packed in cellophane and aluminum foil and put down in the basement; there's plenty to see in the museum, of course, so I didn't feel sorry about being in the empty shack, which wasn't really empty and wasn't a shack, either; I wasted my entire day at Hieronymus Bosch's altar-tablet, no, a shame to say *wasted* in this context, spent the day, rarely have I spent my time better than at this altar of Jeremiah, and I wouldn't have, or it would have been less impressive, had *The Fortune of Satan* been hanging somewhere in the place, and all my energy been directed to that picture, as planned—so I feel that I didn't waste the day in front of Bosch's altar-tablet of Jeremiah but instead *spent* the day, the imagery on the altar-tablet explains all man's consumption and his wasting of God's gifts; it is in fact thanks to the band Morbid Angel and the album *Blessed Are the Sick* that I was such an eager visitor to *Museé royaux des Beaux-Arts de Belgique*, where you often find death metallers scattered like seed about the place; I haven't dressed like a death metalhead since I was seventeen, none of the visitors or staff could tell from looking at me that I'd come to the museum specifically to see the painting by the symbolist Jean Delville, Morbid Angel groupies go on pilgrimages to Bulgeum, to Brussels... Morbid Angel is a mystic band, the band's occult background makes it a powerful band, they gained their knowledge from one single book, as happens so often with the occult, one very general book, full of enigmatic symbols, in the case of Morbid Angel it was the NECRONOMICON, which is actually a forgery, and that might be called its strength: Morbid Angel is based on the philosophy of the mad Arab in the Necronomicon. The Necronomicon was released in a pocket edition in the 1970s, a time when the members of Morbid Angel were growing up in Florida, under constant threat of the atom bomb, a threat that belonged to the adult world, a world they weren't able to deal with, but that they heard about daily, the media saying the world might perish at any moment in an atomic explosion; where might they hide? In a garage with instruments and a large amplifier, little fellows fascinated by the Necronomicon, the *Book of the Dead*, finding shelter from the world's threats, even as the book explained how to open portals and let unspeakable horrors in; that book was the foundation of death metal. The Necronomicon comprises the experiences of a mad Arab and his knowledge of the forces which lie beyond the manifestations of reality; the mad Arab writes that he saw unknown and unmapped lands, lands without place names, he is an ideal character for the writer H.P. Lovecraft, it was as if he foresaw the Cold War, monsters waiting outside the world's limits, waiting to break in and destroy everything we hold dear... the Necronomicon is fictional, a sour mishmash of Sumerian Studies, the heart and brain of the HP-sauce oeuvre I myself read as a teenager who was into death metal: Morbid Angel shared it with me, they had read it and I had to read it, the Necronomicon itself is a hell in Lovecraft's works, a fictional hell, anonymously published as an ancient manuscript, you can arguably trace death metal to a Brit, Sir Ernest Alfred Thompson Wallis Budge, though he himself would hardly recognize that fact: this nineteenth century Brit, Sir Wallis Budge, worked at the British Museum and published the *Egyptian Book of the Dead* in 1899; this became the bible of Aleister Crowley and also obsessed H.P. Lovecraft, who made his own *Book of the Dead,* the Necronomicon, via a concoction of Sumerian Studies and the Egyptian Book of the Dead, and when it was reprinted as a mysterious *Found Manuscript* in the '70s, there were two teenagers in Florida named Trey and David, they lost themselves in it, became dark symbolists overnight, establishing the band Morbid Angel to bring these discoveries into sight. Morbid Angel built its art and creations on a 17,000-year-old heap of lies and fictions which then found their way directly to me, and I swallowed it inside, essential for everything.

Although the band Morbid Angel had four members, two forces ruled it, Trey Azagthoth the guitarist and David Vincent the bassist and singer; Trey composed the music and David the lyrics. David Vincent's voice is an occult growl; he was tall with blond wavy hair like Gunnar from Hlíðarendi, a bit tattered and worse-for-wear, with thick arms, bull-chested, and decorated with tattoos galore, a ring in his nostril, his tone deep and gloomy, he had chosen to lose his way out of guilt, wanted to search the dark woods of his mind, he was a poet with a propensity for sacrifice who shared his gloomy suffering as an act of sympathy toward others and as a cruelty, a solution for the lesser beings who followed him, pained and suffering, the way shadows follow a wolfherd; he was the great mother to these sufferers, blasting out protections for them with his creations. David Vincent was a beast. Trey Azagthoth was swarthy, you seldom saw his face's sunken cheeks, never his eyes, due to his black hair and dark appearance, he was unassuming, his clothes shredded and torn; little was known about him. Trey was the fervor, David the means, but the real wonder is a third, background power which binds the band together, Peter Sandoval the drummer, very pimpled and unpredictable, he seemed to have sold his soul to the devil for his talent and art, he's known as Pete the Feet due to his speed and stamina and outlandishness, and sometimes Peter Strandhöggvir, Peter Coast-Cutter, raining down coastal blows in his music, unpredictable, the drummer's full name is Pete the Feet Coast-Cutter Sandoval, and one might say, The Regular said, that Pete the Feet Coast-Cutter Sandoval is the Robert Johnson of death metal...

Robert Johnson?

Who sold his soul to the devil, one of the lead wethers in Satan's fortunes, a true wild sheep, all those who want to be artists have to sell their souls to the devil, sacrifice everything, including themselves, go beyond all limits, otherwise there can be no art, it's an unfortunate job being an artist, and perverted—with occasional joy, however, some pleasures, actually nothing but pleasure, idle pleasures that erode one's inner being... many people think that art requires suffering, that's not quite right, no art causes suffering, rather art becomes a triumph over pain, the same thing applies to beauty, the same thing applies to truth; O, what a miserable destiny, being an artist... that man there ought to know all about it, the underworld poet Worm Serpent, one of the poets who frequents this place, he wrote the book *The Black on the Shore,* poets are odd screws, most writers aren't poets, of course, upon closer inspection, usually poets are stupid people pretending to be wise, some are poets by nature but do nothing with that, they're maladapted in some respect so fail to nurture their talents, perhaps in a treatment center or job they hate, in order to find the poetic they would need to mute their personality and let their environment swallow them and hope to be squeezed back to life in the asshole of reality, that's my opinion, the true poet goes through the world like a child, as Georges Bataille said about William Blake, The Regular said, Worm Serpent has just published the book *The Buzzing of Existence,* he publishes many books a year and he pesters people on the street so that they are forced to buy them off him, other people can't handle him because he is a dwarf, but also not a dwarf, people don't know what to do, best to just pay and get the hell away, I've seen people buy books and discard them in the trash can on the next street corner, out of his sight, it's sad, there are not many dwarfs left, they've been destroyed, Worm Serpent is a true poet although everyone says

he isn't, that will happen after he's dead, isn't that just swell? He
is, of course, truly mad, but a real poet has to enter the moonlight,
go to the altar of madness and return afterward to mass, it's perhaps not until after death that the poet returns: the mental patient
remains in madness, unable to control his travels; the poet walks
out of the church, the poet does not even need to go into the
church, or so I think Bataille said of Blake, though he never said
that, poets don't need anything but the smallest fragment in order
to describe the entire world, one little seed becomes a whole
field of ideas, and all these ideas the world...the poetry book
Detritus in Studded Tires—Stars in Rubber Heaven, that's the name of
one of Worm Serpent's, *The Wind Does Not Know the Way Home*,
The Low Hum of Flight, *Time and the Phone*, *My Dirtiest Shirt Clean*,
Designer of the Mixmaster, you must collect them, *The Rustle of the
Bag* came out after this and there are many others too, there's no
way to keep up, I usually go on the run if I see Serpent twisting
along the street and am ashamed; it quite destroys a man's day! He
is doing his best; no one can tolerate him now, but when he dies
everyone will compete to acquire his books, to talk about their
friendship with him, about how remarkable he was, though while
he is alive very few people can put up with him, a very few good-
hearted people and only for a micro-moment...Worm is sometimes called *The Venomous Snake*, and he is really happy with that,
presents himself sometimes as a venomous snake, people see him
on the street and think: there goes the viper with its poisonous
tooth, best to flee ... he is a biting poet, said The Regular, both a
word for the poison of a serpent and an ancient poetic locution
for swords ...Worm is a dwarf and not a dwarf, he is a big dwarf,

a short serpent, he is always out on the street downtown selling his books and chatting with people, one needs to be in quite the special mood to meet him, one has to be in an outdoor mood, in the mood to sit on a bench and have nothing to do, moderately pessimistic, then you're ready for the poet, sitting on a bench in the afternoon sun and taking snuff with him and grumbling about how bad the situation is everywhere, in parliament, out in the world, Worm spends all day downtown persecuting people, at dinnertime he goes to the west side of town and rings the doorbell of some influential member of society, a sea captain, a bank manager, a foreman, he gets to eat with one of them, sells a book or is dealt with in the form of a thousand króna bill to go back downtown to sit in a cafe or bar and spend the money. I don't know where he lives; he probably rents a room somewhere up in an attic where he writes poems, and paints, too, abstract symbolist pictures with a naive-ish appearance ... Jean Delville, the Belgian painter who painted *The Fortune of Satan*—the painting I have never seen because the roof leaks in the *Museé royaux des Beaux-Arts de Belgique* and the picture is always down in the basement—belonged to a mighty symbolist movement at the end of the nineteenth century in France and neighboring countries, I've always loved this concept, *symbolism*, the sequence of chords in this concept, they were great eccentrics, these symbolists, Delville joined a simple revival of Spiritism in Europe, it pops in my mind to call them a kind of spiritual impressionist, I'm thinking out loud, said The Regular via telepathy, you're getting my unfiltered thoughts, straight from the barrel ... no, now I've lost the thread ... as soon as you begin to explain something, you lose your thread ... Morbid Angel ... there's an unexpected connection between Morbid Angel and the symbolists, it runs deeper than just the fact that *Les trésors de Satan* by Jean Delville graced the cover of *Blessed Are the Sick*: mysticism, based on emotion and invented information, a fiction, the NECRONOMICON is fiction, and not a lie, there's a big difference there, it is a relationship to pleasure, to dark feelings ... being high ... an exploratory expedition to the source-forest ... Edvard Munch is a symbolist and I reckon Vincent Van Gogh is also a symbolist, although all the art historians in the world seem to me likely to disagree, Van Gogh is usually classified as impressionism or postimpressionism ... you're on the right track when art historians are disagreeing with you ... *The Scream* by Munch, that's the same howling as death metal, though death metal doesn't set palms to cheeks on stage, that would smack of effeminacy, there's significant homophobia in death metal, but it's the same scream, a scream within from the limits of Being, an invocation, an invocation to death after life ... there's a certain art to screaming, or rather to bellowing, there are small amounts of screaming, purer experience, a bellow is a balanced scream, tempered, death metal is the taming of wild destruction, the bellow siphoned from a man so he can retain his sanity, bellows are small screams that prevent screams going quantum like in Munch's painting, which is an effeminate howl, untamed, desperate, it would be fun to write a paper about howling in death metal, to examine the types of howls, the distinction between bellowing and howling and screaming, their characteristics and meaning, the thesis could be called:

about

Bellowing

in Death Metal

especially what's called old

school & sources in / links with *the occult*

Symbolists rejected the overwhelming realism that led everything living to die in art, said The Regular, all 19th century thought, in fact, the symbolists rejected reality, they wanted to get out of the world, just somewhere away, somewhere in hell, realism kills everything with boredom, they said, the symbolists' transfigurations were a response to this boredom, to lifeless manifestations of things; beauty was dying out, because beauty, I think, is barely found on the surface of things, the beautiful, the true and divine, is inside things, the inner area, and that's where transfiguration directs itself, a solution from under the suffocating surface of things...Transformative vision is everything, Bernharður, much more Greek, the idea of transfiguration originates in Christian mysticism, when the body of Christ goes to the angels, the avatar of Jesus lights up inside yet the body's form is unchanging, its external manifestation does not alter, and so too in reality the manifestation of the world does not change after transfiguration, instead things become archetypal or prototypical in the Platonic sense, or, more accurately, the Socratic sense, meaning the idea that things do not die except at worst on the surface, life can be found within, in sleep, dreams, death and so on, it is the road to the world beyond the world...Why is Vincent Van Gogh a symbolist? His absinthe drinking and his aura? Slicing off his ear? ... in my book, that is more accurately a deformation, a distortion, not a transformation, even less a transfiguration, but it is still an illumination from within, the night sky is lit up from within like with Christ's transfiguration ... Kirk Douglas interpreted Van Gogh's existential pain remarkably in the old film, have you seen it? That was such a deep surprise, because it is one thing to be a European artist and another to be an American artist, is it not ... Kirk Douglas playing Vincent Van Gogh! I was skeptical about the movie, to say the least, but when he jumps into the bushes at the peak of his madness at the institution ... the essence of symbolism! ... Van Gogh is really a reverse symbolist, a symbolist in negative or maybe not a symbolist?

Trey Azagthoth is not like most people, no one in Morbid Angel is like most people, in fact no one in death metal is like most people. Trey Azagthoth is a symbolist in the same sense as Van Gogh, who wasn't a symbolist at all, perhaps, or maybe a new type of symbolist, a physical symbolist, for when Trey Azagthoth plays his guitar at a concert he cuts himself with a razor blade, marking an inverted cross and the devil's star on his arm, he contracts and he vanishes behind his guitar, it seems very much like he's getting sexual satisfaction as blood leaks down the strings, that he's raging away on the instrument in some other world, just let others try and do as much! The Regular said, laughing so that his teeth glittered. Trey Azagthoth's form falls into a trance and his inner experience of divinity blasts out the Marshall amplifier! ... symbols ... the language of the other side ... for that matter, one might say that a Trey Azagthoth guitar solo is a tribute to Vincent Van Gogh and the sliced-off ear, perversion as emotional perfection, art, divinity…The venomous serpent's sitting there not saying anything, The Regular said at Circus, the wormy, hearing-impaired poet with his big head just looks at us, hardly even thinking, doggedly fingering the base of his glass, watching us chatting together, not hearing any of it, maybe he's reading our lips, are lips telepathic?…Worm Serpent sits and looks at us and drinks, his same old tweed jacket as ever, smelly and swollen by nihilism; some people go to the bar every day only to sit and drink and goggle at others and to eavesdrop, pretending to be thinking but not thinking, not that I know for sure, Worm Serpent looks like he's thinking, with that gigantic head, that blinding forehead, that fur hat resting on top of his box-shaped head, the venomous snake seems lost deep inside itself, perhaps he's gone deep inside to compose poetry, wandering withered fields of thought within his great head?

The year after *Blessed Are the Sick* was released in the death metal Mecca, Tampa, Florida, I turned sixteen and my mother wanted to get me out of the house: the time has come when you need to look after yourself—but I stayed home and didn't do anything but listen to albums; I was no good for anything. Some man had moved in with us and I didn't accept him, refusing to talk to him, pretending not to see him, pretending he wasn't there, who was this man?…My mother thought it a good solution to send this moody teenager away from the country, people do everything in their power to get rid of children nowadays, there are playschools, kindergartens, elementary schools, so on, you can use student exchange programs to get rid of teenagers, for a year or possibly forever, on the pretext that children gain experience in and knowledge of an alien world, but I didn't want to go anywhere except one place in the world, Tampa, Florida, my mother was astonished at that, but I explained how Tampa, Florida, was the Mecca of death metal, the boiling point of a new world, the world *I* wanted to be in, I did not recognize myself anywhere in our world. Beyond that, I knew nothing about the city of Tampa, Florida, I knew Disneyworld was in Florida, that Icelanders flocked there, thinking it the peak of existence to destroy their children there, I had no interest in the sunshine coast or anything like that but I had Florida on the brain, I wanted to go to Tampa or nowhere, to take a swamp boat out among the mangroves to view pelicans, flamingos, and crocodiles during the day then go to a concert in the evening, although I'd heard that Tampa contains almost exclusively old people, the city pretty much a retirement home for Americans, but I couldn't believe it, how could that be? That death metal flourished from a retirement haven? My mother said I could apply to visit the United States but I wouldn't myself get to decide where I was sent within the United States, that wasn't how things worked. I only want to go to Tampa, Florida, I said to my mother, nowhere else, and so a whole year passed with me refusing to accept the new man in any way, doing everything in my power to protest the situation quite unconsciously, mainly creating chaos and self-destructing so as to disrupt their courtship and attempt to capture my mother's attention, it had just been the two of us and then this man burst into our lives and was trying to supplant me, to get me not only out of the house but also out of the country, you must go and gain experience and become a man, instead of hanging out in the garage all day and night with these long-haired, black-clad good-for-nothings, said the new man, talking about my friends through my mother, you're destroying your hearing producing all this noise, and hearing is one of God's gifts, to be treated with care, next I pressed hard to go to Australia because that was the farthest country from Iceland, might as well go far away if I was going to be smoked out of my country, but that didn't happen, I was too late for the program there or something; then I was filled with a desire to learn about animal life in the rainforests, there was much talk about the rainforests disappearing, dying out, I felt within me a strong urge to experience the rainforests, to help save them, the lungs of the earth, before man destroyed them entirely on his journey to self-destruction, just like a heavy smoker, I pressed hard for a chance to vanish into the rainforest, planning never to return, given that my mother wanted to get rid of me by any means, having chosen this man over me, The Regular said, Costa Rica, it was a short distance to Florida and I could flee there once I was done losing myself in the rainforest, besides, I wasn't so excited anymore about going to Tampa, death metal had dispersed around the world during the past year, was thinning out, I'd missed the revolution, there was no longer the same energy and excitement, everything had been destroyed because it had expanded and spread out, everything had become an after-image of the energy in Tampa, and therefore dead, so no point thinking about the rainforests in Costa Rica, I was too late again, I then got desperate to get away, and now my mother wanted to keep me at home and I wanted out, there were only two countries left with teenage exchange programs,

Argentina and Paraguay, and I did not know anything about these countries, I asked some girl or other in the exchange office which country she reckoned was better, Argentina or Paraguay, what would she do if she was being sent away, and she, whoever she was, didn't need to think about it, she preferred Argentina, so I went to Argentina the winter of my seventeenth year, to a place no one had previously been sent, the southern end of South America, in a small village in the mountains where there was nobody to welcome me. I grew extremely unsociable and sullen and wandered the deserts of south Patagonia, I didn't know a word of the language, it rushed by so fast, I made one friend in the village, a stray dog, he and I roamed the dusty streets and shared packs of cookies in the afternoon, finally I found a home, I wanted to take the dog with me to the home, but it was out of the question, we'd rather beat him, said the father of the household, and he treated me like a dog because I didn't speak the language at all, but indeed I studied the language at an amazing rate, wrote down every new word twenty times, made a long list of terms, copied out grammar tables from a pocket dictionary until I understood it, I always remained loyal to the stray dog out on the main street, and he to me, he came running toward me on the dusty main street, and I tried to have something for him from the kitchen of the home, he was big and yellow, skinny and patchy, it was fun to share a packet of cookies with him, said The Regular, with a far-off expression ... then one day I was gone ... he's definitely dead now, this was so long ago, although stray dogs grow so wise from their freedom and hardships, stray dogs in Buenos Aires, for example, have reached astonishing heights of civilization, they are grouped into classes and each class is a society in which certain rules apply, there's a lead dog, a so-called alpha, all the others are under his power until he's overthrown, often the dogs are also alone when they're strays, one often sees a stray dog come trotting along the pavement, completely in its own world and letting nothing disturb it, determined, headed somewhere, and one thinks: now where is he going like that? The dog has taken a course, has a mission somewhere in the neighborhood; he comes to a large road, stops, looks both ways with a calm expression, and when the street is empty he jogs across it like nothing is more straightforward... I came back home, said The Regular, out to Iceland, as it was phrased in olden days, a changed man, independent, a stray dog amputated from its family, my mother having to mourn a son who was forever lost... at the time there was death metal in Florida and grunge in Sjóttl, the city of Seattle, think of the navigator Sea-Attila in ancient Nordic writings, and then hardcore in Nueva Jórvík... all these were variously seen as signs of the end of times, The Death showed up in Florida, it surprised everyone, death metal chose Florida because human beings were coming to an end there, it was the end of humanity, the end of Western culture, *The Death in Florida*, I'm thinking of writing a book about this, Bernharður, said The Regular, dedicated to Thomas Mann, to people sunbathing as they await death, to Disney, to the graveyard of humanity where Nasa attempts to scurry out of the pit up to the dark abyss, a book about death metal and old folks having a perfect communion.

What happens in transfiguration, a death which is not death but a transformation, is that people become archetypes for eternity, even as they fade quickly and disappear like *rain on the sand*, as the poet Worm Serpent would say; people later try to remember how the deceased was *typical*, an extremely fragile image, everyone wants some influence over her, we all distort her in our minds, certain idioms, particular foods, smells, intimacies...but once she settles into archetype she becomes unbreakable, that's perhaps exactly what happens in a transfiguration: a fragile image becomes unbreakable...for example, a mother who has lost her son sees him always in the hoodie he wore everywhere, a hoodie she was constantly trying to replace with a warm, beautiful sweater she had knit for him, one he sniffed at, she couldn't ever get him out of the hoodie, this hoodie he'll now wear for eternity, up to the day of judgment, to the ends of the universe, in her mind and heart; this detail causes his mother infinite sorrow, at least for the short time it takes to grieve the boy and distort his memory and finally forget him as he was, said The Regular, and remember him as he was not, always in the damn hoodie which symbolizes that and reminds the mother how she was unable to deal with the boy and neglected his parenting and taught him to expect defeat, she disastrously failed at her goal, the goal of all mothers: to bring the seed to its luxurious fruition, where all the shattered dreams still shine whole, the dead dreams living yet, everything ending in universal distortion.

After the transfiguration, said The Regular at Circus, when the body is transformed into a spirit, its archetypical form, like a boy in an ugly hoodie, the *ascension* begins, the heavenly journey of Jesus Christ, as the mother accompanies her son to the State and as is recorded in the Virgin Mary's heavenly journey, or *assumption*, because the son takes the mother up to himself after she has been in the ground and died in Jerusalem; it is said that the admission of both Mary's body and soul and her clothes have become, after the assumption, a truth, a proof, although that doesn't also prove that men have seen her naked before them ... on the other hand, I'm against proof, I do not believe this, that the clothes of the Virgin Mary have been left on the earth is a sign of that she was admitted, naked and alive, to heaven; some theologians want it to mean that she has simply fallen asleep and woken in heaven, and some scholars say that her grave was empty on the third day and her flesh ascended, like the son, and her clothes too, but it is probable that she had transmuted and eyewitnesses watched the image of her spirit being admitted to heaven while they kept the body—not that I mean to contravene John Damascene, the most learned in these studies, the man Catholics call *Doctor of the Assumption*, said The Regular; John Damascene wrote *The Fountain of Wisdom* where he rightly refutes Islam as a heresy though he was a contemporary of its fount—but who am I to exchange words with John of Patmos, who composed the Book of Revelations in exile using God's words, composed it as an encouragement for the survivors of persecution and sectarianism, popular for its poetry and symbolism, this John was named *theologian* and I am not a theologian, not by any stretch, just an amateur, I'm not Thessalonian John or Jerusalem Andrew or Jerusalem Modestus or Geirmundur from Constantinople, the writer of the literary *Mystical History of the Catholic Church*, which describes the symbolism or the "sign-sight" of Byzantine mass form, both ritual and liturgical; Geirmundur from Constantinople fought against the iconoclasm of authority and heresy alike, seeing holy symbols and signs as keys to the divine, Geirmundur was therefore called the servant of the image, the image-friend, the *symbolist* ... and Gregory of Tours, who wrote *The History of the Franks* and had a major impact on Snorri Sturluson—but these guys all wrote about the *Assumption of the Virgin Mary*, said The Regular, and this is becoming too esoteric a conversation if we want everyone to follow along, all I have is my *Book of Homilies* on the bedside table, written in 1200, it must have something of value to its ... the difference is that the Son *ascends* but the mother is *taken* up ... contrasting that, in the beginning the mother gives birth to the son and takes him to her breast; after, the son steals the scene with pretense and self-pity and megalomania, so often the way with sons ... it's the mother, in fact, who's tortured, not the Son, as Augustine points out in *City of God*, I don't remember where exactly, but he does say it, the mother's spirit is tortured and the son's body, he endures it but she cannot tolerate it, she was too sensitive, too delicate for the world of Pontius Pilate, the mother grieves, she has sacrificed her son, truly, not the father or the son himself, the mother is humility in the world, she is taken up to heaven because the father and son waded into the world in a sick delusion that the world is their house, their dwelling, their company, the father is CEO and Managing Director, the son is responsible for operations, moving and selling tickets, managing inventory, marketing, in the end the son runs the company into the ground, the son plans to honor his father by becoming just like him but discovers he can't, the father loves himself and no one else, in reality he hates himself and the entire world and cannot wait to destroy both himself and the world to teach his son a lesson; the son starts to despise his father, wallowing in self-pity, feeling the father has abandoned him because he doesn't reward him, the son doesn't receive an immediate promotion within the company, he has to start with the lowest jobs and can't immediately take the helm, the son first follows the father then wants to get rid of him and take over the company (the world), the son has forsaken his mother in a blind rush to pursue his father, the mother pursues her son and eventually joins the family in heaven on a sticky Chesterfield sofa after her endless fragmentation on the ground down below and they cannot talk to one another, said The Regular. We have made a covenant with God which has force here in our ambiguous human world, it was called the *Old Covenant* because the covenant is indeed old, there are 613 laws which Moses wrote down according to God's voice and word, laws Moses shared in whole with mankind, that is to say, Jews, the elect nation that knows itself as an underrepresented and excluded people, the children of Israel, and God's children should be circumcised on the eighth day after birth, as Abraham was circumcised, and Jesus Christ was circumcised, that is to say castrated and amputated, so pleasure may be destroyed, the king sluggish, the venomous serpent kept in check so the heavens do not immediately collapse and the world remains disrupted a little while, too, until the Day of Judgment, which is coming soon, said The Regular at Circus, you'll have proof before long.

At that the serpent poet turned away from his wilderness, he woke up, I do not know if he gleaned nutrition from his inner regions, the poet Worm Serpent ordered another glass of red wine, his tweed jacket is starting to look the worse for wear, his fur hat awry, more like a wet rag, his galoshes worn on top of his crumpled pants, the poet is clearly in dire straits and seems quite drunk, his big head weighs heavily on his dwarf adult body, Worm Serpent is a vagrant, said The Regular, a dwarf, vagrant poet. He lurched over to us with overcoat hanging over one hand, and held the wine glass like a small cup he had won at bingo, wearing a disappointed expression, resembling a distortion of the intellectual; the poet climbed nimbly into a chair and introduced himself with a polite bow, saying:

Ormur eg var

Ormur eg er

& Ormur mun ætíð vera

með eitraða tönn

& tambúrín hala

einn skríð eg

úr skinni mínu

& skipti um ham.[3]

He crumpled his change into a tattered wallet and pulled out a document he wanted to show us: it certified that the poet was a full

3. *Worm I was*
  Worm I am
  & Worm shall always be
  with poisonous teeth
  & a tambourine tail
  I crawled alone
  out of my skin
  & switched hides.

member of the Rotary Club. If I were not an Icelander, I would have earned the Nobel Prize, said Worm, if I'd written in French or German, I would already have received the Nobel, I'm so isolated, in such a tiny linguistic region, I am alone, stranded... stranded on a deserted skerry... banished... I'm stranded on a deserted rock, banished from the raging sea of languages! said Worm, loud and aggrieved, and some looked up from their sheeps' heads in our direction, I got the worst curse of Babel, born an Icelandic poet, no one understands me, no one hears me at all... Slit your throat, then, said The Regular but Worm got sacredly offended and coiled up, So, what are you writing these days? Worm quickly softened at this apparent attention to his work, I'm experimenting, said Worm Serpent, with writing between sleep and waking ...And it's going well, is it? The Regular asked brusquely and with great disrespect, but the poet did not let himself get worked up this time; sipping many small sips of red wine, he said: This is how poets drink in Paris, many small sips quickly...We looked at this approach to red wine with some astonishment...They (sip) were (sip) prepared (sip) to (sip) let (sip) me (sip) have (sip) the Nobel (sip)...the poet muttered between tiny sips before crying out: Can can can can can can't some gentleman here offer to buy a single book of poetry in exchange for a finger of brandy!?...The Regular waved to the waiter and asked for a bottle of red wine from the Rhone valley, which would work on the poet like the powerful Mistral wind, but Worm Serpent snatched up a book of poetry, *A Journey Within Sight*, shot the cap off his fountain pen with his thumb and wrote the date on the flyleaf with shaky hands and with best wishes from the author. The ritual took a fantastically long time.

We were discussing poetry, said The Regular. Dwarves are done with, answered Worm Serpent, therefore I am a poet. And who is it that writes for you while you're stuck between sleep and waking? The Regular asked, we were just discussing this very topic, the boundary between dreams and existence, it's not easy to hold a pen in that state but one can remember ... I'm crippled, said Worm Serpent, I cannot work, I cannot live on a disability allowance, I cannot live in poetry, I can not ... I catch words and pictures, I set them to memory and process them later ... There's a little of the symbolist in you, maybe, said The Regular, symbolists cease to distinguish between dreams and reality, the boundaries fade away, the symbolist ceases to differentiate between these two kinds of reality, sinks into signs and wanders in darkness and doesn't know where the ideas or memories come from, whether he has had an actual experience or dreamed it, he wanders in the dark, maybe it's better put another way, a symbolist wanders in amazement, he knows these two worlds work together, but he, the symbolist, fears the darkness ... yet first and foremost he desires the darkness and when a person is held by fear mixed with desire, then they must wander ... Wander in existence like I do! cried Worm Serpent, *je suis un grand symboliste!* ... Poets desire solitude but cannot be alone, continued The Regular, ignoring the poet's interruption, they want to form groups, look at the wretched young poets, how poor and afflicted they are ... Van Gogh took symbolism a step further, like true artists do, went one step further, leaving the rest behind to be swallowed by forgetfulness, but Van Gogh did not desire darkness, he longed for the light beyond the darkness, the stars in the night sky, he

desired life, like the novel about him called *Lust for Life I & II*
which you could procure from Bragi for nothing, I recommend
it, Bernharður, take it into Öræfi and read it in the tent out on
a glacier in Mávabyggðir, that'd be tremendous! But no doubt
you've enough to read, toponymy...I cannot think of anything
better than to read *Lust for Life I & II* in a tent on Öræfajökull,
said The Regular, here inside this elegant hostelry there are also
place names which need recording, too, perhaps you can do a little recording when you come back? I'll remain in place here and
can assist you, I have a workspace over there in the corner during
the day, there's no one more knowledgeable about these historical sites than I...everywhere humankind needs something, she
marks it like a dog pissing, I've never tolerated the verse that endlessly gets quoted in newspapers, books and radio, *the landscape
would have little value were it not called something*, this is the most intolerable line in Icelandic literary history, this is the ugliest example of how revoltingly narcissistic writers can become, value for
whom? Farmers? Toponymers? The general public?...The landscape would have *significant value* if it were not called anything,
that's how it should be, otherwise it's so unpleasant, talking about
the value of the landscape only from the perspective of poets and
politicians, it makes me sick, not even economists are that grotesque, but enough now, anyway...I have a lifethirst, too, said
The Regular, moi aussi, said Worm Serpent, we all do, said The
Regular, a lifethirst quenched by sleep...It's perfume, said the
poet, Worm Serpent, *le parfume* ...That's right! The Regular said,
the fragrance opens up dimensions and sends us on to dream-
land...I completely forgot perfume because nowadays there's

just stench, but if anything is symbolist it is perfume, which is nineteenth century, romantic, decadent, all-in-one dispenser ... a bottle ... in the arms of a prostitute in Paris ... dead but dreaming, as it says in the song, that's something for a poet like you to memorize! dead but dreaming, on the other hand I've heard that a great poet has no memory, that's one of the characteristics of great poets, the absence of memory, they have annihilated memory so as to multiply their poetic talents, the romantic imagination is one of nature's loving gifts, Benedikt Gröndal said, isn't that the opposite of memory? ... Benedikt Gröndal was a great poet and scholar of many things and he of all people should know, he was alive in a time of fragrance, today we live in the era of stench dispensers, stench and bottled stench, that's all that's available in stores these days, stench, and if realism, Gröndal also says somewhere, manages to clear away the romantic imagination, then everything becomes empty, that's how he puts it: no poetic fictions, all empty.

Yes, prostitutes in Paris, said the poet Worm Serpent, melancholic with the residue of recollection and dreams, *mon cherie putains*, I could write an entire book about prostitutes in Paris, in the language of the night, it would be a deep book because I am deep even though I am short, perhaps precisely because I'm short, the night is short and deep and weaves me a tranquil cocoon ... wait I need to write this down, where is my pen? ... here, but what? It won't write ... you're duh-dry ... oh, oh, I forgot to close it, I've lost my cap, waiter! Ha-have you a pen? ... It may not be as understood, said The Regular, that prostitutes are somewhat deep, they're just as clueless as anyone, prostitutes are symbolists' *tools*, their devices and instruments, prostitutes are the guards of an alternate reality, Cerberus & Anubis south in the Mediterranean and Garmur at Gnípahell here on the north side of the Alps, prostitutes are the dogs guarding the underworld, conducting the dead, never easily domesticated, the sleeping poet in the arms of a prostitute has received access to the kingdom of the dead, or rather *paid* for access, because prostitutes have to make a living somehow, someone gives her enough to live on, preferably only a little, for who wants a fat, overdressed whore? ... yes, some do, perhaps ... the poet asleep in the arms of a prostitute has received a passport out of true reality, received respite from boredom, oppression, family, work, and taxation, the prostitute is Heimdallur at Bifröst, a doorkeeper to the gods' home; without a prostitute a man is nothing, without a prostitute a man isn't a man ... probably you can't say that these days ... I'm of course talking about prostitutes in a figurative form, as metaphors, a prostitute is a metawhore, something only the future understands ... necessary for distress, necessary for lying at the bottom and finding peace beneath life's routine, what William Blake called *sublime allegory*, being immersed in the heavens, in fact, necessary for maternal care ... necessary for poetry ... maybe a source of identification, for what is the poet but a whore? ... to sleep in a prostitute's embrace is not something everyone can understand, it's only a poet who can sleep in a prostitute's arms, in fact, no one can be a poet without sleeping in a prostitute's arms, only briefly, oh, how short it lasts! ... poets also don't have the means to dally endlessly in whorehouses, perhaps they did in the 19th century but things have changed, men will swiftly destroy themselves exploring the depths, poets aren't built to last, they're destroyed in an instant by internal disasters, each poem is *nuées ardentes*, it is much healthier to toddle about on the safety of surface or wander just one dimension of quotidian life, that's rewarding in its own way; the poet and the symbolist have but a short time for creating and for reporting from the depths before the burning ash chokes anything living in their inner city, petrifying them, before anguish freezes the intelligence, before the poet slits his throat and casts himself into a glacial crevasse and becomes immortal...symbolists explore the depths, explore connections with reality, where and how they overlap, how our world is governed by the underworld, true reality is the consciousness of the world, apparitions, the symbolist wants to delve into the subconscious world to understand the images of things, to return to them, to see through things, to perceive them, a symbolist always has a lot to do, as you can tell, if he lies asleep in the arms of a prostitute, in fact, he is never as busy as when he lies asleep in the arms of a metaphorical prostitute, for he is toiling away in the fields of the underworld, he investigates motor power, in the under-depths there's a kind of ship's engine for the world, the engine room, it's the most difficult space you can enter, no one ends his stay there sane, you cannot stay too long there, I mean in the arms of a prostitute, the world's ship-engine, it would destroy a man in no time, a symbolist must know his goal, that's essential if he's to explore the world's thresholds, the engineer isn't a man but a *daemon*, a devil, impervious to the machine, living dead, a symbolist must come back up on deck, dress himself and pay the prostitute, taking his leave and trusting the underworld's watchdog, even though that's impossible, trusting the machine of the world to continue without his presence, the symbolist has many things to do, he examines what's caught in the nets, he processes the data, he is aboard the research vessel *Bjarni Sæmundsson*, he talks to the captain on the bridge, takes snuff with him, he talks to himself on his way around the ship, he has to monitor everything, everyone is bound fast to his work except him, though he is in a sense responsible for everything, even if no one's willing to admit it, he's reality's supervisor and must learn to trust, it's not possible to steer the ship with a hard hand as in the past, now we need cooperation, he has to rely on a first mate when he goes downstairs to the engine room, he trusts the first mate not only with his life but his very being, no one should go insecurely down to the depths, symbolists needs bodyguards, although they don't know they're bodyguards, so they don't have to worry while at their job, this was confirmed by David Vincent and Trey Azagthoth and Pete the Foot Coast-Shaker Sandóval in Morbid Angel, when they go on stage someone has to ensure they get the peace to work their work... I dream of finding the privacy to write an article on Icelandic symbolism, which hardly exists, and connect it to Belgian symbolism, there are only three Icelandic Symbolists, all totally different, Benedikt Gröndal the poet, Einar Jónsson the sculptor, and Jóhannes Kjarval the painter, these artists have migrated symbolism across the sea to this country, an imported symbolism, and Benedikt Gröndal is probably not a symbolist, only an aesthete and eccentric... it's clear no one knows the connection between Einar Jónsson and Jean Delville, maybe I should just concentrate on that, muttered The Regular, make a novel out of it rather than an essay, or a novel in the style of an essay, an essayistic novel … it probably wouldn't be taken seriously, I'm no historian, but I know a lot about art, if an author is uneducated then he is too *school of life* to be able to write, but if he's educated he is too far *removed from life* to be able to write, writers are either too educated to be able to write or too uneducated to be able to write, too bound up with living to be able to write or too set apart from life to be able to write, said The Regular at Circus, the novel is a world in itself which simultaneously creates and complies with its own laws, all the characters in a novel reflect the character of the author and all their opinions reflect the views of the author, the novel is the author, but the author is inherently *Proteus* or the weather vane of opinion within their own work, there he is outside the world and outside himself, ever-changing, the writer is like the sea and the sea is cold and deep, my dear Worm, the writer is sea-worthy, *the Deep*, and lands upon that image of himself … but what business do the sea-worthy have on land? … shouldn't he hold himself to the limits of poetic fiction, which no breakwater can hold back? … it's also, however, possible to argue that the novel is not the author himself, even that the novel is not really by the author, for doesn't Thomas Aquinas say that: My soul is not me, that is, the soul is not the whole human being, he is so much more, the author adopts a role when he writes, he feels close to his essence and he feels good, he is willing to sacrifice everything, family and friends, just to be able to write even if he never publishes, the novel is the author's role, driven by fantasies and delusions, he shapes himself in fiction, finds his style and finally the style becomes the author's role, his character, the man himself is lost …

Th-this is your theory? Worm asked.

Yes, and I also have another theory about fiction.

G-good. L-let the volcano erupt.

Until now, fiction has at all times been bound up with the spirit, no? So much so that the spirit doggy paddles in the upper atmosphere, sweeps the benefits of art up from the earth to the glory of the Divine, from Aristotle's *Ars Poetica* up to today not much new has happened in this regard, until now, now I've dropped by Circus with my new theory of poetics... it's not enough to read Aristotle once and always be bragging Aristotle this and Aristotle that, one must *always* be reading Aristotle to mention his name, have him constantly present, whetting his knife after each use, most people are forever saying Aristotle this and Aristotle the other but have never read Aristotle, just some other author who has read Aristotle and refers to Aristotle, and this author himself has only read an author who has read Aristotle, actually no-one has read Aristotle, everyone is always saying Aristotle...

A-and what is your theory? Worm Serpent asked, amazed.

Your theory? asked The Regular.

No, your theory, you claim to have a theory of poetics, said Worm.

Ah, my theory!? That poetry is not connected with the spirit, as has always been thought, but is far more tied to the body, I think it might even exclude the spirit, writing is only depen-dent on the body, said The Regular, drawing breath in the ghostly form of smoke from a Bagatello cigar before continuing, the so-called Muse has long disappeared from the literary field and poetic fiction has been an orphan a long while, one knows that writing doesn't spring from the spirit because there is no spirit nowadays, no one has realized that poetry and fiction burst out from the body, that they originated in the material, in real life.

Wh-What to do you mean that poetry and fiction burst out from the body? How does something become spiritual? something spiritual? something spiritual? Worm asked with great effort, no-noble and bursting from the body like you say?

These days, it's highly fashionable in healthcare circles to pH-adjust the body; something you might be needing, dear Worm, people claim unhealthy diets make the body too acidic and as a consequence various ailments result, even all ailments, according to some, acid destroys the body's cells, it's advisable to consume foods that make your body more alkaline to balance the pH value and nurture a natural digestive environment, it should be around 7, seven is a sacred number in this theory as in other studies, yet highly measurable and scientific with no belief systems or lofty ideas obstructing one, and that's why my theory is so strong, because it connects poetics with science again, said The Regular, yeast makes the body acidic, yeast leavens the body, bread, beer and wine and coffee, fatty foods and fast food, all this makes the body acidic, all these pleasurable things, and it's somehow wrong, contrary to conscience, conscience is intimately connected with the origins of farming... alkaline sustenance is by contrast nuts, beans, vegetables and fruits, melons and asparagus, even lemons, the most sour fruit bases the body, in other words everything that seems boring, the basic is good, the acidic bad...

Ha-how is this connected to the art of poetry, du-do I have to puh-ph-balance my body? asked Worm Serpent, skeptically.

There are two types of writing, said The Regular, acidic writing and alkaline writing, if the body is acidic, it prefers acidic writing and an acidic body will generate acidic writing, if the body is alkaline...

... it's drawn to alkaline writing, added Worm Serpent, quick on the uptake.

And alkaline bodies generate alkaline writing, continued The Regular unflagging and systematic in his theory, acidic writing is intoxicated, alkaline writing is sober, acidic writing dives into the deep, alkaline stays on the surface, acidic writing deals with death, alkaline writing focuses on life, acidic writing deals with the suffering of existence, alkaline focuses on the joy of existence, acidic writing is fun, especially when it is highly acidic and relentless, alkaline writing is always boring in a boring way, at least for an acidic man such as myself, acidic writing deals with the inner state, alkaline writing deals with the outer state, acidic writing takes risks, alkaline writing is always safe, acidic writing discovers something new by itself, alkaline writing discovers nothing new by itself, except that alkaline writing which is always never new, you see where I'm going? With this formula you can now select whatever writer you like and place them in either category ... Go on, name someone, Worm.

Rimbaud must be acidic, said Worm.

Rimbaud and Verlaine are both very acidic, said The Regular.

Baudelaire must also be acidic, said Worm.

The French are mostly acidic, it's the wine and French bread which fuels that great literary nation. Baudelaire spoke of the worm inside him that would not die, no matter how much wine he drank and French bread he ate, the worm kept on living, a serpent sitting around his heart like the Dragon Nídhöggr at the roots of the ash tree Yggdrasil. You quickly reach the conclusion that all the great poets are acidic and all the bad poets are alkaline, said The Regular, all immortal poets are acidic and all the forgotten poets are alkaline.

Ho-how can that be? Worm said.

There are physical reasons, said The Regular, the consumption of acidic food or acidic beverages, especially over-consumption, ferments inside the writer, some call it a worm but it's actually a fungus, and this fungus grows and thrives and becomes an autonomous reality, not actual reality but fictional reality, the writer starts to have visions because of this fungus, even going outside their body up to the skies and seeing the world and the self both from outside and inside, the writer finds that truly spiritual, believes it to be some world-spirit controlling the poetic; it's actually a *fungus* that controls the poetic, a particular fungus, *yeast-fungus*, I've called this poetic fungus *Gerjólf*, which is, of course, reductive, a complex process simplified, but all good theories must be distilled so people can follow their mechanics, Gerjólf is a *symbol* for all the acid the body craves, Gerjólf is the death bacteria, it wants to destroy the body, dissolve it in acid and preserve it, because acidic poetics are alive and breeding whereas alkaline poetics are stillborn and infertile. To be fair, let's give the alkaline basic a name and call it *Basólf*. Imagine them as two wolves inside the body. Gerjólf is forgetful and irrational, Basólf is mindful and rational, Gerjólf is excess, Basólf is temperance; this is why acidic writers are often thoughtless and bad at relationships, unruly, alcoholic wind-bladders, often needing to apologize for various behavioral problems... are you at all familiar with this? The Regular said to Worm Serpent, and he was clearly relieved at such acknowledgement... alkaline writers are prudent and controlled and safe to be around and do not need have to have any particular concerns. The muse which poets have served from time immemorial is actually a fungus, a living fungus in the body, the muse is not a goddess in the upper atmosphere but a fungus called Gerjólf, poets have always served Gerjólf when they claimed they were worshipping the muse... poets have had a vague idea of this, in that they call literary talent an *affliction*, a sickness they fervently wish to be free from, whereas most minor poets look up to the muse and adopt assorted, desperate tactics in an attempt to approach her by chance; only little poets without literary gifts want to worship the Muse, that is, Gerjólf, great poets hate Gerjólf because the poetry within them will destroy the soul's temple, so the unsightly spirit of the consumer might be raised up and power the economic cogwheels that trample the poet down into the mire, and Gerjólf himself at that, writers hate literary talents and start worshiping life and get themselves ridiculed. Given all that, it seems poetic to long for death, but foolish to want life.

I'm going to dedicate my next book to Gerjólf, said Worm, perhaps a new religion is emerging!?... in which poets are gods!

Gerjólf was born in the fields and so we should rightly thank the farmer for poetry and fiction and the body's passions, the agricultural farmer's labor birthed Gerjólf. One can see a clear correlation between cereal production in Iceland and written production, both were inactive for centuries, and now the whole country is covered by animal feed production, by ditches and fences, the country is entirely subjected to cultivating grass though not anything edible, except indirectly and dependent on violence against animals; amid this, fiction is entirely ignored... something, however, appears in this regard to do with climate warming and awareness about grain production and human production; still, it's totally different from what was here at the settlement, when extremely pale fields glittered under the sky. Perhaps it's not the best idea to keep on, said The Regular, addressing his words directly to Worm, or you'll drink yourself to death, you're quite free to do so, I personally hope you do, being acidic isn't enough to make you a poet, not all drunks and gluttons are poets, Gerjólf gives you nothing if he's over-saturated, experience has taught us that, any more than if he gets nothing but nuts and celery, because he will die. One needs to tame and constrain the wolf from within so he does not become too large and get loose from his leash, for if he does he will tear you apart from inside. Some think it's enough to drink tons of alcohol in order to be a poet, but the reverse is true, when Gerjólf has been awoken, no bonds holds him, like the ancient wolf Fenris: poets are immediately enslaved by Gerjólf; Gerjólf is a hard taskmaster.

I think we should all go east to Öræfi this weekend, said Kiddi, who otherwise had sat silent during the telepathy, you too Worm, and you, Bernharður, are more than welcome to come stay with me. I thought it was a good offer, but I had decided to stay on the campsite at Skaftafell and study the place names. There's plenty of place names at my place, Kiddi said to me, can't you study them?

On Svínafell is where the swine went in ancient times, murmured The Regular as we stood up and went to the cloakroom; the band had completed *Stabat Mater* by Haydn and were packing their instruments away, we were the last ones to leave and found ourselves next to a pyramid of sheeps' heads and empty champagne bottles that was a high as a person, the pigs back then were not pink and bald with huge asses like today's factory swine, said The Regular as he slipped into his jacket, but dark and furry and with large shoulders and little asses—then he threw himself down on the carpet and lay face down and began to shake, he wept for a while, sobbing, he stood up again, rubbed his eyes, yawned and stuck his tongue out as far as he could, like a dog letting out its tension, he shook himself and went sloppily past us, through a large beige drape, and out through the revolving door, followed by three vaguely female creatures masked by shawls and mascara. We stood confused for a bit then walked out. He was standing outside in the morning light waiting for us. Oh, forgive me, I'm just trying to be entertaining, said The Regular, Bernharður said, interpreted the Interpreter, Dr. Lassi wrote in the report, Bernharður wrote to me in his letter, spring 2003.

III

MYSTERIES

Guilt goes by a winding route, it says in Proverbs, said The Regular on the way over the hill at the bus terminal, it's a long and winding way from Klapparstígur home to Freyjugata via the wilderness that is Öræfi, a six-hundred-and-fifty-kilometer detour... admittedly, I always take the long way home; ever since I was a kid, I've wandered around and goofed off despite the fact that my mother repeated every morning as I left for the day that I must come *straight home*, straight home, my friend, my mother said every morning when I went to school, but I *never* came straight home, I always larked about and I will always lark about, I always take the longest route possible home, I will lark my way to the grave... and yet I also have the feeling I've wasted time, that my whole life has been a waste of time, I wasted time and it's too late to do anything about it, I finished school late, didn't know what I wanted, still don't, I didn't stick to any one job, I've got nothing, I've never been able to have a successful relationship with another person, I have a constant feeling of guilt, I'm young but I feel old, I'm old yet think I'm young... Back then things took longer than today: whenever we could, i.e. during school holidays, Kiddi and I took the green bus out into eternity, at the time the bus took nine hours from

Reykjavík to Öræfi; it now takes four hours by automobile. Still, that was a breakthrough, when the rivers were bridged and the sands, even if it wasn't asphalt nearly all the way, just narrow, bumpy gravel roads, the bus larked about and perhaps still does these days, back then bus trips were very hazardous in winter, one had to stop at great cliffs and cross torrential rivers and put chains on the bus, sometimes we were stranded overnight somewhere in a storm and the bus company was forced to buy us accommodation in a hotel; I'd never stayed in a hotel, what a glory to stay in a hotel, I thought, clutching this foreign sensation to me, as a vacation from reality, I felt I'd finally become an independent being in the world. Being weather-bound inside a hotel in the countryside in a snowstorm is one of the best memories of my youth, said The Regular on the way over the hill, I can always remember exactly the feeling when I've been weather-bound, you recognize your own foundations, can descend to the very bottom, the calm becomes tangible, you read a book and you remember that book, the feeling of reading, the book becomes part of your person and is meaningful for the whole of your life, no matter what the book is, in fact, no matter what you do, reading a book or listening to weather reports on the radio or lying there silent, listening to the storm, life becomes filled with lyrical meaning, the storm isolates your character and holds it together, and before you know it you're fearing the weather has died down, that the bus is leaving, that time is scant. I prayed to God for the weather to worsen, to remain that way for a week, a moderately long eternity, enough to read the entire bookcase in the front lounge, although all the books at the hotel at the time were perfect for that place at that moment.

Our departure from the bus terminal, BSÍ, took place early Friday morning, and we were all there, I, The Regular, Kiddi, and Worm Serpent; in fact, we had not even separated, just went right from the bar over the hill and down to the bus rank with my trunk in tow, making only a brief stop at Guesthouse Northern Lights on Freyjugata, where I cleared my room and settled my account; The Regular had no need to go into his room since all Kiddi's stuff was out east, Worm Serpent didn't need anything but the light jacket he was wearing, indeed, he didn't have anything but the things on him, a worn leather bag with a few copies of his poetry books, a wallet, and the things in his pockets. I'm basically nothing but a dustjacket, said Worm Serpent, evidently distressed, I slip it off and there's nothing more to me. The bus was short and tall, it was the bus used in the winter even though spring had arrived, you never know the weather out in the country, the roads, the bus was green and the words *Eastern Way* were written on it; we were the sole passengers. The Regular sat at the front with the driver; he snatched up the microphone and became a guide for the benefit of me, the tourist.

Our way first lies east over Hellisheiði, The Regular said into the microphone, which is an underrated beauty; on Hellisheiði Eggert and Bjarni marveled at the unexpected beauty as they passed through around the middle of the 18th century. But Reykjavíkers don't see this beauty, they see just mines and outgrowth, things which are in reality destructive and wasteful: the beauty in Eggert and Bjarni's eyes has been dug into and drilled and useless roads crisscross the torn-up moss and lava while endless pipes and power lines and high voltage towers are all over the place, there are also impassable routes and muddy water-holes, there are half-mountains, open-cast mining and nothing but facilities and factories, all monuments to the fate of Icelandic nature. Beyond the heath is Hveragerði, where you find massive hot springs, pillows of steam that rise to the heavens—but a stench lies over the settlement due to the burning sulfur fumes, they swell your thyroid, dandruff falls on your shoulders, sweat beads on your forehead, the poet seeks to shape this into the poetic spirit's dwelling when it is in reality a poisonous vapor, inside the huge greenhouses druggies crawl around the tomatoes, hunting about under the heat lamps, sensitive to cold, the frequent earthquakes cause the greenhouses to explode and broken glass rains on the town, Hveragerðings are readily recognizable by abrasions and scratches wherever they go. Halfway between Hveragerði and Selfoss is Kotstrandarkirkja, which is called Flói, or the Gulf, and there are magical shifts in the light, a profound natural beauty that only artists with honed eyes know how to appreciate, there you find Ingólfsfjall, on which mountain the Icelandic settler Ingólf Arnarson was buried at his own request so he could watch Flói's light show in the afterlife; by the side of the road men are at work destroying the mountain with never-ending mining so that this memorial to Iceland's settlement might crumble, this *holy mountain* sacred to adventurers and poets, this *Northern Parnassus* which is being sundered by systematic work that destroys the nation itself, it's an autopsy of the settler so that we might see the anatomy of our national character destroyed, ensuring nothing can be learned from it, it's one thing to examine the land and another to dig a mine, well... under the mountain is Grýluskyr, blue cliffs in front of which stands Kögurnarhóll, inside which Ingólf Arnarson's ship is buried; the road takes us between Grýluskyr and Kögurnarhóll, there, ideas frequently strike anyone open to them; a young Ludwig Wittgenstein rode through here on horseback with his concubine and had the idea for *Tractatus Logico-Philosophicus*, the solution occurred to Wittgenstein as he rode through the gate between Grýluskyr and Kögurnarhóll, he gesticulated wildly and called out to the glowing moor: The foundations of arithmetic are creaking now, maestro!—because in *Tractatus*, Wittgenstein refutes the teachings of Guðleif Frege, his mentor; Frege was afraid of Wittgenstein and moreover a terrible anti–Semite, so he sent Wittgenstein to Bernhard Russell in the UK, who told him that he should rebuild Jerusalem in Albion and all the Jews should leave for there. Guðleif Frege had spent all his long academic life building a foundational mathematical system for the world and language but when Wittgenstein, Frege's student, was riding here between the blue rocks of the settler's mountain and the ship's tomb, free from Russell, he got the idea for the *Tractatus* and swept his mentor from the table of Western thought... it does not pay to offend Jews, The Regular said over the bus's microphone; no one gets ideas here any more and moreover the moorland has been dried up by trench-digging so it no longer glitters under a lone sunbeam in Fló like before. The *Blue Book* is dedicated to Grýluskyr because it owes a debt to the blue cliffs, in the *Blue Book* Wittgenstein addresses at length *sub rosa* the beauty of changing light and sunbeams in Fló; the academic community has managed to miss that completely.

Then we cross over Ölfusárbrú—the bridge over the river Ölfus—and stop at the shop in Selfoss for ten minutes, as is unfortunately customary. The Regular fell silent for a while as we drove away from the place, everyone wanting to sleep; I saw a sign on the road, it seemed like a coat of arms rather than a road sign, spears and halberds in a cross, the purring of the bus and its dandling suspension had a strange effect on me, the slopes and mountain sights, the map indicating destructive forces all around, Hekla, Katla, I felt like an army of women was besieging us... Now we're driving past Rangárvelli, said The Regular suddenly into the microphone, hoarse and mumbling, Þríhyrningur rises up here, a mysterious triangular mountain about which men know nothing. Then he stopped again, perhaps he had been asleep and had started talking in his sleep, finally we're arriving at the site of Njál's Saga where heroes once rode about the province showing off their ornaments and scarlet robes lined with gold and jasmine, this old dream of mine. I meant to get a hot dog in Selfoss, said Worm, when's the next stop, the poet stood up and eased himself along the corridor to tell The Regular he wanted a hot dog. A stuffed skin tube drowned in sauce! cried The Regular into the bus microphone, at Hvolsvollur there's a large shop, he said, fatherly and reassuring, there's nothing but one big shop and a slaughterhouse, it's a memorial to our Golden Age, a 20-minute stop at the shop which is named after the farm of one of the greatest heroes in Icelandic history, after his fate and history. We drove on, went under Eyjafjall and stopped at Skógar, over which the collector and elder Þórður Tómasson reigns; he played the pump organ for us and sang *Now Lingers Only Peace*, a song by your country's own Mozart, Þórður told me, *Sehnsucht nach dem Frühlinge*, a longing for spring, certainly appropriate since a late snow and cold spell was actually delaying the arrival of spring; we met the regional veterinarian, Dr. Lassi, an imposing woman (Dr. Lassi startles but keeps writing down what's being interpreted) ... a third man, Þrasi, who settled in Skógar, according to *Landnám*, was there in spirit, but the Cultural Heritage Officer for the Suðurlands, a sturdy, strong fellow, and all these gentlemen plus Dr. Lassi sang *Now Lingers Only Peace* to the tune of Mozart as Þórður pumped on the organ with great dexterity, not sparing the knee paddles; the stanza was sung over and over again until everyone started crying, we then sauntered over to the church and sang some hymns as a spiritual salve to clean away all our secular trash, like when Hindus bathe in the cloudy Ganges River, *Praise Our God the Lord*; a hymn especially for me, *Gott erhalte Franz den Kaiser*, first in German and then in Icelandic; and *Psalm over Wine*. We sang: God caused bounteous grapes to grow, wanted joy for a solemn world ... then Þórður disappeared; no one knew what had become of him and the meeting broke up. It's in archivists' natures to disappear and appear to everyone's surprise. After this unexpected concert, everyone returned to the passenger bus full of inspiration from Þórður and Þrasi in Skógar, a daily bread through the centuries. Now we will drive through Mýrdal, The Regular said into the microphone, a moist, green, fruitful valley, past the volcano Katla, she sleeps here, everyone sneaks about in the fields and whispers so as not to wake her, she's what foreign languages call a *tyran*; we'll stop at a convenience store in Vík to eat but they only serve hot dogs and hamburgers, french fries and cola, because that's Icelandic food, although it's not food but junk, we'll pause there half an hour before continuing out onto Mýrdalsandur, which is like continuing out into death and the unknown, that's what going out on the sand is, there will be a jökulhlaup if Katla wakes up, Katlahlaups are such fierce floods that the sand would become a single raging ocean, it's good to be able to enjoy life a little in the shop, to do right by oneself and guzzle down a hotdog before you die on the sand and are washed out to sea in rapture.

Our drive takes us next up to Skaftártunga, a soft tongue in an area of high volcanic activity, beautiful countryside made plump from fertile ash where there are extensive pastures; Eldgjá erupted there in 934, opening up a hundred-kilometer long fissure in the ground between two glaciers which became the greatest lava-flood in recorded history, and after that Katla awoke and began to erupt, destroying settlements, changing the weather all across the earth, causing harvests in Europe to fail because of the cold; lakes froze in Persia and men dropped like flies in many parts of the world. Eldgjá is the earth's genitals, The Regular said into the bus's microphone, with Katla at one end, an enormous hump, and Lakagígar at the other end, from where much stuff has spewed forth, these awful women are quite capable of laying waste to the earth and feeding a new Earth in one fell swoop, so you can just imagine where on the body of Mother Earth we find ourselves situated. One time, Kiddi and I were on the bus in winter passing under the Tunga and had to stop at Eldvatn to put chains on the bus because of the snow and icy roads: at the end there were very steep slopes and sharp bends and a rusty bridge but the lake wrestled its way along…Eldvatn, The Regular said into the microphone, have you heard about little Sigga who swam across Eldvatn? Ten-year-old Sigga was entrusted with getting an urgent message to the nearest farm; there was no one at the ferry dock and Eldvatn was a morass of mud, gray from clay, thick and ugly and scabrous due to glacial activity; it sounds completely implausible, but little Sigga floundered over with the message and no one understood how. Then, another time, when little Sigga was at Svínafell in Öræfi, one early autumn, men were standing about in the farmyard and looking up into the mountain where a starving lamb was stuck on a very steep and narrow rock belt; no one had ever been up there and no one remembered if any of the sheep had gotten itself there before the round-up; after having watched closely and intently and for a long time, everyone was heading to sleep; it was a draining activity, looking up at the rocks, and then they got to their feet bright and early to see whether anyone from the farm would be so foolhardy to risk their life for the blessed creature; but in the dawn men adopted new positions in the farmyard in order to be able to look up to the mountain for the sheep amid the grooves; they were astonished to see she had gone, most of them felt an embarrassing relief at the idea the sheep had fallen to her death, because then they could go back in to get a second cup to drink before applying themselves to something else instead of putting their lives and limbs in danger, but look! said The Regular into the microphone so that we startled, little Sigga who swam across Eldvatn was coming down the slope leading the sheep before her and no one could understand how; since that time this impassable route has been called *Siggurák* and little Sigga who swam across Eldvatn has been immortalized in significant place names which are kept in a drawer in a filing cabinet in the Department of Place Names, The Regular said, standing up and nodding to me, the toponymy student who sat back across two seats, his gams thrown into the aisle. The sheep's throat was immediately cut, rather than allowing her to live, a reward for escaping starvation. That's exactly how it is these days. When Kiddi and I took this green bus when we were little, people on it were heading to the farms, there was still life in the rural areas, the bus stopped here and there and you could see the people who lived on the farms, traveling on the bus or meeting their relatives by the road; now, you never see the people who live in rural areas taking the bus, you never see country folk anywhere, there's no one on the bus heading home to their farms, it's just the occasional tourist using the bus...Well, said The Regular, next we're going to drive over Skaftárhraunið from the Laki Craters, it burned in 1783, the largest lava flow in written history, an eruption that caused the deaths of millions of people around the world, from Britain to Japan; harvests failed in Europe and Asia, there was a revolution in France, the Mississippi River froze, something which had never happened since the Ice Age. A toxic haze of sulfuric acid lay throughout the northern hemisphere for years, it was called *móðuharðindi,* the breathless famine; Jón Steingrímsson the Fire Priest wrote about it in *Complete Writings on the Síða Fire,* often called the *Book of Fire,* a contemporary report on the incident; you, Bernharður, should translate it into German or Viennese some time because it's a brilliant report, the most extraordinary thing ever written here in Iceland, it will admittedly be an imperfect translation of the complete writings of Jón the Fire Cleric because he was a great stylist but you're probably something of a stylist: most anyone who could fled Síða when the eruption happened, but Jón stayed to help the people, and he conducted the so-called Fire Sermon as lava approached the church; the lava stopped before the sermon. Katla burned Tungu, Laki burned Síða and the mother's whole body suffered...After this, we'll stop in a shop at Kirkjubaejarklaustur where the Fire Cleric held his famous Mass, not in the shop itself, there were of course no shops back then, though today shops are the countryside's faith, its cultural centers; the fire sermon was declaimed in a large timber church...you're grabbing a hot dog!?...goddamn it!

Hello, hello—followed by the microphone scraping—one two one two—we've reached Síða where Lómagnúpur gnaps out there on the sand, controlling the limits of fate, this great rock head...this great rock head...Hello?...Yes this great rock head was ground out by an ancient sea and the raging of bygone weather!...only the fortunate are still sane once they've passed Lómagnúpur which looms over the traveler, which casts death's shadow over him, making man a mere trifle in existence, The Regular said over the microphone...here, too, we find Núpstaður, the last town before we drive onto the Skeiðarársandur. Here was where the road used to end, there by the waters, and you had to be escorted across on horses that were suited to water, at Núpstaður the tourist industry managed to change older brothers and self-respecting people into freaks and exhibition pieces, but that's another story, one so sad I can't think about it... here Öræfi in all its glory appears across the sand and the water... and just then I suddenly fell asleep, an uncontrollable sleep, says Bernharður; I dreamed the giant Járngrím had stepped out of the rock Lómagnúpur and stabbed downward with his staff, the road between his legs; the bus ran under his groin out across the sand, he called my name and his voice was cold and deep, then he said *Worm Serpent* something and seemed to want the dwarf dead too, even all poets, he spoke an old language I didn't understand, and when we drove onto the sand, I felt like I was traveling over the open flesh of the earth, that we were viruses in the bus seeking admission in order to drag our mothers to death, the glacial rivers were red as blood and viscous, the surf from the waves striking rocks visible like a dragon's ridged back, the blurry steam snaking up, turning the sky black and yellow while the glacier glowed with the humidity, the bus will meet its end on the sand, I thought in my dream, we're all going to die... through my drowsiness I could hear The Regular had the microphone on and was speaking about paradise, how Skeiðarársandur was paradise, the foundation of life and destruction, that Skeiðarársandur was *real country*, the sand was the revelation of the world, its essence, the spiritual particles of the world stripped bare... Here you can see a great wonder, The Regular said into the microphone, and I woke up in an instant, in the middle of the sands a new forest springs up where human intervention never could, he continued, it's like a fairy tale, it's reason enough to abolish the Icelandic State Forest Service, Skógrækt, immediately, to throw the Director of the State Forest Service into prison for crimes against nature, in large areas birch trees are emerging, they come from the seeds of Bæjarstaðarskógur, the most beautiful forest in Iceland, with full-grown birch trees, with distinctive, upright trunks, and light enough to use for shafts, like spear shafts and pointed staffs, the region's name comes from the nature of Bæjarstaðarskógur. Skaftafellssýsla, this perfect forest on Skeiðarársandur will be destroyed in the impending jökulhlaup and come to nothing, and in that sense perfect.

I looked out the window of the bus at Öræfi; how colossal this glacier is, I thought, the mountains seem small next to it, though they are large and tall and terrible; one sees how under this marvel miniscule houses nap; people live in them, steadfast beneath this snow-covered threat.

Here you see an old refuge hut, The Regular said, associated with a sad story everyone tries to forget. Back when the rivers were the greatest obstacles and the locals accompanied tourists across the sand, they *read* streams, the rivers were like an ever-changing text across the sand, one that constantly needed to be reviewed, they read the waves striking the rocks in the stream, used that to ascertain the state of the bed at that moment, saw whether it was sandy or made up of large stones, they assessed the depth and force of the stream from the current, and in this way they found a way across, for the rivers had no fords, changing permanently, never the same, discussing Heraclitus's river philosophy, ideas proposed and debated for how to cross, fierce arguments flowing back and forth all day, ways across being tested out; everything was bound up with nature's uncertainty, and so the people of the water developed their knowledge and culture, but that's now come to an end with the bridges over the rivers, the fixed fords over ordinary rivers are nothing like this, there was solid knowledge and certainty and no need to wonder, the people of the water saw what others did not see, death approaching on the one hand, a way across on the other; however, a reading knowledge of the language of currents saved many lives each year, the lives of tourists who would otherwise have gotten into danger—but that language is now extinct ... and here we are rushing across an elevated road over a bridge over a river without noticing, crossing the Skeiðará, the greatest destroyer in any of the Nordic countries, The Regular announced over the bus microphone as we drove onto the bridge, she is the head of the Öræfing beast, rarely mentioned by name, they made their knowledge of her into a sport and a science and then an art, she floods approximately every 10 years, the last big flood was in 1996 and was jokingly called the television flood, it sent out a message via a brutal eruption after which a colossal amount of water collected in the glacier; foreign reporters flocked to Iceland, but the Skeiðará flood still had not happened weeks later, the correspondents and videographers grew tired of waiting and went home disappointed, *then* the Skeiðará flooded, routing everything before it with its incredible burden of ice and mass of water, the road vanished as though it had never existed and with it all the elegant bridges across the sand, everything returned to ancient times, and I remember thinking it terribly entertaining, as domestic reporters and freelancers gave detailed accounts of the disaster and sold their copy around the world, the Skeiðará becomes an ocean when it floods, and large blocks calve from the glacier and they rush out onto the sand, borne by the water, when the flood subsides icebergs stand on the sand and can take years to melt, once they are gone they leave so-called *ker* or "pots" in the sand, places that are hollow under the sand, dangerous quagmires, many men and horses have sunk in these pots and in bygone times the route across the sand meandered between such craters, The Regular said over the bus's microphone, and one more thing I'd like to tell you, Bernharður, you must understand, there are so-called channels formed in glaciers, rock belts formed by the glacier moving, you need to know these things: *streaks* on the advancing glaciers, current-born *sediment* in the glacial water, kettle *pots* on the sand. Knowing that, you should always be able to cope.

Then we were suddenly at the Skaftafell Visitor Center; I jumped up and dashed out, making for my trunk which was in the bus's luggage compartment, I'd fixed off-road tires to my trunk for the trip to Iceland, I had thought about staying in the trunk, because there was plenty of room, inside I would have had the enormous quantity of books purchased at Bragi thanks to The Regular's guidance. I also had with me a large sail-canvas tent so I could set up a table and chair and sit down to write and work on my research. I'd taken pains to be well prepared, not wanting to be like some travelers in Öræfi about whom The Regular had told me: not long ago a twenty-six-year-old tourist from the UK went hiking on Hvannadalshnjúk, the highest peak of Öræfajökull, the highest peak in the country, one of the most dangerous volcanoes in the world, wearing just jeans and a leather jacket and without provisions; the farmer's wife at Hof insisted the man pack a lunch but he refused, saying he was going to live on berries, he'd heard Iceland boasted an enormous quantity of berries, but first of all not a lot of berries grow out on the glacier and secondly he was traveling in mid-January, and berries appear in late August, the farmers warned him, told him that at this time of year the weather was evil, the next day they were slammed by a blizzard and the tourist vanished immediately, a search got underway, everyone was called out, a helicopter searching the glacier, many groups of hikers, three snowmobiles called Gusi, Grendill and Kuggur, several snow sleds, the armored dragon itself ferried men between places in hostile weather, the search conditions were terrible, rescue teams from throughout the South, two hundred people, they all looked but the man in the leather jacket was nowhere, a few days later the weather dropped and the snow thawed and the farmer over at Hof was taking out the trash and found him dead below the road. Yet it's common to never find bodies, because many fall into the cracks and end up a microscopic redness under the glacier, disappearing, though anything metal surfaces from under the creeping glacier a long time later, flattened like a pancake; and so, said The Regular, I let you buy all these books in Bragi so you will not end like all the rest, so you can read up before you go out onto the mountain, these days everyone has such sophisticated equipment but no knowledge, in the past, the equipment might have been so-so but the knowledge was greater, when Kiddi went up to Hvannadalshnjúk on Öræfajökull with regional farmers, he did head across in sneakers and jeans, he had thermal underwear with him and put it on over his clothes when he was getting cold on the glacier, because he could not bear the thought of taking off the jeans in the cold to put the underwear underneath, and he didn't think the equipment was poor, the expedition manager, said Kiddi, he was in rubber boots.

I went to the countryside with Kiddi whenever I could, The Regular said, standing in the car park at Skaftafell, Kiddi always just calls Öræfi the country, want to come to the country with me? Kiddi would ask, yes, I'd say and we would go to the country. I began calling Öræfi the country, it quickly became my only country, although strictly speaking it wasn't mine, I didn't have a country, but Öræfi provided the youthful adventures that shaped me as a person for life... I remember when I first came here: I had never been on such a long journey, and when Öræfi faced us across the sand, it was an utter demarcation of the world, glaciers, mountains, canyons, forests, plains, sands, the shore, the sea. First, we went with Kiddi's grandfather to the sheep barn to attend to the sheep, it was a rustic structure with piled walls and gables out on the plain amid overgrown rocks which dated back to the catastrophic floods of 1362; it was constructed out of beach driftwood and has since been torn to pieces, with nothing good set in its place. While his grandfather fed and watered the animals, Kiddi wanted to show off for his new friend, peeling away from the spot in a jeep and reeling around the barn; by one of the corners he drove over a stone boulder and the car pitched onto two wheels and he drove like that too long, I thought, he was leaning toward the slope at the bottom of which I stood, looking up, amazed by it all, Kiddi looking back at me from the jeep's window, concerned, concentrating, I saw it was even odds that either the car would overturn and he would roll down the slope toward me, or else, as happened, the car would thump back down onto its tires, Kiddi drove in a circle and returned the car back to the sheep barn, I came running, we were both scared and sheepish and ran giggling in to help his grandfather attend to the livestock. Because of everything we were laughing so much that we couldn't hold onto the bundles of hay but Kiddi's grandfather did not understand what the hell had gotten into us, although he didn't interfere. Next we walked along the beach, with a rifle and a shotgun we'd pilfered from the farm, we borrowed the jeep from Kiddi's grandfather, because it was small and light the jeep glided across the wet sand well whereas larger SUVs sometimes sank like sugar cubes in coffee, swallowed up, no trace of them ever seen again, the sand was deathly sweet, if you could make a cross-section scan of Skeiðarársand it would be like a hazelnut chocolate bar, I'm just realizing this now, given all the cars and ships in the sand, many kinds, Kiddi always drove the jeep at lightning speed, and sometimes it jumped and we were slung about like two dice in a tupperware, we drove around like this and walked the shore all day, we jabbered on about girls in school, who had the largest breasts, that sort of thing, we jabbered about bands and jabbered about movies, we ran along the shoreline and played with the two dogs who were along with us, we bowled with the spherical floats from fishing nets, we pulled ropes up out of the sand and got burns on our palms, we threw cans into the air and lobbed stones at them, we fooled around, we opened a small bottle we found and tried to analyze its bitter salt taste, was booze, we drew caricatures in the sand, we laughed and lazed about on driftwood logs, we composed little rhymes, Kiddi came up with the words and I arranged them into verses, we saw a group of tiny sanderlings on the beach, we had the idea to shoot at the birds from long range in order to kill some without damaging them too much, because we wanted to stuff a bird and put it in our collection, a sandpiper, but how to kill it without damaging them too much? I asked, by shooting them from long range, Kiddi said, I considered Kiddi a tremendous naturalist and tried to learn as much as possible from him, Kiddi collected and blew eggs, he had a huge egg collection housed in several large ski-boot boxes; he'd lined the boxes with cotton and marked the eggs with tiny handwritten labels, and I myself started to collect eggs and blow them and transplant them into cardboard boxes, just like he did. Kiddi had learned the method off Hálfdán from Tvísker, Kiddi gathered eggs and then Hálfdán helped him, I gathered eggs and Kiddi helped me, Kiddi collected skulls and I collected skulls, Kiddi collected bird feet and stood them taut on corks with pins to fix them in their proper shape, as Hálfdán taught him to do, and I collected bird feet and did the same thing, Kiddi collected skeletons and I collected skeletons, Kiddi collected insects like Hálfdán but that's where I drew the line, I couldn't imagine collecting bugs, I was too spoiled for that, being raised in Reykjavík. Kiddi studied theory with Hálfdán from Tvísker who was generous with his knowledge and treated little Kiddi as an equal, taught him handcrafts and explained his own work, inducted him into study, and Kiddi shared the knowledge he got from Hálfdán with me, The Regular said there in the carpark at Skaftafell, not without pride, Hálfdán is the greatest ornithologist and entomologist and botanist who ever lived and

he's completely self-taught, which makes all the difference, there
have been several great natural scientists in Iceland and Hálfdán is
one of them, at the beginning we should mention the poet Eggert
Ólafsson and also Bjarni Palsson *landphysicus*, they pioneered modern natural science, then Ólaf Olavius, also your doctor friend
Sveinn Pálsson, Jónas Hallgrímsson the poet, the poet Benedikt
Gröndal, followed by Þorvald Thoroddsen and Dr. Helgi Pjeturs
though they quarreled about móberg tuffs and breccia rock, a
reasonable dispute, and next Bjarni Sæmundsson after whom the
research vessel was named, then Hálfdán from Tvísker and then
Kiddi and finally me. So you see how short the thread is between
me and Eggert Olafsson, Hálfdán taught me through Kiddi,
Bjarni Sæmundsson taught me through Hálfdán and Kiddi, Dr.
Helgi Pjeturs taught me through Bjarni Sæmundsson, Hálfdán
from Tvísker and Kiddi, Þorvald Thoroddsen taught me through
Dr. Helgi Pjeturs, Bjarni Sæmundsson, Hálfdán from Tvísker and
Kiddi, Benedikt Gröndal taught me through Þorvald
Thoroddsen, Dr. Helgi Pjeturs, Bjarni Sæmundsson, Hálfdán
from Tvísker and Kiddi, Jónas Hallgrímsson taught me through
Benedikt Gröndal, Þorvald Thoroddsen, Dr. Helgi Pjeturs,
Bjarni Sæmundsson, Hálfdán from Tvísker and Kiddi, Sveinn
Pálsson taught me through Jónas Hallgrímsson, Benedikt
Gröndal, Þorvald Thoroddsen, Dr. Helgi Pjeturs, Bjarni
Sæmundsson, Hálfdán from Tvísker and Kiddi, Ólaf Olavius
taught me through Sveinn Pálsson, Jónas Hallgrímsson, Benedikt
Gröndal, Þorvald Thoroddsen, Dr. Helgi Pjeturs, Bjarni
Sæmundsson, Hálfdán from Tvísker and Kiddi, Bjarni Palsson
landphysicus taught me through Ólaf Olavius, Sveinn Pálsson,

Jónas Hallgrímsson, Benedikt Gröndal, Þorvald Thoroddsen, Dr. Helgi Pjeturs, Bjarni Sæmundsson, Hálfdán from Tvísker and Kiddi, and Eggert Ólafsson taught me through Bjarni Pálsson, Ólaf Olavius, Sveinn Pálsson, Jónas Hallgrímsson, Benedikt Gröndal, Þorvald Thoroddsen, Dr. Helgi Pjeturs, Bjarni Sæmundsson, Hálfdán from Tvísker and Kiddi, and so I feel often like I'm talking to Eggert Ólafsson when I'm talking to Kiddi, though I didn't think that back then because we didn't have a clue who Eggert and Bjarni were, we were only eleven, but when I think back ... I pointed the gun at the middle of the group of sanderlings on the beach and fired, after the report I ran with Eggert to the target, small sanderlings writhed about fatally wounded, some with only one foot, others with one wing, bleeding and carrying themselves lamely. Swelling with fear and excitement I fired another shot immediately on the run from close range in order to end this heap of suffering on the sand, after the second pop there were no birds, just a hole in the sand and feather ribbons wafting slowly through the air like artificial snow ... silence on the sand ... Eggert Ólafsson was angry with me, Bjarni Pálsson, because I had destroyed the raw material for stuffing, because I had been so excited, unable to control myself, you never have any self-control, Bjarni, said Eggert; moreover, in the excitement I'd handed him a loaded, cocked rifle and Eggert looked down the barrel and was lucky not to receive a ball through his head, which would have been an irreparable loss for the nation in future ... for all this, Kiddi got angry and Hálfdán too and all the other natural scientists were pissed at me for not being suitably scientific.

When we were not set a task or chore, shoveling out the stable, picking up trash, stacking bales, we'd ride around up to the mountain and each day was an adventure, we went on a mission out into peat landslips looking for fossils, we looked for nests and recorded the birds we'd see, if we saw or found something important, for example the time we found a dead Eurasian woodcock in the woods, then Kiddi rang Hálfdán from Tvísker and gave him the account, I found it incomparably more fun learning the difference between an Amami woodcock and a Eurasian woodcock than shoveling shit from the outbuilding. It was big news in Öræfi the time Kiddi saw the white dove flying over the mountain slopes and heading east over the outbuilding, a great wonder, no one had ever seen a white dove in Öræfi before, we immediately decided to try to catch her, and found it wasn't enough to throw a coat over her the way we caught the pigeons down by the pond in Reykjavík before taking them home by bus; the white dove was afraid and kept itself a fair distance from the farm, we each grabbed the blade of an old plough, hurried over to the storage shed, applied ourselves diligently to using the grinder, sparks flying as we sharpened our blades deliberately to razor sharp tips at the top, and then we went on the prowl, fishing about in the low willow bushes. We saw a white dove flutter out of a thicket, arc around the barn, and land somewhere in the low grass beyond; we were filled with tingling anticipation as we crawled along the ground, all the way around the barn where we reckoned our prey had landed, almost in ecstasy we saw a flash of white in a bush close by, I trembled all over with excitement, Kiddi sprang to his feet and launched the metal spear with all his strength, I jumped to my feet too, and saw the spear had stabbed through the dove which lay motionless in the bush, dead... we looked on, amazed at what had happened, Kiddi had managed to harpoon the dove, in that great shot's time the world had changed, it was like we could do anything, this world was not such an uncontrollable force after all, we ran over in silence, celebrating only internally for now, trying to act like professional hunters though we couldn't contain our joy, and it turned out to be a white can... a white can in the bush, it was like someone was silently baiting us, I thought God was tricking us, but I was afraid to say the word God aloud in this situation, that's not what hunters do, the iron spike had gone through the can and pinned it to the earth, Kiddi took the can out of the bush and for a long time we looked at the way the spear had punched through it, although we had unintentionally stumbled on the can, we were still filled with awe, we were still great hunters, we looked around us, saw a dove on top of the barn, it took off and flew east along the mountain, perhaps it would visit Hálfdán from Tvísker? She'd get a milder reception there than from us; we ran home and Kiddi asked if he could use the phone and he rang Hálfdán and said he should expect a visitor.

Out past the mire beyond the hayfield, almost all the way out to Skeiðarársandur, Kiddi and I went past a skua nest where an Arctic skua flung himself down at us to protect the eggs; it was light-colored, a variant on the true Nordic variety, much rarer than its dark-feathered cousin, this would be great for you to taxidermy, said Kiddi, I picked up a stone, threw it at the bird as he dived on us, my shot went wide, I threw another rock the next time he dived, it also went past him, it was easier said than done, hitting a bird with stones while he flung himself at us at high speed, screeching, and this went on for such a long time, the skua hurtled at us, I threw stones, the skua dived, I threw stones. Belatedly, when patience was running out and we were about to set off back home, I took a big rock and threw it angrily and hopelessly in the air toward the skua, a dismal thump could be heard as the stone struck its chest, the skua fell to the ground, still alive, we ran to him in a hurry, I was super excited and said we needed to wring its neck right away, so it wouldn't suffer, I'd learned from Kiddi that one should always try to kill animals quickly so they don't suffer unnecessarily, and there was the skua on the ground suffering because I had thrown a boulder-sized stone at him, how do I wring its neck, I asked Kiddi in a frenzy, quick! show me how to wring its neck so he isn't in pain any longer, I cried, Kiddi said it would be best to strangle him, it would damage the skin to twist its neck, I didn't know quite how to do it, do it for me, strangle it, strangleitforme! and Kiddi went in front of me and picked the skua up and I looked on in confusion while Kiddi strangled the skua, it black eyes stared at me in terror, its beak open, its tongue stuck out, its life taking a long time to fade away. The skua's gaze has followed me ever since; sometimes I think that from that moment I brought a curse upon myself, some evil. This moment will be on my conscience forever, The Regular said in the car park at Skaftafell, finally he was dead, Kiddi handed me the bird, we went back past the mire, it was a half-hour walk to the meadow where people were making hay, we were shirking our duties, I held the skua in my arms like

a small infant, I was simultaneously happy and sad. You're holding it too gently! said Kiddi indignantly as we walked into the
meadow, I grabbed it by the feet and tail and dangled it noncha-
lantly the way a real hunter does, we were embarrassed that we
were slacking and not helping farm. I put the skua in the freezer
until we could get to the taxidermist at the Icelandic Natural
History Museum near the bus station, Hlemmur. It cost a fair
bit, and those conscripted into child labor as part of the farming
life didn't get paid—but to gather funds we hunted mink. The
country magistrates and farmers encouraged children and teenagers to hunt and kill all minks and foxes to protect sheep and
the Icelandic ecosystem; we were the watchmen of the natural
republic, we received 1,500 krónur for a tail, which was a lot of
money in those days. I paid the taxidermist 2,500 krónur for his
work on the skua, Kiddi and I had hunted four adult mink in the
summer, you got nothing for pups but they were numerous so we
killed a few by striking them on the head with a stone, the magistrate gave each of us 3,000 krónur for our four minks, I dropped
500 on treats at the Skaftafell Visitor Center where there was a
store, I bought a hamburger and ice cream and cigarettes which
Kiddi and I shared that whole summer.

Kiddi and I wanted to kill Great Skuas, The Regular said
in the carpark, we borrowed the jeep to go over the sand out
to Ingólfshöfði, a really hazardous journey across quicksand and
deep ravines, guided only by stakes standing up from the water,
we had to keep on their right side and gun the gas the whole
time so as not to sink into the sand, it was part of the culture back
then to kill Great Skuas and gulls, ideally in late summer when

the young were typically almost adults but not yet fully fledged, but fat and lazy, we took clubs with us and knocked the young dead under the fierce air raids of their parents, the skua grows big and is a daredevil, fierce and bold, no one can wander the sands during mating season without its attention, the skua is large and powerful, stout-chested, it throws itself at you at high speed and drives you away with fierce strikes of its claws, sometimes with its whole torso, many tourists come off the sand bloody having risked entering the territory of the Great Skua during breeding season, they are stitched back up at the Visitor Center, at other times the bird prefers to winter out on the wide ocean, being a seabird and eating everything he comes across, carcasses and all, he chases and kills any bird he has a mind to and a variety of animals far up into the country, I had a big kitchen knife strapped to me with haybale binding, I felt I looked the part of the hunter, ready for anything, you had to keep your eyes open, you had to look out in all directions, each time a Great Skua flung himself at you you had to throw yourself down between the tussocks, the whining over your head indicated how narrowly you had escaped his strike, once I jumped up and threw the kitchen knife after a skua as he wheeled back toward me, preparing his next dive; the shaft pierced him but the skua did not yield ground, he kept turning and descended again and struck his talons on my the forehead so that I was thrown back and stuck fast between tussocks, I yelled to Kiddi, mortally wounded, bloody in the face, that I had almost hunted an adult skua with a knife! ... in from the skua nests on Ingólfshöfði, Great Black-backed Gulls also laid eggs, the beneficiaries of the Great Skua's military-style patrols, a gull would sometimes fling himself at you, but only in a shallow arc, not coming close but orbiting instead, screeching, hoping that God and the skua would scare the child-murderers away from the breeding ground, we killed seagulls too, it was a dying tradition in the country, nobody ate seagulls any more except Kiddi and me, we plucked them and singed them and baked them whole inside the oven, getting a lot of attention for our seagull-feast, but usually finding ourselves sat alone at our banquet table. One year we came back from the sand with a jeep full of birds and brought food to the whole farm, The Regular said in the carpark at Skaftafell, but Kiddi and I were the last of the 1100-year-old tradition in Öræfi of hunting skua and gulls for food, Ingólf Arnarson began that when he was based on the promontory but Kiddi and I were the last. We stopped once we got interested in girls in Reykjavík and all those things that put a stop to a man's culture.

✝

Now the bus was leaving, said Bernharður, wrote Dr. Lassi, and Kiddi and The Regular and Worm Serpent were stone surprised that I was going to stay in Skaftafell, Kiddi had a newly-built farm in Hálsasker with partitioned rooms on all floors, there's plenty of room for everyone, but I was stubborn and wanted to be left alone, the night before had been quite enough social life for me, I told the entourage, now they were all hopping mad that I wanted to be where the tourists were, hardly any Öræfings go into Skaftafell any more, said The Regular, only tourists, Skaftafell is no longer Skaftafell, it's a distortion, come with us! There's a chieftain's place in Svínafell, where Flosi lived, your friend from *Njáls Saga*, it's not right for a chief like yourself to stay on the campsite at Skaftafell, a chieftain, an aristocrat, a prestigious scholar from Vienna, in Hálsker you'd have your own private room with views out into the infinite, it is absolutely doomed being on a campsite where you can't see a thing but the next person's ugly tent, with us you'd have the whole of Öræfi to yourself. I'd already decided to stay in Skaftafell and would not change it.

You don't want to stay in Flosi's cave? asked Kiddi, there's a view of the entire Skeiðarársand and you'd have the whole ocean and the sky as your property.

It's a tempting offer, I said.

This is an appalling trunk you have, said Worm Serpent, he'd had a drink or two and had stopped stuttering, it reminds me of my grandmother's trunk, but I have to admit that it's many times larger, and with off-road wheels!

Don't you have any bags? I asked Worm.

Just my jacket, said Worm, it's all I have, baggage is spiritual, my baggage is an affliction, two large canvas sacks full of the past and my afflictions ... Oh, Ö-Öræfi inside me, an empty city, ruins and sorrows ...

I bid farewell to the men at the bus stop and said I would stop by Hálsasker on my way east, but for now I needed to attend to my studies.

Well and good! The Regular said, loud and clear.

A man is composed of everyone who's shared his path, I told myself, overwhelmed by my weighty trunk, an extension of my body, but it's nothing compared to Captain Koch's luggage, I tried to cheer myself with that, the trunk on its sturdy tires nonetheless rolled gently forward, at the campsite I found a secluded spot, inside my trunk I had a comforter, a camp stove, pots and pans and plates and cutlery, a whetstone, a compass, matches, a telescope, wool clothes, stationery, notebooks, diaries, papers, study books, dictionaries, books that I couldn't travel without according to The Regular, the travelogue of Eggert Ólafsson and Bjarni Pálsson, the travelogue of Sveinn Pálsson, the travelogue of Ólaf Olavius, the travelogue of Þorvaldur Thoroddsen, the travelogue of Dr. Helgi Pjeturs, it is obvious that one cannot stuff such tomes into a backpack so you need a cumbersome trunk for your journey. When we went to Bragi's bookstore, The Regular made a list of the materials I had to have on a research expedition to Fingurbjörg in Mávabyggðir on Öræfajökull on Vatnajökull in Öræfi in East Skaftafell district in Iceland, as he put it, The Regular said those words firmly to Bragi, the bookseller, told him I was going on a toponymical research expedition to Fingurbjörg in Mávabyggðir on Öræfajökull on Vatnajökull and he wanted me to take without fail every issue of the journal *Skaftfellingur*, all the volumes of the history journal *Blanda: Knowledge Old and New*, the complete magazine *Goðastein* which the civic leaders in Skógar have put out for a half a century with distinction, the region's culture would be impoverished without them, Bragi arranged this all with one move and made me a big package and many little ones, miniature constructions of great beauty and quality, wrapped in construction paper and tied together with hemp rope and netting and placed in this hellishly large and cumbersome trunk which I'd had to leave outside because it wouldn't fit into the store, which was too crowded with books and knowledge, I'd parked the trunk in a parking space and put a ten-krónur piece in the meter, then I returned with the additional purchases of many publications Bragi and The Regular deemed necessary for me to bring to Öræfi, *Findings of the Alþing,* forty volumes, *Government News,* fifty volumes, *Broadcast News,* 100 issues, *Anthology of Charters,* 200 issues, the complete magazine *Weather,* I tipped the whole lot into the trunk and Bragi was glad to be rid of them, he danced and sang amid his stacks and waved his snotrag so that mucus flew out of it in all directions, I said goodbye but the cumbertrunk belched horribly as it digested all these books, as if threatening to vomit them back up over Bragi.

After I'd got set up, turned on the camp stove and put the kettle on, I took a selection of books from the trunk and first read the travel books conscientiously, I wound my way through books by Árni Óli, *Exploring I–XV,* books which apparently cover everything the nation has forgotten; *Annals, 1400–1800,* a refreshing and tasteful stash, *Espól's Yearbooks,* 11 installments, the Registers, aka the *Icelandic Charter Collection* in 16 thick volumes containing letters and deeds and judgments and settlements and other records pertaining to Iceland or Icelandic people from the earliest times to the year 1590, as it stated; there was also the agricultural newspaper *Freyr,* 80 bound volumes, a *Historical Narrative of Mail Delivery,* volume I and volume II, there was *Skaftafell Customs & Place Names, Country Perceptions,* reprinted, also the *Diaries* of William Morris from his time in Iceland, *County Proceedings 1749–1752,* Árni Magnússon's *Land Registrar,* which admittedly omitted the Skaftafell region because Árni was afraid of Lómagnúpur and stopped at that point, he was deadly afraid he would meet the mountain giant Járngrím and become fated to die before he finished the work, Arni was scared for his life because he had substantial work ahead collecting all the manuscripts he could and rescuing Icelandic culture from destruction but laying waste to it in the process, there was also *Women's Studies*, the Sheep Markings List for the Skaftafell District west & east, sixty volumes on unbound sheets that dispersed all over the place in the trunk, The Sheep, The Land, the Nation; The Sheep and the People; Livestock Reports from the South; and the Markings List, 300 issues, Skaftafell district and her citizens and occasional visitors, Skaftfell poetry & skaldic poetry & glosses, one volume, *Hikes & Round-ups I–V, Non-Hikes and Non-Round-ups I–IV, A Different Age, A Better Time, Agricultural Progress for Eternity, Progressives, Sweet and Happy*; the complete magazine *The Mink*, comprising three paper-thin installments brimful of information, the articles Lupine, Friend or Foe? The Book of Tvísker, The Glacial Writings, Skaftafell in Öræfi, Iceland's Thousand Years, The Mountain Book, The Sand Book, The Bird Book, The Flag of Iceland, Icelandic Biographical Dictionary, Distinguished Icelanders … there was no end to it, there were many more books in the trunk than enumerated here, no wonder the trunk was so heavy to lug about, and to set a bow on my account I must mention, last but not least, *Grímnir*, a magazine of place name studies, published by the Toponymy Room at the National Museum of Iceland, every issue and volume was in the suitcase, 1980–1996, I considered this a treasure, a great discovery on the part of The

Regular and Bragi, even if it was only three small volumes; things proceed slowly in the world of names. Then the kettle boiled and I wanted to go and drink tea and think of home and think my way up into the mountains, to think about Mávabyggðir and think about women; mostly, though I wondered, as I gulped down the tea, why had Bragi thrown so many books about sheep into the trunk? I couldn't consider myself a real man without having read all of it; then I'd be ready to travel up to Mávabyggðir like the rest of the Yule Lads.

Not until I had finished reading all the stuff from Bragi would I be spiritually willing to go to Mávabyggðir, I said to myself, not until I understood all this, so I don't end up like those found dead down below. Then Edda the ranger came to charge me and I stone forgot my journey and laughed carelessly at the campsite in Skaftafell and let my studies slide. On the afternoon of Saturday April 12th I left on foot from Skaftafell's Visitor Center, pulling my trunk behind me, in a good mood as I waded Skaftafellsá and Svínafellsá, ignoring the bridges, I walked past Freysnes, where there's a hotel and a supermarket and a gas station serving boiled hot dogs and hamburgers in buns and a great smoky smell. Further east lies Svínafell, where Flosalaug is heated by the burning of tourist trash in an old fox farm; beautiful blue clouds lie over the settlement like the spirits of murdered foxes. Here, in Svínafell, is the best weather anywhere, the sources say.

As I walked out of Skaftafell National Park, I was amazed to come across the Öræfings, Eggert Ólafsson and Bjarni Pálsson's *Travelogue* still with me; according to The Regular they are great friends to men, animal lovers, plant lovers, lovers of stones, Eggert and Bjarni both say that Öræfings are the most perfect men in Iceland, gentle, silent, quiet, the least polluted; they speak the clearest, most perfect language due to their isolation.

I threaded my way south in Destrikt, which is down in sandstone flatlands; tourists can rent horses there, because government subsidies to farmers are certainly not enough to get by on. I rented 5 horses. These are all strong water horses, the farmer at Destrikt said, the tourists usually get nags, but because you are going to go to the glacier, I will equip them with spiked hooves and snowshoes. I wanted to pay him in euros but he did not want to see them, just krónur! What the hell would I do with euros? said the farmer, black with grease, barely paying attention to me, busy trying to loosen a screw from something. Fortunately, I had a whole stack of hundred-krónur coins I'd won on the one-arm bandit at the bus terminal the morning we left, and I offered the farmer the coins, it was the only Icelandic currency I had, they were not worth as much as the euros, they'd said so at the bank, he struggled and swore at the stuck screw and said he had never been to a bank and did not want to as long as he lived, banks are coffins, he said, sweaty from the screw. Perhaps it's the other direction, I said, but the farmer's patience cracked and he snapped at me, do you think I don't know which way to screw!?...Then he said he needed material to cast nails anyway; he led me into his smithy where he dumped all the hundred-krónur coins down into the container and melted them and began to cast nails but told me to scram with my trunk and said he would grab hold of both my nipples if I didn't treat the horses well, twist them, rip them off, but where did you learn

to speak Icelandic? the farmer asked...back home in Vienna,
I said...You speak like a horse with its mouth full of bread, he
said and laughed deep down...I said I had come to record place
names...Record place names? asked the farmer outraged, record
the places names for whom? They're fixed to the mountains and
everywhere, they stand written there, they won't benefit anyone
in books, place names are only useful to those who own livestock,
you don't learn place names unless you use them, what's that you
have in your hand? It's a walking stick, I answered the farmer, I
read that you couldn't go anywhere in Öræfi except with a good
walking stick...That's a broomstick! he said and shook violently,
are you planning to sweep the names off the mountains? You're as
good as dead if you're going to walk about in the mountains with
this reed, you need a proper pole, for damn's sake, you can bor-
row this one, he said, and handed me a big pole, I had read about
such broad Skaftafell staffs in some of the books, I don't remember where...This is a handsome stick, I said, trying to hold it
confidently...This isn't a *stick*! Never call a pole a stick, a pole is
a pole and not a stick, you can call this broom handle of yours
a stick, in my eyes it's nothing but the stalk of a pole, it might
just suffice to pick my teeth...Then the farmer took my walking stick and broke it into pieces and threw it into the fire so that
the hundred-krónur coins simmered...It seemed strange to me
that all the shelves and slats of the smelter were clear, but the floor
was covered with tools, so that I was standing on tools, the man
seemed to know exactly where the tongs or screwdrivers were,
the crescent wrench, every nut and every bolt even though he
threw everything away from him in such a way that being nearby

was high risk ... It's good to get the hundred-krónurs; I was really short of nails, said the farmer in Destrikt, there's a boy here, some fool Southerner from Reykjavík and he is cleaning the nails out of rotten wood for me and fetching me the nails but he is so lazy and has taken so long doing it that I'm forced to cast more nails ... this boy thinks he's here on vacation, he just wants to laze about or wander off in the mountains, watching birds and staring into thin air, but there's plenty of tasks to do and no need for a dreamer, we must collect the timber that was used to shape the concrete for the new outbuilding and clean the timber of its nails, not count birds on the sand or measure the height of the trees in the woods, if he wants to do that he ought to go into Tvísker country, where men lie in bed all day and pick their noses and nothing achieves anything.

    I set two horses in front of the trunk and climbed on it, using it as a wagon; I left the other three tied to the tailgate behind. I took a big Vienna Cake and gave it to the farmer when I left; that cheered him up and he danced about on the slope with the cake. I hurried back to Hálsasker, where they all were, The Regular and Worm Serpent, having a high old time at the farm. The farm is named for the place, said Kiddi, the place name "Hálsasker" is composed of two geographical phenomena, háls, or neck, and sker, or skerry, a neck indicates a slope or a hill, a skerry usually means a crag in the sea, but here it has a special Skaftafell-ish meaning, a rock that is cut out from itself, though you can't find a rock outcrop here any longer, there's no crag because everything has grown ... Sker has transcended its meaning of a sea-crag, said The Regular, just as on land the neck transcends the body, that's

what a sker is on land, for example a low, flat rock in the vegetation, a belt of rock, of bare rock, on the glacier, that's the idea of
sker, the surface of sker, which goes beyond its original meaning
to become a symbol, where before at the edge of the neck there
was flaky, naked rock there's now abundant growth, especially
angelica, back in the day you had to go all the way to Hvannadal
to get angelica, now no one collects this medicinal herb any longer, angelica is really healthy, a useful herb, good-tasting, similar
to cumin, the root has saved many from hunger and was thought
a delicacy, the leaves saved people from scurvy, it's always said
that lamb saved this nation's life over the centuries, but angelica
protected people's lives, today no one thinks about it although
it blossoms across the meadows, angelica is chopped down and
thrown away, not even good for animal fodder, considered ugly,
this weed instead gets torn up at the roots or poisoned; it's a
shame, all this angelica, say modern farmers, since they know
nothing about herbs, just toxins and chemical powders ... today
you get laughed at if you eat something that grows in nature.

Back-solutions is common in toponymy, right, Bernharður,
asked The Regular, and sometimes correct, but also sometimes
idiotic ... don't you have the *Annals* in your trunk? We can just
open it up and review things, that's an excellent starting point, it'd
be refreshing to look through the Annals 1400–1800 over coffee,
the Annals have it, said The Regular. In 1362, Öræfajökull
destroyed all the Province's names and the Province itself, I mean
its name, no volcano had ever before done that anywhere in the
world, so if the place name came from after 1800, old men would
know how it came about, would have learned from their

grandmothers or grandfathers...the old reckonings...here it is!
I think...the year 1586 saw three moons in the sky with one
solar ring, that winter the strange event took place at the sacred
site of Hólar in Hjaltadal: a teenager, Vigfús Jónsson, a priest's son,
who had been in school but now worked for the printer, cut his
own throat over the altar in the Holy Church; the year 1611 witnessed a darkening of the sun, a sad event befell a husband in
Sámsstaðir in South Iceland, Jón Símonsson, a god-fearing man,
an honest, upright and well-behaved man, he laid hands on himself early in the morning on Saturday, January 19th, the next
Sunday he got to his feet with the other locals and prayed as
usual, after which he left home and didn't return, people searched
for him that night and found him dead in the morning near the
farm, his right hand was a bloody stump, beside him lay a knife
bigger than a butcher's knife pooling in the blood and on his
neck there was a big gaping wound all the way into the bone; on
February 24th a man cut his own throat at Fljótshlíð, he was
called Þorvarður, from the south, he was wounded with a food
knife but was saved; a priest from the north, Rev. Stefán
Guðmundsson, at Undirfell in Vatnsdal, stabbed his own throat
with a food knife, greatly indisposed and evilly tempted, he died;
the water in Reyðarfjörður turned bloody; a woman in Suðureyri
gave birth to a deformed child and immediately stabbed herself
with a knife, soon after, her husband drowned himself in the sea;
the monster in the Hvítá was clearly seen by many, looming out
of the water like a colossus, the serpent moved up and down
along the riverbed but had a base camp in a thunderous whirl-
pool or bottomless hollow; in 1619 at Hlíðarend in Fljótshlíð a

man who was alone cut his throat and died; another stabbed himself to death in Landeyja, not far away; a woman cut her throat in Laugardalshólar in October; 1620 witnessed a large bloody color in the sea around Eyjafjörður; in the year 1621 a man hanged himself, Tyrfing by name, from Vatnsholt in Staðarsveit; in Flatey one Sunday around mass after people had confessed and were going to sip from the chalice, a man rushed out from the church and drove himself into the sea; a man hanged himself in Fljótshlíð; in 1623, three weeks before Christmas, a water-serpent was seen in the Hvítá two evenings in a row after sunset; the first evening he rose up as two curves across the river, breaking up the ice, so the river flowed on land, the second night the worm rose up in a coil near the middle of Hestfjall; that year a man hanged himself at Hlíðarenda, Gísli Jónsson by name; in 1624, a woman hanged herself at Eyjafjall; 1626 at Hlíðarenda a boy was whipped and branded, he went and hanged himself; in the winter of 1630 a woman killed herself in Stærra-Árskógur, she was granted burial within the church yard because her daughter was so mournful; that year a man stabbed himself in Stokkseyri; in 1631, a woman lost her husband in Svarfaðardal, she grieved him angrily, stabbed herself in the neck with a knife until dead, returned to haunt her sister-in-law into taking care of her son, ruined everything she had, her specter caused great misery and terror; in 1634, a man hanged himself in Staðursveit, his name was Ásmundur; a boy hanged himself at Hlíðarenda; in 1636, Helgi Kráksson from Hrútafjörður hanged himself; in 1638 a man in Ströndum jumped into the sea and committed suicide; in May 1639 the farmer at Langholt in Flói, Hallur Jónsson, wanted to burn a fire on his estate and as he set the fire it spread wide onto another man's estate and the land burned on the next thirteen estates in a row west because the wind came from the north and as a result he was rebuked because of the damage caused, he felt that so heavily that he ran out into the Hvítá trying to commit suicide by having the serpent swallow him; a man saw and swam out after him and reached him but a few days later he cast himself almost automatically down a deep sinkhole, he drowned and was found dead; in the fall, a man became possessed in the Westman Islands, he was seized and bound on crossbeams in the air by the National Church but had so much strength in him that he burst the bonds and was annihilated; in 1644 a boy hanged himself in Steingrímsfjörður; in 1645, a man ran out of Akranes into the sea and drowned himself; the sun was observed darkening in unnatural ways, becoming red as blood and black as terror and terrifying to look at, shortly after the mood grew dark and still more omens followed; on Christmas Day a man ran out in the middle of mass into the Rangá to take his own life; a man killed himself out west in the town of Staðarsveit; in the year 1648, in the autumn, a man indulged himself in an attempt on the life of Bjarni Bjarnason at Ingunnarstaðir in Skálarnesmúlakirkjusókn and so he cut his own neck with a knife, yet recovered from the injury a winter later; in 1650 a man drowned himself in the sea in Vestfjörður; in 1651 a man harmed himself in Hrútafjörð; in the Fall, a woman harmed herself in Höfn by drowning herself in the river beside the meadow and was buried in an unmarked grave near where she was found; 1652, a girl drowned herself in the Norðurá because of temptation; 1655, a young girl flung herself from the seacliffs in the south, dying immediately, found dead on the cliffs; 1656, a man hanged himself in Álftanes, Jón Halldórsson; 1658, two women harmed themselves; one stabbed herself to death but the other cut her throat to the bone; a boy in Vestfjörður hanged himself in the lambhouse and was found dead there; in 1658, a wife committed suicide in Tálknafjörður; a boy hanged himself in Króksfjörður; 1659, a man hanged himself down below Jökull; a man hanged himself out east at Síða one holy day in December and another in Flói cut his own throat on Christmas eve; 1660, a man cut his throat out east; another hanged himself in Flói; a girl in Flói did away with herself; in 1664 in Vestfjörður a man hanged himself with a child's shirt; a boy hanged himself in Steingrímsfjörður; a symbol was seen in the air that looked like pulsating jellyfish and many honest men entered the final sleep; in Þorlákshöfn, a woman drowned herself in the sea, she was known as Kossa-Dóra, her name was Halldóra Ólafsdóttir, the wife of Jón Jónsson, from Staðarhraun; right before Christmas a comet with a long tail was seen; in 1665 another comet; a boy of 14 hanged himself in Borgarfjörður, west of the Hvítá; on November 5th, a Sunday, a boy left the sermon and hanged himself; 1668 a man ended his own life in Álftanes; in 1670 a man hanged himself with a horse tail, that took place in Hruttarfjörður; in the year 1671 a man in the East Fjords had a child with his own flesh-and-blood daughter, he was called Jón Eiríksson from Skálanes at Seyðisfjörður, the girl ran away from him and exposed his compulsion, then she unwillingly went back to him, he destroyed himself a week later by undressing on a boulder and throwing himself into the water; the daughter, Margaret, was finally absolved after the matter had been referred to the district for investigation, afterward she was freed from execution at the national parliament because she was not all there; Oddný Jónsdóttir, out east in Grímsnes, had been married two weeks when she stuck into her belly a sausage knife she'd left in bed that evening, she got out of bed and took the knife out of her side and cut her throat immediately after; in 1673, a woman stabbed her own neck with a knife out east in Laugardal and soon died, she still received absolution and the sacrament before death, drifting away soon afterward, she was the mother of the man whose wife slit her throat in Grímsnes; beneath Eyjafjall, a man argued with his wife one night because she did not want to go to bed with him and in the morning he found her dead, having hanged herself; 1675, a disturbed person killed herself, Eyjólfur Björnsson's wife in Hallfríðurstaðir out in the north near Myrkársókn, she got out of bed in secret at night, leaving her husband, and proceeded to drown herself in the Hörgá below the farm, she was found dead there in the morning, as a result she was buried outside the church yard on the bank where she was pulled from the river; in the year 1676 a man cut his throat, he was called Bjarni Snorrason, he lived in Hjalla and was buried in open country; in 1679, a resplendent man on a fiery horse with a drawn sword was seen in the sky; 1680, a laborer at Tjörn in Svarfaðardal was found dead in an outbuilding with a cord around his neck; the cord was bound around his neck and knotted so tight people thought another person had been involved; a man cut his throat in Kjós and died the following day, he was called Gísli; another man slit his throat at Rangárvellir, living for two days; 1688, this year many follies occurred, according to the Fitja Chronicle, said The Regular, despair and doubtful temptations, a woman drowned herself in the spring at Miðfirð; 1690, a man cut his throat because of his troubled conscience, Ari Magnússon, from Fellströnd in the west; 1692, an impoverished man out east in a rural district got sick from rancid lard, he got an ax and hobbled into a single-room house, he was found dead there with his foot cut off; 1699, a farmer ran naked out of his bed during the night and was found dead in the morning in a lake near the town; 1701, during the spring, it rained worms all over Austurland, the worms ate flora and grass and were the most damaging and destructive visitor, at first the worms were small but quickly grew because they ate everything they came across and were soon the size of a stubby finger; in Austurfjörður a man hanged himself, a woman in Loðmundarfjörður ran out into the sea; also, a man ran into the sea at Reyðarfjorður; also a magistrate at Eyjafjörður; that same year, the farmer at Moldbrekka ran out of bed away from his wife and drowned himself in a stream, in 1702; Solomon Jónsson was the man's name and he was the hospital chief in the Westfjords, he came to Rif under Jökull and asked for accommodation, he said he was mad from insomnia and wanted to sleep in a one-room house so he could be free of all the noise and uproar that night, in the morning when they checked on him Solomon had hanged himself in the fishing gear which hung about the house, and he was buried outside the church grounds; another man hanged himself out east in the fjords; in 1703 in Breiðafjörður a man cut his throat from folly, yet he still died; the same year a councilor in Viðey left his bed one night barely dressed and was found dead on the shore after walking into the sea; in 1705, a man hanged himself in the river at Önundarfjörður; another cut his neck with a knife at Rauðamel and died a quick death; the assistant cook on the ship Stapa threw himself out of the window during the voyage and died; the farmer Guðmundur Magnússon hanged himself at age 51 in Álfadal in Ingjaldssandur in Ísafjörð district; a man whom age had bent double hanged himself in Eyrarsveit; in the year 1706 at Leysingstaðir in Húnavatnþingi a man cut his own throat, though didn't kill himself, after being urged to by a devil, he healed and got back on his feet; in 1708, a man killed himself with a knife in Hörðadalur; during 1709 the country experienced a plague and a third of the population died, said The Regular, it was as if the plague chose people based on esteem and took only women, children and distinguished folk and good people but left alive the poor vagabonds, the needy, the wretched and feckless people, a decent man, Jón Tómasson, a resident of Dvergastein in Álftafjord, lay close to death from the disease, he told his wife before he died how to put his body into the ground, he wanted to be dressed in his finest clothes, shoes on his feet and a cap with its hood folded back on his head, the way one should set a cap, a black-sheathed knife in his right hand and white gloves on his hands, don't use a coffin, my dear woman, Jón told his wife, this wasn't all effected as he'd asked and after Jón died and was buried his wife fell ill, many people believed he had gone back and visited her, she went to his region, though he had forbidden her to go there, and when she arrived at the farm, she walked into the farmhouse and hanged herself; a small boy hanged himself in Laxholt in Borgarhrepp; in 1713, in the middle of summer, a middle-aged man by the name of Guðmundur Þorsteinsson from Rauðamel, out west, cut his throat with a scythe; in 1714 a man killed himself in Miðfjörður; in 1715 Jón Magnússon from Víðidalur, the brother of the professor Árni Magnússon *antiqvitatis*, hanged himself in a hay barn; the next winter Magnús Sigurðsson slit his throat with a hay-scythe at Skegghaldsstaðir in Miðfjordur valley and died soon after, sixty-five years old; in the late winter of 1716 a girl intentionally stabbed herself with a needle, lonely and despairing, she lived for two nights and repented, she received the priest's blessing and died well; at Rútsstaðir a woman slit her throat, lived for three days, then died; a man from the south who had sworn at a priest in a pulpit and been severely reprimanded by the priest afterward asked forgiveness from the priest, but the priest did not want to forgive the man so he went out to sea and drowned himself; in 1717, a twenty-year-old boy hanged himself from a hay barn in Víðidal, he was called Guðmundur; in 1720 Þorleif Bessason came to Möðruvellir to buy himself a girl, he got out of bed during the night in his underwear and drowned himself in a brook a little way away, he'd been anxious about being able to afford a wife; a man in Vatnsdal drowned himself in the river; in the winter of 1721, two men in the Westman Islands committed suicide, one ran off a cliff, the other drowned in the sea; 1723, the district magistrate for Árnes, Grímur Magnússon, walked out of his house and threw himself down a well and drowned, a church priest had taken his blood and found nothing wrong with him although the magistrate had been very ill for a period of time, the magistrate had invited the priest and some others to dinner that day and when everyone was seated at the table the magistrate tried to leave and sent his servant to wait table, he ran as fast as he could and threw himself into the well, he was found right away standing on his head dead in the well; Jón Snorrason the book-binder was sick, he fled his bed in the night and was found dead in the Þjórsá; in the year 1724, in the spring, at Arnarstapi, a woman, Margrét by name, harmed herself when she jumped down into Kerið, the Cauldron, which lies below the cliffs, though she'd always been a cautious person; 1725, a housewife hanged herself at Stapa because of strife and anger, Guðrún Guðmundsdóttir, she took the key to her room and locked herself inside, she set one chest on top of another to lay the snare, pushed the upper one away from her feet and was found hanging there when the room was broken into; 1726, in the winter, February 5th, a girl drowned herself in the sea in Fúlavík in Gullbring district, Steinunn Jónsdóttir by name; a young man ran out of the sea-shelter and drowned himself, his name was Leif Jónsson and he lived near the Bakkaá in Tjörnes, that happened on the first Tuesday of the month by the old calendar, 26th March by the new, he wasn't found although there was a search, he had been told the morning before that he was to be a father, although blameless, and in late spring bones washed up on the shore that people thought were Leif's and which they buried outside the cemetery; at Miðnes, a girl disappeared from her bed one night, she ran into the sea and committed suicide; in 1728, a merchant ran out onto Skutulsfjorðureyri, Birk was his name, he threw off his blanket during the night and cast himself into the sea from the cliffs, he had quarreled with the magistrate; a woman hanged herself in Vesturhóp, Bergljót Bjarnadóttir, between 20th and 21st January, she had previously cut her throat but then been healed by *monsieur* Jón Magnússon; in 1729, a merchant drowned himself at sea at Skutulsfjörður, he was in dispute with a magistrate about the scales that had weighted forty kilos of fish, the load was sealed away and a pound taken off the merchant and the magistrate sailed off by ship, after this the merchant experienced great insomnia, on the morning he was meant to settle the payment he disappeared from the door of the administrative building and was found in the sea close to death; in the year 1731, on the 26th day of Decembris, Runolfur Þorvarðsson harmed himself at Höskuldsstaðir in Laxárdalur, he cut his neck with a knife, he was found alive there in the small house, Reverend Þórarin from Hjarðarholt was called, he came quickly and pardoned Runólf in confession, there was some awareness but no speech, he could write yes and no in chalk in response to the priest's questions, he received absolution and the sacrament, Runki died the following day; 1732, a man ended his life in Herdísarvík; 1737, a woman who lost her husband in a bitter storm drowned herself in the river where he disappeared; 1740, 5th of June, Pentecost night, at Arnarstapa, a man did himself in by running into the sea by the landing, he floated up, sank again, and died, he was later hooked by pole from a ship, he was allegedly in debt for small hand-knitted garments which he'd traded for ½ pound of tobacco, it was said he'd stolen the knitting and so he ran into the sea and did away with himself; on the morning of August 5, 1741, Oddur Sigurðsson the respected lawyer was found dead in his bed, he had gone to bed the night before and no one had heard him during the night, his neck-scarf had been tightened until he choked, he had repeatedly tried to commit suicide; 1742, in Rangárþing, melancholy thoughts led a magistrate, Nikulás Magnússon, to drown himself in a ravine, Nikulás left his bed one night and waded east in the Öxará at the Heathen Law Rock, a teenage boy saw him and wanted to help him but the magistrate drove the boy away, the boy, frightened, went in confusion back to Þingvellir and called for men to help but by then the magistrate had disappeared, three days before Nikulás had sent a message to the lawyer Magnús Gíslason, along with some documents and money, asking him to take care of his son, Þorleif, because within three days his life would be over; they first searched his tent, then looked for a body, and at the ravine's edge north of Þingvellir meadow they found his silver flask, several papers, and his handkerchief, all dripping wet, this led one man to look in the ravine, Nicholas was fished out and his body taken to church the next morning, some foolish men thought he had been conducting magic or spells, but things were utterly different, all his life Nikulás had been insane, never violent or evil-minded, on the contrary he suffered from too much gaiety, which especially went together with drinking, but now and then he would become reserved and sometimes morose, this happened during that year's parliament gathering, he was constantly joyful and excited both night and day until his mood changed while he slept one night, he got to his feet and drew his blade, a *hirschfænger*, it was long and sharp and he wanted to do himself some damage, his servant boy woke and was able to obstruct him so he didn't kill himself, but for the following days he was beside himself and hardly spoke to anybody and things ended badly, as previously explained, he was buried in a cemetery at Þingvellir (even though he had walked or thrown himself into a water-cleft out of folly or *mala conscientia*) out of kindness to his impoverished heirs, or else his estate and money would have been forfeit to the king, men thought he was fearful a case he had with the land registrar would affect his reputation, ever since this cleft has been called Nikulásargjá, a rough place in winter, a common spot for horses to die; a man from Skaftafell district who lost all his money one severe winter was so sorry about his loss that he slit his throat; Hrómundur Jónsson the smith was found after his place was searched, he had a strap with one end around his neck and the other tied to a stone which the dead man had kicked away, he was buried outside the cemetery by his master, a magistrate came to the site and exhumed him and saw from the mark on his throat that the death was caused by strangling with a leather belt and that there were stab marks on the body, his nose had bled, so he was taken from the cairn and his master was sought, being suspected of the murder and allegedly a criminal; east in Múlasýsla a man harmed himself, cutting his neck, he had suffered the loss of a lot of money, which led him to a very troubled death; in 1745 at Þingeyrir a man harmed himself on New Year's Day, he had previously been preoccupied; in 1746, a man hanged himself in Melasveit; 1747, a man killed himself alone in a lake in Stokkseyrarhreppur, he had been in custody for a time because of his deranged spirit; during the year 1757 the attorney Einar Jónsson Thorlacius cut his throat in Berufjörður as people were kneeling in church for Mass, the person next to him saw what he was doing and his knife was taken away, he lived half a month, repented and died; a man in Múlasýsla deliberately stabbed himself in his abdomen, lived for two days, repented and died; the year 1760, an old woman at Háeyri at Eyrarbakka threw herself down a well and killed herself, having long had a mental illness; in 1771, in an unfortunate event under Jökull, a man cut himself or stabbed himself in his neck and bled to death, a man named Bjarni Jónsson; a woman under Jökull cut herself to death in a similar way; 1772, a man hanged himself in the district of the Bishop of Skálholt; just before the winter nights arrived, a laborer named Guðmundur from Hvammur in Svartárdal disappeared one night from his bed, he was alleged to be somewhat sick, he was finally found by sheep-herders in the valley in the so-called Þjófagil, he had jabbed himself to death in the neck and was buried outside the cemetery; a lone farmer in Rangárvellir criticized his son's work in the cowshed, though not overly, he went back to his farm but it turned out the son hung himself in the cowshed; up north, a fire burned in the ocean; in 1774 the deputy lawman Magnús Olafsson, who was often near death from blood loss, stabbed himself with a knife; Bachmann, the surgeon from his land quarter, spent a long time healing him during the spring, he lay there over midsummer, then recovered; out west on Vatnseyri a Danish sub-merchant named Hauchsheim hanged himself with his neck scarf, no one knew why, a destitute father of many children from Vatnsnes, Tómas, hanged himself midweek, the Sunday before Tómas had received the sacrament after requesting it from a priest, Tómas was Þórðarson and lived in

Ásbjarnarstaðir, he was deranged and hanged himself from a nail driven into an outbuilding at Sauðdalsá; 1775, Guðmundur Einarsson, district administrative officer at Akranesi and a decent man, cut his own throat, then he had a fit of conscience and because his jaw had borne some of the wound he clung to life by God's grace and the assistance of Mr. Bjarni Pálsson land-physicus, who had immediately been sought, he pieced together the windpipe and mended the wound swiftly, the neck felt even better than before; a woman from the south slit her throat; 1776, in Hólárgil in Skíðadal a poor, pious man named Sigurður Jónsson hanged himself from a small tree; on the 11th of April, 1778, the Saturday after Palm Sunday, a workwoman named Solveig, from Miklabæ in Blönduhlíð near Rev. Oddi Gíslason, fatally cut her throat, her mind tormented, the workwoman and the priest had fallen in love but then she learned that the priest was going to marry and she lost her wits, the Rev. Oddi was told about Solveig and she was still alive when he came and as he saw this horrific sight he fell into a swoon, but when he came round she was dead, she was buried outside the cemetery, left to lay out north to south as is the custom for a suicide, those dead lie unregistered in church books, Miklabæjar-Solveig did not lie still in her grave, The Regular said, but walked the region with blood spewing from her neck, 8 years after Solveig's death, Rev. Oddur drowned himself, that year another woman killed herself the same way at Möðrufell in Eyjafjörður; in the year 1781 an exceptional event occurred, a single man up north at Tjörnes, Torfi by name, conscientiously drowned himself in the sea, having scruples that his innocent son would be bound to an oath because of what the merchant had himself lost in Húsavík; in 1782, in the summer, a man in Barðaströnd, Magnús, suffered an outrageous death, he stabbed a hole through himself with a scythe, he laid himself down entirely willingly on the scythe so that it went into his shoulder blade and out of his chest, he came home from this gutting and sighed these words, *God be merciful to my sins*, then died; in the Fall, a man called Oddur from Kasthús on Álftanes harmed himself, he was walking back home from another farm where he had gone to sharpen his knives, which he carried in a bag, he was later found dead between the farms having stabbed three knives between his rib-bones; a woman north of Svalbard drowned herself out of madness, she was called Kristín, she found her husband's extravagance unbearable; 1783, a mishap occurred when a married woman disappeared from her bed and her husband in Eyjafjörður and was later found dead there in the river, she had done away with herself because of her conscience; another woman, the wife of the farmer Guðmundur in Eyjafjörður, wanted to drown herself, she was found before she could and brought home scarcely aware; a recently married farmer at Jökuldal did himself a great injury by sticking a knife below his chest into his stomach after his wife had nursed a child for a few days, that happened around Christmas; a man cut his throat in Múlasysla; 1786, a man killed himself out of insanity; the winter of 1787, Jón Eiríksson, council member and chief ambassador of Iceland in Copenhagen, our greatest patriot and patron, a champion of the land, a reformer and society-builder, would spend long periods confined to his bed and room, afflicted by an ongoing melancholic sickness, all the while he still wrote and engaged in debates and fought against the oppression of the businessman and inequality in our land and resource exploitation and corruption but he had to endure obscenities from the king's men, including that he was an unremarkable man who had betrayed the king out of about 8000 *riksdaler*, one day Jón Eiríksson the councilor was driving home from a parliamentary debate when he asked his driver to drive down to Langebro, as if he wanted to go there to shake off his somber mood and breathe fresh air, at the bridge he rushed out of the cart, leaving behind his fur coat and watch, asked the driver to wait, walked onto the bridge, and in an instant he had thrown himself into the sea, the driver shouted to a nearby boat and they hauled the councilor out of the sea alive but senseless and brought him to land where doctors examined him, his head was smashed to smithereens and he had a gaping wound from having crashed into the bridge's stone pillars, he was considered incurable and lived only until evening, he was buried honorably in the Church of Our Lady, he was a scholarly man who particularly focused on ancient studies, unflagging in his studies, the causes of his death never became fully known, the annals say, The Regular said, maybe it was his war against Danish rule, and especially her secretariat, mixed with an uneasy conscience as to the shameful truth, his melancholic illness which had long afflicted him, together with other dispositions and the unrelenting and troubling contradictions in his domestic situation, such as that his wife's drinking was more than moderate, his rejection by his disrespectful sons, perhaps his daughter's conceited behavior, or it seems truest that he was burdened by all of this together and by the suspicion that he had been appointed to the chamber due to his great intimacy with Skúli the Chief Magistrate as much as his extensive work in Icelandic industry and his fierce fight for Icelanders' freedom from the powerful Danish trading monopoly, Skúli wasted the king's money, which the aforementioned secretariat, their nemesis, wanted brought to light, and the demise of councilor Jón Eiríkson, the high-profile and high-ranking Icelandic aristocrat, a steadfast lover and a merchant, was a magnificent loss for Iceland, regret poured over all the well-to-do Icelanders whom he had devoted his life so earnestly to furthering and the royal Icelandic Scholarly Society lost its president, he was missed with great mourning, the esteemed Jón was 59 years old; that year, in the Fall, a woman in Suðurnes hanged herself after being intimidated by another man who, out of fear, removed her head before she was buried outside the cemetery, Skúli exhumed her and saw how the head had been taken off the body and set by her ass with its nose to the crack, the man said he'd done this in fear so she did not come back like she had threatened to, Skúli caught this man and his son and sentenced them to time in jail; in 1788, a farmer in Svarfaðardal hanged himself, he slung his rope to the trelliswork and was found lifeless there in the snow in the morning, having killed himself in psychosis; 1789, some widow who lived beneath Jökull, Guðrún Steindórsdóttir by name, threw herself off 40-meter-high cliffs and was found below unharmed and conscious, she then lay bedridden and a girl watched over her, she fled her bed and the farm when the girl went away, she was found in the morning naked and entirely lifeless under a ship's side; 1790, an insane woman committed suicide in Jökuldal; 1793, a man threw himself into the sea—but let's end this tally here, said The Regular at Hálsasker, and may God bless all these suicides and self-harmers in Iceland, allow them their good names, but you should note that no Öræfing is named in this account, though all other regions of the country are.

†

It's great to get out into nature once in a while, said the poet Worm Serpent, drawing in a deep breath which ended in a hacking cough; he lit his pipe and breathed easier, his lightweight dustjacket fluttering in the wind. He pulled his fur hat down to his bushy eyebrows so all the fur ran together, it was like the poet's eyebrows had spread over his whole head... outsider, dwarf, poet, I thought to myself. Ah, yes, it's good to be here, Worm, said The Regular, people are always talking about going out to nature when you really go *into* nature, you go out of the house into nature, you cannot go out of the house out to nature, that's just confusing, one goes out of the city, out of the car into nature... ah, here are the perfect conditions for writing my essay on symbolism, Belgian symbolism, not any old symbolism, and Icelandic symbolism if anything exists that can be called Icelandic symbolism, and Einar Jónsson, sculptor and symbolist, here I finally have peace because there is no agriculture to please the State, here you can have an institute like at Tvísker... here a man can get inspiration from a rock... you'll see! Worm! you! lads! out from the rock my title rolls along like a meteor down the landslides:

EINAR

JÓNSSON

HIS SCULPTURES

& BELGIAN SYMBOLISM

INC. J. DELVILLE & HIS OCCULT KIN

& MEANINGS & INFLUENCE OF *LES TRÉSORS*

ON EINAR JÓNSSON ESPECIALLY ALDA ALDANNA

(*THE WAVE OF THE AGES*) ALSO WHY NO-ONE HAS DUG

INTO THIS OR KNOWS ABOUT THESE FOUNDATIONAL CONNECTIONS

It strikes me as peculiar, said Worm, to use eighteenth-century style in the title of an article about nineteenth-century material, but The Regular got angry and said: You are speaking out against Móskriður! And he curled up into a ball like a slug and rolled down the slope at Hálsasker, then jumped up the way a rolled-up spring mattress does when released; landing on his feet, he said:

EINAR JÓNSSON

&

SATAN'S TREASURE

Satisfied? Is that really better? The Regular asked Worm Serpent. Much better, said Worm, nice and simple…We need simplicity, always, to suit simple souls, The Regular said, rather than letting content and style go hand in hand, you're probably right, dear Worm, the baroque dazzles me, this essay concerns sculptors, and the style is supposed to be chiseled, no blockiness, no ricketiness, that's cubism, what happened to the cubists in literature?…maybe a kind of diamond structure, because triangles and pyramids relate to symbolism and all the mysteries, some higher eye I've never comprehended, yes, the all-seeing eye, the text will be in the style of Einar Jónsson's sculptures, the subject, thank you Short Worm.

You get so sleepy, deeply tired inside your head, being constantly immersed in beauty, The Regular said, the Öræfings are indeed as calm and perfect as Eggert & Bjarni say, they live in such a beautiful environment, ugliness makes men aggressive, discourteous, arrogant and repulsive and insipid, sharp, witty, sarcastic; the sources in your trunk suggest that there's no equivalent good weather as in Svínafell, even though there's nowhere in the world where there are dwellings closer to the glacier than there, that provides Svínafell with its beautiful weather, said Kiddi, contributing to the debate and then falling silent, he's such an Öræfing that he can fall asleep in mid-sentence when he is talking to someone and finish that sentence sometime later in the day. When he was little, a tractor blew off a slope and over the house, its hood was later found far out on the sand, crumpled together like a caramel paper. Violent gusts came down the mountain, said The Regular. One time, Kiddi was on the way out to the duckhouse when he heard a great din, and saw the forest high in the mountain had toppled over and was heading at speed for the farm, he started to run, going at a clop up the hill to the duckhouse, he wanted to save the ducks because he's a great bird-lover, the ducks are my friends, Kiddi interjected before dozing off, he dashed into the duckhouse and started to flush out the ducks, but maybe that wouldn't help so he began to drive them back in, just then he heard a violent hissing approaching at thunderous speed, he felt like the mountain had become a coffee pot and the coffee was boiling and the coffee pot was going to burst from the pressure or a giant goose come hissing at a run with outstretched wings and tongue stuck out and he did not know whether he was coming or going! ... it burst into the hut and whipped it into the air so it flew up high, floating up in the air a long time, the whole house tumbling back and forth and crushing some ducks under it which really displeased Kiddi, from the duckhouse he could see far and wide across the countryside, out to Ingólfshöfði, across Skeiðarársandur, up the mountains and valleys, the hills, the cliffs, all the impassable routes, everywhere Kiddi had gone on the annual round-up, he thought to himself, I've been here and I've been here, I've been here, and he was pleased with himself until a duck walked past him and said, as the house blew past Illukletta in Hafrafell: You've not done the round-up here ... then the gust died down, the hiss fizzled out, but hot rain poured into the house like coffee into a cup, the duckhouse landed high up in the woods, Kiddi stepped safely out but all the ducks had been crushed, they were eaten that evening and everyone got cheerful, the duckhouse's journey roused a lot of attention and the event was written about on the back cover of the newspaper *Morgunblaðið*, Sunday, 14th October, 1990, and you can see from the news this isn't an exaggeration, this gale rolled up the asphalt on the national highway all the way to Svínafell and a tourist bus was blown away, shattering all the windows and cutting people to death.

I've never been so fascinated by anything in all my life,

said The Regular at Hálsasker, as much as the hovercraft on Skeiðarársandur which the gold-seeking prospectors used, it remained a lone, deep dream, somehow impossible, I don't even know if I saw it with my own eyes or just heard Kiddi talk about it and so see it vividly before me, I feel like I've sat inside the hovercraft and felt it lift off the earth, the awesome noise of the engine as it starts up, how it glides over the whole sand and the rivers and quicksand, like being on the back of a ghost or dragon, at that moment it felt like the most amazing vehicle in the world and the most impossible, it had to save everyone but was saving no one, it had to be from the future but was recent, like a sailing wagon from the 18th century; a forgotten dream napping inside oneself, stirring slightly sometimes like a dragon on its gold, filling you with bliss, raising everything up into the air.

During the war years, a balloon was seen gliding unmanned from the ocean out past Svínafell and heading into the mountains, said The Regular. The next day more balloons could be seen and men stood on the slopes to look at them, some floated up high while others headed low into the valleys. Children and adults leaped up and chased the balloons into the wilderness. The balloons were made of light material, yet dense enough to hold water well, so-called Zeppelin fabric, said The Regular, and the balloons were double-layred, the inner white and the outer made of the same material but with aluminum on the outside. The balloon that floated across Svínafell was found high in Hvannadal and was carried home in small pieces, most people took two or three trips to carry precious material home. The balloons had a lot of twined cable which people felt would be good for bridle reins; after the Öræfings started sewing raincoats out of the balloon materials it was mentioned that they rather stood out, going around the province in silver-colored garments and with twine bridle-reins, the garments aroused some wonder among those who did not know the custom, and around that time a teacher from Reykjavík went to the county and stayed at a farm in Suðursveit that had an impressive library, that evening he took down the book *Invasion from Mars* to read, it's a tale of invaders from outer space in silvery garments and how no earthly army could stop them, he was late getting up the next morning and when he checked on the weather he saw men in silver-colored clothes heading to the farm, he startled, but got his natural color back when he was told that these were men from the next region, Öræfings. During the war years, all kinds of stuff and trash drifted to the shore, as at other times, The Regular said, in amongst the driftwood, which had always been a significant amount, there now drifted more than timber: planks, boards, cylindrical posts, beams, various scraps of wood, and much more than that washed up, car wheels, rims and tires, hub caps, bits of rubber, lifeboats, unmanned boats, gas tanks, flasks, bottles and cans, various little things, and other stuff drifted in, dozens of landmines arriving at the shore and exploding as they crashed into the beach, smoke columns rising up high from the sand, visible from the farms and dispersed over about 500 meters, these were button mines, later there were almost exclusively magnetic mines, many mines drifted in at Ingolfshöfði and the blasts were heard all over the region and the farm houses quaked when the booms echoed off the mountains.

During the winter of 1982, high winds and violent storms and hurricanes traversed Öræfi; the harried inhabitants couldn't remember comparable weather, The Regular said, there were many broken telephone poles and electricity poles, windows cracked and roofs blew off in most towns, vegetated lands were damaged by flung gravel, the *Eastern Way* bus was out east, loaded with passengers heading home for Christmas, but the weather was so bad buses couldn't get back or forth, its windows shattered in a hail of rocks and everyone had to stay put for the night in a violent storm of rocks and broken glass, sheltering under floor mats, there was a man taking a trip in a passenger car when a rock hail smashed all the windows in the car, the man was heading to a farm but his car was flung into the air and blown off the road, he said in an interview that he had been afraid he was going to be blown out to sea, that the force of the wind had been enormously weighty, had beaten him down, he crawled along the road with a pocket flashlight in his jaw for many miles before he came, lacerated, to shelter in the bus that was on the road; that saved his life. The Skeiðará flooded and did a lot of damage to vegetation and structures; it changed the landscape. By then, there were as many foreign tourists as domestic ones. That same winter Halley's comet was seen in Öræfi, some cows and sheep went mad and had to be put down, dogs were inconsolable and howled and whined at this comet in the star-studded winter sky as the glacier glowed and muttered; one evening Flosi from Svínafell saw a floodlight on the mountains as he walked home from the outbuilding but when asked for details he did not want to talk about it, it's nothing, said Flosi, said The Regular, but men knew it meant something was bound to occur in the region and they waited apprehensively for the days to lighten. A farmer in Hof was walking home from the next town one evening, he was engulfed by thick fog and darkness and couldn't see where he went, then a kernel of light appeared in front of him, swinging low over the ground, the size of a child's head, with sparks coming from it, the illuminated head lit up the road and accompanied the farmer, then the head disappeared and he reached home. Perhaps it was ball lightning showing him the way, though nobody knew what it was. The comet was first seen out west before Christmas, it had a long radiant tail that reached up into the air, it looked as though it was going to crash to the ground, but it rose up fast day after day, all the way through the end of February, and learned men tell us that comets portend tumult, a sign of transformations both spiritual and worldly, comets are omens for battles and bloodshed, these learned folks say, for the earth's fruitlessness, for terrible hunger and disease, both for humans and animals, one night red northern lights could be seen, which did not bode well, the moon was marked with a cross and three suns floated in the west, and now people felt it was enough, in one sunset there was a glowing red cross rising high into the sky, it lasted only a short while and few saw it, then the crossbar disappeared and only the post remained, more people than just Flosi experienced the floodlight and saw lights and symbols in the sky, people were taken aback and there was fear across the nation when all of this was spoken about and reported by the papers, the week before the month of Þorri begins, late January, a great snowstorm crashed to land and two men came riding into

Skaftafell, frozen statues stuck to their saddles, their faces black
with frostbite, when the ranger tried to remove one of the bodies from the horse's back, its hand fell off but its torso stuck fast,
then all the man's limbs came loose and fell to the ground, breaking into a thousand pieces, there were reports of a fish out east
with a man's countenance but a fish's body, it had hands instead
of fins and that monster went all around the region, there was an
ugly flu in the North and the Netherlands during the winter the
comet was in the sky, meteors crashed down onto the glacier and
rolled down the mountain side, they broke apart with a boom,
illuminated, then vanished down into crevasses with a din, clocks
rang of their own accord and corpses recited horrible quatrains
on their biers and from their graves, especially those who weren't
silver-tongued when alive, men were seen in the sky, the earth
quaked, cracks opened and the water in them ran blood-red, a
stench rose up from them, deadly to people and animals, especially to birds flying overhead and diving down from the sky, one
evening that winter Kiddi and I were with his great-grandmother
in the room in Svínafell and we were looking out onto the sand
as lightning flashes crisscrossed it and we watched terrified, said
The Regular, especially because Kiddi's great-grandmother
seemed to dread everything that was happening, she was 100
years old and had seen everything and we didn't think she feared
anything, the lightning didn't let up until the morning, when the
weather passed over the farm, and then the phone began to ring
automatically, although nobody was on the phone and it was out
of its cradle, flashes spat from the radio and the coffee machine
poured coffee from itself, the toaster toasted bread, the kettle

boiled water, the oven baked, then there was thunder and lightning and the house started shaking. That winter, Kiddi and I read *Wonders of the World*, *Flying Saucers*, *Guinness Book of World Records* and *The Annals of Gísli Oddsson*, and we became uneasy and afraid of the world. Sometimes in the evenings people said: there's a light on the sand. I always got a strange feeling in my breast at that, and we ran to a window to see the light on the sand, was it someone coming to the region, would they drive past, going further east? Who could it be? They would have to stop at Skaftafell, even though the area's more built up now, this is an uninvited guest, I thought with a half-unusual feeling, coming into my world, where I'm still totally alien, here where I'm a foreign body totally without rights, a stranger, people would turn to one another, usually everyone knows who's coming, but Kiddi and I kept hanging out at the window and watching the car lights, back then it was news to see a light on the sand, now there's a constant light from traffic over the sand and it's only news if there's no light to see, now everyone only walks over to the window to see no light on the sand, but that almost never happens. Once again the Skeiðará flooded, making a big gap in the road, and ice floes rolled all over the sand with din and booms. That summer the treasure ship *Het Wapen van Amsterdam* was found, said The Regular, the nation sprang into frenzy and excitement and followed the news closely in the newspapers and on the radio. The very same day, two Swiss sisters were traveling around the East Skaftafell region, young and carefree, one was twenty-one years old, her name was Lucette Marie, her sister, Marie Luce, was twenty-nine years old, they were young, well-to-do ladies in search of adventure before life's seriousness took over, they were enchanted by the untouched nature, the wide expanses, the freedom, they'd traveled through the country hitchhiking for three months and had gone a long way, they rambled around as they pleased, they took jobs in a freezing cold plant out west to earn a little money, everyone they met on this journey had good things to say about them, they were so open and beautiful and joyful, got on extremely well together. This particular Monday they were about a kilometer outside the village of Höfn in Hornafjörður, which is the east part of Eastern Skaftafell region, a green Mercedes Benz came driving past, on top of the car was a sign which read FÍB Road Service, it was an employee from the Association of Icelandic Automobile Owners, the man in the green Merc offered the girls a ride, asking where they were headed, they said they were on the way to Jökulsárlón, he picked them up and said he would drive them there, Lucette Marie sat in front but her older sister Marie Luce was in the back, the driver of the FÍB car asked where they were from and they told him, he himself had never been so fortunate to go abroad, in fact, he did not especially want to go abroad, though he had nothing against going to Switzerland, yet on the other hand, said the driver, that would probably be too much for me, what did they think about the mountains and Vatnajökull, they said they were extremely impressed and couldn't wait to see the famous glacier lagoon, Jökulsárlón, they felt Icelanders were lucky to have such untouched nature, it's all so *free*, said Lucette Marie, and the man looked at her in amazement. The FÍB man drove them all the way to Jökulsárlón and the journey took an hour, most of it silent, with the sisters watching the glacier, the mountains, and the rural farms on the right side of the road, but also looking out the windows on the left side at the sand, the shore and the sea, and when Lucette Marie looked at the sea, the FÍB man felt she was looking at him. All three parties' scant English put a limit on communication. The FÍB man drove off the road along a small trail to a sandhill and parked there, taking a break from driving to walk to the lagoon with the sisters, a cool breeze confronted them together with the spectacular view of ice floes on the lagoon, from time to time they could see seals stick up their heads and look inquisitively at them, the sisters were highly impressed, Lucette Marie took pictures of her older sister in front of the lagoon on her *Olympus Trip 35*, inside it was black and white film that she was going to have developed, along with many other films, Lucette Marie was going to start studying at the Basel Academy of Art in the autumn following the trip, she'd always taken pictures and developed everything she took in a dark room, Marie Luce had a beret on her head in the pictures and was in a thin coat that fluttered in the breeze, Lucette tried to get some shots of the seals but they appeared too far away in the 35mm lens, just black and bent shadows in the glacial water, it was the seals who greeted them that day, the FÍB man got tired of waiting around and offered to take the girls further but the sisters said they were planning to stay at Jökulsárlón, in Slysavarnarskýli, the so-called shelter hut. The FÍB man offered to look into it for them and they accepted, a little while later he returned, saying that the shelter was full, but they shouldn't panic because he would drive them to another shelter, at Skeiðarársandur, which is all the way at the end of the Öræfi region. On the way out to the car, the FÍB man told the sisters that the shelter huts weren't for tourists, they were strictly for people in hardship, places of *refuge*, not hotels, what if all the tourists stayed in huts for free? The tourist industry would get no money, nor would the State, which gets money from foreign exchange income and taxes, it is tax evasion against the Icelandic state, staying in the shelter huts, said the FÍB man, those refuges are for the shipwrecked, for those in danger, you aren't in any danger, right? The FÍB man asked the sisters, but he would still make an exception to the rules, only once, if they did not mind, they praised and thanked him, shame-faced and taken aback, Icelandic friends had advised them to go stay in the huts, they said, that's idiotic! said the FÍB man on the way out to the car at the Jökulsárlón, it's beyond idiotic! tourists ought not to stay in the shelter huts, the shipwrecked should stay in the shelter huts, what if shipwrecked men come to a shelter hut and there's a lot of tourists and no space for them, or if all the emergency shelters have been used and all the warm clothes taken, they are sacred houses, said the FÍB man and his voice broke, holy houses, but I will make an exception. There was not much chattering in the car on the way from the lagoon to Skeiðarársandur. It was around 8pm when they arrived at the Skeiðarársandur refuge house. Lucette and Marie thanked the man for the journey and went into the hut to get settled in. The FÍB man drove back east. The Swiss girls got ready to sleep, find-ing the shelter house fitting if rather dilapidated; they chatted and browsed the books. It's great to get such a long vacation from work and everything, said Marie Luce, among other things, it absolutely saves my life. At 11pm the FÍB-man came back and wanted them to come out to the car, the sisters were asleep and were rather unhappy the FÍB man had come back again, he said there was a police officer around who claimed they had been smoking hash... Come with me, said the FÍB man, but they had not been smoking hash, said The Regular, just lying in bed reading and going to sleep, they kindly asked the man to leave, thanked him again and asked him to kindly leave them in peace now. Then the man stormed away and went to his car, they hoped he would clear off but then he came back to the refuge hut and said, "This is your last chance to come with me!" He had electrical wire and a shotgun with him and wanted to tie the girls up with the wire and lead them out. They struggled with him and the older sister, Marie Luce, scuffled with the man but the younger sister ran out in confusion. The FÍB man struck Marie Luce in the head with the gun shaft, she fell to the floor, then he repeatedly beat her head until she fell unconscious on the floor, her face in a pool of blood, next the man ran out after Lucette and shot her in the back from 35–40 meters; she fell to the ground. The FÍB man walked over to her and pulled her to the car and put her in the back seat, then drove down the highway. He drove the car east. Lucette was still alive and lay fatally wounded in the back seat, she struggled up with great effort, saw the back of the FÍB man at the wheel, the night had taken hold of the vehicle, she looked through the back window and saw car lights on the road, she opened the back door and threw herself out the car. The FÍB man braked sharply and ran out to look for her. A commercial vehicle approached, the driver saw the green Merc out of its lane and slowed down because he saw a man standing outside the car, he wound down the window and heard a terrible emergency cry from a girl who was crawling away from the car all bloody. What's going on? asked the truck driver, with a trembling voice, he was a young man, under thirty. There's been an accident, said the FÍB man, I ran over her in the dark. Lucette crawled to the lorry and climbed up the steps and gripped the mirror with her hand and yelled at the driver: Help me! He's killing me! He's killing me! What's going on? asked the truck driver again, his voice even less sure, but the FÍB man repeated that there'd been an accident, he had driven over the girl in the dark, she was dizzy from the impact, in shock and senseless, he was trying to calm her down and get her into the car, he had been trying to call for help on the car's telephone but it was somehow broken. Hurry to Skaftafell to get help, said the FÍB man to the truck driver, find a doctor and the police. When the truck driver was about to drive off, the girl hung fast on the driver's side door and shouted: Help me! He's gonna kill me! Help me! Get the girl off the car so I do not drive into her, said the truck driver. Then the FÍB man pulled the girl screaming from the truck. The truck driver drove away, he looked in the rearview mirror and saw that the man was standing over the girl and holding her by the automobile, then the image receded and vanished into the night. A few moments later, the FÍB man took Lucette Marie in a choke hold and pulled her back toward the car, he opened the trunk and stuffed her in. The truck driver ran into another truck at the bridge across Skeiðará and asked him to contact the National Phone Network to report the accident, but the driver said he did not have the radio phone connected because of new regulations that prohibited doing so while the radio phone system was being updated. Then they drove off in their respective directions, the truck driver noticed car lights in the rear-view mirror, wondering where the car was coming from, because he had not seen anyone on the sand, the car drove behind him all the way but didn't turn into Skaftafell like the van but continued eastward instead. The park rangers at Skaftafell were finishing their work at 1 in the morning and saw the truck arriving at a dreadful speed and braking hard, the driver jumped out saying that an accident had occurred at Skeiðarársandur and asked the ranger to call a doctor and the police immediately, they were connected to the police in the region, who were based at Svínafell, and who arrived within a few minutes. The rangers took the police out to the sands to the scene of the accident. Nobody was there, the car had disappeared and there was nothing to see. They continued west over the sand all the way to Gígjukvísl and turned back there. Did this mean that the man had himself driven the girl to get her medical care, should they assume that, that everything had turned out for the best? Just then someone staggered out of the darkness into the light-cone of the automobiles, waving; the police attendant braked and a girl collapsed, exhausted, against the hood, her face covered in blood, her eyes staring panic stricken at them, she had a major head injury and was bleeding a lot. This was opposite the shelter hut at Skeiðarársand. They sped directly to Skaftafell with Marie Luce and got her under a doctor's care so her wounds could be tended right away, she had five ugly lacerations on her head. Marie Luce was able to describe what had happened with incredible accuracy and clarity, despite being in shock. Immediately there was a search for a green Merc from the Association of Icelandic Automobile Owners, and the authorities in East Skaftafell Region already knew who the driver was, using the description of the older sister to work out the man and the car. The car that drove behind the truck must have been the green Merc. The night's search bore no results. The car was found at 9:00 AM Tuesday morning at Hafrafell up by Svínafellsjökull. The FÍB man had jumped out and run into the mountains armed, said The Regular, Lucette Marie's body lay in the trunk compartment of the car, badly used and with a gunshot wound in her back, it was thought she had died sometime in the night in the trunk, she either suffocated or bled out. Extensive searches were conducted on Svínafellsjökull and nearby, and the chief magistrate of East Skaftafell district, Friðjón Guðröðarson, operated with great assurance, warning the people on the nearby farms and telling the farmers to check around and take care in the outbuildings, he secured a helicopter from the Coast Guard to come participate in the search, he warned tourists at the camp site in Skaftafell and forbade all hiking in the park, he got the Scout Rescue Unit from Hafnarfjördur to assist because they had a powerful search dog, a bloodhound, the only one in Iceland, named Perla; a stranger creature had never been seen in Öræfi. Friðjón Guðröðarson stood in the parking lot at Skaftafell; he was a tall man with big, thick, tinted glasses, wore his tinted glasses both inside and outside, it irked many that he always wore the sunglasses, even in meetings and at the office, he had a dense black beard and was thick-lipped, his hair flecked with gray, he was trim, wearing a trendy suit and a spotted tie. The bloodhound, Perla, began searching at the green Merc and immediately took a heading up Svínafellsjökull, she raced up the trail to a huge crater that was about 100 meters deep, it was thought that the FÍB man was down there. Due to the time and the darkness, it was decided to wait to rappel down the glacial crater until the morning. At dawn, just as two zealous men from the province were getting ready to rappel down into the glacier, Perla found another trail that led away from the crater and west from Hafrafell up under Illukletta; the searchers came to a shelter built against a small cave a little way up the mountain. The Scout Rescue Unit went to investigate and saw the man in the cave, he had blocked the way and closed up the cave with small trees and vegetation, and he lay there dozing with a folded rifle and a shotgun in his lap. The scouts bid him good morning and asked whether he wasn't cold, the man half-woke and looked up, then a scout said: I'm going to take your rifle, friend. The FÍB man assented and extended him the weapon. The scout seized the cold barrel, but the FÍB man clung to the shaft, and their eyes met. Be careful, the FÍB man told the scout, it's loaded. Then he let go of the shaft, and the scout took the rifle and disarmed it. And the gun, the shotgun, said the scout, but the FÍB man took it and emptied it himself, saying, I'm not going to use this on you, lads. These days were dark over Öræfi, the nation struck by dread, because the news appeared alongside the awesome progress taking place in Öræfi, the magistrate Friðjón Guðröðarson informed the media as soon as something happened, honestly answering the media and telling the truth since it couldn't damage the investigation, which was in reality no investigation, it was quite unprecedented to be so open to the public, the custom was to fight the news or baldly lie to the media, which does great damage to the story of the future, said The Regular, we are not in some gangster-game here, the magistrate Friðjón Guðröðarson told journalists in Reykjavík by telephone from Skaftafell Visitor Center, from where he controlled the operation, we know who the man is and he knows who we are, everyone in the country is a known entity, he's just Friðrik Albert, he knows we're looking for him and we just need to find him before he does any more damage, although I do not believe he will, said the magistrate. Friðrik Albert had often pretended to be a cop on the highway and stopped cars for driving too fast, although the person was going the legal speed, he took the law into his hands, pulling people over; he was thought a bit of a fool. The treasure ship was found and the murderer was found, the nation celebrated. The murderer was declared not a murderer but a sick man; the treasure ship turned out not to be a treasure ship but a rusty trawler, The Regular said in Hálsaskeri.

My mother lay in the City Hospital for 2 weeks, I said, and had to undergo three operations on her head. Flugleiðir, the Icelandic airline, offered to fly my family out so we could come watch over her, grandfather and grandmother went, I was left back home with my father. My mother took all the newspaper stories home with her, they were very accurate and detailed about the events, thanks to the magistrate in East Skaftfell district, Friðjón Guðröðarson, she did this because my father asked her to. She was a changed person when she came home, said my father, he said that repeatedly over the years, sometimes it seemed to me that he was the one who had changed, not her. I later pored over all this data.

†

The brothers met me at Tvísker: Hálfdán, the ornithologist; Helgi, the inventor; Sigurður, the author; and Flosi, the glaciologist. They were determined I should travel on horseback, pulling my oversize trunk behind me. Where are you headed exactly? they asked. Up into Mávabyggðir, I said. And you're planning to take your trunk up to Mávabyggðir? Yes, that's the plan, it has all my tools, everything I need. You're clearly mindful of Captain Koch, said Sigurður, but no one has traveled through Öræfi with as much baggage as he did, the size of your trunk notwithstanding.

I was invited onto the farm and the brothers set out numerous cakes on the kitchen table, a sponge cake, a Christmas cake, a layer cake, assorted other kinds I didn't even know the names of. I was able to fish out of my trunk a Viennese cream cake my mother had baked and I set it on the table; it was pretty crushed because the cake plate had broken under the weight of all my books. That doesn't diminish the taste, Sigurður said. We had the best cake party, rabbiting on about sundry issues, mostly old, lost things. It was time well spent.

I didn't want to accept accommodation with the Tvísker brothers, having already inconvenienced and troubled them enough; they probably have lots of guests stay with them, lots of ignorant people like me, inquisitive travelers. The time has passed when you can walk up to someone's farm for food and shelter; these days, people just want to be left in peace to watch TV, free from strangers, they don't want other people around, they don't even want themselves there. But Tvísker is more like a college than the home of farmers, inventors, and scientists: all sorts of ignorant folk compete to ingratiate themselves, wanting to see their collections and milk their knowledge. I decided to over-night in my trunk, having got permission to park it on the farm-yard. Before I went outside, however, I was not able to restrain myself from doing what Kiddi had said I ought to, that is, get Hálfdán to show me his insect collection, which he did very happily, pleased by my interest, I could have spent many hours in front of those glass cases, all the beetles and butterflies mounted to the backing with tiny needles, their little machine-written labels displaying the Icelandic and Latin names. Hálfdán showed me his invention, an insect suction device, and gave me a demon-stration; it was a small device Hálfdán had thought up in his younger years when he was just beginning to collect insects. They often got damaged when put in a tin, so he constructed a clear plastic jar with two rubber tubes through the lid; you bend one of the tubes down to the tiny creature and stick the other into your mouth and suck, so the creature gets sucked down through the lid; at the end of the suction pipe inside the jar there's a filter so you don't inhale the insect, and then you can examine the insect close up and safely in the jar before return-ing it to nature unscathed or adding it to your collection. After that, he accompanied me out to the farmyard. It had begun to get dark, the weather cold but calm. He showed me his light trap under the mountain ash on the east side of the house, checking what it had caught, various remarkable things. Then we walked back. I said good night and crawled into the trunk like a larva. I felt good. I enjoyed snuggling up to myself on my soft mattress, wrapped in my down comforter amid my books, feeling the cold from outside. I wrote down in my diary everything that had happened that day. In the morning, I had been to Sandfell, the next destination east of Svínafell, which looks beautiful though the sources in my trunk deem it ugly; when we were at Hálsasker, near Sandfell, The Regular told me about the bare, scant vegetation and the place's gray tones, which few have appreciated, at least until recently, when a sign with information about the place was installed. Sandfell dates back to the Settlement but it's deserted now, The Regular said, a woman settled there because her husband was lost at sea on the way over to Iceland, her name was Þorgerður and she was a woman of strong resolve. In Sandfell there is an old cemetery with a single great rowan tree in which two ravens nearly always sit, croaking. Once, a beautiful cluster of houses stood there, the last in the traditional Skaftafell style; all the others had been demolished and levelled to the earth, turf houses and gabled farmhouses, and when the rivers were bridged and the road continued past Sandfellsbær and the president was planning a visit in his fancy car, a fire was set on Sandfellsbær, and the structures were flattened by bulldozer because people were ashamed of them, there hadn't been enough progress, and thus the last idiosyncratic construction methods in all of Öræfi were destroyed, right as we were celebrating 1100 years of settlement in the country, right as the ring road opened. We burned up and tore down anything old, flattening everything, to let the present see itself. But 1974, the year we attempted to please the president of the republic with a fire set by the Ministry of Agriculture at Sandfellsbær, our anniversary year during which we levelled the ruins with a bulldozer, that was a special year through Europe, a year dedicated to conserving houses; people didn't realize that the president was an archaeologist and a former Icelandic park ranger; needless to say, the gesture didn't suit him especially well. Twenty years earlier, before he became president, he'd rescued the turf church in Hof from destruction; today, this small church is the most precious gem in Öræfi, one of the most beautiful churches in Iceland. Objects and relics that weren't destroyed in the fire or by bulldozer and might be used for farming got scattered across the region and disappeared; for example, the altar from Sandfellskirkja ended up as a cabinet in an outbuilding; it's no longer in use, has vanished. It wasn't long ago that ancient houses existed in Sandfell and Svínafell; it was said they dated to the 11th century, much larger than was later customary, built from old red spruce, or so Eggert and Bjarni say in their *Travelogue*, these structures were preserved and restored through the centuries until Progressives set fire to them, flattened the ruins, smoothed turf structures into meadows to produce grass to produce animals to industrialize farms—and now nobody knows where those big, ancient halls stood. After 1974, Sandfell has been so haunted that no one gets any peace there for any length of time. One time, there were road workers in tents near the rowan tree and the two ravens were extremely uneasy; that night, everyone woke up to resounding hoofbeats, but couldn't see anything in the night. The following day people asked around, but nobody had been traveling during the night, never mind several people on horseback; it was something supernatural. Nowadays, many tourists come by bus to read the sign, said The Regular there in Hálsasker, the main reason people travel is to read signs, he said, on the sign at Sandfell you find information about how remarkable this place is and how remarkable the destroyed house was. There's ample parking. There's human shit in the cemetery, people crap among the graves because there's no toilet at the sign everyone is reading, all those millions of tourists shitting out on the land all the burgers and fries they felt compelled to eat. Runki from Destrikt was surprised by all these white flowers in the cemetery he did not recognize, he thought they were newly-discovered plants, he was going to call Hálfdán and let him know of this remarkable find, but when he walked into the yard, he saw it was toilet paper fluttering on the graves in the wind.

A true story, said The Regular, in the past, the foreign tourists who came to Öræfi were European noblemen and geniuses, lords, earls, princes, scholars, and philosophers; now it's a hollow, trashy rabble! In bygone days, foreign relations were much better than now: Öræfings knew foreign languages, Latin, Hebrew, Dutch, French, English, Danish, German. Today, no-one here knows any foreign language even though there's a thousand times more foreigners than locals—except for Flosi from Tvísker, who reached great perfection in English by listening to English language education programs on the Icelandic Broadcasting Service for several decades. I don't know where they'd be without him. Back when, Öræfings could manage on their own, lived sustainable lives, they had enough to clothe themselves, feed themselves, make tools, they could sustain their existence, so says the naturalist Þorvaldur Thoroddsen about his arrival in Öræfi in the 19th century, and it's still the case, it's likely the only self-sufficient place in the whole country, exactly as it was when Sveinn Pálsson came to Öræfi, when Eggert Ólafsson and Bjarni Pálsson came to Öræfi, and Jón Steingrímsson the Fire Cleric tells the same story, he wrote the praise poem "Öræfingahrós," a panegyric from the Fire Cleric to the Öræfings, he found the people *ideal*, the epitome of the language, the epitome of the body, the epitome of the spirit, the epitome of morals, the epitome of culture. And in this place, travellers found their peace.

I decided to rest the horses and let them eat a little grass in Sandfell; they found the trunk rather cumbersome, but wouldn't let anything bother them, they were truly strong, unstinting horses, as I had read about Captain Koch's. For my part, I decided to lay under the rowan, but the ravens cawed irregularly, so I crawled down into the trunk and fell asleep for a bit. I tried to decide whether to read the sign or not. Then I wrote down in my diary everything that had happened since the morning.

I woke up that night and didn't know where I was. I heard all sorts of scratching in the dirt and a strange chirping in the farmyard, I felt something that could fly land on the trunk, I heard first a whistling, then a little thud on the lid, the sound of a claw right across the lid, a scratch, more like a smack, and then again, a loud chirp, a tongue clicking. The ravens, probably. Early in the morning as I dozed I felt a knock on the trunk; I jumped up, but there was nobody there. Seeing a light in the kitchen, I hurried over, chilled to my bones, poorly-rested. The brothers were all in the kitchen, and they gave me moss milk, which they have for breakfast every day, they told me, ever since they were very little; they credit their good health to moss milk, although they're all as old as dogs.

Did you sleep well in your trunk, fellow? Sigurður from Tvísker asked, it's a really handsome trunk, are you going out onto the glacier all alone? That's not very wise, but you should be safe if you travel carefully over the crevasse area, it'll surely be covered by snow this time of year. Eggert's *Travelogue* says that the glaucous gull, *laurus hyperboreus,* lays its eggs in Mávabyggðir, Hálfdán chimed in, I don't know if that's still the case ... Or Eggert and Bjarni's *Travelogue* says about *their* trip east to Öræfi, Sigurður corrected, men had newly-arrived with eggs when Eggert and Bjarni showed up, it's a remarkable pathology to always imply Bjarni and only say Eggert, Eggert Ólafsson's *Travelogue* when Bjarni's part is no less, you ought to say Eggert and Bjarni's *Travelogue,* Sigurður insisted, Eggert and Bjarni say this or that in the *Travelogue,* not just Eggert ... Hálfdán leaves Bjarni out because he was the one who shot the birds, said Sigurður. But Eggert made a book of birds, said Hálfdán, amused, an account of birds, sketches of birds ... Are you writing a Travelogue? ... *The Travelogue of Bernharður Fingurbjörg,* not such a bad title, I thought, the Tvísker brothers are so famous, so much has been written and said about them that I suspect it doesn't matter if I scribble something about them too, I thought, maybe something foolish, when it comes down to it nothing accurate ever gets written about anyone, a person's character is always wrong and misrepresented, even if you write about yourself, your character is made to say something it has never said or thought, everyone is always making people tell things they never told, do things they never did; that's how it's always been done, writing about humans, dead and alive, humans get described mistakenly, made to use words they have never spoken, made alive when they're dead…That's *folktales*, said Sigurður, and culture, much was said and written about Einar from Skaftafell and his giantess, who some reckon wasn't a giantess, just a criminal come south from Landbrot; a certain image of Einar emerges in these writings and it would be pretty miraculous if it were at all similar to the Einar who actually lived in Skaftafell. This means we've now got *two* Einars from Skaftafell: one dead, so nobody can know anything about him, the other living on in folktales and able to constantly change and multiply himself as more people write about him, but fortunately most of the stories are the same, since everyone mimics what others have written, Sigurður said; we can never know if Einar from Skaftafell as we know him through stories is at all similar to the Einar who really lived in Skaftafell, and it's probably all much of a muchness.

There used to be great black-backed gull nests in Mávabyggðir, and even barnacle geese, said Hálfdán, as we all sipped our moss milk; birds and insects and plants are continually settling the land. He gave me an insect sucker and told me which tube I should suck and which I should aim at the insect, if I saw anything special on Mávabyggðir I should let him know, if I remembered to. It's been a long time since I went there, he said, no one goes to Mávabyggðir any longer. If memory serves, my last trip there was in 1940, when we brothers went, out of curiosity, wanting to check out the settlement sites and birds' nests and even the out-law sheep, what used to be called feral sheep, outlaw sheep are sheep which have been out so long that they have become a special species, or sub-species, dissimilar from other sheep in Iceland, in the whole world really. By the way, I went down to the sand this morning to look for birds, and saw a gull. To find one's way up Mávabyggðir, said Sigurður, follow the strip on the glacier which goes from Breiðárlón up to Mávabyggðir; there's another strip coming down the mountain, so you shouldn't get lost. Do you have enough provisions? Don't you want to take this layer cake with you?

I picked up the ancient military survey map and went over the route with them. The glacier has retreated significantly, said Sigurður, a large lagoon has now formed in front. I often headed east with my father to Breiðármerkurjökull to cut ice stairs, a route for horses over the glacier, said Sigurður; he was in charge of the route, that needed doing every time someone went across because the glacier was so unstable, it pressed forward then retreated and many crevasses emerged thanks to the changing water level, and naturally there was no bridge over the Jökulsá, it was always impassable around midsummer, the only way was to detour via the glacier, which usually took three hours, nowadays it takes three seconds to cross the bridge, I sometimes went along when my father accompanied people over, and we checked out the glacier's pace, he said he wanted me along for entertainment, we liked being together, and one time when I was ten years old, in 1927, my father was expecting the mail carrier and his brother and was planning to head east to bring them over the glacier; Jón, my father's brother, was a teacher in Svínafell, where my father grew up, that day the rains were extremely severe and the glacier difficult to traverse, so my father decided to wait and hope they would not head out onto the glacier in such weather. We sat at home all day, my father very nervous, felt sure something had happened, I tried to be cheerful for him, tried to amuse him, but he alternately sat there dejected or else paced the carpet. The more the day wore on the more uneasy he grew, coming to regret not having left that morning; now it was too late. That night the mail carrier arrived with two women and said that there had been an accident on the glacier, we started off as soon as it got light, the weather now good, the mailman said what had happened, and my father asked repeatedly for details: the accident had happened when my uncle Jón was headed west over the glacier with the mail carrier and two women, he and the mail carrier were cutting stairs in the ice for the horses while the two women were standing below holding the horses; then something seized Jón and he walked down the stairs to the women; they were cold standing there in the rain; Jón took the horses and the women walked up the stairs to where the cutting was being done, wanting to help out. That saved their lives because at that moment the glacier above the horses burst apart, splitting, crashing down in large pieces, submerging the horses and Jón, my father's brother; three horses were rescued alive after much effort, the other three were crushed between floes in the collapse and died. The mail carrier and the women looked about in the darkness for Jón but could not see him, they went home to Tvísker, soaked and shivering, they searched the next day but didn't find

Jón, my father kept looking, although the others stopped and he frequently searched for him in later days. I would go along to see if we could do anything to retrieve what we'd lost. One day the next year my father and I were there checking the road and suddenly saw a horse's head protruding from a high glacial wall, and my father knew the horse, it was the horse the mail cargo would have been on, we went and got a crew to chop the ice and as we were striking at the ice, giving it a sturdy blow, we saw one of Jón's feet, shortly after that we reached the body. Under the horse's body we found a coffer, mangled and crushed to pieces; inside were six small postbags full of money, wet and stinking, because pressure inside the glacier had burst the horse and its intestinal fluid must have leaked through the glacier over the mail, which was rescued and cleaned; the body was driven by cart to Kvísker and a coffin built around it, then moved to Svínafell, and buried in Sandfell. People guessed that Jón had lived for some time after he became trapped in the glacier because his body wasn't badly injured; when we found him, we saw he had lain down to his last rest with his arms folded and his hat over his face.

At that moment, the phone rang in Tvísker and Sigurður got up, left the kitchen to pick up the handset, and said: It's for you Hálfdán. Hálfdán went to the phone, I heard him say, Yes, naturally, naturally…Then he returned and said, It was Kiddi, he found a dead bird that he thinks is a Eurasian woodcock because it's a little bigger than a common snipe, he's going to bring it here around coffee-time today. Isn't Kiddi your friend? asked Sigurður. Yes, I said, yes, we travelled east together. Do you use the internet? I asked. Sure, Sigurður answered, sometimes it hurries things along, although you find a lot that's wrong, I'm the only one who uses it as a tool, though I'm the eldest. He writes reams on the computer, said Hálfdán, he has always diligently adopted modern technology. Sigurður contended that Öræfi had entered the present when the phone lines were laid across Skeiðarársand in 1929, not when the bridge was consecrated in 1974; 1929 broke the isolation, 1974 created something else, something I cannot comprehend, perhaps the only thing that happened was that mice came, before then it was considered the only province in the world without mice, said Sigurður, you couldn't have cats, they all died of boredom, interjected Hálfdán, although a single mouse was found in a mansion in 1941, the first mouse known in Öræfi, no more mice were seen until nineteen sixty-something, then one was seen in Skaftafell; both mice were likely brought with the mail or in someone's luggage and then slipped out, but after bridges crossed the sand, mice became widespread in no time and the cats had quite enough to be getting along with. Hannes, the rural post carrier at Núpsstað, once saw a mouse's trail in the fresh snow at Núpsvötn, he followed the trail to the river, and saw where the mouse had reemerged on the other bank, and Hannes barely wondered about how small a distance the stream had taken the mouse downstream. But the phone meant security, said Sigurður, it became possible to call across the sand and send people to help or as escorts, we could inform one another about impassable routes and ever-changing rivers, about whether the Skeiðará was flooding; the phone saved lives. Now perhaps there's too much talking into such devices, I don't know. Then the phone rang again, as if in protest. Hálfdán went and answered it. When he returned to the kitchen, he said: That was the University, wondering why I keep sending them empty matchboxes. They aren't empty, I send them little flakes I find on the glacier and want chemically analyzed, but they must overlook the flakes; maybe they evaporate on the way.

I bid farewell to the Tvísker brothers in the farmyard, all looking happy. They thanked me for the tart and I thanked them for the cakes, the hospitality and the dissemination of knowledge. You go east to Breiðamerkurfjall, Flosi called after me, and up to the glacier there via the rock strip. I looked back and couldn't see anyone in the farmyard, come to think about it I never saw Flosi, you should indeed head a little way north, the voice in the farmyard said, a voice in my head, and then you'll hit Mávabyggðir ... *Adios!* ...

†

It was a great wonder to come upon dry, bare land when my map told me it should be entirely concealed by glacier; I felt like I was under the map, in a Borges story. I had the military survey map from 1903, made according to Captain Koch's measurements, and I could see how many kilometers the glacier had retreated in 100 years. There are no place names here, I pointed out to myself, just eroded stones in varied colors, tremendously large rocks the glacier has hauled along then left behind, this is new land, I noted, Sigurður from Tvísker told me there was once a great forest here, the hero Kári Sölmundarson lived here after the burning of Bergþórshvoli, an incident told in *Burnt-Njáls Saga*, the glacier destroyed this green earthen landmark and then unveiled it again anew, the way a theatre curtain reveals a new scene after the intermission.

I summited a steep slope and saw two glacial lagoons facing me at a distance, the nearer is called Fjallsárlón, the farther-off Breiðárlón, both of these lagoons had formed in the foregoing decades after the glacier began to retreat. There was fog in the middle of the mountainside. I was amazed at how the two valley glaciers descended from the clouds, rough and hideous as they crept across the land. I needed to head between the lagoons to get to Breiðármerkurfjall; a glacier river flows between the lagoons; whereas I crossed by cable car, before you had to go right out onto the glacier to reach the mountain. I ferried the horses over in the car because I didn't want to get them wet walking the glacier; I took one horse on my first trip, quite a tight fit in the iron car's cage.

Every time I looked at the survey map of Öræfi, my thoughts turned to Captain Koch. Koch was extremely popular in Öræfi, and lived on people's lips long after his passing, as Sigurður told me in Tvísker when he saw me with the maps. He was tough and tenacious, qualities Icelanders could appreciate in foreigners; little annoys an Icelander more than a whiny traveler. He principally earned admiration by staying for many weeks in a tent on Skeiðarársandur during the coldest months, enduring sandstorms and terrible weather; he set up cairns and took measurements. Captain Koch's first acquaintance with Iceland was difficult, said Sigurður, but he never showed any fussiness. One time, he accompanied his guide to the Skeiðará during a surge; there was a storm from the north and a hoar frost. The guide went into the river first and it crashed right over him so he was soaked through by the time he hit the other bank. Koch did not care to ride the long way drenched so he tore his clothes off and tied them behind him and the horse swam across the Skeiðará in the raging northern weather with him naked on its back; for the rest of the day Koch rode in dry clothes, warm, while the guide shivered with cold and wet and rime. Sometimes his path would be completely impassable due to sandstorms, and the horses couldn't eat because the feedbags were full of sand, so they loitered there hungry and trembling for days on end, the surveyors keeping up a steadfast shoveling because their sleeping quarters risked falling into the sand; the tents were torn open, and the sea came far up into the estuary, meaning the men couldn't drink the water. Their mouths and noses filled with sand and their provisions spoiled. When the weather subsided, they could go back to measuring, every day they had to ride the estuary and rivers and glacial floods on the sand, and it was rough hardship, and then snow came, but it was barely a bother compared to the sand's buffets. People wondered how Captain Koch was so efficient and quick to learn the conditions, and they were delighted his adoption of and love for the Icelandic horse. After that, Captain Koch went up Öræfajökull to survey and lived there in a tent for 6 weeks; he had with him an Öræfing draftsman and guide, Þorstein from Skaftafell, a brave man who was an experienced traveler. Koch made his first attempt to use horses on the glacier there, but it did not go well because of the heavy going and the snowmelt, it was largely awful weather, a cheerless retreat. Koch was unable to get the horses up to the high glacier, and he had to seek out supplies from the camp store down below the glacier when provisions ran short; during that trip he couldn't make it back to the tent the same day due to the inclement weather, and Koch and Þorstein got rained on, then a darkening blizzed, and they lay out exposed all that night, thoroughly wet, lying in hay sacks; it seemed impossible humans could have survived such a thing, and the newspapers in the South wrote about it enough that it became well known.

The stories surrounding the military survey map are a gold mine for my doctoral thesis, I thought there in the cable car, place names are symbols, I told myself, and a shiver ran through me, I was overjoyed, it was nothing less than an *awakening* there in the car and I instinctively quit hauling myself, stopping halfway across the water. The cable car dipped deep and slow, holding me and the horse I'd named Fuck-red, Fuck for short. *Place names as Symbols*, I noted in my notebook there in the bouncing cable car with Fuck, nothing more, I stared at those words, place names as symbols, a complete world had opened for me as I finished writing these words, place names as symbols, I said out loud there in the bouncing cable car above the thundering glacial water, there for the first time I realized that there was a real chance of finishing my thesis. I'd grown afraid that the trip to Mávabyggðir was a cloak for my lack of imagination and my regrets and absence of research, but even if I didn't finish the thesis, the searching and discovering mattered to me above all, the process of being in motion, increasing my range, with uncertainty as my constant light... all of a sudden, I felt unsafe there in the cable car above a floating death, cold and beautiful, felt fearful of the symbols, of the world beyond the symbols, a streaming glacial water running with symbols, with place names ... there was probably nothing beyond the symbols but the universe in all its emptiness and fortune of oblivion. I put my hands to my head and yelled; my pen fell down into the water. Fuck bolted, I yelled out like Munch's *The Scream* there in the cable car above the symbolic glacial waters, the sun reddening the eastern sky and turning the glacier into swelling blood, the gray-green glacier bulging under me, and Fuck and I were bouncing about in the open air terrified by the void behind the symbols ... I hauled us across in a flurry and threw my body onto the dirt of the other bank to calm myself.

Shortly afterward, I fetched the rest of the horses, one by one; on each crossing, I received some inspiration. On the second, the Belgian symbolism became more prominent in the landscape; on the third journey, the way names cloak things; on the fourth trip, how naked symbols are; on the fifth journey, I involuntarily wrote *Einar Jónsson* without really knowing who that was. By the time I had finished moving myself, the horses, and my trunk across I was greedy for ideas, I went back alone in the car, hauling myself out over the river, ready with pencil and notebook—but nothing happened. Perhaps I lacked a horse, so I went to get a horse and bring it out in the cable car and wait for inspiration. I switched the pencil out for a pen, but nothing happened, except some rather unremarkable twittering from the world of ideas which soon passed ... I tried to concentrate on the twittering but it was utterly meaningless. I grew uncontrollably sad, full of hopelessness.

In the most desolate place on earth, where once there had been a glacier out past Breiðármerkurfjall but now there was nothing except filed-down scree and rocks, gray, dark, cold, there in the shadow of the mountain as though on the bottom of the ocean, I went past a sign. Although I'm usually a sucker for signs, I felt compelled to avoid reading this one. I'm not going to read the sign, no way, I said to myself, I'm going to go past the sign, pretend I cannot see it, I wasn't going to go through desolation and wasteland to do something so despicable as go and read a sign. Perhaps it's a sign about Kári Sölmundsson's farm? I thought. No, Sigurður from Tvísker had told me about that, no way you can trust a sign in such a situation; what could possibly be on a sign in a place like this. Recently, there was a glacier here; now it's retreated, leaving just gray, red, and blue, no place names, nothing could have happened here, nothing could be so remarkable to look at that it required a sign, not here in this place no one visits, a place without stories, it probably says there was a glacier here, something like: Nothing has ever happened here. I don't need to read the sign, I know what it says, the sign is absolutely foreseeable, I'll just go past it, absolutely ignore it, since nothing remarkable is written on it, it says nothing I don't already know. I plodded toward the sign and looked angrily at it:

"Praise to the Lord"
By the big rock
on the slope
Sigurður Björnsson
was saved

FROM AN AVALANCHE

8TH NOVEMBER

1936.

THE FLOOD TOOK SIGURÐUR

BY THE HILLOCK

AT THE TOP OF THE SLOPE.

HE THEREFORE FELL

212 METERS

AND STOPPED 28 METERS

BELOW THE GLACIER,

IN A HOLE

A STREAM

EKED—

BACK THEN THE GLACIER

REACHED THIS HIGH.

That cheered me. I looked up. Fog had settled on the middle of
the slopes and the gray of the rock the glacial tongue had lain
across had taken on infinite tones, glistening matte and foggy,
moist and warm, hard and friendly, gray and colorful. All of this
touched something lost inside me; joy trickled through me. An
excited joy, full of anticipation. The joy of life. Walking alone amid
the glacial deposits became life's highest pleasure. Picking up a pen
and a notebook out in nature: pure happiness. What happened
to the place names here when they went under the ice in the
Middle Ages? I noted the sign down in my notebook. Would it
be possible to dig the place names up out of the old sources, paste
them back into nature? How painful it must have been, seeing

the glacier crawl over Kári Sölmundsson's farm and destroy the earth. Icelanders today willingly drown their wilderness, The Regular had told me, dunking their highlands and uninhabited areas under water, flooding them with dams to create cheap electricity for criminal foreign corporations and for murderers and misanthropes and those who loathe nature and life itself, as he so mildly put it; what became of the place names in the lakes the dams made? I noted, perhaps they're in the bottom of some drawer somewhere at the Place Name Institute, have they lost all meaning having lost their utility? They're forgotten, they've disappeared into the archive's dark cubbyholes, dropped out of everyday linguistic use, no longer part of descriptions, vanished from maps ... yet even if place names lose their usefulness, they don't lose their aesthetic value, in the archives, on obsolete maps, in old books; the country itself is a manuscript, that's the essence of toponymy, I noted, pleased with myself there by the sign. I need to contact the Place Name Institute and ask what's happened to all the names that got drowned by corrupt politicians in cahoots with foreign criminal enterprises, the lost children of nature, it's somewhat unclear whether there is an institute still working on behalf of all the place names, probably it got closed down before the country was drowned, generations have learned that landscapes would be worth little if they weren't named something, and that made it possible to discard the place name registry and drown the country ... but place names survive ... *Place names rise from the depths,* I noted down, standing by the sign.

Palm Sunday, 13th April. Temperature: 2 degrees. The wind in the east. Unbudging fog, now and then seeming to lighten slightly, to get sucked down into gullies and ravines, sucked up into cliffs, dragged off the mountain. I had brought a map of the glacier, it was all white, nothing to see on it except a unique, transitory contour line, no place names, no land. *The symbols of time*, I also noted down, there by the sign, the site of time, the place names of time... *Topo-time*... the phrase came to mind in English, for some reason, I noted it down, Topo-time, in my notebook, tópótími in Icelandic, topozeit... better in German, I thought, *topozeit*... it would be best if the term settled into its German form within the academic community. I allowed myself to dream, sitting there on the trunk by the sign, topozeit, I repeated it a hundred times to myself and each time the concept deepened, I didn't know exactly what it meant, but had a feeling, that's how it always goes in creative studies, intuition, it was something big, important, you can build on the concept, for example: topozeit-geist... I knew that topozeit and topotime and tópótími were something crucial, a new concept, a key to mysteries, the essence of my doctoral thesis, its expectation and solution, if I managed to do the groundwork for this new concept, lay out this concept of mine, Topo-time could become well-established within toponymy, then later within philosophy, sociology, history, the whole of the humanities, and finally more widely in scholarship, then the media, on into popular language, in the end everyone will begin saying topotime this and topotime the other, politicians will say that an idea would be subject to topotime in the budget bill; there was true topotime in the news from the South this weekend, the renowned regional reporter from the Icelandic National Broadcasting Service would say; hardly anyone would be able to express themselves without mentioning topotime—but by then it wouldn't be possible for topotime to make any headway, I thought beside my trunk at the sign, the concept would have long become distorted, divorced from its origins, toponymers would long have ceased using topozeit and topotime, scholars in general would have quit using the term, individual writers and politicians and lawyers would make a show of topotime but that, too, would be on the decrease; everyone would be done getting drunk on the topotime concept, and it would enter oblivion, never completely understood, although the concept would have completed the definite process all words and concepts and phenomena go through over a longer or shorter period of time, topotime would have gained life-experience, it would persist, as a place name does, a resolute thought in human history, a place name inside language; indeed, after the term has long been forgotten, and someone feels that humanity is wading into a new error, there would be this low whisper: topotime ... topotime ... and then the whispering would get a bit louder: topotime, topotime, and soon scholars and writers would again compete to say topotime ahead of one another because all of a sudden, everyone is saying topotime, in time and out of time; all this I noted in my notebook by my trunk at the sign near the foot of Breiðármerkurfjall.

Also this: in my mind, I see Kári Sölmundarson in the smithy whetting his weapon while Sigurður from Tvísker comes down the chimney head first. They have a lot to discuss. Sigurður had used the name *Káratindur,* after Kári Sölmundsson, for a peak approach that had recently surfaced from under a glacier in these parts; in fact, Sigurður from Tvísker is the greatest toponymist in

Iceland, although no one appreciates that fact; he's the poet of the land, he roams far and wide about the mountains in his scholarly pursuits. Many cliffs have come to light since global warming caused the glacier to dwindle, since agriculture, since the population explosion … Sigurður is to thank for the names that can now be found on new maps: Heljargnípa, Drangaklettur, Hellutindur, Sveinstindur, Sveinsgnípa (both after Sveinn Pálsson, who went out onto Öræfajökull in 1794 and whose name had not been given to anything this whole time, this topotime), Tindaborg, Hvannadalshryggur, Dyrhamar, Súlukambur, and Veðrastapi, all now well-known place names that people believe have existed since olden times, though some aren't more than thirty years old. There was a beautiful crag or ridge which recently emerged from the glacier, right next to Káraskeri, named after the Tvísker brothers: *Bræðrasker*.

✝

I stepped out onto the glacial tongue and held my breath. At first the ice was full of grit, easy to cross, suiting the horses, with their spiked horseshoes, and the trunk; I myself was wearing spikes, and went at an oblique angle up the so-called Mávabyggðarönd, the streak of boulders extending from Mávabyggðir down to the lowlands, scree the glacier has scraped out the mountains, the best signpost providing there isn't much fresh snow. It lay there, quite clear, while I was on the advancing glacier; a maze of clefts and ice-prisons lay right in front of me, I needed to thread myself along a narrow channel, deep blackness on both sides as hundreds,

if not thousands, of geese flew up in an arrow, high in flight on
the way to the blue sky above their nesting ground, they were
newly arrived, like thousands of other birds heading northwest
during the past few days. Beyond the land, the sun broke through
the clouds, sending rays of light beaming down to the moving
ocean. I heard many small streams underneath me in the glacier,
it was spring, trickling water everywhere. The fog still sat on the
mountains, but on the glacier, there was light inside the fog, and
I expected it to be bright once I reached high altitude, expected
I would head up through the clouds. My route up the glacier
would pass thousands of those singular "glacier mice," the moss
balls that roll about the glacier. An existential shiver traversed me
as I walked out into the white wasteland: I was heading to meet
my youth, lost for sure yet still pregnant with meaning for me. It
was snowing and the wind ramped up, coming from the northeast,
slanting against me, and soon the streak disappeared and everything turned white, I might direct my heading any which way in
this wind, I was barely able to see the compass, there was nothing to aim at, I could hardly see out my eyes. I wandered about
alone snowblind and in snowlight, constantly needing to break
the ice which clung to me, the ice-spatterings which hampered
the horses, these horses are so hairy and unique and but tremendously resolute, yet I regretted having taken them onto the glacier, perhaps I would have to shoot them like Captain Koch had if
they gave up dragging the trunk, but I had of course clean forget
to bring a gun along with me. A person compiles appendixes until
he breaks down under them, I thought in my snowblindness, your
baggage is your self. Captain Koch and Dr. Wegner took six tons

of hay and fodder to Grænlandsjökull for the sake of the horses, I had two hay sacks for mine, which the rear horse carried.

I could not find us a direction forward. I switched over to skis and felt the going was better. I could not make headway so I changed over to snowshoes. I was worried about the horses, they had sorrowful expressions, who was I to drag these creatures onto the glacier, but maybe they are happy getting a break from Runki from Destrikt, I thought there on the glacier, perhaps their sadness is really an expression of pleasure, probably they miss the torment, it's the same with humans as horses, I didn't know how much time had passed, I had probably been going for many hours, I was forced to stop regularly, often and for short periods, to get myself a mixture to drink and a bit to eat, to give the horses their feed bag, but it was difficult to stop, only a little further, just a little further, I told myself time and time again in the snowblindness, it will be interesting to see how I fare with my toponymical research in the blindness. When I finally stopped, I realized the frost had spread via my sweat to my flesh, I did some Müller technique to limber up and prevent the shivers plaguing me. I gave my beasts of burden a frozen tart from Vienna; best practice in the cold is to have something frozen, I told them, fire against fire, frost against frost, that is a Tyrolean trick. They were feverish for the sugar, inhaling the tart.

I walked for hours yet found no way forward. The wind kept on blowing from the northeast, blowing, drifting snow, the temperature dropped to 9 degrees frost, but despite the wind's chill I was overheated from walking and had to remind myself not to go fast but to keep a steady pace, ever gaining newer and newer

height, what insanity to attempt this journey alone, dragging my
beloved creatures with me, lugging my trunk with me in order to
be just like Captain Koch, I'm no Captain Koch, I told myself in
the snowstorm, I'm just a *National Geographic* subscriber ... I talked
to myself and asked the horses several questions, I thought about
explorers from the past century, I was hypnotized by the crunch
of snow underfoot, now and then there was a little visibility and
all at once I saw a peak rise up from the ocean of ice, a bare cliff,
at first I thought it a mirage ... no, it's the Mávabyggðir! ... then
everything went white, the earth disappeared from under me and
suddenly I was in open air, eternity, my mind rushed home to
Freyvang in Vienna into my mother's arms, I was broken apart by
a sense of guilt, I wanted to beg forgiveness from her for how difficult I had been as a child, how hopeless as a teenager, I wanted
to beg forgiveness from her for having once dunked her rubber
gloves in the cleaning bucket so they got soaked inside, I knew
mom hated that, rubber gloves dunked in cleaning water, I had
heard her say so once, and so I did it, perhaps she hadn't really
meant it, I was angry with her, she'd done something to me,
I don't remember what, it seemed to me that the most insig-
nificant things in life are the most important things in life; rubber gloves in cleaning water had in fact been a turning point,
not the death of my brother, Tómas, or so I thought during my
fall, I'd never recovered from having soaked the rubber gloves in
the cleaning water, from this crime against my mother, not ever,
while I was floating in the darkness, why had the cleaning bucket
been standing all by itself on the tiles and my mother nowhere
to be seen? or the cleaning woman, my mother always helped

the servants, there's the pail, I thought as I fell, steaming, fresh cleaning water, yellow rubber gloves on the rim, half resting in lather, and I took the opportunity in my rage and submerged the gloves, I recoiled when my hand went under the boiling water, my guilt was accompanied by a boiling hot whip-crack, it was a jerking, a yanking on the rope I'd bound to the lead horse, I was now hanging in open air upside down above the abyss, I needed to get the horse train to back up and that would lift me up, I started to whistle and call and it was ominous to hear how all my sounds were dampened, my voice quenched, it's the depths of my guilt, I thought hanging there over the abyss, and I sank still further, memories surfaced of my birth, my mother's vagina, I was making every effort to wipe this picture away and all the while I was sinking down and lower and the crevasse was narrowing, I looked down past my breast and saw, up at the top of the cre-vasse, a horse's head peeking down, it was Fuck, I yelled: FUCK! But then everything went black, the edge of the fissure gave way under the horse, he fell into the ravine, a big overhang falling with him, and we plummeted together deeper into the crevasse, me upside down and the horse above me. The snow was packed around me, hardened like concrete, said Bernharður, interpreted the Interpreter, wrote Dr. Lassi in her report, or so Bernharður wrote to me in his letter that spring of 2003.

IV.

THE FOLLOWING

Bernharður Fingurbjörg was taking a sound and well-deserved nap when I took a break from writing the report, Dr. Lassi wrote, it was 3¾ at night, the sun was rising over the glacier, the sky pale, the air clear; all the able men and farmers from most of the nearby farms had been summoned to Freysnes for deployment in order to apprehend one or more wild sheep on the mountain, as decreed by the State. I wanted to be part of the crowd, so long as I could be more useful than useless, even though I wasn't being paid by the Nature Conservation Board like the rest, I just wanted to take the opportunity to see this unique species before it was exterminated, as the law mandates. I even hoped to get the species named after me: *Ovis Lassi*. But it was to be a mournful journey. Three guys had come from the city, one an Öræfing for sure, the other two rather badly prepared, one a dwarf in a dustjacket with a fur cap, the poet Worm Serpent, a notorious outcast and embarrassing person, while the third seemed to me the most wretched, wearing worn-out, tattered clothing from the First World War, he was called The Regular, god only knows where he turned up from, rather sullen in expression and disinterested.

None of the farmers was concerned with firearms licenses; rather, they all carried shotguns and rifles baldly over their shoulders, following the laws of nature. They were mostly old bachelors with rusty fox-hunting rifles, sheep guns, and blunderbusses. Jakob from Jökulfell was unusual because he was carrying a camera, but he is an artist.

I, Dr. Lassi, a regional veterinarian in the south of Iceland, set off from the location at sunrise on Easter Sunday, April 20th, 2003, leaving from Freysnes along with farmers from the region, trying to find wild sheep in the mountains. The intention was to get there ahead of the helicopter someone had caught wind was being sent on behalf of the Ministry of Justice—the State, that is—in order to eliminate the wild livestock in the National Park. There was a slight frost and it was tranquil, ideal weather for implementing such laws, men had brought ropes so they could descend cliffs onto the icy surfaces or traverse the crevasse regions in the glacier; each of them had his Skaftafell staff in his hand, what's usually called a *pole*; without one, it's tantamount to going about naked in the mountains, a pole is an indispensable tool for running at speed and managing steep slopes, doing pole vaults over streams and fissures that are otherwise totally impassable for humans, poles like these have been used ever since Settlement, some even say *for* settlement because the land-spirit Járngrímur in Lómagnúpur holds a staff, at least in our coat of arms. Men arranged themselves by the hotel, each with his pole, and you could hear the sound of the group appreciating how long the poles were, how thick, heavy and so on, some had poles that were new this year. Beech is good for a pole, said

Muggur, it's a durable wood yet lightweight, or you could use oak or birch, larch, pine. Muggur melted down iron from car suspensions and from springs, from rotisseries and other circular bits of iron, the spike is inserted into the underside of the pole and consists of four teeth or springs called weathers, Muggur told me, they reach out to the spike to hold it in place, there's a nick in the spike where it forks like a snake's tongue, inside it there's molten hard metal; finally, three bands are bound around the bottom of the pole to prevent it from splitting. As it grips the scree, the spike gets sharpened and thus maintains itself with use, and so the spiked pole is sustainable, lasts a lifetime, like good smithing used to, Dr. Lassi wrote, today everything's disposable trash, not good for shit.

I showed up that morning to the round-up with a broomstick I'd found in a closet at the hotel, reckoning I'd done well to remember to bring a stick. Not only did they laugh at me, the broomstick was disappeared, a worn-down pole set in my hand, so thick my hand barely fit around the stick. I drew their attention to that, and discovered it's a big no-no to call a staff a stick, a staff is not a stick, I was told, but a pole. I was greatly amazed how poorly-dressed everyone was, in light jackets and old jogging outfits, jeans and sneakers. In their eyes, I looked wishy-washy, wearing my wax raincoat and my large fisherman's hat on my head in case it started to snow. Little Interpreter showed up energetic, sturdy and animated. Edda the ranger was there, standing with the so-called The Regular, who seemed preoccupied with getting to meet Sigurður from Tvísker, even as he was trying to divert attention away from himself, tripping over his own feet to introduce the poet Worm Serpent. In ancient times, a Worm lived in Svínafell, said Sigurður, which emboldened the poet. The Regular smiled a distant smile, as though he had grown old along the way. One of the greatest Icelandic chieftains was named Worm and he was a poet, a peacekeeper during an era of great violence, Sigurður was saying, the worst Iceland has ever plunged into, a time everyone fought against everyone and civil war erupted, that was no further back than the 13th century. Worm Serpent gleamed; emotional, he took off his fur hat and put it to his heart, as though he felt Sigurður was talking about him or his spirit. According to *Svínafellsaga,* for example, said Sigurður, it seems Worm had a heart attack at Þingvellir: the story says he experienced a pain in his arm and died soon after. Worm Serpent fondled and squeezed the cap, terrified and in shock, he felt he would suffer the same fate, he felt a pain in his breast, it ran down his arm, he was done for, he would have a heart attack and Sigurður here had set it off, I'm never going back to Þingvellir, Worm Serpent said to The Regular. Then Worm's wife got with child, *Svínafellsaga* says, Sigurður said; she gave birth to a boy named after his father, Worm Wormsson, he became a goði—a chieftain—as his father's heir, and traveled as the last Icelandic chieftain on behalf of the King of Norway in 1264, Worm Wormsson was the last bastion of independence of this free nation, the king gave him authority over half the country, but he drowned shortly after, along with his whole ship and its crew, in Norway, just 29 years old, and with his death the ancient chieftain's lineage in Svínafell vanished into the darkness of history... I'm 29 years old! said Worm Serpent; he immediately fainted in the hotel lobby. The poet was carried over to a couch; he was left there awhile as the rest of us went out to search for the sheep.

We, this little armed band, had not gone far into the mountains when Runki from Destrikt caught sight of the silhouette of a sheep high up on a mountainside, a shadow image standing there gravely still and puffed up and bare against the morning sky; for a good while, no one saw anything else except Runki, I can't see a thing, I said, some thought it was just the image of a sheep on the cliff, we stood there watching for an eternity, no creature could hold still this long, Hálfdán from Tvísker grabbed the binoculars he had around his neck. Isn't it a sheep? I asked. For sure, naturally, of course, said Hálfdán, a sheep with a thin neck, long haired, white with a dark nose, from the looks of it, possibly horned, a badger-faced moorit, a white back and a moorit belly ... no one dared dispute that, everyone knows that Hálfdán can detect a winter wren from a mile away with one eye while the other finds an insect behind a stone, Runki from Destrikt did not dare dispute the color analysis made by the natural scientist from Tvísker, although I could see he longed to, his mouth itching, vibrating, Runki urged everyone from their spots and he himself started running with his dog up a narrow gully over loose scree, we did not follow on foot but leaned forward on our poles to watch him tear up the rocky slopes, climbing the cliff, running along ledges and jumping over lavafields across the ravine. Runki was adept with his pole but the white-yet-dark sheep stood still as a headstone, the morning sun frowning behind him, casting his silhouette sharp against the sky, an awesome sight. Runki approached quickly, the dog sniffing at his heels; Runki was wearing brand new sneakers he'd got at the Cooperative in Fagurhólsmýri and he moved surely and swiftly, he had already reached the white-dark sheep and it seemed to us he was going to stumble headlong into it, we heard a screech echo across the morning calm, Runki had sent the dog ahead, Get up! Runki shouted to the bitch, Get up! *Jasmine!* echoed in the mountains, Right! Jasmine! No! Come-bye! Right!...The farmer from Destrikt deftly commanded his bitch, waving his hand like an air traffic controller, and she immediately ran up the cliffs like a trout in a stream, much to the amazement of we on the ground below hearing the commands. But then the sheep disappeared, nowhere to be seen, and now the bitch Jasmine was standing on the ledge, confused and uncertain against the sky, far more disheveled than the sheep who had stood there only a moment before. Then Runki reached the edge of the mountain and also stood silhouetted against the sky, looking around him with his baseball cap, the least still of the three, he ran in circles, to no end, the white-dark sheep had evaporated, wild sheep are famous for their disappearing act, Dr. Lassi wrote, they re-appear somewhere else, utterly unexpected, behind a person, like a guard in an art gallery, scaring the person out of their wits, Runki came back along the cliff slopes, somewhat dejected, and the sheep appeared on the ledge again, again standing out against the sky, it was like he blinked, I was convinced the sky and the sheep were light and shadow alternately, all of us down below on the ground hollered and called out, Runki whirled back to the place and now tried to come upon the sheep from above but it disappeared again just before Runki appeared on the ledge, Runki stood there for a long time and scratched his head under his deer hat. Finally, he returned empty-handed, in a foul temper, deeply ashamed, blustering at his bitch who was the target of both her master's embarrassment and caresses.

The following dogs had come along on the journey with us to find the wild sheep on the mountains: *Sámur*, named after the most famous dog in Icelandic history, the dog owned by Gunnar from Hlíðarenda, the hero's most trusted friend: when Gunnar was buried, Sámur sat day and night on the mound and howled until he died of sorrow, the mound was then opened up so Sámur could be with Gunnar, it's said Gunnar opened his arms in the mound when Sámur arrived, and threw out all the possessions so that the mound would never be robbed by the country's rabble-rousers, and thus the two friends would remain undisturbed by archaeologists and desecrators and grave robbers; among other things a halberd flew out, killing two men along the way, everyone wanted to own the halberd and thus began Iceland's karmic journey, right down to its seabed, the poet Eggert Ólafsson last had the halberd, it was on the boat when he sailed across Breiðafjörður with his bride and their household possessions, because they were moving after the wedding, on board there were ancient manuscripts and ancient gems, and then the woman fell overboard, and Eggert jumped away from the steering wheel to go after her, and the boat tipped on its side and sank, Iceland sank there, and with Eggert Ólafsson went the last hope of our god-forsaken land, and Gunnar's halberd was lost forever, but Gunnar and Sámur enjoyed their peace in their mound, Dr. Lassi wrote. Two place names are associated with Gunnar's Sámur: Sámsból and Sámsreitur. Sámur has been the most popular dog name ever since. Gunnar's Sámur came from Ireland, a wonderful dog, a companion as good as any zealous man, he had human intelligence, it says that in *Njál's Saga*, Dr. Lassi wrote, Sámur was loyal to Gunnar, their lives intertwined, Sámur was probably an Irish wolfhound, they are indeed gigantic, slender hounds, perhaps from Ancient Egyptian stock, and were used to protect sheep herds against wolves, but then fences took over from dogs, fences took over from both shepherds and dogs, fences have destroyed a lot of culture. Men treated the dog poorly in their attack on Gunnar, and it is an ugly and sad chapter in *Njála*, writes Dr. Lassi, you're hard done by Sámur, my foster-brother, Gunnar said, awaking to his howling, Sámur's howls seemed so intense and loud, the like of which people had never heard before, the dog had been struck in the head with an axe after biting the crotch of one of the attackers, and ripping off his genitals, all to defend his master; I must confess the terrible fact that I've always enjoyed reading that part.

Our Sámur, heading the pursuit, is heavy-built and hairy, black on top but light brown underneath, he seems to be a mix of Icelandic and German sheepdogs, he has light eyebrows similar to the dog Kafka, although he is a Shäfer; Sámur is the senior member of the dog pack, the leader in the search for wild sheep, the alpha animal, intelligent and resolute. The next in the hierarchy is *Kátur*, who is gray all over and mottled, a somewhat diligent, efficient dog, a workman, obedient and gentle and child-friendly, a dog who enjoys little better than shepherding. Kátur is from an inscrutable breed and so is a true Icelander. *Lubbi* is a careless, inferior herder and not everyone was happy he had got to come along, some said he didn't serve any purpose, that he got underfoot and was no use, he got an ugly reception from Runki, who thought the world of his own *Jasmine*, a Border Collie bitch, extremely obedient and gentle and the best shepherd, but fearful of her master; I don't blame her, everyone was a bit afraid of Runki, men and animals alike. He had learned dog training from some videotape, which seemed outrageous. Dog training?... Dog training by video tape?... you can get anything these days! said Muggur from Bölti. It's a certain fact that no dog in the Icelandic countryside had ever before received training, all the way back to the Settlement, Dr. Lassi wrote, hitherto the rule has been that good herders are obedient by chance alone, farmers will repeatedly kill their dogs until they get an obedient and good-tempered dog and then keep them; dogs have always been worthless, it's *chance* that dictates whether one has a good herd-dog in Iceland. Runki from Destrikt's bitch understands language fluently and has a big vocabulary, he stumbled upon a honey-pot with this bitch, the other farmers said, but Runki had broken his back training this dog, watching the videotape every single day for weeks, his wife got to choose the name Jasmine, which feels modern, but he always feels ashamed when he calls the dog...Jasmine! Come-bye! Runki shouts all day long to his dog, Come-bye! Jasmine! he calls and looks around embarrassed, scratching his butt frantically, grinding out old lumps from his arse-hairs and shaking them down his pants legs; Destrikt-Runki can send his bitch in whichever direction he orders and he stands up on a hill with a little pennant and an umpire's whistle, flapping his hands like a traffic cop and blowing the whistle and Jasmine translates from across the ridge and gravel, she crawls up the cliff and down into a lava tube, Runki comes running after her, shouting: Right! Right!...Jasmine! Come-bye! Left!...stop! Jasmine! Stop! No!...you devil!...the two of them do the work of many men and have been a breath of fresh air within the shepherding world. Flosi from Svínafell remarked to old Muggur: Runki has a most excellent dog. I thought it was a cat, said Muggur, snorting a pile of snuff from the back of his hand, I was really surprised what good control he had of his cat.

A strange fact, one I've never seen it discussed, is that Gunnar from Hlíðarenda's dog had a Biblical name, *Sámur,* at a time when paganism reigned in Iceland, Dr. Lassi writes, Sám, or *Samuel,* God's name in Hebrew; Sámur may also have come from medieval Persian studies, the dog being dark in color because *Sam* is an ancient Persian legendary character translated as *sá myrki,* the dark one; Nordic Vikings, the so-called *væringjar,* wandered far and wide in Iran and learned the indigenous language in order to conduct business and talk to kings, being merchant vikings who believed in the free flow of money; today, it's quite the opposite, I must interject at this point, Dr Lassie wrote, today's banksters, free-market vikings, can't talk any languages, have no courtesy, and never travel; in Icelandic, *sámur* is sometimes used instead of other words for black, dark, or even unclean, as it is in Persia; it can be intimately related to the Turkish-Mongolian word *shaman* or spirit doctor...Could it be the Nordic people sought sheep in Persia and brought them home to breed? Dr. Lassi's report questioned; merino sheep were at one time found in the mountains of Persia, they originally lived in highland pastures and avoided human interference; they are famous for the quality of their wool, they have wool that does not prickle, it's said, the merino sheep brought over for breeding in the 18th and 19th centuries caused the *psoroptes ovis* disease, and the species died like flies, precipitating a tough crisis, a famine ... So the third possibility concerning this Sámur of ours, the one I personally think most likely, is that his name comes from the original Indo-European word meaning one, *einn*, which later became the verb *sameina,* to combine, the German word *sammeln*, to gather together as one, and so a perfectly chosen name for a herder ... aren't we used to knitting scarves from dog hairs? I asked, instinctively connecting Bernharður's scarf and these canine thoughts, don't we comb dogs in the country? I know hair and wool require very different treatment or is it the case that the wool from wild sheep is different from other wool? ... These days, people have other things to do with their time than comb dogs, said Runki from Destrikt, shocked, although it's something people get up to on the farms where everyone is stressed-out, heh ... The wool of a wild sheep is denser, said Fippi from Núpstaður quietly, softer, stronger and warmer and more useful, wild sheep is in all respects better than domesticated sheep.

I'm wearing underwear, I said, then hesitated, leaving my sentence hanging. The Tvísker brothers looked at me because they are attentive listeners and intelligent and courteous men, but they didn't meet my eyes like some louts, they instead gazed down to the ground with composed expressions, waiting for what I wanted to say, the district veterinarian, so they might consider it. I'm wearing underwear made from merino wool, I said to the men, finally, which I got from my wife as a Christmas gift. I asked for this underwear especially because my wife cannot abide wool and always gives me something worthless as a Christmas gift, this underwear was advertised clearly as Icelandic apparel and I thought it was time for Icelanders to be making their own underwear again as they had done for 1100 years until they became new-monied plebs; that Christmas Eve, however, I discovered this special Icelandic underwear is made with Turkish wool and sewn in China, it was written absolutely shamelessly on the label under the declaration about it being Icelandic clothing, I got angry with the clothes and threw them away in the corner, and my wife was angry about that, it's all so different from the good old country which we in the older generation recognize, it took me time to be reconciled to these thin, artificial tatters, I told the men, but now I'm proud of these quality goods, a luxury, they don't itch you underneath and thus I can hardly believe merino wool caused the disease in the 18th century; I quickly unfastened my pants and allowed the farmers to finger the wool that did not prickle, to feel how soft merino is ... Oh-ooh, it cannot be high quality wool unless it prickles, said Flosi from Svínafell.

†

I grew amazed at the fellowship between the one who went by The Regular, his friend Kiddi, and the dwarf who fell unconscious in the lobby. Those three came into the hotel room the night I was getting ready for the trip, they seemed to know the patient, Edda the ranger was with them, hanging out with The Regular. Freysnes is your home now, my one-legged friend, just like Freyvangur, The Regular said to Bernharður there on his death bed, smiling as if he had looked forward to saying this, you can lay here as long as you want and read, not everyone has it this good, all you have to do is be, so what if one of your legs has been sawed off, what does that matter? I would give both legs to get to stay in a country hotel for a few months ... one-legged and one-buttocked, dear friend, a *gelding*, that's what you've transformed into, both a spiritual gelding and a physical gelding, that's why you are a *superman*, I'd just enjoy this, the insurance company is going to pay your hotel costs or the state or the travel agency or the embassy or some other damn place, even though it's all one what you are doing with your doctoral thesis, that you went up to Mávabyggðir, that's not really remarkable here, in fact, nothing is remarkable in Öræfi, said The Regular, it's not remarkable that Dr. Lassi amputated you here in the hotel in Freysnes, it's not at all remarkable or surprising that you're alive, you're just not at all remarkable, so you can entirely relax, Bernharður my friend, and don't think you're someone special.

The Regular laughed and Bernharður smiled. We all wanted to comfort Bernharður, I pointed out he'd have a nice view out the window if he sat up, he should be able to enjoy it while we were out getting the sheep, although it's a disaster seeing the lupine on the glacier moraine, seeing how the desolation which emerges from under the glacier cannot be enjoyed and left to heal in peace, that's a sad sight, being as it is, what do people really have against rocks? are people scared of rock? does the brightness of the rock remind the multitude of death? is the rock a remembrance of death? … man thinks he loves nature, but he really hates nature, he only loves what is cultivated by human hands, the forest, the meadow, the field, he merely tolerates grass, level meadows, the earth is subsumed by animal feed, not by kindness and caring but murder and cruelty, the farmer is no pillar of society, said The Regular by the window, the farmer is a hangman, a state-sponsored land-hangman and a tormentor of beasts, it's entirely evident everywhere, the farmer rips apart the land and drains the moorland and destroys birdlife, he blames the mink in the ditches for the death of the birds, but it's the farmer who kills the birds with the ditches, the farmer kills both the mink and the birds, he shoots the foxes, the farmer kills all the animals, he dries the land where it's supposed to be wet, floods the land where it should be dry, he cultivates meadows and fields to destroy nature with their monotony, eliminating animal species that have been there a million times longer than man has been on earth, it's agriculture that's destroying the earth, both its spirit and its work, greed, it's all becoming clearer and clearer, evolution and progress is what destroys the earth, the agriculturalist thinks that he is keeping humanity alive but he's actually eliminating it, it cannot last forever, the economy is cracking, epidemics will gush out, nature will burst apart, we must manage to learn from this, not even the farmer can live on his production or, rather, he cannot live on his destruction, although he considers himself the prerequisite for life on earth, he's remunerated by the State for killing animals and the ecosystem, all so he can buy tractors and quad bikes and many cars and jeeps and trucks and excavators and backhoes and bulldozers and combine harvesters and all kinds of other devices that cost trillions and which he uses to destroy the land, he can build the largest house in the country, and that provides him cover for torturing animals, intelligently-raised creatures appear senseless to him, property and materials, money, cattle, and if the farmer loses a lamb he loses his money, he blames everything else, fox, mink, the weather, he finds the money he lost within the State, he finds it in the slaughterhouse, said The Regular at the hotel window in Freysnes, if I lose five thousand crowns on the heath, I don't require the State to pay me back, if a raven steals my wallet, I don't shout whining to the media and demand the State provide compensation, it's really the State that has destroyed the land and killed all the animals, the farmer is only the State hangman ... indeed, some farmers have become forest farmers and been given State subsidies to plant trees which destroy the undergrowth, added The Regular, still at the window, they get poison from the State to kill the moorland and heaths to plant alien trees that destroy all the undergrowth, they call themselves good and think they are doing good when they are doing evil, State reforestation is a god in a community like the Ministry of Agriculture, the critic of reforestation or of the Ministry of Agriculture is taken and burned at stake, he's met with fury and ferocity, such criticism is not welcome in society, the lamb is sacred, the only free creature in the country, it is everywhere, the Icelandic lamb is holier than cows in India, if you drive into a lamb and lose your child in the ensuing car accident, as has often happened, you get fined for running into the sheep and have to

pay the farmer for his damaging loss, a lamb that was on the way
to the slaughterhouse; how easy it was in an unforested country
to impress on the nation that forestry was an advance, people are
afraid of panoramas and beauty and feel ashamed they live in a
treeless country, their impression is that culture lives in the trees
like monkeys, that a treeless land is an uncultured land, that there
are no mysteries, no treasures, no fairy tales, no castles, people are
ashamed of living in such a poor country, such an uninhabitable
country where no forests grow, it is true that the weather here is
plenty good enough for forest, little matter when Skaftafell was
sold, said The Regular at the window in Freysnes, when Ragnar
performed his unexpected work abolishing eleven hundred years
of his family history in Skaftafell, reaching all the way back to settlement, the Icelandic Forest Service fought hard to buy the earth
at Skaftafell so they could breed a new forest there, with foreign
pine trees and fir trees; if they'd succeeded, the Director of the
Forest Service, working for the State, would have destroyed one
of the largest natural pearls on earth, yet Ragnar didn't want an
exotic new forest but to protect the land in its natural form, so
that future generations could enjoy staying in this magnificent
nature, so Ragnar sold the State the land on the condition that
everyone was given equal access to the estate and that everyone
could enjoy the beauty in perpetuity, *as far as human power can
achieve,* Ragnar stipulated in the condition, said The Regular, one
eruption like 1362 and everything would be a wasteland again,
that's the beauty, that's why I come to Öræfi every year because
true beauty is perishable, I'm incomparably grateful to Ragnar
for opening up the area to the public and making such a big

sacrifice which stretched back to Settlement, because what is beauty? The highest quality? Everyone has the right to enjoy nature, without beauty this world would be unbearable, everything would be empty, gray and dead, many people, of course, have no sense of beauty and are spiritless, they cannot enjoy it except as a way to the balance their own delights and greed, many find an unknown force drives them to destroy nature like, for example, the Director of the Icelandic Forest Service, who offered Ragnar a fortune under the table, an amount of money that none of his relatives all the way back to Settlement had ever seen before in one place, as if he had found the gold ship, it was the public's tax money the Director was waving about, with this sort of money you can do whatever you want, Ragnar, said the Director, you've slaved away enough here in this vegetation-poor country, these miserable *Wastelands*, go to the Canary Islands and enjoy life in your family's bosom, you've never been anywhere, now's your chance, take this money and enjoy your twilight years in peace and calm, save your relatives from the daily grind and invite them to drink with you at Klöru Bar in the Canary Islands, where the Minister of Agriculture and many other change makers enjoy the nightlife, you can do that too, the Director said to Ragnar in Skaftafell. I don't want to suffocate the land, said Ragnar, alter it with imported plants and human hands, Sitka spruce, Russian larch, Alaskan aspen, but to have Icelandic trees, birch and rowan, willow bushes, the existing forests ... These are racial prejudices! cried the Forestry Director, you are standing in the way of developing our national mentality, Ragnar, I'll take this to the newspapers, how you're standing in the way of the future, it reminds me of the nationality-cleansing by the Third Reich, will there be a *crystal night* in Skaftafell? Sitka spruce and Alaskan aspen grew here before the ice age and the leaves of such trees have been found in the wasteland, you know that well, these trees have the *right* to be here, like the Jews in Israel ... Well, fellow, said Ragnar, I hadn't thought I would accept a bribe and sacrifice the land, only wanting to protect nature as it is, everyone ought to get to come to Skaftafell and enjoy its nature, I had no plan to sell the beauty. This angered the Forestry Director, who wanted to shut the country down and went so far in his plans for revenge that an entire army of men and women all across the country does nothing but plant trees, said The Regular by the hotel window in Freysnes, it was the Director of the Icelandic Forest Service's revenge, and this army carries out its idiotic propaganda in the media on behalf of reforestation, everyone becomes a fool for reforestation, people are afraid of rock and sand, of everything that gives insight into nature, they want to dress the country in foreign clothing, they have even got scared of the wind because it threatens economic identity, sitting under shelter is a sign of prosperity, sitting under shelter and stuffing oneself, said The Regular, the wind has become the nation's chief enemy, and the Icelandic Forest Service plants and plants trees to shelter and protect the economy, the wind is poverty, reforestation is supposed to rescue us from the humiliation of wind gusting around homes and cottages—but forests provide only shadows and mud, nothing else, and isn't there enough of that in human nature? asked The Regular, the whole nation has gone crazy for reforestation and mad for shadows and mud, the nation has become shadow and mud, there's nothing but planting another and another tree so you can be happier, and soon ten thousand trees, twenty thousand trees around your summer house, five hundred thousand trees, ten million trees, an idiotic fear of death is nowhere more obvious than in all this reforestation, planting trees in a straight line, making quadratic forests, is that supposed to be civilized? asked The Regular at the window, these square forests are evidence their purpose is to fight nature, to fight themselves, reforestation destroys vegetation, the worst thing you can do is imitate nature because that's impossible, reforestation amounts only to self-denial and self-destruction, unless people really believe they're restoring the forest that was here during the Settlement, with poplar and spruce, and thereby regaining their ego? Do we need to timber the land from mountain to shore with square forests? For shame, I always feel happiest out on the hearth in a hearty breeze, said The Regular at the window, trees are for man alone, a man gets caught up in this hell like underwear in a zipper; a wide expanse is meant to look back at a man, what about untouched beauty? untouched nature? Isn't that the world's best quality today, getting to enjoy God's creative work, the number 1 artist!...What is the Director of the Icelandic Forest Service doing, strutting about improving on God's creation (number 1 artist!)? ...They ought to shut down the Icelandic Forest Service, as soon as possible, and establish the *Icelandic Neglect Service* instead, in order to protect nature the way it is so we can learn from it how the world works; that won't happen with reforestation and the cultivation of meadows and sheep and pork farming and fur farming; eroded soil gives us an insight into life, lava and black sand make one drunk with poetic joy, eroded soil, lava and black sand provide insight into life as a creation, and everyone wants to struggle against this insight into the creation of life … alas, I guess I'm like the thistle, I'm most content with barren trails … let's not talk about lupine, my dear Bernharður, said The Regular at the window, it's a plague, a lost war we're waging against ourselves, I grow infinitely sad when I see lupine or even hear about it, lupine is a blue sorrow, a sign of our self-esteem, a low self-esteem, the lupine itself is such a beautiful plant, magnificent, but it's abused for destructive purposes like the reforestation, used against the heath and the marsh and nature in its entirety, it was the Director of the Icelandic Forest Service who brought lupine to Öræfi 50 years ago, we weren't in any mystery about it, lupine has already wrecked many more regions than the miserable eruption of 1362, but she does so quietly, lupine behaves exactly like a virus, a cancer, exactly like man, it squeezes itself in and destroys everything from within and a million-fold; an attempt was made to conceal the rock when the bridges opened in 1974, to hide the glacier-waves, memorials to every glacier that has stretched out its tongue, to hide the sand, to hide the heaths and the gravel beds, to hide these monuments to time and nature's power, filthy children, the waves are unrecognizable and impassible because of lupine, you can no longer go on a walking tour of the waves and skerries and examine the rock as you did in the old days, said The Regular at the window. The Tvísker brothers have tried various methods to eradicate this nasty plant and recover the old heaths but without success, the seed is stored in the ground for at least half a century, like a lost tent hidden in a glacier, the lupine springs up unexpectedly all over the place, disperses with terrible speed, kills and destroys everything that exists, both vegetation and desolation, as pyroclastic flow reveals in slow motion ... Everything that's called *cultivation* ... cultivation is anti-nature, anti-life, anti-God, all this reforestation and sheep farming and horticulture, first and foremost I'm opposed to all cultivation, said The Regular at the window of the hotel in Freysnes, I am all in with God and nature, humans, animals, plants and rocks and glaciers and the wind; I'm all for the wasteland.

†

The badger-faced moorit sheep was being debated below the cliffs, Dr. Lassi wrote in her report, what sheep could this have been, did anyone know they had failed to bring such a creature home from the mountain during the round-up last fall? Was this a wild lamb? Was it really so long-legged? Some people thought that the sheep they were trying to get from the National Park must have its roots in the Núpsstaður forest, must never have been domesticated, they were descended from the famous wild sheep of Núpstaður, which stayed out all year round for centuries, perhaps from the Settlement, wild sheep that were never housebroken or fodder or cultivated in any way but lived freely in birch forests at the glacier's foot and up in the mountains, the wild sheep was always a special breed, said the men, tall and sedulous and plump, notorious for being able to disappear when someone was trying to get it. It was always considered a delicious sheep with a good flesh. Too much feed and attention only yields lazy, indifferent sheep, the way all Iceland's sheep have become, *indifferent*, I said there under the crag, Dr. Lassi wrote, indeed, there's still a few of the very ancient leader sheep about, sheep which are so wise and weather-aware, with an excellent sense of direction, sturdy and daring, the leader sheep is a genuinely unique species of lamb, and it's found nowhere in the world except Iceland, because there were attempts to eliminate it, it's in our nature to eliminate everything special, but fortunately that didn't happen, so-called leisure farmers saved the stock, which is indeed peculiar, these long legs, a slender, stretched face, thin wool, intelligent-looking eyes, I've always found the leader sheep to be almost a mix of goat, dog, and Nordic Studies professor, I said there under the cliffs' shadow, wrote Dr. Lassi. The leader sheep has a built-in barometer that makes it an excellent meteorologist: if a storm is coming the next day, the leader wether refuses to leave its shelter, the leader sheep heads across to the mountains, gathers the herd, finds its way in snow-fog to the upper heath, through the weather, blindly, it breaks its way through snowdrifts and the sheep follow after in a streak, leading men and creatures safe and well to shelter and pasture; little copper balls jingle on their horns to maintain constant focus, the leader sheep is studious but hardy, good for the going, erect and nimble and accompanied by its herd, better in all its qualities than the lazy, cultivated sheep. The wild sheep is fat and shy, the leader sheep is lean and gentle, the lazy sheep is ugly and annoying, Dr. Lassi wrote in her report. The badger-faced moorit ewe Runki from Destrikt chased disappeared and wasn't seen again, not at first, showing up later in an entirely different place, which seemed miraculous, the wild sheep is so talented it can hide itself in lava tubes and lead men out on lone journeys, can return to the slope and head them out to the cliffs, where they fall to their death, their bellies bursting so that the entrails scatter far and wide over the rock, and it's hard to clean up the trash, and it's best to let the fox lick it up and clean the rock.

Again a sheep was seen on the cliffs, it was black and blended into the mountain, Runki said it was at a dead end, but some disputed this, without further debate, without a long-winded deliberation which would never lead anywhere, he tore away from the place again with Jasmine but stopped before he got too close, vanished down somewhere with her, prowling about with his bitch, peeking here and there, then he pulled the rifle off his back and aimed it, took aim and shot, the crack rushed onto the mountain and up the glacier and ran in a big circle around the mountain hall, I followed the sound with my eyes, turning around in a ring, and then we saw the lamb falling down the cliff to the rockbed where its carcass remained. Now the air became thick, and nothing peeked out from the mountains, I felt the spirit of the mountains, alive and ghostly, the dogs slow and tangled about our feet, fearful-eyed, as though death was awaiting us up ahead; a cold shiver chilled through me, we flocked single file over the loose stones, if your foot slipped it was a long fall down. The mountain fog gave us an advantage over the helicopter that was on the way. Why do we risk ourselves for some lamb or other? I asked myself, we considered ourselves a rescue operation, we must *save* sheep from the mountain, from outdoors, from the inclement, bring them under human control, within the law, but this was no rescue operation, it was more like a hunting trip, a military raid, any sheep approaching civilization from these free mountain ranges would be slaughtered, the rest shot from a distance. Nobody is allowed to eat the creatures, I have to make sure that State laws are enforced, that all the carcasses are disposed of in the trash incinerator that heats Flosalaug; such is the fate of the most singular and wild livestock in the world.

Sheep should simply be wild, I thought under the cliff, Dr. Lassi wrote in the report, I should be sitting at home with my wife and not taking part in this foolhardiness, drinking coffee and reading *The Settlement in Skaftafell District* instead of toiling away here in precipitous scree moseying about with this cumbersome pole I have no idea how to use, on this deathly stony mountain ridge, this Hafrafell with its evil Illukletta and mystical X... in reality, farming should be banned, I thought as soon as I looked at the weeping, cracking glacier, we were now far inside the wasteland at the root of the glacier, the Öræfings slid down the scree with poles under armpits, using them as a third leg, going fast but gently, bumping over large rocks and floating a dozen meters at a time down the steep slopes as though they were mountain goats. I felt heavy, cumbersome, a layabout. The sheep should be free, I thought, looking out at the cracking glacier, we should ban farming and sheep rearing and get rid of the *horfellislögin*, the laws against wild animals starving, we should instead let sheep take care of themselves, we should stop interfering in everything, if it dies it dies, if it lives it lives, the wild sheep here are a chosen few, this wild sheep is *elite*, the gods selected the sheep to turn away from man and starvation laws and *búfjárlögin* and the State as a whole, the circle of compensation, they should be remunerated with *life* not death, the wild sheep have nowhere to be, people fervently seek to eliminate anything free in this country, to exterminate a whole species, and so all farming as we know it should be shut down, government subsidies for industrial farming, it's no longer right, I thought there under the rocks as I looked about the creeping glacier, Dr. Lassi wrote, the whole country taken over by meadows to produce dry fodder for creatures who are going to be slaughtered; before 1362, cereal was grown in the Province for humans to eat, and today only to fatten animals for death. Sheep are intelligent creatures, not idiotic as people always say; if a sheep doesn't want to go home, if it chooses to be out in winter, to forsake, that is, the conditions and behavior it encounters on the farm, then the sheep has will, has chosen for itself, the sheep's shyness stems from experience, what's shyness but an acquaintance with man? Humans use this stupid starvation law as an excuse, we've become ironically conditioned to tormenting animals, wanting to shoot sheep in the name of animal welfare and humanity, to run them off the rocks because farmers didn't get to inject poisons or toxins in them and give them trash to eat at home in the extermination camps, a.k.a. farms, what's a farmer but a torture guard, an executioner of animals? I grew up in the countryside, my parents were farmers, and I have gone to all the farms in the whole South of Iceland, my parents were tormentors of animals but they were simply performing their duty, they were not evil by nature, just low-minded and with bad taste, my parents were Eichmannic animal torturers for the State and I am an animal torturer for the State, whole generations are stuck in this torture mire, extermination is our ever-present guiding light, always the only solution, under our own shadow of uncertainty we extinguished our pork stocks, we practically extinguished the Icelandic dog, which was saved by a foreigner, quite frankly, we extinguished our goat stocks, chicken stocks and there's more we might tally up, we want to eliminate the foxes and the mink, the vegetation, we really actually want to eliminate the country, ourselves, we're ashamed even though we act like we don't know shame... Icelanders are a mixed-up nation of hunters, Dr. Lassi writes, greedy, scared, and short-sighted, we should protect wildlife by leaving it alone, instead of constantly competing to destroy them, there's clearly something wrong with us, the wild sheep brings some vice in our character to the surface, something we do not want to face up to, some old black shadow in our soul, the wild sheep is our subconscious, I thought under the cliffs as I looked out on the creeping glacier, Dr. Lassi wrote in the report, because we want to eradicate this darkness, although it's never really possible.

I looked up from these musings of mine, sluggish and gloomy, and noticed that they had managed to corner the wild sheep and tie a rope around its horns and neck, they were in full swing trying to get her down from the glacier, Dr. Lassi writes. Then I saw old Muggur from Bölti walking along the mountain ridge with a damn ram on his shoulders, looking like nothing less than a giant troll with broad chest, the Tvísker brothers had gone high up on the slopes to pick grasses and write in notebooks, to look through their binoculars and gather samples. Kiddi came upon his grandfather on top of the glacier, and his bitch lying there, giving birth in the snow, he took each puppy and placed them in his lunch-box, packing them together well and propping them up with soft bread, then he set the lunch box back in his pack and continued walking. They were chatting together when Runki came running down the mountain slope with a large collection of wild sheep, nobody could be in the way or it would frighten the sheep; we scattered in all directions. Runki was making all kinds of gestures with his whole body, giving coded signals we mustn't frighten the sheep, it shouldn't have been possible to drive a herd of wild sheep ahead of a man, according to theory, but he repeatedly commanded his bitch Jasmine with his pole first right then left now up and out and she rushed to and fro, working hard to hold the sheep together, I cried out and ran to help, so did some others in the area, we arranged ourselves so that the sheep couldn't escape onto the glacier, into Illukletta, they were so frenzied in their shy anger that it was mesmerizing to see, the group swept forward like starlings at sunset over the Paris skyline, I had to hit myself on my thigh to avoid getting stuck in a trance and staring like a troll at a clear sky; I was ready, I had taken up a stance like a goalkeeper...The sheep tore toward the Tvísker brothers who rose and swung their poles and shouted and called, quiet and gentle, they are mild men, it is not in their nature to scream, Runki drove the sheep with great intensity and speed down the scree...The Regular clearly had no idea what was going on and stood there in the middle of the heath, with Runki yelling: Get away! Get away!...Then The Regular ran toward the sheep, and they scattered in all directions, smashing through all our defenses and escaping out into the wide expanse. Runki and The Regular came together. What the hell are you doing, boy! Runki hurled invectives at The Regular, who stood there gasping and puffing and leaning over his pole, the both watched the sheep disappearing hither and thither, rushing up gullies and ravines, up slopes, out onto the glacier... I'm protecting nature, said The Regular. I ought to thrash you, Runki said, lifting his pole, but The Regular sped away from his swipe like a mink and set off down the hill, Jasmine staring and looking at her master, bewildered, as his eyes narrowed with dark rage.

I'm *olly olly oxen free*, The Regular mournfully said to me shortly afterward, Dr. Lassi wrote, I don't stand a chance against these warriors, and you know what, those old men are spryer than me, I was assigned a spot further down the scree near a promontory some way further from the summit and had to stand in the way there, and seeing that no sheep had come from the promontory and escaped past me back up ono the mountain, there was no chance any of the sheep were on the promontory; I was delighted with my role, said The Regular, I sat down on a rock and had some coffee and some cake, from there I had a great view of the sand and the mountains and the glacier, I rather regretted not having Worm Serpent with me so we could shorten the time by talking poetics or composing rhymes, he was further down, he's quite bad at hiking, a wretch, really, I took a sip here and there, let my mind roam the cliffs, now and then felt a spell of dizziness so had to roll onto my belly and clutch the moss tight, and then I got bored and decided to find out whether I couldn't better amuse myself on the killing trip.

Kiddi was positioned a long way into the cliff belt, chasing a wild ram, Kiddi saw that he was heading for a tight corner or would get thrown off the cliff bridge and splattered down on the cliffs; he ran as far as he could onto a very narrow ledge near a precipitous landslide and glided hundreds of yards down, Kiddi saw where the ram went below him single-file around a corner, heavy but agile, when he came around the corner there was no ram there and no egress and he thought it must have fallen down, then as he stood there Kiddi became of the wild ram which had raised itself up on hind legs and now hissed and smacked its tongue, startling Kiddi, the ram took to its feet and drove him back, almost off the cliff, butting his side so that Kiddi's foot slipped off the ledge and floundered on the loose gravel; Kiddi took off his rope and threw a snare around the horns and pulled hard, he fastened the pole to it, the ram stormed away from the place and dragged Kiddi on his stomach across the rocks, Kiddi flung himself to his feet and ran past the ram and led him by the reins from the impasse back to the heath.

The Regular and I stood and watched and thought, amazed, Dr. Lassi writes. No one goes to herd the wild sheep like when the lazy sheep are rounded-up from the mountains ready for slaughter, as Runki had tried to, blaming The Regular for his failure; the wild sheep must be tamed, said Jakob, one and only one lamb at a time, it requires a lot of skill and comprehension because it runs counter to everything men tend to set store in; the wild herd is frenzied from anger and fights for its life, there is a certain trick to reining it in that, done right, can harness its strength, use the sheep's strength to direct it down the mountain—not unlike the Japanese martial art *aikido,* where agile old men treat trolls like empty cardboard boxes, I inferred from Jakob, and nobody was better at this than Jakob from Jökulfell, it was a pleasure to watch him on the slope, he relaxed at just the right moment and flung his rope so that beautiful waves formed along the line, mesmerizing people, then the ewe took to its feet in the direction Jakob indicated and if anyone could have spoken, the only word they'd have been able to use was to mention Jakob's *art*.

The weather in the mountains was clearing. I was done pursuing wild sheep; I never meant to take part, just wanted to see this special sheep, analyze it and give it a name. I followed along with the Tvísker brothers, I watched Hálfdán inch forward along a green border on a harsh and stony scree, a hot stream must run there, I could see things growing where Hálfdán was while everything was barren where the others were. And then several things happened at once. Hálfdán looked around, stooping a little, his expression benign, glancing up at the sky, then at his watch, he fished out his barometer, his thermometer, his compass, he stood and thought and looked around, walked a few steps, rolled a stone over and found a beetle which had never before been found in Iceland, a new species. Runki from Destrikt was amazed by Hálfdán's useless toil and his eccentricity given how all the sheep had scattered, demanding that he must help with the sheep or be left behind or do whatever he damn please!...Yes, of course, Hálfdán murmured, the beetle there in his hand, and set off. I went over to Hálfdán and got to look at the find, the beetle was so small that she could hardly be seen by eyes alone, Runki shouted and tried to herd the men to herd the sheep, everyone seemed rather unaccustomed to such hullaballoo and not best pleased but then the men heard the helicopter approaching, flying low along the glacier's foot and curving toward the hills, her whistling and clapping sound reverberating everywhere in the mountains, the National Coast Guard helicopter flew up the mountain to us and the members of the police Viking Division started shooting at the wild sheep from the helicopter, we all dived for cover behind the rocks and couldn't do anything except watch the events with shocked surprise, the State was now involved in the matter, the State, which was opposed to wild animals, so the Minister of the Environment had asked the Attorney General to send the Viking Division with the Coast Guard helicopter to destroy the livestock on humanitarian grounds, in the name of animal welfare, per the statutory duty the State has to maintain the Icelandic biosphere and follow animal welfare laws, starvation laws, laws about preventing sheep disease; a lot of bloodshed followed, and it was ugly to behold; the marksmen of the Viking Division were quick to shoot all the animals that had been gathered in one area thanks to the diligence and drive of Runki from Destrikt and many other zealous lads and old men, but now we were a ways away, no longer able to do anything. This went on for a while. The helicopter flew big circles, ferreting out the flock with its thunderous noise; some of the sheep fell from cliffs and broke apart on the glacier; others died from breathlessness. Kiddi saw a ram up on the mountain and immediately sprang after him, wanting to get ahead of the helicopter and capture him alive, desperate to save the wild sheep from both State and Reality; it was the last wild ram, and Kiddi knew Runki had a ewe lamb inside his sweater, it was a predetermined plan, Kiddi kicked hard across the gravel bed and tussocks and scrambled up the mountain slope and jumped over the gully, leaping onward with his pole; Runki sent Jasmine after him to help, and together they cornered the ram which was fat and lumbering while Kiddi and Jasmine were both tremendously sprightly. It was the most arresting thing, a beautiful sight, we stood and watched through binoculars, which seemed to me the most sensible and thoughtful and, most of all, the best view, Dr. Lassi writes, according to Hálfdán, the ram had variously colored body and legs, with a white line from his nose up its snout, ending with a star on his forehead; his neck was gray back to his sides and to the upper thighs, but he had moorit socks, gray-flecked, he held his head high, his fiery eyes a bright white on his big, long-necked head, that exactly was the appearance of the last wild ram, he was grumpy and wary, proud, erect, and stern; everyone agreed they had never set eyes on so beautiful a creature. This was something other than a white, lazy normal sheep, wool dangling, dragging behind it, Dr. Lassi wrote in the report. The helicopter pilot had caught sight of him, Jasmine crept and shifted around the mottled ram, Kiddi lassoed up the hillside in the meantime and came face to face with Hosi the ram who stood and looked at Kiddi with threatening eyes, frozen there, Hosi had Kiddi in his sights and meant to butt this lout to death, Hosi stamped down his foot, knocking the stones from under him, Kiddi lowered his pole and placed it in his armpit and rushed down the gravel terribly fast, it seemed like a triplet of Kiddis were there but the helicopter swung up the valley to meet them and the members of the Viking Division loaded their rifles, Hosi stood still, not budging, Kiddi stepped hard on the ground, preparing his feet for flight and he indeed leapt high and far, a somersault finishing with a half-screw to land beside the ram, Jasmine jumped away in terror but Kiddi seized Hosi by the antlers, wrapped the rope around one hand, bound the ram's horns, and then ran then back down the scree…The helicopter swung over them like a wasp and then headed down the mountain and disappeared past the cliff, we thought they were done, the noise was dying off, silence returned to the mountains' kingdom. Kiddi came triumphantly down the slopes, leading Hosi behind him, sometimes stumbling on the way back to us, Hosi reluctant on the line, lumbering in his wake, finally Kiddi had to use all his strength to drag Hosi to us, the large and great and final wild sheep. The little ewe lamb in Runk's windbreaker peeked out silent and half-fearful from the neck hole. When Kiddi finally reached us with the ram, gasping and stumbling, he could see from our expressions that all was not right: looking back, he saw that Hosi was dead.

†

The sun was in the southeast, high in the sky over the tranquil glacier, Dr. Lassi wrote, concluding her report, an intense, bright blue, the crater silent for now, to the north lay ice-sheets extending across the plateau to the horizons, white deserts, thick and old, creeping down the cliffs and gullies, passes and valleys, down to the lowlands, and from under them rivers run southward out to the sand, wild and merciless, all the way out into the ocean that receives everything in its silence. Far out there Ingolfshöfði slumbers in a mist of fog on the sand, singular, a symbol of a new beginning. We set off back down into the everyday newslessness, Dr. Lassi wrote. Hálfdán had put the beetle gently into an empty matchbox and thought of a name.

The horse falls down into the fissure after me and the trunk comes down with him and stops right above me as I lie there with my head propped up on some kind of ledge. After a long time, I reach out and manage to free myself with great difficulty and turn around; exhausted, I crawl inside the trunk. Once inside, I turn the light on. I sing the Austrian imperial hymn to Joseph Haydn's tune because it's the only hymn I know and I want to sing myself alive like Sigurður sang his hymns to live, but no one hears me, there's no brother to reach out a helping hand. People can no longer provide their own salvation. Despair is inevitable. Nothing happens. The days pass and I keep singing this one hymn. I pass my time writing you this letter you will definitely never get, it keeps me occupied, in fact, it is my salvation.

Forty days and forty nights have passed. One continuous night. All the supplies in the trunk have long since been used up; the fuel and gas for the stove have run out. For two weeks, I have only drunk water. I do not know how deep into the fissure I fell, how deep in the glacier I am, maybe a kilometer, maybe more, maybe less. Fissures in the upper glacier do not narrow like they do further down the advancing glaciers, it says somewhere in the books in the trunk; they can reach all the way down to the base of the glacier, where death is the only exit route. It's been a long time I thought I heard a helicopter, which gave me weak hope, I even thought I could hear a gunshot, probably it was nothing; now I only hear in my dreams. The silence is so great that she has become a suction. A stimulating noise in my head. I ate what I could off the horse and remarked every time I tasted the soup how delicious he was. It lasted a long time, but now it's all long gone. I've writhed around in guilt, about the horses, my mother, my brother, myself. I've been thinking whether I could cut off my limbs to eat them, gradually devouring myself to nothing. Fade away that way. What was at first a narrow crack has now become a splendid ice cave, and as it has enlarged, the possibilities of climbing up and out have diminished, although they were zero to begin with. There's enough water and the temperature is steady, but cold. At first, I was afraid of the thunderous noise, scared of the dangerous cracks high up in the glacial heaven above me, afraid of the glacier's movement, afraid I would be crushed to death; now I can say the thundering calms me to sleep like a distant music as I lie under my pelt in the trunk, which I do most all the time, not knowing if what I hear is thunder overhead or something taking place inside the limits of my body. I have carved the cave with the cake slice to warm myself up after sleeping, shored up the trunk on a plinth, fashioned a toilet, a kitchenette and a single spice shelf where I keep the cumin, during such activity I always sing the same hymn, varying the lyrics, improvising all kinds of adaptations, I eked out my liquor quite some time, and used to sing the hymn over Brennivín. Joseph Haydn, I've been thinking a fair bit about Joseph Haydn here in the ice cave, I wish that I could take Snorri's-Edda to Schönbrunn Palace in Vienna and listen to Symphony No. 45 and wander about the streets drunk before saying goodbye to home as I float down the Danube on a raft all the way to the Black Sea ... *Farewell* ... journeying home ... Otherwise, I mostly crouch in the trunk wrapped in a pelt, having stretched the sail-canvas tent across to keep the wet out of my abode ... I will write to you as long as I live, my strength is gone and I feel death nearer inside me. These three days I have coughed up blood. The glacier gives back what it takes, they say. I am putting these papers in a well-made chest, an old Swiss lunchbox from the army, I think it's actually bulletproof, in the hope the glacier will give the letter up at some point. It won't matter anymore. You probably won't be alive. I've managed to disconnect my mind from reality as I'm ebbing out. Is life anything but this? I have kept myself from my cold fate in this glacial crevasse these 40 days and nights by thinking about how everything could have gone another way, if I had been the fortunate person who crawled, exhausted, into the Skaftafell Visitor Center, bitten by a wild sheep and amputated by an angle grinder, lying in a dry and warm bed in a hotel instead of falling through a snowy ceiling down into a fissure and awaiting my death for weeks on end under a cold blanket. Today, Ascension Day, 29th May, 2003, now when my appreciation of light and my provisions have been used up and it is complete darkness, I have decided to take my razor blade and let him dance across my neck so I can go visit my brother, and thus I take leave of all my friends in this letter. After I have closed this box, I will fold my hands and say goodbye to this world without place names.

Your friend,
Bernharður

EPILOGUE: THE FUTURE

As everyone knows, Öræfajökull erupted twenty-five years ago, destroying the settlements all around the glacier and laying waste to the largest national park in Europe. Things are still being rebuilt today, following the destruction, everything put back as before. We've never witnessed such a great volcanic eruption; geologists reckon it is comparable to the 1362 eruption. First, people became aware of three tremendous thuds and it was already too late, a gray-white swollen cloud could be seen proceeding with terrible speed down the glacier, within minutes all those who were based in Öræfi perished in a single instant, mostly foreign tourists; the rush immediately cast everyone into statues which have been preserved for all time at the regional museum of East Skaftafell district; they are exhibited there and attract many visitors; they're the bedrock of the community. The deaths of tens of millions of people around the world can be attributed to the eruption. Dry fog crossed the ocean and first lay over Britain and then the whole continent of Europe, then south to Africa and Asia Minor. The haze sat for a long time over the landmasses. Riots broke out in the Arab world and recalled events from the beginning of this century, though they did not lead to anything except the deaths of many people and continued corruption and terrorism. War still surges on; it hasn't been possible to make the twenty-first century the century of peace, as was intended at the beginning. Many people suffered the consequences, as in the past. Öræfajökull became famous in the world in an instant, grounding all flights across Western countries for 18 months, despite the new technology of jet engines that were supposed to persist through ash clouds. The white, light, rhyolite ash of Öræfajökull proved different from what foreign scientists had previously known and considered. The effects of the eruption were prolonged, unceasing, some say even irreversible. Hoarfrost made war on hot countries while cold lands heated up, causing an ominous destruction of vegetation and the collapse of ecosystems; the northerners fled southward, but the southerners fled northward. Crops were destroyed almost everywhere for many years. Such horror and famine followed as the West has not seen for centuries. European markets crashed and there were fights over shipping routes in the northern part of the continent; many things remain uncertain. The collapse rebuilt the tourism industry in Europe and kept the Chinese in the West, as in the past, with treasury agreements and monopolies and inferior merchandise; they are still trying hard to buy Iceland, which has become pretty much all one big national park; there is an on-going quarrel in the Restored Icelandic Parliament at Þingvellir as to whether wasteland has any meaning or any value, there are quarrels about symbols, the meaning of symbols, about what lies beyond symbols and their meaning, there are quarrels about the financial value of wastelands, people listen to scholars but pay no heed to them, nobody understands anything and nothing changes, no more than before. The Chinese operate unscrupulous mining over large areas within the protected space which escaped the glacier, erecting a so-called luxury hospital and a luxury village there where rare metals are processed for the luxury sector. This is called progress and progression, our only alternative is to sink back to the darkness of the Middle Ages, they say at the Restored Parliament. Others maintain we should not upset the land-spirits with the yawning snouts of large-scale machinery, and the nation is split like a serpent's tongue in this matter, as in everything else, being split is what defines a nation nowadays, as always.

Tourists have begun to visit Öræfi again, the Province, Héraŏ, as it is called now, and everything is headed straight down the same road as bfore. Destruction is the basis of the tourism industry here, as it is elsewhere. Large white pumice hills attract them; the ruins of towns, petrified people, memories of the disaster. The vegetation has manifested an admirable tenaciousness, the slopes fragrant with birch and willow, the birdlife more diverse than ever before; limpid streams trickle down the slopes, and sand and gravel turn to peat. After things warmed up, the deathly mist disappeared, the glaciers began to retreat faster than the most pessimistic forecasts and fires burned, the valleys written about in the chapters of *The Book of Settlement* opened up again, there is now fertile moorland and blissful weather; butter drips from every blade. The vegetation has reacted amazingly quickly to the glacial rock slopes, and scientists from all over the world compete to monitor the settlement of plants in the desert;

the entire area is popular with the public. Vatnajökull has been given its former name again, *Klofajökull*, the Split Glacier, and new roads now lie around the valley between various parts of the land; scholars tell us how many contemporary things are redolent of the Settlement era.

Many things emerge from under the glacier which were lost in the course of time; it's a popular sport for people to look for relics using metal detecting equipment—there's practically a gold rush. West of Mávabyggðir, below Hermannaskarð, the equipment of a someone who half a century ago undertook a solo research trip onto the glacier came to light: various ancient metal items, crampons, tent pegs, a glasses frame, and what was thought to be a trowel but turned out to be a silver cake slice. No bodily remains were found. Then a box came to light filled with the letters which appear in this book only slightly modified and adapted. This is all on display in what was once called the Skaftafell Visitor Center but is now called something else—because everything gets called something else at some point, or else nothing at all, and only then can it be left in peace.

Auth.

THE PLACE OF TRANSLATION:
SIX MISADVENTURES IN LOCATION

I.

"What do you do if you get lost in an Icelandic forest?"

"Stand up."

The first Icelandic joke I ever learned relies on classic Icelandic wit. Practical rather than hilarious, it's faintly embarrassed about Iceland itself, and not immediately meaningful to non-Icelanders. You need to know forests are few and far between in Iceland to get the joke.

Arboreal scarcity is a recurring Icelandic theme. Recently, I've been reading my three- and five-year-old daughters *How the Ladies Stopped the Wind*, by Bruce McMillan. In it, tenacious Icelandic women persist in growing trees to shelter their homes, despite obstacles including hungrily-grazing sheep, bemused cows, and an over-abundance of chicken manure. But, as one of the characters in Ófeigur Sigurðsson's Öræfi remarks, "reforestation is supposed to rescue us from the humiliation of wind gusting around our homes and cottages."

Both joke and story fear something's wrong with the Icelandic environment. In 1874, on the 1,000th anniversary of the settlement of Iceland, Friðjón Friðriksson wrote to President Ulysses Grant. He and several co-signatories, all born-and-bred Icelanders now living in the U.S., requested that Iceland's 70,000-strong population be allowed to repopulate on mass to Alaska. "Neither trees nor grain can now be made to grow" in Iceland, Friðjón complained, "it has become more and more barren." Friðjón's failed petition wasn't a stab in the dark: in 1868, then U.S. Secretary of State William H. Seward had received from the mining engineer Benjamin Pierce "A Report on the Resources of Iceland and Greenland." That document led to an 1869 *New York Times* article headlined "Iceland.; Rumored Plan for the Annexation of the Island to the United States."

The question of whether Iceland can extend hospitality to those who live amid its glaciers and volcanoes has been a concern since its settlement. A largely apocryphal story holds that Iceland was named to deter future migrants (especially unwanted Norwegian overlords), with the icier Greenland, so named in order to tempt settlers. A different root for Iceland's name is explained in *Landnáma* (*The Book of Settlements,* Iceland's foundational literary text). According to that book, Hrafna-Flóki Vilgerðarson, a Norwegian Viking, landed in the West Fjords in 865 CE; hiking up nearby mountains, he gazed out on the glacial pack ice at either Vatnsfjörður or Ísafjarðardjúp and named the country Ísland, Iceland. A more recent theory traces the naming to a group of Irish monks who pre-dated the Norwegian arrivants; one, stunned by the island's beauty, gave the place the name Jesusland, in the form Ísuland, from the Old Gaelic word for Jesus.

In all three versions of Iceland's naming story, we see the humans who confront its geology, topography, and geography attempting to find the language that could contain its wonder, tumult, and extremes. "Land of fire and ice" runs the tourist slogan: a place you could as easily get burned to a crisp in a geothermal zone as frozen to a statue amid endless glacial ice. The Icelandic word for stories is also its word for history; Icelanders have long known that place is narrative. That a recent tourist board promotion invited visitors to rename Iceland (entries included Endless Night Land and Best Country to Grow a Beard Land) suggests some hesitation about the existing state of affairs alongside a confidence in the power of place names.

II.

Translating *Öræfi* has meant traversing the path between word and world, exploring the ways language is a land-gauge. The fiction of translation is physical: a translation is a creation in which one geography gets moved to another, Iceland to the United States, or wherever and whenever you are now holding this copy of *Öræfi—The Wasteland*, a title that remembers the bridge a translation needs. Translation is not, as some would have it, a betrayal, but it is a displacement.

Finding the region Öræfi is easier than translating it. In Reykjavík some years back I bought a map of the area: it is mostly white, empty. By reputation, Öræfi is a wilderness, inhospitable, a wasteland. Like most Icelandic place names, though, Öræfi gains its name through narrative—through story and history—more than etymology. Eyjafjallajökull, the ice cap that erupted in 2010, disrupting European air travel, is composed of the Icelandic words for island, mountain and glacier. Its name only makes sense as a micro-story: the glacial mountain from which you can see the islands—the Vestmannaeyjar, just off the south coast of the country. So too with Öræfi: it is a name that replaced a former name, a reminder of the power of volcanoes and glaciers to wipe clean the human slate.

Ófeigur's Sigurðsson's *Öræfi* similarly sustains itself on the way words and events can get covered over. The whole of the narrative proves a fiction, an invention, one which overlays Austria and Iceland, Vienna and Reykjavík. Our narrator, Bernharður, finds himself at a guesthouse on Freyjugata in Reykavík; there he meets the Icelander Gestur, whose name means guest, and so recalls the maiden name of his mother, Geist—which also implies ghost, for everywhere this novel is haunted by past events. Little wonder that Bernharður lives on a street in Vienna called Freyvangur. Even as his mother's own troubled history visiting Iceland plays out, backdrop to his own adventures, the words that shape his world shuttle him between places, between past and present.

Öræfi is at heart a thriller about a man contending with extreme elements, an adventure story featuring a lone figure out on a glacier. It is also a history of Southern Iceland, an eclectic annal to volcanic eruptions, to glacial melt, to Icelandic suicides. It is briefly an homage to the intersection of death metal and Belgian symbolism. At every moment, it is a love song to toponymy, the study of place names. It is a work of environmental consciousness, debating reforestation and cultural preservation.

More than any of this, though, *Öræfi* attempts to see whether the page can give us more experience of place than the image. Bernharður ends up in Iceland because of a story he read in *National Geographic*; that encounter, definitive of Bernharður's life, places us as readers in an uneasy position, knowing what we know of the consequences of his reading, what it inspired in him. We first meet him in a sorry state, and things worsen from there. The veterinarian and would-be-savior Dr. Lassi, who stands in as Bernharður's unlikely field medic, laments her missing library, frustrated in her attempts to understand Bernharður's story because she lacks key books to consult. Gestur, the Virgil to Bernharður's Dante, had loaded up Bernharður's Tardis-like traveling trunk with journals, articles, and guides, warning him that to be unread about Öræfi is to dice with death. For all that Öræfi's pages bubble with sulphuric gasses and leak glacial floods, they remain pages, which is also to say trees, which is also to say places you might get lost. And getting lost, in Öræfi, never ends well. Reader, you have been warned.

III.

Why, then, did I find myself, in May 2017, my tent pitched yards from the very Visitor Center Bernharður tells us he crawled into, leg gouged by a wild beast? Why had I brought along my two girls, both under four, and my wife? Just what was waiting for me along the hike up towards the relentless Vatnajökull, whose finger glaciers Morsárjökull, Skaftafellsjökull, and Svínafellsjökull reach down towards the coast, hooking as if they might pluck Route 1—the only road around the island, the only road out of here—off the map entirely?

After three days of incessant rain, the sun had finally pushed on through, and our yellow tents were backlit in the kind of illumination that makes you realize why humans have so long prized gold, that useless metal. Behind the tents, I could see the canopy of birch and rowans that comprise the Bæjarstaðarskógur, an Icelandic forest you could just about get lost in, providing you trained a bit first, as though for some kind of anti-orienteering Olympics. Bernharður had been here; had stood at this site and looked east, past these trees to the menacing Hafrafell cliffs. On them I could see the Illuklettar, or Evil Rocks, as he had seen them. From such topography we get the idea that land can be forbidding, foreboding. Illuklettar seemed to roil and lash out, a fraught ocean preserved in stone.

This, and not my empty map, was *Öræfi*, Several Icelandic words that share the form *ör* connote violence: darts and scars. The adjective *æfur* implies vicious anger. *Öræfi*: a scar that's angry enough to lash out. To call it that might not be precise linguistics, not a direct replication of language, but here in a pyritic sun, a gentle forest sloping ahead of me, I could see why Bernharður had been daunted—and could see why translating *Öræfi* as some kind of raging injury would do justice to the word. I could see, in other words, why the novel that bears the region's name begins with Bernharður detailing the

large, open wound in my thigh, reminiscent of a caldera, and I thought I saw glowing lava well from it, a burning current pouring itself out like a serpent writhing up my spinal cord towards my head which was becoming a seething magma chamber

One of the most ancient truisms of creative writing comes from the Roman poet Horace: *Si vis me flere, dolendum est primum ipsi tibi.*

If you want me to weep, it's your sadness you need to show me first. The narrator must be visibly sad if the reader is to become so. But how to show sadness across translation, when translation requires us to travel so far between places?

IV.

My favorite English translation of Horace's adage, "if you want me to weep, / First show me your own eye full of tears," is quoted by Bertolt Brecht, as translated by John Willett, based on a translation of Horace into German by Johann Christoph Gottsched. A displacement, and then some. Brecht hated Horace's idea of art— he called it "forced emotion," decried its falsity. Yet this collaborative, free-ranging translation of Horace, who mentions nothing about eyes or showing them, reveals something about the way translation might work as the reflection of place.

There in Skaftafell National Park, I was tracing some of Bernharður's foosteps just as he had been tracing the explorer-soldier Captain Koch's. I opted to forgo Bernharður's extensive luggage and his train of Icelandic horses, traveling instead with a 360° camera and two car seats. It seemed the way to bring Öræfi across from Iceland was not only to help the novel's Icelandic words into English, but to be in as many of the novel's places as possible.

The point, I realized, was to find a way for my eye to contain the sights that Bernharður's had. That to show the reader my own eye full of Evil Rocks and endless black sands wasn't to show off vague emotions—the abstract tears Brecht lamented—but to reflect a set of images across distance. To replicate Freyung as

Freyjugata, as it were, or *Öræfi* as *The Wasteland* via an em-dash—
that punctuation mark which both pushes words (and worlds)
away from one another and means they're roped together, working in series.

My own travels took me, like Bernharður, to the streets of
Reykjavík, to a drive out east across the flinty metal bridges
Öræfi narrates being installed to complete Route 1's ring around
Iceland, ushering the modern into the untouched wilderness,
bringing tourism and mice. As we drove through hail, I risked
the circuitry of my 360° camera to capture the landscape moving around me. As our car sped along the single-lane highway, the
rivers a quiet trickle beneath us, I wanted a way to bring Iceland
back with me. I think Bernharður did, too.

V.

The 360° camera wants us to believe its image isn't flat. A 360° image
is to still photography what the globe is to the atlas. A globe
allows us the full sphere, whereas the atlas admits a geometric
problem: the Earth laid flat distorts itself. Everything's out of
place, a photo excerpted from its environment. Bernharður's aunt
had been photographing Iceland when she and his mother ran
into trouble. His response? To follow the language of maps, to see
land in terms of the words that have shaped it. Landscape, after
all, isn't an objective reality: it's the way we perceive the world
around us. It's the story behind both the atlas and the globe.

The geologist Nick Warner explained this to me another way
as we looked out at the Stampar crater row in the South West of
Iceland, where during the Reykjanes Fires of 1210–1240 AD four

different lava fields formed across the two westernmost volcanic systems on the Reykjanes peninsula. Becoming a geologist, he said, isn't just about acquiring the terminology that helps articulate the earth's shape; nor is it just about understanding the processes by which a particular formation has arisen. At some point, geologists stop seeing the earth the way the rest of us do. They start seeing geologic history replaying itself before them, their eyes tiny movie theaters in which an epic sweep of natural history unfolds, a tuff cone forming at the shore during a surtseyan eruption, magma coming into billowing contact with water.

Show me your own eye full of tears—or full of geologic time playing out. *Öræfi*—*The Wasteland* comes into being because of the way volcanic eruptions laid waste to a region once called Heraÿ, or The Province, despoiling it, ridding it of places by ridding it of place names, only to in time give fertile rise to new flora and fauna. "The Wasteland" is a perspective, a way of seeing. And all our ways of seeing are also our ways of speaking, of giving the land we're seeing to the language that will translate it across distance.

VI.

To translate, then, is to be on location: both to get lost in the forest and to realize what it might mean to stand up within it. When I tell new friends that I translate Icelandic, they almost always ask, So you must speak it really well? What I should say in response is that I hope I see Iceland really well.

To talk about seeing Iceland, though, isn't uncomplicated. There's an Icelandic saying some trace back to the father of the

Norse gods, Oðin: *glöggt er gests auga,* meaning that the guest's eyes see more clearly than the resident's. The connection to Oðin is fanciful, reliant on that fact that he, like Bernharður's guide, The Regular, went by Gestur, among other names. The link in *Öræfi* between Gestur and Oðin gets lost in translation. In its place, we get "The Regular," a known entity, a fixture, someone who frequents a place. How clearly are we seeing here?

Out in the field, there in Bernharður's wake, I discover it's impossible to take a 360° video without the videographer showing up. At the base of the image lie the lines that ridge my fingers, the bulk of my hand interrupting the scene. Panning the black sands over which Bernharður drives on the way to his fateful adventure, you see me there, wearing the raincoat I bought to hike Ben Nevis, somewhat impromptu, a decade ago. I'm wearing, too, a white 66° North Iceland hat, which always makes me feel 50% local, 50% tourist eyesore. Filming, I try to hide myself, the finger-length camera held atop my head. The result is a strange image reminiscent of nothing more than the 1988 ZX Spectrum Microprose soccer game: a head, two arms, nothing more. Raindrops dot the image, interfering with what might be a seal head bobbing about in the glacial waters of Jökulsarlón, where glaciers calve and drift out to sea, out to where they can't be seen.

Perhaps the point isn't to hide the videographer. Video, first person singular, meaning I see, from the Latin. Graph, also Latin: writing. The rain bows our tents' roofs. Like Koch and Bernharður before us, we're freighted with too much luggage, can't really fit it inside the tents alongside our four bodies. Pressed against the tent's edges, our bags take on water, imported maca-roni shells going tacky, shoes dampening. I do my best to keep the 360° sealed in Ziplocs, only to bring it out in downpours, desper-ate to capture the surreal blue of icebergs against the ashen slopes leading down to water. I let the rain in, and the videos I write to my hard drive bring that rain with them, flecked evidence from the trip. When, a week after my return, my laptop is destroyed by a freak torrential rain in Red Hook, Brooklyn, it seems that the rain has followed me.

In the end, you can't remove the I, or the eye. In the rare image where I almost conceal myself holding the camera, my shadow stands on the sand, which isn't black enough, quite, to hide it. If translation is being on location, it is also *being* on loca-tion, present in place and words, land and language. The amazing Icelandic Literature Center and the Writers' Union of Iceland offer residencies to translators, helping us spend time in Iceland, not just to work with authors, not just to immerse ourselves in the language, but so we can be on location. Can let sites be sights. I'd love for more of translation to be so site-specific. It takes a rare book like Ófeigur Sigurðsson's Öræfi to make the locations of translation visible. Whatever befalls Bernharður, places and names alike live on because of what he notices, what he records. The eyes of the guest aren't clear—they're flecked with rain—but they're novel. And what they see, the reader sees too. Reflected, which means distorted, which means we have to look a little closer, and maybe, finally, we get to see a little more distinctly.

There, in Öræfi, at Hotel Fresynes, Bernharður lies waiting. His story needs a translator: in the novel, her name is Interpreter.

Nothing happens without her. By the time you find out where Bernharður really is, and has been, what you've got is a story of how place is language, and how language is translation. Sometimes, you can't see the words for the trees until a book brings them to light.

ACKNOWLEDGMENTS

Thanks to Dr. Nick Warner for his insights into the geology of Öræfi and Southern Iceland. The students who took the *Writing and Knowing the Land: Abroad in Iceland Study Abroad* course at SUNY Geneseo in Summer 2016, taught by the translator and Dr. Warner, helped bring the area to life with the wonderful ways they saw and wrote about Iceland's people, trees, and places. A special thanks to Lizzie Pellegrino, who served as research assistant and geological consultant for the translation, providing much needed information about pyroclastic flows, glaciology, and also Rick and Morty. This translation is for Jess, June, and Rosie, who are always ready to share and delight in Iceland with me.

Research for this translation was supported by funding by SUNY Geneseo and the Geneseo Foundation.

Ófeigur Sigurðsson was born in Reykjavík in 1975. He is a graduate of the University of Iceland with a degree in philosophy. He made his poetry debut in 2001 with *Skál fyrir skammdeginu* (*Cheers to the Winter Darkness*), and published his first novel, *Áferð* (*Texture*), in 2005. Since then, he has published six books of poetry and three novels, in addition to his work as an accomplished translator. Sigurðsson was awarded the European Union Prize for Literature in 2011 for his novel, *Jon*, making him the first Icelander to receive the prize. His novel *Öræfi: The Wasteland* was published in Iceland in 2014 to great critical and commercial acclaim, and received the Book Merchant's Prize in 2014 and the Icelandic Literature Prize in 2015. He currently resides in Antwerp, Belgium.

Lytton Smith is the award-winning author of four books of poetry and several translations from the Icelandic, including Jón Gnarr's childhood memoir trilogy, *The Indian, The Pirate,* and *The Outlaw* (Deep Vellum); *The Ambassador* by Bragi Ólafsson (Open Letter); and *Children in Reindeer Woods* by Kristín Ómarsdóttir (Open Letter). His translation of Guðbergur Bergsson's *Tómas Jónsson—Bestseller* (*Tómas Jónsson, metsölubók*) was published by Open Letter Books in 2017. He is an Assistant Professor of English at SUNY Geneseo in upstate New York.

Thank you all
for your support.
We do this for you,
and could not do
it without you.

DEEP
VELLUM

DEAR SUBSCRIBERS,

We are both proud of and awed by what you've helped us accomplish so far in achieving and growing our mission. Since our founding, with your help, we've been able to reach over 100,000 English-language readers through the translation and publication of 32 award-winning books, from 5 continents, 24 countries, and 14 languages. In addition, we've been able to participate in over 50 programs in Dallas with 17 of our authors and translators and over 100 conversations nationwide reaching thousands of people, and were named Dallas's Best Publisher by *D Magazine*.

Deep Vellum is a 501c3 nonprofit literary arts organization founded in 2013 in Dallas's historic cultural neighborhood of Deep Ellum. Our mission is threefold: to cultivate a more vibrant, engaged literary arts community both locally and nationally; to promote the craft, discussion, and study of literary translation; and to publish award-winning, diverse international literature in English-language translations.

As a nonprofit organization, we rely on your generosity as individual donors, cultural organizations, government institutions, and charitable foundations. Your tax-deductible recurring or one-time donation provides the basis of our operational budget as we seek out and publish exciting literary works from around the globe and continue to build the partnerships that create a vibrant, thriving literary arts community. Deep Vellum offers various donor levels with opportunities to receive personalized benefits at each level, including books and Deep Vellum merchandise, invitations to special events, and recognition in each book and on our website.

In addition to donations, we rely on subscriptions from readers like you to provide the bedrock of our support, through an ongoing investment that demonstrates your commitment to our editorial vision and mission. The support our 5- and 10-book subscribers provide allows us to demonstrate to potential partners, bookstores, and organizations alike the support and demand for Deep Vellum's literature across a broad readership, giving us the ability to grow our mission in ever-new, ever-innovative ways.

It is crucial that English-language readers have access to diverse perspectives on the human experience, perspectives that literature is uniquely positioned to provide. You can keep the conversation going and growing with us by becoming involved as a donor, subscriber, or volunteer. Contact us at deepvellum.org to learn more today. We would love to hear from you.

Thank you all. Enjoy reading.

Will Evans
Founder & Publisher

PARTNERS

SUBSCRIBERS

Ali Bolcakan
Andrew Bowles
Anita Tarar
Ben Nichols
Blair Bullock
Brandye Brown
Caitlin Schmid
Caroline West
Charles Dee Mitchell
Chris McCann
Chris Sweet
Christie Tull
Courtney Sheedy
David Bristow
David Tomlinson &
Kathryn Berry
David Travis
Elizabeth Johnson
Ellen Miller
Farley Houston
Frank Garrett (Anonymous)
Hannah McGinty
Holly LaFon
Jason Linden
Jeff Goldberg
Joe Maceda
John Schmerein
John Winkelman

Joshua Edwin
Kelly Baxter
Kevin Winter
Lesley Conzelman
Lora Lafayette
Lytton Smith
Mario Sifuentez
Martha Gifford
Mary Brockson
Matt Cheney
Michael Aguilar
Michael Elliott
Mies de Vries
Nathan Wey
Neal Chuang
Nicholas R. Theis
Patrick Shirak
Reid Allison
Robert Keefe
Ronald Morton
Shelby Vincent
Stephanie Barr
Steve Jansen
Todd Crocken
Todd Jailer
Wenyang Chen
Will Pepple
William Fletcher

FOUAD LAROUI · *The Curious Case of Dassoukine's Trousers*
translated by Emma Ramadan · MOROCCO

LINA MERUANE · *Seeing Red*
translated by Megan McDowell · CHILE

FISTON MWANZA MUJILA · *Tram 83*
translated by Roland Glasser · DEMOCRATIC REPUBLIC OF CONGO

ILJA LEONARD PFEIJFFER · *La Superba*
translated by Michele Hutchison · NETHERLANDS

RICARDO PIGLIA · *Target in the Night*
translated by Sergio Waisman · ARGENTINA

SERGIO PITOL · *The Art of Flight* · *The Journey* · *The Magician of Vienna*
translated by George Henson · MEXICO

EDUARDO RABASA · *A Zero-Sum Game*
translated by Christina MacSweeney · MEXICO

MIKHAIL SHISHKIN · *Calligraphy Lesson: The Collected Stories*
translated by Marian Schwartz, Leo Shtutin, Mariya Bashkatova,
Sylvia Maizell · RUSSIA

BAE SUAH · *Recitation*
translated by Deborah Smith · SOUTH KOREA

JUAN RULFO · *The Golden Cockerel & Other Writings*
translated by Douglas J. Weatherford · MEXICO

SERHIY ZHADAN · *Voroshilovgrad*
translated by Reilly Costigan-Humes & Isaac Stackhouse Wheeler
· UKRAINE

DEEP
VELLUM